MANSIONS OF
THE MOON

ALSO BY
SHYAM SELVADURAI

Novels
Funny Boy
Cinnamon Gardens
Swimming in the Monsoon Sea
The Hungry Ghosts

MANSIONS OF THE MOON

SHYAM SELVADURAI

ALFRED A. KNOPF CANADA

PUBLISHED BY ALFRED A. KNOPF CANADA

Copyright © 2022 Shyam Selvadurai

LIBRARY AND ARCHIVES CANADA CATALOGUING IN PUBLICATION
Title: Mansions of the moon / Shyam Selvadurai.
Names: Selvadurai, Shyam, 1965- author.
Identifiers: Canadiana (print) 20210259914 | Canadiana (ebook) 20210260025 |
ISBN 9780735280625 (hardcover) | ISBN 9780735280632 (EPUB)
Classification: LCC PS8587.E445 M36 2022 | DDC C813/.54—dc23

Jacket & text designs: Talia Abramson
Jacket images: (grass) Vertyr / Shutterstock, (moon and temples) Terd486 / Shutterstock;
(plants and flowers) Alex Illi / Shutterstock; (texture) Annie Spratt / Unsplash Images
Title page image: Alex Illi / Shutterstock

Printed in Canada

10 9 8 7 6 5 4 3 2 1

Penguin
Random House
KNOPF CANADA

For Rishika Williams (Loku)
Fellow traveller on the Path;
patient reader of numerous drafts;
අඹ යාළුවා

And Andrew,
for happiness, for love, for home.

Fools,
who don't know things
as they really are,
revere the mansions of the moon
and tend the fire in the wood,
thinking this purity.

THE THERIVADA
(Songs of the Sisters)

CONTENTS

This I have heard, mitto: A woman, thinking a river calm and peaceful, enters it with a blissful mind, intending to cleanse and rejuvenate herself. Yet, once she has waded in, she finds herself caught in a strong current and swept along. Helpless, she watches her clothes on the shore become specks in the distance. Soon, the river narrows, the banks drawing close, and she sees grass, sawgrass, reeds, creepers and bushes, all hanging into the river. As she goes past the grass, she tries to cling to it, but it breaks off in her hands. She clings to the sawgrass next, but it cuts her hands. She clings to the creeper, the reeds, even the bushes, but nothing can withstand the current and she is carried along by the river.

DUKKHA I

THE HOT SEASON arrives and stays. There is thunder and rumbling in the skies, an occasional drizzle, but not the deluge needed and longed for. When Yasodhara goes out with her aunt and the Manager of the Fields to look at their plots beyond the city walls, she sees, with her expert eye, that the paddy, if it does come to maturation, will have fewer than usual grains on its stalks. As always, she watches with longing the women workers in the raja's fields, wanting so much to join them, but knowing such a thing is impossible now, given her status in the palace—though her heart aches with her desire to feel the cool earth between her toes, as she did in her youth.

One morning, Yasodhara wakes to the shriek of an owl, and this sound, unnatural in the daytime, fills her with a foreboding that is only heightened by the heat, sharpening her nerves to a knife's edge. So, when she looks up from picking flowers in the walled garden and sees her aunt hurrying towards her, face contorted with worrying news, it is as if she's been expecting whatever calamity is about to come. Prajapati reaches her and takes the flower basket from her hands. "Come, daharé." She leads the way to a bench under a tree, and Yasodhara suddenly finds it hard to breathe. Once they are seated, Prajapati wipes the sweat from her upper lip, then holds both Yasodhara's hands in her own and regards her sombrely. "Oh Ushas, I don't know how to say this . . . It's Siddhartha. He's alive."

Yasodhara snatches her hands back. "But that can't be! He's dead!"

Prajapati gently shakes her head. "He's reappeared in the city of Rajagaha. A messenger from the emperor Bimbisara just arrived for your uncle with the news."

"But that's not possible. No ascetic who's taken a fast unto death can last ten years."

"Your uncle, *I*, wanted you to know, before the news spreads." Her aunt blinks at her. "He is staying just outside Rajagaha with a hundred samanas who follow him. The Buddha, the Awakened One, is, evidently, how he wishes to be called. But awake from what, no one knows."

Yasodhara, her mind numb, gets up, then sits down, then gets up again. In the silence, she can hear, beyond the garden walls, the sounds of the young concubines practising their music in the courtyard, the *swish-swish* of the swing. After a long moment, she wipes her face with her shawl, takes up her basket and goes among the rows of plants as Prajapati follows. "A hundred," she murmurs. "That's a lot."

"He's been living these past years in a little forest hamlet called Uruvela. Claims to have found a new path that he calls 'the Middle Way.'"

"Middle Way . . ." Yasodhara squats to pick some flowers off a jasmine bush. Her calm, she knows, is unnatural.

"Something to do with Four Great Realities and the notion of everything burning, everything being on fire. The messenger wasn't very clear on this at all."

"And the Maharaja Bimbisara has no doubt embraced this Middle Way." She grimaces, bitter.

Prajapati raises an eyebrow. "As well as the entire court; the wealthy merchants; even the Dasas. Yes," her aunt continues—nodding at Yasodhara's surprise that the Dasas, so low that they exist outside the caste structure, are allowed to practise Siddhartha's new philosophy—"the Middle Way is open to everyone, no matter their varna, not just to us Khattiyas and the Brahmins."

Yasodhara stands and remains unmoving for a long moment. Then, before she can help herself, she cries out, "I wish he was dead, why is he alive, why?" Ignoring her aunt's appalled look, she wraps her shawl around herself and hurries towards the archway and out of the garden.

In her room, she paces, fingers twisting the pleats of her dhoti, then sits on a stool, leaning forward, hands clasped tightly on her knees. "Yes, yes," she murmurs, "why isn't he dead, why?" Whatever ground she has gained in the last ten years, whatever little stability and happiness she has found, is slipping away from her. No—he, her former husband, has snatched it from her. As if to confirm this, she hears her son Rahula shouting, "Ammé, ammé," as he runs down the corridor.

Rahula bursts into the room, face fractured with shock, with wonder. For a moment he says nothing, seeing that she has heard the news. Then he whispers in awe, "He's alive, ammé. Ayyaka says he is a renowned guru, that he is the favourite of the Maharaja Bimbisara. Has thousands who follow him like . . . like . . . a raja. Ayyaka is going to invite him here to Kapilavastu. My pita is a famous man throughout the Middle Country!"

Yasodhara laughs. She crouches over, unable to stifle her mirth, tears running down her face. Prajapati rushes in. She pats a frightened Rahula on the shoulder, and guides Yasodhara, now sobbing as well as laughing, to sit on the bed. "Ushas," she says gently, and signals Rahula to bring his mother a cup of water from the pitcher. Once she has taken the cup, Yasodhara gulps a first mouthful, then sips slowly, shoulders hunched, wiping her eyes with her shawl, appalled at her outburst, depleted by it. Finally, she puts the cup on the floor, straightens and turns to her son. "Rahula, you are ten now, old enough to face up to the truth. Putha, your pita will not come to see you. You should be prepared for this. Look how he has gone first to the Maharaja Bimbisara, the most powerful man in the Middle Country. All he's interested in is his own glory."

"Ushas," her aunt murmurs, indicating Rahula's dismayed face. But Yasodhara turns on Prajapati. "What I am saying is true, pitucché. Think: he has been alive for ten years and never sent us any word. Think: all these years we mourned his death, all these years his son believed he was father-less. I lived believing I was a widow. And, while we suffered here, he has been glorifying himself." She turns to Rahula again. "Puthā, your ayyaka's hopes are in vain. I know your pita, he won't come." Despite the pain seeping into Rahula's face like a dark dye, she continues, convinced she must make him see the truth. "It truly hurts me to say this to you, puthā, but I cannot, will not, have you hope, only to be disappointed." She reaches out and takes him by the shoulders. "I'm sorry, but you must accept this. Your pita doesn't care about you or me." Then she starts to weep, drawing Rahula close. Soon he is weeping too.

⚘

The next morning, Yasodhara, befuddled by lack of sleep, is in the palace granary with her aunt, squatting before a large clay jar, scratching the level

of the mung beans on the side so they can't be stolen by the kitchen workers, when Prajapati nudges her. She turns to see her brother Devadatta
limping furiously across the courtyard towards them, his war-damaged
leg dragging like an oar through water. She nods to her aunt, hands
her the royal seal to press next to the scratching, and goes to intercept her
brother at the door, wanting nothing discussed in front of the granary and
kitchen workers.

She takes his brawny arm and they walk a short distance away. She is
glad to see him, glad to see the anger in his swarthy face, which matches
her own. The only one whose absolute love and loyalty she can count on.

"How are you faring with this news, bhagini?" Devadatta asks grimly,
examining her closely.

Yasodhara shrugs. "I wish he had died, I really do. I can say that to you,
bhāta, but no one else understands." He nods. Their dhotis brush together
as they walk along, side by side. "The women of the quarters think me
cruel, unwomanly, for saying such a thing, but I have a right to feel that way.
Ten years, bhāta, ten years he was alive and let us believe he was dead. And
our Rahula. At least knowing his father was alive would have given him
that pride a boy can only get from knowing he has a father. I was rendered
a widow, when all the while I could have still been a married woman, with
all the status it brings."

"You should know that our uncle is planning to invite Siddhartha to
visit and spread his teachings here. He is inviting him officially, as our raja."

She frowns to say she already does know.

His weather-beaten face flushes. "They shouldn't invite him, he doesn't
deserve such an honour, given the way he abandoned you and Rahula. I
don't care about this Middle Way he preaches, selfishness and self-interest
are at its core. Which doesn't surprise me. And what is this nonsense about
understanding dukkha?" His lips curl in contempt. "How can understanding dukkha help you to wisdom?"

Yasodhara shakes her head. She doesn't understand either. "Dukkha,"
depending on its context, covers everything from dissatisfaction, to irritation, to annoyance, to great suffering. So why does understanding dukkha
(what exactly is there to *understand* about it?) lead to "deathlessness," another

bewildering term? Is Siddhartha claiming that he has found a way to avoid death, that he will never die?

Once Devadatta leaves, Yasodhara goes back to her work, miserable and feeling helpless. Things are moving and changing and, though these changes affect her profoundly, she cannot do anything about them, is nothing but a seedpod carried along by a river current.

That night she dreams she is seated on a bench in the walled garden weaving a long rope, the finished parts falling from her lap to the floor, where they coil about her feet. Unknown to her dream self, a she-jackal sits beneath the bench, gnawing on the rope. There is something nauseating about the way it sucks the rope down its throat.

When she opens her eyes the next morning, she immediately cries out, lifting her arm to block the light coming through the window—a physical thing slashing at her. She falls back on her pillow with a groan, arm over her face. The illness that periodically overcomes her is back.

For the next few days, Yasodhara rests in her darkened room, a damp cloth over her eyes, nauseous and unable to swallow anything except water, paralyzed by an extreme sensitivity to light. Lying there, as if pinned to her bed, she is wretched and angry at this weakness, whose appearance and disappearance she cannot control; and at Siddhartha, who is responsible for the illness, which only started a decade ago—after he left. Memories of her former life as a girl, as a young bride, arrive now to torment her, reminding her of who she was then and who she is now. She will see no one, not even Rahula, though she can sometimes hear his voice in the corridor talking in hushed tones to his grandmother or the other palace women. The sound of their voices, though muffled by the door, causes her to screw her eyes tight, as if voices too are a form of light. Her only succour is the Yakshi of Kapilavastu, to whom she prays, begging to be relieved of this distress.

The illness, as always, leaves her as suddenly as it arrives, and one morning Yasodhara awakens cured and ravenously hungry. She eats, then immediately orders a palanquin. She will visit the Yakshi of Kapilavastu, to thank her.

The shrine is within a pleasant city garden, frequented only by women. Yasodhara makes her way through the garden towards the Yakshi's abode, a samitr following with a cockerel held upside down by its legs. The deity's home is a wooden hut with a thatched roof. Yasodhara enters the dark interior, lit only by a few lamps, and stands, hands clasped, gazing with love at the Yakshi's red clay image. The plump naked deity, with her fanged smile and pendulous breasts, squats over a large clay pot, birthing good harvests, healthy children, good luck, good health and the release of the rains. The pot has a hole in the bottom, through which flows saffron water or blood from the sacrifices, dribbling along a shallow drain in the clay floor and out through a hole in the wall. The rusty stench of dried blood mixes with the perfume of the saffron water and incense sticks; flies buzz about in the pot, the tiny *thwoks* of their bodies as they hit the clay interior echoing in the chamber. Once the samitr slits the cockerel's neck over the pot, there is a great gush like pattering rain. After the bird is bled dry, the samitr leaves, taking the cockerel. Yasodhara, alone finally with her beloved, prostrates herself on the clay floor, hair loose about her shoulders and face to show humility. She lies like that for a long time, forehead resting on the cool clay floor, weeping silently with the relief of an injured child in its mother's arms.

When Yasodhara finally leaves the hut, she takes a moment to knot up her hair again, lost in thought. She is remembering that sixteen-year-old girl who came one day into her parents' room—summoned, she was sure, to be chided for racing a male cousin around the ramparts—only to find her feet starting along the path that has brought her here. *Where is that girl now?* A pang of loss and longing rises in her. *Dissolved like froth on the river.*

Froth on the River

1

Beginnings

"AH, COME, COME, Ushas," Pamita said briskly, summoning her daughter with a crooking of her finger.

Yasodhara paused in the doorway, taking in her petite mother seated cross-legged on the bed, back erect as she wrapped spices in a betel leaf on a small silver tray. Her father, Dandapani, lounged beside his wife, his long frame stretched out like a cat in the sun, chewing a packet of betel, wearing a look of contentment.

From her mother's solemn expression, Yasodhara was sure her parents knew that she had raced her cousin around the ramparts in a display they considered unseemly for a girl her age. So she came forward slowly, trying to think what lie or excuse she might plausibly invent. As she reached the bed, however, her father took her hand with a smile and pulled her to sit beside them. "Don't worry, dhītā, you're not in trouble. The contrary."

Her parents exchanged a look, then her mother said, still in that brisk tone of hers, "Ushas, we've received an offer of marriage. For you." They nodded sympathetically at her astonishment.

"But who?" she cried after a moment, unable to recall any young man who had showed interest recently.

"Siddhartha!" Pamita clapped her hands and cackled as if she thought the whole thing a good joke. Her father grinned too. "Delivered on his behalf to us by a messenger sent from Savatthi," her mother continued. "Can you imagine? A *messenger*!"

"That boy," Dandapani murmured, shaking his head indulgently. "Truly in his own world, living by his own rules." The proposal should have come from his father or stepmother.

She scrunched her nose in astonishment. "Siddhartha? But . . . why me? I don't understand." The last time her cousin had visited their city was three years ago, and, unlike in their early childhood, no real connection had formed between them. Siddhartha, thirteen then, remote as ever, had been more interested in a renowned Brahmin visiting the city than in his cousins. And he was even more distant from her now, having been in Savatthi for the last three years, studying in the court of their overlord, the Maharaja Maha Kosala. "I simply don't understand."

"But what do you think, Ushas?" Dandapani asked eagerly. "Are you at all interested? It would be a good marriage between our royal houses. And you are now sixteen, after all, time for marriage. Siddhartha's a decent young man. As you know, I'm very fond of him."

Pamita smacked her husband's shoulder with her palm fan. "It's not you who he's asking to marry, beloved."

Yasodhara shook her head, too bewildered to know what she thought or felt.

"There is no hurry to respond, Ushas." Her mother reached out and gently pressed her arm. "And, anyway, I've told the messenger that, even if you're interested, there must be a period of courtship. Siddhartha must visit over the next few months, to see how you both get along. Though you've known him since childhood, you haven't been close for a very long time."

"But I still don't understand. Why me?"

Her parents shrugged and then they both laughed. "You know, it *is* Siddhartha." Her father twirled his hand in the air. "A mind of his own, one that doesn't work like regular minds. I mean this sending of a messenger . . ." If her parents weren't so fond of Siddhartha, they would have been insulted. "Well, think about it, Ushas," her mother concluded, "and let us know."

Once Yasodhara left her parents' bedroom, she went to her own room and sat in the window well, hugging her knees, watching the life out in the royal square: the comings and goings of the inhabitants of the mansions off the square, the few noblemen who sat on cushions in the open, pillared

santagara, debating some matter of state as workmen re-thatched the santagara's straw roof with its sharply slanting sides.

Born a month apart, she and Siddhartha had known each other since
they were infants. Their nicknames, Ushas and Surya, had come from the
way her cousin had tottered after her in those early years, like Surya, the
Sun, following his beloved Ushas, Dawn, across the sky. Once past early
childhood, they'd grown apart, though the nicknames stuck. Yasodhara
had moved into the world of her girl cousins and the raucous games they'd
played with her brother and boy cousins: catch and hide-and-seek, and a
variety of mischief such as playing tricks on old servants, tearing along
the wooden platform that ran around the city's ramparts, swimming in the
Rohini River. Each year Siddhartha's stepmother, Prajapati, returned in the
spring to Ramagama, her hometown, to see her brother Dandapani, bringing along Siddhartha and her daughter Sundari Nanda. Other cousins from
Kapilavastu also often came along with Prajapati, and then the games were
particularly raucous.

Though Siddhartha had sometimes joined in these pursuits, he spent
most of his visits trailing her father, whom he hero-worshipped. Dandapani
was patient and gentle with the boy's precocious questions, and allowed
Siddhartha to go with him to the santagara to hear matters of state debated
or to be present during court cases brought before Dandapani, and even
to accompany him on his trips out into the kingdom to see about various
matters. Her father was flattered at the attention but also drawn to this boy
who was preternaturally intelligent, able to grasp things well beyond his
years, able to remember and quote the Vedas. Yasodhara had also come to
understand that her father pitied Siddhartha because he was despised by
his own father, Suddhodana. For Suddhodana, his son's failure in the manly
sports was shaming and unforgivable, and there were many times when
Yasodhara had witnessed her uncle humiliating Siddhartha in front of a
gathering. She had also, many a time, seen the bruises on Siddhartha from
a whipping and had pitied him herself. Yet Siddhartha bore these beatings
and humiliations meekly. When anyone expressed outrage on his behalf,
he would say things like, "But it's true, I am shaming my pita. I am failing
in archery and spear fighting," speaking in a strangely judicious tone, as
if talking about someone else. This objectivity, rather than winning him

sympathy, alienated people. She knew that his nickname among the servants and slaves was "ghost."

Suddenly now, she recalled a long-forgotten incident with a swan. It had taken place during a visit she and her family had made to Kapilavastu, the city where Siddhartha lived. Her brother Devadatta and her cousin Mahanama had shot at a swan that was flying by, and one of their arrows had injured the bird. It had drifted down lopsided, the flap of its wings sounding like a washerwoman snapping open sheets, to land near where Siddhartha was crouched, playing a game of chaturanga by himself. Yasodhara and her girl cousins were playing with their dolls close by under a tree and they watched, fascinated, as Siddhartha gently took the bird in his arms and removed the arrow, wrapping the swan in his shawl, its red cotton turning black as the blood soaked through. Soon, Devadatta and Mahanama rushed into the garden looking for their kill, bows slung across shoulders. Seeing Siddhartha with the bird, they ran up to him, crying, "Leave that swan alone, Siddhartha!" "How dare you touch it!" They stood over him, arms on hips. Mahanama grinned menacingly, his incisors sharp like a goose's, while Devadatta's swarthy face radiated righteous outrage. Siddhartha continued to quietly staunch the bird's blood. With an exasperated grunt, Mahanama grabbed his cousin roughly by the shoulder and shook him—but now the swan began to snap its beak at Mahanama and he quickly stepped away. "The bird is not yours," Siddhartha said with a shrug. "Not while it's alive. I claim it. Our fathers are gathered in the pavilion, let them decide."

Yasodhara and her girl cousins trooped after the boys, interested in the outcome. When they arrived at the raja's pavilion, they found Dandapani, Suddhodana and the Senapati of Kapilavastu seated on cushions, chatting. The children trooped up the steps towards the men, Siddhartha bearing the swan. Dandapani and the senapati were amused at the interruption, but Suddhodana was irritated.

Siddhartha put the swan down before his elders.

"Mātula," Devadatta said to Suddhodana, "since we are here in your kingdom, and you are its raja, I ask you: Who does this swan belong to? The one who shot it or the one who found it?"

"The one who shot it," Suddhodana replied promptly.

"But it's a wild animal, pita," Siddhartha said earnestly to his father, "and so doesn't belong to any of us, because it's not dead." Then he quoted the Vedas, to back himself up. A flash of astonished admiration passed over the faces of Dandapani and the senapati that a boy of ten would know such an obscure verse by heart. Suddhodana, however, was angry. "My son the scholar," he cried with a forced laugh. He gestured to Dandapani. "As our guest here, you are pre-eminent. You rule on this."

But, before Dandapani could speak, Siddhartha said quietly, with an apologetic grimace at his uncle, "Actually, it's our senapati, as the representative of our maharaja, our overlord, who is pre-eminent, pita."

With another short laugh, Suddhodana gestured playfully for the senapati to speak. The senapati stood and bowed deeply to both rajas, humbling himself before them. Then he sat down and, after arranging the folds of his dhoti, nodded to say that Siddhartha's reasoning about the swan was correct. The man's chin had lifted, eyes hooded, as he examined the boy.

Yasodhara wondered now, as she gazed out her window at the square below, what Siddhartha's relationship with this senapati, the maharaja's general, had been at that time. Were they already friends, or was that moment the start of the friendship? Whatever the case, when it came time for the biennial picking of a young nobleman from the cohort who were between thirteen and fourteen, to go to study in the Savatthi Court, the senapati bestowed this great honour on Siddhartha. Suddhodana was furious. His choice had been his nephew Mahanama, whom he was already grooming as his successor. But the senapati, ignoring his recommendation, had picked Siddhartha. This had finally and completely turned Suddhodana against his son. He believed that Siddhartha had plotted to humiliate him. And it didn't help that Siddhartha, in these past three years at the Savatthi Court, had become the favourite of the maharaja. In the court of Maha Kosala, Siddhartha's contemplative intelligence, his quickness in assessing a situation, were recognized, valued and channelled into what those talents were good for—the administration of a state, diplomacy and policy. His failures in the manly sports of hunting and horse racing and weaponry did not matter in the Savatthi Court. Theirs was the age of trade, not war, Yasodhara's mother often told her, and the talents a future raja most needed were the ones that Siddhartha possessed. Besides becoming the favourite of the emperor Maha Kosala, who treated him like a son, Siddhartha had also caught the eye of the regent, Pasénadi, and had quickly become the uparaja's friend.

To Yasodhara, Siddhartha now seemed so distant, barely the cousin she knew, this rising star in the maharaja's court. So, why had he chosen her? She sat in the window well pondering this for a while. Then, with a quiet "yes, I see," she grasped his reason. He loved and admired her parents. Though it had been some years since he'd followed her father around, the memory of her father's kindness was likely still with him. He also loved his aunt for her motherliness towards him. Yasodhara recalled how Pamita had always been gentle with Siddhartha because his own mother had died giving birth to him and his stepmother Prajapati, though not unkind, offered him no love and no protection from Suddhodana's cruelty. *Yes, yes, that is it: he's marrying the family, not me.*

Yasodhara had been absentmindedly ripping at a tassel on a cushion and now she pushed it away with a *tttch* and got up from the window well. She gathered her bathing things for the midday bath and sacrifice, annoyed and offended by the thought that Siddhartha wasn't picking her but her family. Yet, over the course of the day, the more she pondered his reason for choosing her, the less insulted she felt; and the more swayed she was towards saying yes to meeting him. After all, her parents' marriage, which was the model she aspired to, had started in much the same way: a strategic decision by her mother, who had made it known to Dandapani, through another girl cousin, that if he was interested, she wouldn't be averse to a proposal. Pamita liked his family and wanted to escape her own harsh one in Kapilavastu, but also saw in Dandapani a potential future raja. With the marriage, love had come. Also, friendship and companionship. Siddhartha, Yasodhara knew without a doubt, would treat her well. If nothing else, his respect for her parents would make him considerate towards her.

When she told her mother all this, Pamita smacked her palms together, gratified. "Ah, Ushas, then I have trained you well! You are truly my daughter!"

"I have one doubt, though." Yasodhara scrunched up her nose, folding her arms under her shawl. "He is very remote, like a Brahmin in a forest.

I won't marry some man who lives in his head all the time, ammé, who'll barely say a word to me."

"You're right to be cautious about that, dhītā. You don't want a dry, parched husband. So let's arrange for you to spend time with him and see."

⚓

Pamita and Dandapani sent Siddhartha word that his proposal was conditionally accepted, so long as their daughter was given time to fully make up her mind. They invited him to visit at the end of the rainy season.

Yasodhara hadn't seen Siddhartha for so long that when she came downstairs to the courtyard of the women's quarters—aware that her mother had paused on the steps above to watch from a distance—she couldn't stop herself from lifting her eyes to him. He examined her back in a frank, friendly way. He was greatly changed—no longer the pudgy boy she had known three years before. Unlike most sixteen-year-old boys, he wasn't gangly and awkward but was well formed, slim and quite tall, his skin smooth, without any pimples. Why, she thought in surprise as she examined his face, he's handsome! And he was, in a delicate, fine-featured way, his wrists not much bigger than hers, a stem-of-an-amphora neck, a pronounced clavicle that fluttered with his breath. He was dressed simply, in a white dhoti and plain red turban, the red sash around his waist with no embroidery. His bare upper body was not dusted with camphor, as was the fashion among men, and his necklace was a simple pearl pendant, while his earrings and armbands were modest circles of gold.

They greeted each other shyly, bowing. "Ñātiké," he said, blushing, "I'm happy we are meeting."

"Yes," she said, blushing back. "I am too."

He gestured that they should proceed out of the women's quarters. He had, for their first meeting, requested that they go walk about the city. They left the palace and set off across the royal square, a well-born slave (a widowed noblewoman fallen upon hard times and forced to sell herself) following at a short distance as chaperone.

"You know," he said after a moment, smiling and nodding at her, hands clasped behind his back, "I've always loved your city."

"Have you?" she asked, surprised. "But Kapilavastu is much larger. And Savatthi even grander."

"Ah, but that's why I love *your* city better." He laughed shyly, giving her a quick, friendly glance.

"You must tell me exactly what you love, then," she replied with a matching laugh, feeling suddenly easy with him. She'd thought he would be tongue-tied and awkward like most men who live in their heads, but in fact he wasn't remote at all. His shyness was actually charming because of his niceness, his friendliness. And mercifully, he wasn't one of those shy men who looked for any opportunity to put a woman down as a way to buttress their own awkwardness.

"In your city—the city of my late mother, so there's another reason to love it!—you can walk everywhere because of its size." He waved his hand to encompass their surroundings, breathing in deeply as if smelling a flower garden. "Here, no strangers arrive to set up businesses, to build homes. Trades pass from fathers to sons. Why, even your ganikās can trace their lineage back to their great-grandmothers, some even further!"

"And how would you know about our ganikās, Surya?" She laughed quickly to say she was teasing him about the courtesans, taken aback by her own boldness.

She saw a flash of admiration in his eyes at her wit, then he laughed too. Yes, yes, she really did like him.

He took her hand. "It's strange, isn't it," he said casually, as if he had done nothing surprising, "how our nicknames from childhood have stuck."

She nodded, shy at the feel of his hand in hers, a small vial of warmth tipping within her.

"Do you think we were meant to be together? That it was destined by the gods?" He bent to peer at her earnestly. She lowered her eyelids and blushed, tongue-tied. Mistaking her expression, he made to drop her hand, but she quickly closed her fingers around his. "Ah, Ushas," he said softly, as if she had given him a gift.

They stopped before a garland-maker's shop and he bought her a lovely string of jasmine and blue lotuses. When he put it around her neck, she blushed again, still amazed at that instinctive way she had grasped at his fingers. What had made her do such a forward thing? She didn't know, except to say that she'd felt comfortable enough to do so.

Siddhartha, she noticed, was welcomed wherever they went. The merchants, the Vessas, remembered him well from his previous visits. He had always taken a genuine interest in the work of the various artisans, in the lives and troubles of the shop owners, which was unusual for a member of the ruling Khattiya caste—Siddhartha squatting beside the artisans and asking to be allowed a turn at whatever craft they were doing, helping shop owners wrap up goods and count out change. Although somewhere in the back of her mind Yasodhara had known this was his habit when he visited Ramagama, for the first time she was seeing for herself his relationship with artisans and merchants. The Vessas congratulated him on his success in Savatthi, for they had heard, like everyone else, that he was a favourite of the Maharaja Maha Kosala and that the regent, Pasénadi, had taken him up as a friend. Many of the older men said, "I'm not surprised, daharā, it's what I expected." To her, Siddhartha had been a loner; now she was witnessing his popularity among these people.

He made a special detour down a little road, wanting to introduce her to a potter he was friendly with. Once they arrived at the shop, though, the potter's son informed them that his father was ill and in bed. "I would like to see your pita, if he will see me," Siddhartha said, his tone suggesting the humble potter would be honouring him. The son nodded and bowed, gesturing for them to follow him into the shop. As they made their way through the dim store, Yasodhara looked around, intrigued by the hanging pots and plates tied to each other by thin ropes, the shelves crammed with lumps of clay and shards of pots and potting tools. She had never been in the back of a shop before; merchants always brought their wares to her and Pamita as they sat in their palanquin outside.

They soon emerged into a shabby courtyard, cluttered with pots and a rickety charpoy. Naked children were playing, and a woman was cooking by a large hearth. Yasodhara had never seen such shabbiness, yet Siddhartha seemed perfectly at ease here. When they went into a dim room to see the potter, Siddhartha didn't balk, as she did, at the odour of sickness and unwashed body. Instead, he took the old man's hand and spoke softly to him, calling him "dear mitta," as if he were a Khattiya nobleman rather than a humble potter. From the doorway, she watched his comfort, his grace with these people, feeling intimidated, unworthy of him.

Once they had left and were back in the street, Yasodhara became silent, withdrawn, and Siddhartha said softly, "What is it, Ushas?"

She was quiet for a moment, thinking how to express herself without sounding coquettish or plaintive. Finally, she gathered her shawl about her. "Ñātaka," she said, addressing him formally as "cousin." "Given your success in Savatthi, you have many choices. I am puzzled you have chosen me."

He nodded and paused a moment, frowning over her question. Then he smiled. "I chose you because you can ask such a question plainly. Because I knew you could." Then added with a small, teasing grin, "Ñātiké."

"But how? How do you know? You hardly know me at all."

"Not so, Ushas. I have known you all my life. I remember you well from all my visits to Ramagama."

She peered closely at him and saw that he was sincere. He really did appear to remember her well, to have made his assessment carefully. Though what he was assessing she didn't know, since they had spent so little time together during his visits in latter years. After a moment, she nodded, then smiled and took his hand, her gratitude and happiness making her bold.

They were passing an alley. On impulse, she glanced back and, seeing they had left their chaperone quite a distance behind, she pulled Siddhartha into the laneway, drew him to her and kissed him. After a gasp of surprise, he put his arms around her and kissed her back. Her mouth opened and their tongues touched briefly before she broke away with a giggle and took off back to the main road. It wasn't her first kiss; she'd experimented with other boy cousins.

As Siddhartha joined her, he nodded happily. Seeing this, she understood that she had tested him on impulse, and he had passed. Rather than judging her badly, his quick beseeching look said, *Don't break my heart, it is yours.*

When they returned to the palace and she went to see her parents, Yasodhara didn't need to say anything. They saw her answer in her flushed, radiant face.

2

Siddhartha and the Nigantha

AFTER SIDDHARTHA HAD left Yasodhara at the women's quarters, he made his way towards the ramparts, in need of solitude. He scaled the ladder up to the platform that ran around the inside of the fortifications and, nodding to the soldiers, began to walk around the wooden stockade, hands clasped behind his back, lost in thought, pausing occasionally to look over the thatched roofs of the city, or sometimes to look in the other direction, beyond the ramparts to the Rohini River and the boats and barges there, to the Dasa hovels clustered beyond the moat and, even further in the distance, the fields of paddy and the artisan villages.

What he was thinking about was an evening six months prior, when he went with the Maharaja Maha Kosala to listen to an ascetic in the palace gardens.

The maharaja's interest in the various ascetic schools that had suddenly sprung up in the Middle Country was known to everyone by then, but the old man never talked to anyone about his interest. The court assumed, as Siddhartha did too, that the reason for his silence was that he was fully aware of the heretic nature of these schools; aware it was unseemly, *wrong*, for the Maharaja of the Kosala Empire to be interested in any practice that denigrated the ancient Vedic ways and the sacred thrice-daily sacrifices that fed the gods and kept them strong—kept the sun rising and setting, the rain falling, the wind blowing, the moon lighting their way at night. The maharaja was courting the anger of the gods, who could punish not just him but the entire empire with drought, hurricanes, forest fires, famine, disease and other forms of disaster. Thus Siddhartha had been surprised, and not a little flattered, when the old maharaja asked him to come with him to see the ascetic. "Daharā," Maha Kosala said as they walked together to the pavilion where the ascetic awaited them, "I want to hear your thoughts, your challenges, to this new creed." He gave Siddhartha a sombre look. The maharaja was saying he was hoping Siddhartha might, through his challenges and questions, break him of his fascination.

The pavilion in the royal garden was brightly lit with many lamps, and when they came up the steps they found the naked samana seated cross-legged, his shrivelled sex in his lap. The samana's emaciated body was covered with dust, ribs pressing against thin grey skin, knee and elbow joints painfully bony. He was a Nigantha, and so was slowly starving himself to death to extinguish all possible rebirths. Seeing them, he gestured to a water pot in the pavilion. "Thirsty." He didn't wish to gain any further negative karma by lifting the water pot to his lips and destroying the tiny life forms within. Siddhartha picked up the pot and held it up to the ascetic's lips. Many sticks of incense had been lit in there, but he could still smell the man's stench of urine and dried feces. "I see, O samana, that though you won't pick up the pot yourself, you see no contradiction in destroying the life forms by ingesting them." Siddhartha glanced at the maharaja, who nodded subtly to encourage him, his eyes glittering as if Siddhartha were his favourite horse and he was backing him in a race. The samana smacked his lips and said nothing, refusing to take up the challenge.

After Siddhartha put down the empty pot, he stepped far enough away to diminish the smell and examined the man curiously.

"Ask me what you will, sāmi." The Nigantha gestured at him with his palms open. He smiled thinly to say he knew Siddhartha had been brought to challenge him, but also to let Siddhartha know he was unflustered.

Siddhartha had come prepared: "Mitta, if you must take up the samana's life, why not follow our Vedic ascetic ways? It seems to me much more useful to go, like our samanas, into the forest and, through your mortifications, increase your power at the sacrifice and thus bring strength to the gods and good fortune to us all. Wouldn't that be a worthier path? After all, what does starvation to death achieve for anyone?"

"Ah, but that is the false path, sāmi." The ascetic keenly studied Siddhartha's face, as if looking into him. "Listen, sāmi, I am tired of dragging this body around. Truly, I wish to end my cycles of suffering. Truly, the thought of another birth, no matter how fair, horrifies me. For, even in the most pleasant of lives, as we know, there is suffering. We grow old and sick, we sorrow and hurt. We desire beyond any possible fulfillment. Lose the ones we love most, the things and places we love most. Our bodies that we so cosset become our enemies with age and sickness. But the wisdom of non-action stops all this."

"But this life, which you disparage, mitta, also contains joy and laughter," Siddhartha said, less certain. "It contains love."

"Ah, but even then, the sorrow is ever present—the constant way life, moment to moment, disappoints us." He gave Siddhartha a piercing look, for he had seen his sudden uncertainty. "Then there is the truth that the very things we are sure will make us happy, that we are sure will fix what ails us, when we finally get them, come tainted by other things we could not have anticipated. And so they fail and disappoint us. Indeed, they bewilder us in their failure to satisfy and please."

The ascetic was waiting for Siddhartha to retort, but now he was unable to speak, his mind crowded by the ascetic's words. They had touched a truth he was already aware of: this apprenticeship that he'd wanted fiercely, that he'd worked so hard to get, that he was sure would cure all that troubled him, had failed to do so. Failed to fix his inclination towards pensiveness and make him the outgoing, brilliant person he'd always longed to be. Instead, though outwardly successful and loved and admired here, he still remained the same brooding, lonely person within, his new success a mask he wore.

The emperor was watching him keenly. Siddhartha gave him an embarrassed, pained smile to say he had no answer.

"The path I choose brings great suffering, sāmi," the ascetic continued in triumph. "But this suffering ends all further suffering. It all ends, sāmi, all ends! And one whispers joyfully with one's final breath, 'I am thus gone!'"

That night Siddhartha was unable to sleep. Passing examples of suffering from his own life flitted through his mind. There was the mother he had never known, whose death he felt guilty and responsible for because his father often reminded him that Siddhartha had killed her to gain his own life—sometimes calling him "little murderer" as he beat him, saying he had robbed him of the love of his life, robbed him of his happiness. People thought it odd that he saw his father's point of view when beaten or humiliated by him, but Siddhartha always felt strangely sorry for him. Now, for the first time, his sympathy made sense. During those beatings and humiliations, he had become aware of his father's suffering, a suffering caused by his own pride and ambitions, his own fears. This insight he could now put into words because of the ascetic. When Siddhartha's father cried out, even as he brought his whip or stick down on him, "You deliberately humiliate me," there was often a catch in his voice, sometimes even a glistening in his eyes. Suddhodana truly believed that his son hated him, that he plotted to humiliate him. His father, the raja of a prosperous kingdom, gifted with every comfort a man could want, was still dissatisfied, still angry, his dignity so fragile he would beat his own son to shore it up.

Then there was Siddhartha's stepmother Prajapati, who coldly, scrupulously did her duty by him, so distracted and burdened by her husband's thousand abuses that she had no affection to spare. Her husband constantly reminded her that he had only entered into his double marriage with her to secure the sister he loved, and that the wrong sister, Siddhartha's mother, had died. "Why are you alive and not her?" he would cry to her. "Why have the gods played this cruel trick on me?" Then there were the concubines he installed in the women's quarters for his pleasure, burdening Siddhartha's stepmother not just with their presence and the arrogant contempt with which they often treated her, but also the difficulty of getting rid of them or pensioning them off once her husband had grown tired of them. She, the devi, the pre-eminent woman in the kingdom, was also unhappy. In fact, everywhere Siddhartha looked now, it seemed to be the same—people writhing in their suffering like snakes in a pit.

And yet, starvation to death and emaciation and filth were the answer to nothing. This he knew beyond a doubt. He could never imagine taking that path, and was repulsed by the fanaticism of the ascetics, their blindness to the gaps in their logic, such as drinking water but not drawing it or lifting the pot to their lips. There was also the vanity of their ambitions, the way the different schools competed for the patronage of rich

Vessas and nobles, the way they derided each other. He had witnessed a few knockabout fights between ascetics of competing schools; had even heard of murders by rival ascetics. There was nothing holy or sacred or compassionate about them or their harsh philosophy.

A few days later, Siddhartha went with the maharaja to see another ascetic. He went because he hoped that being in the presence of the samana would cure him of his attraction to the questions these philosophies had raised in him. This man was from the Ajivaka school, one not very different from the Nigantha, except that these ascetics prescribed death by thirst and dehydration, which meant they died much faster than the Niganthas. As Siddhartha crouched by the ascetic, who lay spread out on a mat under a tree in the royal park, he studied the man. The samana was so emaciated that his torso had collapsed against his spine, and the knots of his elbows and knees pushed painfully against his ashen, papery skin. The maharaja was crouched by Siddhartha too, and they leaned in close to hear the man whisper his creed about suffering and escape, his eyes glazed as he approached death. All around them other Ajivaka ascetics, also in stages of emaciation, crouched or lay on mats, all watching their guru die with fierce attention and ardour. Siddhartha was repelled, and yet, even as he felt this repulsion, he found himself listening to the dying man, seeing the truth in what he said about suffering, and frightened by his attraction to this truth, because he didn't know what he was supposed to do with it.

Later, as they were walking towards the royal chariot, Maha Kosala took his elbow. "I know what the court thinks. I know they believe that my visits to these ascetics are as if I have become besotted with a common vesiyā." He shrugged as if to say how could he, the emperor, not know what the court said, given that his spies were everywhere? "I know they say: 'Look at the maharaja!'" He gestured to his rotund stomach, his double chin. "'How can the maharaja, of all people, who demands twelve dishes at each meal, even think he can live off grass, even think he can starve himself to death? How can the maharaja, who walks nowhere, ever think he can walk for yojanas barefooted?'" The old man squeezed Siddhartha's elbow. "But, daharā, the maharaja does think he can. All the time."

"Ah, sāmi," Siddhartha said, searching his face, "can you really see yourself thus?"

Maha Kosala was quiet a moment. "The attraction is real and grows and grows. One day, I suspect, I will walk away from all this." He swept his arm wide to indicate his empire, and Siddhartha saw in the old man's eyes that he was haunted by this calling that he was finding harder and harder to resist.

"And you too, daharā, you too now feel the calling." Maha Kosala nodded at Siddhartha's surprise. "Yes, yes, I see it in you. And I blame myself. I asked you to come with me hoping—because I recognize myself in you—that you would help cure me. But instead, I fear I might have given you my disease."

Siddhartha gazed at the maharaja, worried. It truly frightened him that, like Maha Kosala, he might be drawn irresistibly to this path, and someday find he had no choice but to follow it.

A few nights later, Siddhartha went with the uparaja Pasénadi and his closest friends, Bandhula and Karayana, to the house of the courtesan Kusuma. The night proceeded as it always did, with singing and dancing by the ganikās while refreshments were served. Kusuma, plump and lovely, wandered among the gathered noblemen, who flocked here because of Pasénadi's patronage. She greeted them each in her motherly fashion, pinching cheeks and biceps, tousling heads, teasing and laughing with them. The uparaja's party were separated from the others by an archway, set in a little raised alcove that could be screened off by curtains, when needed. Pasénadi and Bandhula were already sprawled among bolsters and cushions, cuddling their favourite ganikās, who fed them food and wine, some of the liquid dribbling down their chests. The men and the ganikās giggled and flirted, the women licking the wine off the men's chests. Siddhartha sat sipping from his goblet of wine and examined his friends.

At twenty, Pasénadi appeared to be a man who had everything. His love of the sensual life was reflected in his muscular rotundity. And yet, he was trapped in a loveless marriage, a political union thrust upon him. His wife Ubbiri was the sister of the new Magadha emperor Bimbisara, and Pasénadi had been wedded in a double marriage, Bimbisara marrying the uparaja's sister. Ubbiri, so Pasénadi had told Siddhartha, shuddered with disgust every time he made love to her, trembling like a trapped hare beneath him. Nor did Pasénadi find love and affection in his various trysts. They were nothing but amorous taking or buying, the exercise of his privilege as uparaja. Behind his bluff, hearty manner, he was lonely.

Then there were Bandhula and Karayana, uncle and nephew, though only a year separated them. Bandhula, twenty and brawny, had the restrained inner fire of a military man sure of his capabilities. Handsome in a broad-faced way, the oiled, shaved head of a warrior suited him well. He had recently, along with Pasénadi, quashed a rebellion in a vassal state and so was a man much admired in the army and in court. Yet there was a restless ambition to him, and his brooding gaze always sought, it seemed to Siddhartha, the next success just out of his reach. His dissatisfaction was a burden to nineteen-year-old Karayana, for the two men were bound in an amorous relationship of the kind that sometimes springs up in the army. Karayana, whose knobby shaved head and gaunt face made him look like a rain-soaked crow, loved Bandhula with an ardour that wasn't quite returned. And so there was about his manner the wry cynicism of a cuckold bolstering his dignity.

Kusuma's wanderings had now brought her to their alcove. She nodded with approval to see her ganikās pleasuring Pasénadi and Bandhula, then turned to Siddhartha and Karayana, who sat apart, cross-legged. The courtesan let out a fond little sigh. "Can you never find satisfaction in this house, mitto?" she asked, then pouted, mock-hurt. "After all, how will this look for me, who claims to have the best?"

"Indeed," Pasénadi cried heartily, joining this well-worn routine. "You both insult our lovely hostess."

Kusuma leaned close to Karayana and murmured loud enough for Bandhula to hear, with a glance for his permission, "Mitta, I've just acquired a lovely Yavana slave boy from Thebes, the spoil of some war. Would you not be tempted?"

Karayana laughed and shook his head, then said what he always said: "Think of me as a mere escort, a servant who has accompanied his masters." He gestured to Pasénadi and Bandhula.

With a gentle tutting, the ganikā turned to Siddhartha. "And you, mitta? I suppose you too are going to give me this servant-master argument?"

He laughed sheepishly.

But Kusuma, consummate ganikā, saw immediately his hesitancy, even before he was aware of it. "Ah!" she cried. "I have the perfect one for you."

Siddhartha laughed again, shaking his head.

Pasénadi and Bandhula sat up, astonished. "Why Siddhartha," the uparaja cried, "you're finally one of us!"

Karayana, too, turned to regard him with surprise.

Before he could protest, Kusuma, with unexpected strength, grabbed his arm and pulled him to his feet. "Yes, the perfect lovely girl for you!" She bustled him off and Siddhartha let himself be led, giving his friends a shrug and a rictus of a laugh.

"It will be on my charge," Kusuma whispered in a businesslike tone as she led him along, looking around with expert eyes for the ganikā she had in mind. For here was truly something she could add to her list of boasts and important clientele: the son of the Raja of Kapilavastu. She leaned in closer: "I am guessing that, apart from the obligatory visit to a ganikā at thirteen, you haven't . . . mitta?" Siddhartha nodded, blushing, then gave that strained laugh again, playing more drunk than he was to hide the chaos of his feelings.

Kusuma paired him with an eighteen-year-old ganikā who was gentle and friendly, and who, Kusuma felt, would help him overcome his diffidence. Yet Kusuma needn't have worried about his being shy or too nervous to perform. Siddhartha was desperate to lose himself in sensual pleasure, wanting to get away from this malaise that haunted him. He made love again and again to the young woman, crying out as if in pain each time he climaxed.

Finally, Siddhartha fell asleep exhausted and woke towards dawn, the ganikā asleep beside him. In the grey light, he could see lines of weariness and sorrow in her unguarded face. The kohl had spread into wide smudges around her eyes, making her look ill and emaciated, and the collyrium on her cheeks was streaked down to her jaw. Her hair was flung about, and her breasts rose and trembled poignantly with her breath. There was dried spit at the corners of her mouth, and the sandalwood oil perfuming her body mingled with the odour of his semen and their mutual sweat and saliva. He eased himself out of bed, groped for his dhoti, jewellery, turban and shawl and crept out. In the corridor, as he hastily pleated his dhoti, he could hear snoring and snorting coming from the other rooms, the pained *creak-creak* of someone making love again at this hour, the faked cries of a ganikā sounding like she was calling out from deep within a well. There was a fug of male sweat and farts in the corridor, even the faint odour of defecation.

In the main reception room, Siddhartha found that an orgy had taken place, and now men and women were sprawled out on the mats and rugs, their bodies contorted around bolsters and cushions. They looked like corpses in a battlefield, drained of blood in the dawn light. And again, that odour of sweat, saliva, old food and wine mingling with the stink of various perfumes. He looked in briefly on his friends, easing aside the curtains of the alcove. Pasénadi and Bandhula lay naked and spread-eagled in the arms of two ganikās. Karayana had fallen asleep in a corner, curled into himself like a little boy. As Siddhartha examined his friends' slack faces, he could see suddenly the old men they would become, traces of age already in their faces, the first very faint lines that would deepen and spread. He turned to regard his own face in a mirror, seeing also in it the old man he would become.

Siddhartha escaped the ganikā's house and set off through the quiet dawn streets, shoulders hunched, his feet clomping against the beaten-earth road. This defect in him—because yes, he saw now it was a defect—had only grown stronger from his attempt to escape it. But what could he do? And then, for some reason, an image rose in his mind of Yasodhara's father Dandapani, lying on his wife's bed, watching through hooded eyes his beloved wife seated cross-legged beside him, energetically making him a packet of betel or embroidering a shawl or blanket, as they discussed the affairs of the day. The memory was from his visits to Ramagama, when his uncle and aunt, knowing of Siddhartha's loveless existence in Kapilavastu, often invited him to join their family in the evening. There, seated on the carpet by his uncle and aunt's bed, playing a game of chaturanga with Yasodhara or Devadatta, he would observe with interest the couple's companionship, the way his uncle sought the advice of his wife; watch how his aunt steered her husband, sometimes gently, sometimes firmly, towards the correct solution around some matter of state. Of all the men Siddhartha knew, the person he felt closest to temperamentally was his uncle—a man also prone to pensiveness, who would have wandered along byways of thought and lost himself if his vigorous, practical wife had not reined him in. And then Siddhartha thought of Yasodhara too, bent energetically over some task with her mother, the way she led the girl cousins in their games with the boys; thought how she had inherited her mother's vigour and practicality.

The very next day Siddhartha sent a messenger to Ramagama asking for Yasodhara's hand in marriage.

3

Dark Clouds

OVER THE NEXT few months, Siddhartha came often to visit Yasodhara, making the day-long journey by horseback from Savatthi. Her affection grew for him, but it was not a besotted love. There was a private spirit in her that prevented her from giving over completely to any other person. And one of the things she soon came to like best about her cousin was that he didn't press in on her; didn't try to master this private spirit, like most men would have. During his visits, he would spend time with her, but also go off with her father, or sit talking with older statesmen in the santagara, or visit a Brahmin he was fond of who was an expert on the Vedas. While most women would have been jealous, resentful, of his other interests, she valued this about him. Her private spirit needed to breathe, to live, to be left alone. She wondered if this was what he had noticed about her all these years—if he had recognized this shared independence.

Then, on his last visit to her before their marriage, as Yasodhara came down to the women's courtyard, she saw that Siddhartha was agitated, his smile pained. She took his hand and they walked in silence along some side streets until they came to a ladder which led up to the wooden walkway that circled the ramparts. The sentries allowed them access, recognizing them. Once they were up and had walked some distance from the sentries, she turned to him and waited, head cocked.

"It . . . it's nothing, Ushas." He looked away under her steady gaze, then stuck a finger under his turban and scratched his scalp. "I . . . I'm just worried. About returning to Kapilavastu. My pita is still upset at me for being chosen to go to the maharaja's court." He made an impatient gesture, then cried out passionately, "How I hate going back there!"

She stroked his arm soothingly. "But what do you think your pita will do?"

"Not give me a post."

She laughed in disbelief. "Of any kind?"

"Yes."

"But how do you know that?"

"I've heard . . . one of our amicis who came to visit the maharaja on state business warned me. I trust the man. He is fond of me."

"But that's ridiculous. Of course your pita must give you a position."

"Yes, yes, and then I too will be a fly stuck in the honeypot of power." He threw a hand up with great agitation. "That is all that awaits me, the honeypot of power."

She frowned, studying his bitter expression; she had never seen him like this before.

"But we're all stuck in this honeypot of power you speak about," she said quietly. "Myself, my parents. And it isn't like that at all, Surya. We have a good life, we all do. In which we do much good for the janata."

He smiled, but in disagreement, picking at a splinter on one of the rampart logs.

"Surya, tell me your thoughts. We are to be married soon, let's not start dissembling already."

He pulled at the splinter, stripping off a length of wood. "A good life? And yet, didn't your pita, this very day, have to sentence a thief to have his nostrils slit, his left ear cut off?"

"But that's what a raja does! You're surely not suggesting that he should have let the man go? That thief violated the woman he robbed."

"But still your pita had to administer the punishment. Sit there and watch the punishment take place."

She wanted to say, "Yes of course, who else?" but remained silent. She didn't know what he was getting at or why he was in this strange mood. "But Surya," she said carefully, after a moment, "surely if you're raja one day, you too—"

He cut her off with a laugh. "Me, raja? Not if my pita can help it."

"No, no," he added after a moment, "the Niganthas and Ajivakas are right. The world is full of suffering and no matter what we do, we always end up at that place of suffering. Our dreams die, the people we love die, our very bodies let us down, grow old and sicken. Any effort is useless because it always ends badly."

Yasodhara gaped at him. "But why, in the name of all the heavenly apsaras, are you bringing up these ascetics? I . . . I don't understand. Surely you don't, you *can't*, believe these heretics with their gibberish about karma and rebirth?"

"The maharaja believes in them."

"Believes or is entertained?" She studied him, her gaze challenging.

Siddhartha brooded, staring at the Rohini River below, then he sighed, winced at her apologetically and took her hand. "I'm sorry, Ushas. This is all very stupid of me. I think I'm just sad my time in Savatthi is ending, and worried about what awaits me in Kapilavastu . . . worried because . . . Because I want to offer you a life you are worthy of." He said all this earnestly and she examined him for a long moment, trying to discern if he was telling the truth.

After a moment, she nodded—but mostly because she felt him coming down from his agitation. "You *will* be given a position. You're marrying the Koliya raja's daughter, your father's sister's daughter. My uncle, even if he toys with you for a bit, will give you a position."

They walked back to the palace holding hands, a conciliatory silence between them. When they reached the palace entrance Yasodhara said softly, "By the way, I happened to run into the son of that potter we visited. I inquired after his father . . . and he told me he's dying. I wonder, Surya, if you should go see him."

"I will go immediately." And suddenly she could see he was vitalized.

Later, when Siddhartha returned, he was flushed and at peace. The visit with the dying man seemed to have driven away his fears and doubts.

"Yes," Yasodhara thought as he took her in his arms with a little murmur, "how much like my pita he really is. This tendency to get lost in tangles of thought, and needing to be led back to himself, to his task, by ammé." It made her happy to feel she had the same relationship with

Siddhartha as her parents did with each other. He was a good man, like her father. But, just like her father, Siddhartha needed a good woman, a strong woman, to keep him on the correct path. She was that woman.

Yet, as Siddhartha had predicted, once he returned home to Kapilavastu he languished, unemployed. A spy brought to Yasodhara and her parents the story of Siddhartha's return, and how, when he'd presented himself to his father in court, Suddhodana had cried, "Ah, Siddhartha, welcome, welcome back to our humble court. We must seem like peasants compared to the glories you've enjoyed in Savatthi!" Yasodhara could picture her uncle sitting on his throne, his brawny frame, his foolish, petulant face, his habit of running his fingers through the thick mat of hair on his chest; she could picture that brilliant grin of the bully that must have lit his face as he made fun of Siddhartha.

Her mother's other brother, Amitodhana, and his son Mahanama, favoured by Suddhodana to succeed him as raja, had also been in attendance. For though Suddhodana was the real raja, the triad of them ruled together and were present as a united front at all court gatherings. Oh, she could imagine her cousin Mahanama's delight at this humiliation of Siddhartha—his round face merry, those sharp incisors framing his grin; and her uncle Amitodhana sitting in that fastidious way of his, hands clasped, knees pressed together, his smile pinched and sneering.

After that sarcastic greeting, the spy told them, Suddhodana had turned away and begun a conversation with an amici who had come about an issue in the treasury, Amitodhana and Mahanama also joining in the discussion. Siddhartha had stood there, waiting for his father to address him again, but once the amici had left, Suddhodana summoned the next petitioner, and then the next and the next. Siddhartha stood all morning in front of the court like a servant, a slave, his face burning with shame, as petitioner after petitioner approached his father and the other two members of the ruling triad, each petitioner studying Siddhartha avidly so they could describe his demeanour when they spread word of his humiliation. When it finally came time for everyone to go away and bathe in preparation for the midday sacrifice, Suddhodana rose and left without a glance at his son.

Since then, Siddhartha had passed his days doing nothing, waiting for his father to assign him a position in the court. This would not happen, Yasodhara realized, until Suddhodana thought his son had learned a true lesson in humility.

The spy also told them that the uparaja, Pasénadi, hearing of his friend's plight, had petitioned Suddhodana to give him Siddhartha for a position in the Savatthi Court. Suddhodana had sent back a hearty message saying he needed his brilliant son at home, and had great plans for him.

When she heard all this, Yasodhara was frightened. All along she had assumed that Siddhartha, once married, would be given an important position in the Savatthi Court, where she and he would live. After the spy left, she said plaintively to Pamita, "Why doesn't Maha Kosala intervene? After all, he loves Siddhartha. Why doesn't he order my uncle to send Siddhartha to Savatthi?"

Pamita smiled thinly. "A man cannot tell another man what to do with his son, Ushas. If the maharaja did that, it would be a public humiliation for my brother and fray relations between their kingdoms."

Yasodhara picked glumly at the folds of her dhoti. "I hoped that . . . Oh ammé, Kapilavastu? Am I to live in that palace, under my aunt?"

Pamita bent forward to regard her keenly. "Ushas, if you wish, it isn't too late to break the betrothal. There are many young men who—"

"Not marry Siddhartha? Oh, ammé, how is that possible!"

Pamita smiled at her outrage. "Well then, your decision is made."

After a moment, Yasodhara nodded slowly. Yes, it seemed that her decision was made, however difficult the consequences. She simply couldn't imagine a life without Siddhartha.

During this time their neighbour, the Moriya raja, sent a complaint about Devadatta. He had been caught hunting in a patch of Moriya forest that bordered their kingdoms in the northeast. Without permission. Worse, her brother had refused to leave when asked.

This was serious. That piece of forest had been seized back and forth by the Koliya and Moriya kingdoms, until finally her father had signed it over to get rid of the aggravation.

That evening, when Yasodhara was in her parents' room for their evening ritual, the chaturanga board laid out between her and her father, there was a sharp rap on the door.

"Enter," Pamita called out.

Devadatta strode in, frowning, and stood some distance from the bed, as if a stranger.

"You need not have knocked, puthā," Pamita said mildly.

Devadatta made a slight gesture with his head to dismiss this; and when his mother beckoned him forward by patting the mattress, he came and stood by the bed instead, one hand on the bedpost.

"Is this complaint from the Moriya raja true, puthā?" her father asked, though he already knew the answer.

"Yes, I did hunt there."

"Why? You know better." Pamita slapped the mattress impatiently.

"It's our land. We should never have given it up." Devadatta snorted. "Cowardice. So yes, I do hunt. In *our* forest."

Pamita and Dandapani exchanged a worried look.

"It is not for you, puthā, to decide this, nor to provoke the Moriya." Dandapani leaned back, examining his son sombrely. "They are a touchy people, the Moriya, always ready to pick a fight. It is a worthless track of forest, for which we won some important water rights in the treaty."

"The vana-dasa, with whom I was hunting, don't recognize these borders and treaties. The forest, to them, belongs to everyone. I was their guest so I abided by their rules."

"I order you not to do it again," her father said firmly, with a glance at his wife, who nodded. He held out his signet ring to be kissed.

Devadatta glanced at it briefly, then turned away with a contemptuous huff and stalked out.

Her parents looked at each other helplessly and then at Yasodhara. She nodded, jumped off the bed, shuffled into her leather slippers and ran after Devadatta.

She caught up with her brother as he was crossing the courtyard of the women's quarters. Grabbing his arm, she diverted him through an archway into a small private garden used by the women. He allowed himself to be led, but once they were in the garden, he shrugged off her hand and strode away before throwing himself under a flowering red cotton tree. She came and squatted in front of him, regarding him seriously. "Bhāta . . ."

Devadatta played with one of the fallen red flowers for a moment, then let out a sigh and ran a hand over his forehead, pushing back his turban. "It's our forest," he said stubbornly, but she could tell he was relenting. "Our pita is a coward. He's not fit to be raja. Our uncle, Suddhodana, would never have allowed any forest in the Sakiya Kingdom to be ceded."

"No doubt he wouldn't have," Yasodhara replied dryly, for her uncle was rash and obstinate. They sat in silence for a while. Then she added, reaching out to straighten a pleat in her brother's dhoti, "Promise me you won't do it again, bhāta. You will gain nothing, except force our pita to summon you before the Council of Amicis for censuring and punishment."

He gnawed at his thumb for a while, then nodded, not meeting her eye.

But news of Devadatta's deed soon travelled through the stables, and from there to the infantry and the lower ranks in the army; it travelled because Devadatta boasted of his incursion and condemned his father's cowardice. Other hot-headed young men, who also felt their talents unrecognized, took up his cause to win back the forest.

Some days later, Devadatta led a second incursion into the forest. The Moriya raja, anticipating this sortie would happen, had stationed guards in the forest. There were arrows shot, spears thrown, before Devadatta and his band withdrew. Fortunately, no one died and only a few men were wounded.

This time, Devadatta was summoned before his father and the Council of Amicis. As punishment, he was stripped of his sword and placed under palace arrest, confined to the courtyard where his room was. He was forbidden to visit the stables. The other young noblemen received a similar punishment of house arrest; the infantry who had participated were whipped and put into solitary confinement for a week by the senapati.

Now Yasodhara was truly worried, realizing that anger which had been building up in Devadatta these past five years had found a focal point.

Until he turned thirteen, her brother had believed unquestioningly that he would one day be raja, succeeding his father. He was brave and strong and brawny, well ahead of his contemporaries in spear and sword fighting, archery and horsemanship. It therefore came as a shock to him, that year he turned thirteen, when his father did not select him to go to the Savatthi Court. Instead, deferring to the choice of his Council of Amicis, Dandapani had sent one of their sons instead, a decision backed by the Senapati of Ramagama.

Devadatta was devastated—above all because he knew their father had not fought for him. Nor had their mother prevailed upon her husband, as she was quite capable of doing if she thought he'd made a wrong decision. Pamita and Dandapani believed that Devadatta would make an impressive warrior and even perhaps one day hold a senior position in the army, but they also felt he was too impetuous, too easy to anger, to be raja or even an amici. There were bitter meetings between her parents and her brother, Pamita and Dandapani imploring him to understand their case, Devadatta furious and hurt. But, in the end, her parents could not really defend themselves to him. They had not backed him. They had put the future of the kingdom—the state and its populace—ahead of their son.

Because he believed his parents had betrayed him, Devadatta stopped coming each evening to gather with the family in Pamita's room. He spent more and more time in the stables with the grooms and mahouts, and also with the foot soldiers. Soon the stables became his true home. Here he was loved and admired unconditionally for his warrior skills and also for a very special way he had with animals, able to calm an unbroken horse, the only one allowed by a cow elephant to touch her newborn calf. It was something wonderful to see Devadatta ride a horse without bridle or saddle, pressed into the horse's mane, arms around its neck, man and beast blended into one. He also started to spend time with the vana-dasa who lived in the forests, often going for days to stay in their villages.

The rains arrived, ushering in the Vassa season, the air so humid that breathing was hard. Bed legs were kept in buckets of water because snakes and scorpions, flushed out of their holes, often took refuge in houses, hiding under duvets and pillows or up in the rafters. A ceiling of muslin was hung to prevent them from accidentally falling on beds and carpets, heads and floors. The constantly dark, looming sky made Yasodhara melancholy. She fretted about Siddhartha, who, two months since his return to Kapilavastu, she learned still did nothing with his days, spending most of them in his room in the men's quarters, or walking about the city. Like the dark skies of the Vassa season, her uncle had cast a darkness over her future.

But finally Vassa ended, and it was time for her marriage. A messenger arrived to alert her family that soon the moon would be in conjunction with the constellation of Aghas, and they must prepare to be in Kapilavastu on that auspicious day for the wedding.

Since Pamita, like the rest of the family, would be gone a few weeks, it fell to her and Yasodhara to make sure the household could function well in her absence. A widowed aunt, who lived with them, would be the woman of the home until they returned, but she was too old to handle all the complex household duties. So it was left to Yasodhara and Pamita to decide which servants and slaves would come with them; to make sure there were enough grains and pulses for the household brought in from their granaries outside the city walls; that there was adequate feed for the elephants, horses, cattle, goats and chickens from their storehouses, also beyond the city; that there was adequate firewood from their forests, enough incense and ghee for the sacrifices. Endless meetings were held with the heads of household departments to make sure everything would function smoothly. Helping her mother with these duties, Yasodhara was aware that soon she wouldn't be part of such tasks at home anymore. Every time she thought about this, a sadness rose in her, and also worry and fear about the life that awaited her in Kapilavastu.

The evening before they left, the carts were loaded and the royal chariot made comfortable with cushions and carpets, while the chariots of those accompanying them were lined up behind it. The initial part of the trip would be unpleasant, as it had to be made in two hurried dashes. They had to arrive at the first shrine in time for the morning sacrifices, and then reach the next shrine in time for the midday sacrifice. Any delays or failures to do the sacrifices on time and correctly would result in penalties for the travellers, paid by a day of fasting, or a goat or oxen sacrifice. Not doing the sacrifices on time could also anger the gods, who might impair the journey, sending rain or floods or disease, or even curse the marriage.

On the day of departure, Yasodhara awoke in the sixth part of the night, well before dawn. Her face, like Pamita's, was hollow with anxiety, as they both worried they might be late for the morning sacrifice. The women hurriedly got dressed and made sure everyone else was in their conveyances. A messenger was sent ahead on horseback to alert the priests who lived in the village near the sacrificial sites.

As the royal convoy made its way through the sleeping city, Yasodhara and Pamita peered out through the slats of the chariots' bamboo blinds to make sure there was no light in the sky yet. They cried out in wretched exasperation when the convoy came to a halt beyond the moat. The royal elephant, on which Dandapani rode at the head of the convoy, was refusing to move for some inexplicable reason. Devadatta, who had been released from palace arrest for the wedding, was summoned to the front. He stroked the elephant's trunk, spoke softly in its ear and then gently led it forward by the lower lip, much to everyone's relief.

Soon the convoy reached the first shrine, performed the morning sacrifice, had a hurried meal and rushed off again to arrive in time for the midday baths and sacrifices at the next shrine. Once the midday sacrifice was over, a ripple of softness moved through the travellers, like a breeze through a paddy field. The sacrificial shrine was in Lumbini, a park beside the Rohini River that had been landscaped by Sakiya and Koliya ancestors with an eye on the midday sacrifice and the frenetic travel required before it. The park's canopied trees were in flower at this time of the year and the convoy relaxed beneath them on the fragrant, flower-strewn grass. There were a few pavilions along the riverbank, and Yasodhara, Pamita and Dandapani rested in the one set aside for the raja's family. It was now too hot for travel.

Yasodhara lay on carpets and cushions the serving women had spread out, propped on one arm, alternately watching her sleeping parents and gazing out moodily at the river, where Devadatta was bathing the royal elephant to cool it down, a hawk he had trained recently and called Rama circling overhead. The park was busy with female pilgrims who bathed in the river or rested under trees, for Lumbini was famous as the home of the Yakshi of Lumbini, drawing devotees—mostly women—from all over. The Yakshi was visited by barren couples and by pregnant women who sought safety for mother and child during birth. She was also visited by wives who were struggling with adulterous or cruel husbands. Women of the royal

Sakiya and Koliya families had once come to this park to give birth under the protection of the Yakshi but, ever since Siddhartha's mother died in childbirth here, it was deemed unsafe to travel at such a late stage of pregnancy, and so the royal women came earlier to petition for protection.

Yasodhara had been planning to visit the Yakshi after her afternoon rest, but fidgety with worry about the future, she decided to go now. The shrine would be deserted at this time because of the heat, and she would have the Yakshi's ear for as long as she wished. With a quick glance at her sleeping parents, she crept out of the royal pavilion and headed towards the wooded path that led to the Yakshi's shrine, feeling relief at the prospect of unburdening herself by confessing her fears and worries about Siddhartha and asking for the Yakshi's protection.

She was alone on the path, and a tranquility soon stole over her. Light from the overhanging trees speckled the trail, leaves rustled above, the *tree-tree-tree-tree* of a green bee-eater stuttered in the branches. She soon reached the shrine, by the edge of a pool: a simple mud hut with a concave mud roof, built into a banyan tree whose roots, as they made their way back to earth from above, had draped and twined around the hut so that it was as much a part of the tree as the tree was a part of it. The earth around the shrine was red from the offerings made to the Yakshi—goat and fowl blood, red saffron water—and the outer walls were smeared with saffron paste and blood in veneration.

Before she entered the hut, Yasodhara loosened her hair from its plait and arranged it to lie all about her shoulders and face in a gesture of humility. When she stepped inside the shrine, she took a moment to let her eyes adjust to the dark, which was broken only by little clay oil lamps lit by devotees. Through the haze of these lamps she gazed at the clay image of the Yakshi, who stood against a carved banyan tree out of which she seemed to grow, right leg cocked over left, one hand raised to grasp a branch with which her fingers melded, the entire image smeared with red paste and blood. Yasodhara prostrated herself and, in a long, murmured whisper, unburdened her fears and concerns about Siddhartha, about the new life that awaited her. She begged the Yakshi to change Siddhartha's prospects, to free him from the stagnancy he was held in, because only when he was happy and at peace could she be too.

When she finally left the mud hut she felt better. She stood outside the shrine re-plaiting her hair, listening to the calming sound of the wind tinkling the leaves overhead.

In the eighth part of the day, when Surya the sun had begun to tentatively make his way homeward to his beloved Ushas, the wedding party began the last part of their journey to Kapilavastu. Soon, they reached a bridge of boats across the Rohini River at a point where the water was low enough that the horses and royal elephant could be walked across. Once the horses were unhitched, soldiers hoisted the shafts of the chariots on their shoulders and guided them across the bridge, while Devadatta led the royal elephant through the water, the grooms following with the horses. On the other side was the Sakiya Kingdom, where the local rashtrika awaited them. This rashtrika washed Dandapani's feet, greeted him with the Vedic verses to welcome guests and offered him the traditional cup of curd mixed with honey, ghee and spices.

As she watched the ritual, Yasodhara thought, "I am now in the land of my new home." A tremor went through her. She turned to her mother and found Pamita regarding her, eyes welling with tears.

Her brother came to stand by Yasodhara, smelling of horse and elephant and mud. When she let out a muffled sob, he put his arm around her and whispered gruffly, "Come, come, bhagini, you're going to your marriage, not your funeral." He gave her a brotherly grin, part jeering, part loving.

She smiled through her tears. "Oh bhāta, if only you were staying with me! Then I wouldn't be feeling so nervous, so lonely." Devadatta pulled back and gave her a sharp look. She regarded him too, wonderstruck at this sudden possibility. "Try, try to stay," she whispered. He nodded, frowning as he considered this prospect.

The rashtrika accompanied the royal convoy to the end of his district. He waited there until Dandapani dismissed him with the appropriate verses and then handed the convoy over to the rashtrika of the adjoining district—who performed the same set of welcome rites before accompanying the entourage to the end of his own district. In this way, they moved forward until finally, towards the end of the second part of the night, they saw ahead in the moonlight the massive wooden fortifications of Kapilavastu, its brass-studded gates fifteen times the height of a man. Horsemen with flares were waiting before the bridge across the moat and, when the royal convoy reached them, they spurred their horses and galloped ahead, cracking their whips to command the slaves along the way to light flares. Soon the clay road before them was orange from the flicker of torches.

Yasodhara had been to the city a few times before but, as their chariot went through the gates, she saw it anew. This was her future, her home. The streets were as busy now at night as they would be during the day back in Ramagama. The wavering flares and lanterns carried by pedestrians, the flaming torches before shops, made the people of Kapilavastu look, she thought, as if they were inhabitants of an underwater naga kingdom—something submerged and floating about their movements, as if they were pushing slowly through water. And such misery on display! Of a kind they didn't have in her own city: beggars squatting with their little heaps of belongings; a skeletal woman relieving herself over a drain; vesiyās picking their teeth in front of doorways, their voices as they called out to men like metal spoons scraping the hardened crusts of rice from pots. Dogs and pigs nosed through piles of refuse whose odour made Yasodhara press her shawl to her face. She noticed that her mother, too, was gazing out with distaste. Her mother had no fondness for Kapilavastu and was surely reliving the years of her childhood when she had lived here in her loveless, competitive family, until she was sixteen and escaped to Ramagama through marriage. Pamita's distaste for Kapilavastu increased Yasodhara's own fears. The harshness, the filth, the smell surrounding her, seemed all at once like a premonition of the life that awaited her.

The avenue broadened as the entourage approached the palace, the poverty falling away, the thatched roofs of mansions rising grandly around them. Finally, they were in the royal square with its great pillared santagara in one corner, where issues of the kingdom were decided by the sangha. A high audience hall dominated the centre of the square, vertiginous steps leading up from three sides to a rostrum, where Suddhodana held hearings for the lower castes, their requests delivered up the steps by runners.

The royal convoy passed through the first thorana of the palace into the courtyard of government offices, then through another thorana to the stables courtyard, where their hosts awaited them in a cluster at the centre, lit by flares.

Yasodhara watched the figures in the group as they drew nearer and nearer—her uncle, her aunt Prajapati and Siddhartha's half-sister Sundari Nanda. Her new family. She drew her shawl tight about her.

Suddhodana's figure was most brightly lit, two flares held up on either side of him by soldiers. The brilliance of the flames threw her aunt and cousin into shadow, as if he, Suddhodana, consumed the light at their expense, which shimmered off his brawny frame and golden skin, the thick black hair on his chest and forearms glistening like singed coconut fibres. When the convoy stopped in front of him, Suddhodana grinned, teeth brilliant. His strength, his vitality, increased her nervousness.

Yasodhara and her parents dismounted from the chariot. Suddhodana came forward with a clay jug of water. "Bhata," he cried to Dandapani, "I welcome you and your family to my home!" He performed the guest rituals for Dandapani, washing his visitor's feet, offering him curds and then a cow to honour him.

Once the rituals were over, Suddhodana turned to Pamita and cried, "Bhagini!" He took her face in his massive hands and kissed the top of her head.

"Bhāta," Pamita murmured and bent to touch her brother's feet briefly. Then she turned to Prajapati and said with genuine pleasure, "I am blessed to see you, bhagini."

Prajapati smiled, and it was as if a lamp had been lit in her long, bony face. The women embraced tenderly, Prajapati's elaborate hairstyle trembling, top-heavy on her thin face and neck.

Now it was Yasodhara's turn to go forward and greet her uncle. She forced a smile as she bent to touch his feet. She must please and placate him so he would free Siddhartha from his bondage. But she feared her smile was a grimace and, when she rose, she found her uncle regarding her with knit brows. He took her by the shoulders and examined her with a grave, wounded look, his hands heavy and damp on her skin. She lowered her eyes. "You are the daughter of my beloved sister. You will want for nothing in your new home." He let her go with a little shake of her shoulders. She kept her eyes on the floor as she shuffled backwards, sensing her parents' worried gaze on her, still feeling his clammy hands.

Devadatta now went forward to greet their uncle, and Suddhodana's face flushed with delight as his nephew bent to touch his feet. When he straightened up, Suddhodana grabbed him in a playful wrestler's lock and cried approvingly, "What's this I hear about you, you feral bull? In trouble? You must come and tell me all about it." Devadatta laughed proudly; but Yasodhara saw her parents exchange a brief glance. The last thing Devadatta needed was encouragement and praise for what he had done. Suddhodana now noticed Rama circling close above. "But what is this?" Devadatta held out his arm with pride and the hawk came to perch on his leather forearm band. Suddhodana clapped his hands together in admiration.

The men and women now parted, going to their separate accommodations, slaves leading the way with flaring torches. Yasodhara's aunt Prajapati and cousin Sundari Nanda led her, Pamita and the other noblewomen of the convoy to the women's quarters. As they passed through a warren of courtyards, Sundari Nanda fell in step with Yasodhara and chattered away about all the men who had come seeking her hand. "Oh, I am so tired of them asking, asking," Sundari Nanda said, and tossed her head. Sixteen like Yasodhara, she was vain about her beauty and thought no man good enough for her, the daughter of the raja. Yasodhara was happy to let her cousin chatter. She was still shaken from the interaction with her uncle and needed time to gather herself.

Though she had been inside these women's quarters before, Yasodhara took in the building anew, thinking again: *This is home.* The structure was not very different from the women's section in her own home, with two upper floors of wood and a ground floor of wattle and daub. The building wrapped around three sides of the courtyard and on the fourth was the boundary wall. A verandah ran around the ground floor, lit by flaring torches in brackets on posts. Under the torches stood the women of the quarters, waiting to greet them. As these women came down the steps to the courtyard, Yasodhara studied them carefully, even though she had met them in passing on previous visits. They were now part of her world. The two older relatives, Tissa and Utara, were kind and motherly as they greeted

Yasodhara, touching her face and shoulders, their gaze telling her that they saw her apprehension and that she could count on their support in her new life. The orphaned spinster cousin, Mitta, refused to embrace her, bowing formally with hands clasped, mouth puckered as if she'd tasted something sour. And there were the two concubines her uncle had at the moment. The first one, Sumana, long passed over by Suddhodana, whispered kindly in her ear, "If you ever need any advice, daharé . . ." Her eyes twinkled merrily. The other concubine, Upasama, still enjoyed the raja's favour and thought herself above the other women. She greeted Yasodhara with a frosty nod, her haughtiness thinly concealing her envy. How am I to bear life with these women? thought Yasodhara as she gazed at them.

Greetings done, Prajapati showed Pamita and Yasodhara to their room. No sooner had the door shut behind all three when Pamita took Prajapati's hand. "And how is Siddhartha, bhagini? We are a little worried for him and—"

Prajapati laughed lightly and took back her hand. Not meeting her guests' eyes, she ran a long, bony finger along the coverlet. "What is there to worry about? Siddhartha is one of our most capable young men, with a great future."

"Yes, but he hasn't been offered a position, pitucché," Yasodhara blurted. "Why, if he is so capable, hasn't he been given a posting?"

Prajapati looked at her hands with a faint smile to show that she had noted her niece's angry tone. Then she lifted her eyes to Yasodhara and said, in the sing-song tone of someone trying to be reasonable with an intransigent child, "He will be given a position equal to his talents. Of that I am sure. My husband, your uncle, will ensure that."

Yasodhara's face flushed with anger, but Pamita gently touched her hand. "I am sure you're right, ñātiké."

"Ah, it's good to have you here, Pamita," Prajapati said with warmth. She kissed her cousin on the cheek and left the room.

The moment the door closed, Pamita said softly, "Ushas, you're starting on the wrong footing. With my brother, with your aunt. She will be your mother-in-law after tomorrow. Be careful. I will not be here to protect you. And why this anger? We all know my brother is just toying with Siddhartha. Of course he will be given a position soon."

"I don't care, I don't care," Yasodhara cried, anguished. She threw herself on the bed in tears.

Pamita sat beside her and stroked her back. "You have to be patient with your aunt, Ushas, make allowances for her. It's not easy for Prajapati. Your uncle never loved her, only marrying her so he could also marry your late aunt. And then, when Maya died, it was poor Prajapati who had to bear the brunt of nursing Siddhartha as well as her own Sundari Nanda; bear the brunt of your uncle's anger and sorrow, him saying to her, to the court, that the wrong sister had died. It takes courage to bear such contempt, to bear the humiliation of the concubines my brother has installed here. You don't know the difficulties she's had, buying off and getting rid of women once my brother has tired of them. Try to understand, Ushas. The trod-upon are often self-involved to protect themselves. Try and be a good daughter-in-law."

But Yasodhara threw up her hands impatiently to say she had heard all this before and didn't care.

There was a knock on the door. Pamita called out "Enter," and a serving woman came in and bowed to them. "The young sāmini has a visitor."

"Who?" Yasodhara cried breathlessly, sitting up. Perhaps it was Siddhartha, ignoring the taboo and come to see her before the wedding.

"Your cousin, Anuruddha, sāmini."

For an instant Yasodhara was disappointed, but then she jumped off the bed and shuffled into her leather slippers, adjusting her shawl, her hair. Of all her cousins, she loved Anuruddha best. He had come, she knew, to cheer her up with funny stories about his friends and their pranks, and to distract her from her fears. She nodded to her smiling mother and headed out the door.

Downstairs in the women's courtyard Anuruddha stood, carrying a torch, handsome face glowing with welcome in the flickering light. She went to him without a word and wrapped her arms around his tall frame, burying her face in his bare chest. "What's this?" he said with a laugh, as her tears wet him. He wrapped his free arm around her and she felt him handing the torch to someone else before he put his other arm around her as well.

When she was calm, she pulled back with a laugh and wiped her cheeks with her shawl, ashamed. "Bridal nerves."

Anuruddha gave her a comforting pat and then said, with a mischievous grin, "But I have a surprise for you."

He turned to the man behind him, who was now holding the torch. Signalling from the stranger to her, he said, "Ñātaka, ñātiké."

Yasodhara understood immediately. This was her cousin Ananda, who had arrived here about a year and a half ago from Takkasila. She smiled and bowed, taking a good look at this relative whom she'd only heard about: he was in his early twenties, with a long nose that gave his face a melancholy look, and pockmarked cheeks. "I knew of your arrival here," she said shyly, embarrassed he had witnessed her tears. "I'm sorry to hear of your mother's death."

Ananda nodded to acknowledge this. Then in a kindly tone that told her she should not be embarrassed, he said, "And I've heard of you, ñātiké, through my half-brother." He gestured to a grinning Anuruddha.

"All favourable?" she asked with a little laugh.

"Nothing but praise." He smiled and instantly his face changed into that of a cheerful person, before returning to its long-nosed melancholy.

"And you, cousin," she said, turning back to Anuruddha. She pointed to the circles under his eyes. "I see you've been spending too many nights at your ganikā's house."

Anuruddha laughed and shrugged as if to say, "What am I to do?"

"Oh, let's go somewhere else!" she cried. "I'm already sick of the women's quarters."

Her cousins raised their eyebrows at this, and she shrugged and gave a bitter, resigned laugh.

"The gotra courtyard is empty at this hour," Ananda said and led the way with his torch.

Yasodhara followed, arm linked in Anuruddha's, all the while surreptitiously studying this cousin she'd never met. She knew his story well: the son of her uncle Amitodhana from his first marriage, Ananda had been exiled, along with his mother Mrgi, to Takkasila when Amitodhana had taken a much younger second wife who didn't want the first wife to be in the same city. There, Ananda became an apprentice to a merchant and, under his master's tutelage, rose to become his assistant and then a partner in the business, for the merchant had loved him like a son. But then, a year and a half ago, a plague had swept through Takkasila and Ananda had lost both his mother and his master. Rendered destitute, he'd had no choice but to return here. Her uncle Amitodhana had taken him in grudgingly, and now he lived among the senior servants.

They found the gotra courtyard deserted, mats and cushions and low tables already laid out for the wedding tomorrow. Ananda put his torch in a bracket on one of the verandah posts and the cousins sat on a mat among cushions, surveying each other gravely.

"How is he?" Yasodhara asked finally in a whisper.

The men looked at each other significantly. Then Ananda said, "Always with a little smile on his face, as if the world is nothing but pleasant."

"Pride," Anuruddha added.

"Oh, why does our uncle hate him this much? Why, when Siddhartha has done him no wrong?"

Ananda raised his eyebrows wryly. "No wrong? Why, Siddhartha has done his father significant wrong. Look at his success at Savatthi. What a way to insult his father."

They sat in gloomy silence for a bit. Then, to cheer her up, Anuruddha, as she had expected, told Yasodhara about his friends and the pranks they all got up to at night: bawling the name of a girl from a noble family outside her window, even as the paramour urinated on the family's wall; knocking over sentries who had fallen asleep on their feet outside homes; stealing into the santagara to mix up the members' mats and cushions that were stacked in designated corners; daring each other to pinch little trinkets from the courtesan Vimala's house. Yasodhara laughed at this, happy to be distracted, though not entirely approving.

As a boy, Anuruddha had been thoroughly spoiled by his mother. One day, so the family tale went, he was playing marbles with some other boys, gambling on cakes. He kept losing and kept sending home for more cakes. Finally, his mother sent a message through a servant: "There isn't any cake." Anuruddha sent back a message saying, "Well then send me the there-isn't-any cakes."

When Anuruddha was done with his stories of mischief, Ananda tried to cheer her up too, telling her about his travels with the merchant Mendaka. He described the great Lavanasagara Desert which he and his master had often crossed on their travels, and how the sand was so hot the caravan of carts could only travel at night, guided by desert pilots. Travelling in the desert was like sailing the oceans, he said, and one went guided by the stars. He entertained her with a story of how, one night, the desert pilot fell asleep and the oxen, left to their own devices, returned in a circle to the place they had departed from. When the merchants awoke, they were in despair. This night's travel should have brought them to the end of the desert, and now they had run out of water. Mendaka, however, calmly walked about the dunes and found some grass growing in a certain spot. Sure there was water below, the merchants dug to many cubits—but then, to their further despair, hit rock. Mendaka remained confident that water lay just below the rock. He set about with Ananda to split the rock and soon released water that quickly filled the hole.

As Ananda told her this story, Yasodhara watched the way his face lit up at the memory. "And here I am worried about my petty troubles," she thought, "when this man has suffered such loss. What kindness to try and distract me from *my* concerns." His kindness restored her to herself and, when his story was over, she leaned forward, drawing her shawl about her, and said, "And in Kapilavastu, have you made friends among the merchants? Have you met anyone who will be generous to you, like your master?"

He gave her a sharp look but, before he could reply, Anuruddha cried, "He has, he has!" then clapped his hand over his mouth as Ananda gave him an admonishing glare.

Yasodhara smiled, seeing there was some secret between them about this benefactor. She was curious about who it was and why their identity was a secret. Yet, not wanting to probe and feeling the moment growing awkward, she changed the subject and questioned Ananda about the great western city of Takkasila.

Later, when her cousins walked her back to the women's quarters, Ananda said suddenly, "I will be your friend, ñātiké, in your new life here."

Yasodhara smiled to show her gratitude. Still, she did not feel reassured. Ananda was a disinherited son; he wielded no power or influence. Once her cousins were gone, she stood in the murky courtyard, looking up at the lights in the second-floor windows. Their reflections on the bathing pond made the water look as if a slithering, scaly beast waited just below the surface.

4

A Woman's Lot

THE NEXT MORNING, once her mother had dressed her, Yasodhara asked for a few moments alone. She stood before the mirror gazing at herself, her image foreign and formal in an embroidered red silk dhoti, heavy shawl woven in golden thread, bodice cloth tied at her breasts and behind her neck in elaborate knots. The ends of the cloth hung down her back and were weighted with little gold bells. They lay cold against her spine. Her neck, ears and nose felt stretched by the heavy gold necklaces, nose ring and earrings she wore. She leaned in to carefully smooth the sandalwood paste under her eyes, which hid dark circles from a sleepless night. She didn't regret the lost night, however, because it had brought her to a decision: this was her wedding, the only one she would ever have, and she was not going to let her uncle, her aunt, anyone, prevent her from revelling in it. She would not give them that victory.

When she came down into the front courtyard, the bridal palanquin awaited her, draped in ribbons and jasmine and marigold garlands. She smiled at her mother, studiously ignoring the gaze of other female relatives. Pamita helped her into the palanquin, then patted and arranged the pillows so she was comfortable. When the slaves lifted up the palanquin, Yasodhara held her hands up and with glittering-eyed triumph cried, "To my wedding!"

As the slaves jogged towards the quarter's gate, she could hear, from beyond the walls, the restive crowd. The moment the guards flung the gates open, a roar went up—"Pamitadhītā! Pamitadhītā!"—Daughter of Pamita.

They were claiming Yasodhara as one of their own, through the lineage of her mother. She lifted her arms high in acknowledgement, to say that she was indeed one of them and, at this gesture, the roar increased doublefold, the cry of "Pamitadhītā!" like a rumble of thunder travelling down the road lined by the janata of the city. This is the royal wedding they have looked forward to, Yasodhara thought. I will give them something to remember.

And so, as the palanquin made its way in a circle around the royal square and along the streets of Kapilavastu, she waved, standing up sometimes to lay her hands on children the women held out of windows, hoping her luck and good fortune would come to them. The sounds of cheering and shouting, of drums, conches, whistles, soon seemed to dissolve the edges of her being, and she melded into the sounds, into the crowds and their heat against her skin. Her palanquin was littered with flower petals cast down from the upper storeys of buildings they passed, red banners fluttering in windows. Many jostled forward to touch her hands or clothing. Merchants held out their purses for her blessing.

When the bridal procession finally reached the palace courtyard that housed the government offices, the palanquin was lowered to the ground and Yasodhara stepped out. Her father and mother were waiting for her, along with her brother and the retinue who had accompanied the family to Kapilavastu. Pamita came forward, smiling at Yasodhara's flushed, triumphant face. She adjusted her daughter's shawl and bodice cloth, and picked out petals from the folds of her dhoti and also the few that had stuck to Yasodhara's bare midriff, shoulder and arms. "You do me proud, dhītā," Pamita whispered, and kissed her. She could see that her father was barely keeping back his tears. Devadatta was clearing his throat repeatedly. When she was ready, her family led Yasodhara through an elaborately carved thorana and along a short passage to the gotra courtyard.

As they entered, a conch sounded and everyone rose. The verandahs and floor of the courtyard were crowded with members of their Gotama Gotra, clan members who had come from all over the Sakiya and Koliya Kingdoms. Seeing their avid faces turned towards her, Yasodhara felt her excitement and triumph flip over into nervousness. She gritted her teeth, stuck out her chin and fixed her eyes on the verandah at the far end. There Siddhartha sat, hidden by a curtain of red cloth until the auspicious moment.

Anuruddha was holding the red cloth in place and, at the sight of him, she felt a rush of affection and gratitude towards Siddhartha. Anuruddha was no special friend of his, but he had selected her cousin for this honour because he knew she loved Anuruddha. Yes, yes, she and Siddhartha would be happy. How could she have thought otherwise? She gathered her shawl around her shoulders and went through the crowd, keeping her gaze down as she was expected to, but with her back straight. Her parents guided her to the other side of the curtain and, when she reached it, she snuck a quick glance at Anuruddha. He winked and grinned as if to say, "Isn't this all ridiculous?" But she knew he was really saying, "All is well, your worries are for nothing." She pressed her lips together and smiled back. For a moment her eyes travelled to the right to take in Ananda standing on a nearby verandah. Their gaze met and he nodded, his eyes telling her the same thing as Anuruddha's.

The Royal Head Priest now came forward to direct her on how to sit—facing the east, her right hand resting by the curtain. Once seated, she glanced at the curtain and Siddhartha's dark form on the other side. A conch blew, there was a roll of drums and Anuruddha snatched away the cloth. She longed to look at Siddhartha but knew she must not—such a strain to keep her head from turning. The priest came forward, took her hand and offered it to Siddhartha. She waited to see how he would hold her hand; when he took it entirely in his palm, not just holding her thumb, she was so pleased the tears sprang to her eyes. He was asking the gods for male *and* female children, because he knew, because she'd confessed to him, that though she must perform the duty of giving him a male heir, what she really longed for was a little girl so that she could have the same relationship with that child as she had with her own mother. He had not forgotten! He was a good man; she was lucky. There was another drum roll and the Priest cried, "Svaha!"

They turned to look at each other—Siddhartha so handsome in his turban looped with jasmine garlands, his golden shawl, his strings of pearls and emeralds around his neck, his two large emerald earrings. He was smiling at her, and she read in his eyes—*I have been unhappy, but the sight of you has restored me.* She nodded to say back, *The sight of you has restored me too.*

The priest touched Siddhartha's arm to tell him he must get on with the ceremonies. "I take hold of thy hand for happiness," Siddhartha said, and stood, tugging gently on her hand to rise with him. They followed the priest down the steps to a cleared area, where a fire burned in a shallow pit dug for the occasion. She gazed at the fire, awed. This was their marital fire, lit from Siddhartha's parents' marital fire that burned always in the sacrificial enclosure, which in turn was lit from his paternal grandparents' fire, and so on, going back generations.

There was a millstone to the west of the fire and a water jar to the northeast. Siddhartha led her in a route around the fire, their path also encompassing the water jug and millstone. As they went, he chanted the marriage mantra: "I am ama, thou art sa, thou art sa, I am ama. I am heaven, thou art the earth; I am saman, thou art rik. Let us both marry here. Let us beget offspring. Dear to each other, bright, having well-disposed minds, may we live for a hundred years." Each time they passed the millstone, he instructed her to step on it with the mantra, "Tread on this stone. Be firm like a stone. Overcome enemies. Trample down foes."

They did this three times, then Yasodhara went to stand over the fire with her hands cupped together. Devadatta came forward and, with a grin to say he shared her happiness, poured clarified butter into her palms until it flowed over, causing the fire to hiss and sizzle, feeding the gods. She kept her eyes on him, her beloved brother. He then poured fried grain into her palms, which she cast into the fire. She repeated this action three times, while Siddhartha chanted, "To god Aryaman the maiden offers sacrifice. May he, the god Aryaman, loosen her from her father's place and not from the place of her bridegroom. Svaha!" He repeated the same verse thrice, each time substituting the name of another god for Aryaman.

Her hair had been tied in two locks, joined by a strand of wool. Siddhartha untied the wool, then loosened the right lock around her shoulder. "Now from the noose of Varuna I free thee, wherewith Most Blessed Savitr hath bound thee." He untied the left lock. "Hence I set thee free. I make thee softly fettered to me so that thou might live blest in fortune and sons." Next, he held her hand and together they took seven steps in a northeasterly direction. With each step he chanted, "May you take the first step for strength. The second for vigour. The third for bounteous wealth.

The fourth for comfort. The fifth for offspring, the sixth for good seasons. May you be my friend with your seventh step. May you be devoted to me, may we have many sons, may they reach old age. Svaha!"

The priest came forward, brought their heads together and poured water on them. As they raised their heads, shaking off a shower of drops, a cheer went through the gotra courtyard. This was taken up by those outside the courtyard, and from there travelled in waves out through the city where many drums beat and many conches sounded at the marriage of the raja's son. Yasodhara turned, laughing, to Siddhartha and they embraced. He sighed with happiness as he drew her even tighter into his arms, their bodies breathing against each other for a moment before the embrace was broken by the arrival of her parents, his parents, her brother and his stepsister, who took turns blessing them.

That first night, the moment she and Siddhartha were left alone, seated on the bed—Pamita and Prajapati nodding and smiling as they shut the door behind them—Yasodhara said, laughing, "Ah, Surya, here we are, married!"

"Did you think we wouldn't be?" he asked, laughing too, his eyes shining with pleasure at finally having her to himself.

But then shyness and solemnity stole over them, neither knowing how to proceed to what must come next. "There is no hurry, Surya," she said, gently squeezing his hand, "the night is before us."

His face worked for a moment, then he cried out softly, "And yet you are the one who says that to me, when *I* should be the one offering *you* that comfort. Here I am distracted, even on my wedding night!"

"What is it, beloved, what?" She touched the side of his face.

"My pita. How he enjoys humiliating me, stripping me of all I accomplished in Savatthi." He took a deep breath to control himself, then turned and drew her into a passionate embrace, burying his nose in her neck.

"Surya," she whispered and circled him with her arms.

After a moment, he gently broke from their embrace, then took her hand and kissed it. At the feel of his breath on her skin, a tingle travelled all the way up to her chest and she shuddered slightly. He saw that shudder and, keeping his luminous gaze on her, he gently turned her hand over and kissed her wrists. His lips travelled up her forearm, barely touching it, his hot breath on her skin. When he got to the inside of her elbow joint, he brushed his lips over her soft skin, then ran his tongue in a circle. She sighed and warmth tipped over in her solar plexus. He leaned closer and kissed her shoulder. "Come, Ushas," he whispered and lay back on the bed. After a moment, she slid down too until they were lying on their sides facing each other. After a moment, he reached out a shaking hand and touched her face. She held it to her cheek. Then drew him to her and kissed him.

After they had kissed awhile, he sat up abruptly and blew out the lamp. In the dark, she heard the rustle of his dhoti as he took it off, the clink of his jewellery being removed. Now she was nervous, afraid of the pain to come, even though Pamita had assured her it was quick and sharp and then passed. She could smell his odour, released with the removal of his clothes and jewellery: sandalwood mixed with sweat, and a smell that was uniquely his, like freshly planed wood. He lay back down on his side, facing her, eyes glittering in the dark. His breath, inches from hers, smelled of wine and the cardamom sweets at their wedding feast. He reached out and gently pulled open the knot of her bodice cloth. The air on her breasts hardened her nipples. He stroked her face and left arm. Gradually his hand wandered down her body and she understood from the skilled way he touched her breasts, her nipples, the way his hand moved with sureness to unravel her dhoti and then between her legs to the centre of her desire, that he had likely been for tutoring to a ganikā in the city. The thought was with her briefly, but then it was subsumed by her pleasure, which spread like the balm applied to her body in the winter, both warm and cool at the same time. When she sighed, he knew she was ready and whispered in her ear, "Ushas, I will love and protect you all the days of my life."

He entered her and she felt a sharp, hot pain, which then slowly changed to the warmth of pleasure. Her hands, which had gripped his sides, loosened their hold. Beneath her palms, she felt the soft skin over his ribs move as he began to thrust gently into her.

The act was soon over. With a little cry, high like a boy's, he collapsed on her and they lay breathing against each other's wet skin. After a moment, he slid out of her and lay on his back. When his breath subsided, he drew her to him and held her tight, kissing her hair over and over again, whispering,

"Thank you, thank you." She pressed her face against his chest, speechless, overwhelmed, still aroused from the experience.

They drifted into a brief sleep, then awakened, reaching for each other again. This time their coming together was better, with more understanding of each other's bodies, and Yasodhara felt both the rising of desire, and a release from it. In this way they passed the night, briefly falling into rich sleep then, awakened by the other stirring, grasping for arms and limbs and waists, eyes half-closed in the dark as they began all over again.

⚹

They had been married a week when the time came for the traditional visit to a ganikā to discuss any problems in the marriage bed. Yasodhara was excited at the prospect—a rare chance to enter that glamorous world of courtesans.

The day before the visit, she was kneeling on the floor going through her wedding gifts, holding up a gold flagon to the light to admire the twinkling rubies embedded in it, when her mother bustled into the marriage suite saying briskly, "Ushas, your bhāta will not be taking you to see the ganikā tomorrow." Pamita nodded to acknowledge her surprise. "Devadatta doesn't know Kapilavastu's ganikā houses. Anuruddha will take you. And Ananda."

Yasodhara sat back on her heels and examined her mother. There was something else to this break with tradition.

Pamita perched on the edge of the bed and gave her a subtle smile. "And when you come down to the women's courtyard tomorrow, you are to call Ananda 'bhāta.' And he will be calling you 'bhagini' from now on."

"Ammé?"

"You will see, Ushas." Pamita gave her a sidelong mischievous look to say Yasodhara would have to wait and figure it out.

The next morning, Yasodhara spent an inordinate amount of time in front of the mirror, grimacing at her image as she tried on various combinations of jewellery and shawls and waist sashes. Now that she was about to meet women famed for their beauty, she was dissatisfied with herself, wishing she wasn't so slim and lacking the voluptuous curves of true beauty. Finally, when she heard her cousins' voices down in the courtyard, greeting her mother, her aunt and the other women of the quarters, she gave a small laugh of defeat, a shrug at the mirror, and left the room.

As she came down the stairs, Anuruddha, leaning rakishly against the newel post, grinned up at her and winked to say, "What an adventure!"—looking extra handsome because the kohl rimming his eyes threw his long eyelashes and large eyes into relief. Ananda stood beside him, solemn, as if he was indeed her brother, weighted with the responsibility of making sure this marriage ritual went well.

As she descended further, she could see the women of the quarters seated on mats in the courtyard, doing various tasks, her aunt and mother on a charpoy, embroidering opposite ends of a shawl. Hearing her footsteps, they turned to watch her descent. "Ah, Ushas," Pamita said mildly, "enjoy your day."

Yasodhara was not fooled by that mildness. She had reached the bottom stair now and Ananda came forward, took her hand and, with a little bow, said too-loud, "Bhagini."

Her aunt Prajapati looked up sharply, first at Yasodhara with Ananda, then at her mother.

Pamita continued her embroidery.

After a moment, Prajapati, with a slight tucking in of her chin, returned to the shawl as well.

And now Yasodhara understood. Subtle diplomacy. By arranging for Yasodhara and Ananda to call each other "brother" and "sister," her mother was sending Prajapati a message: I don't trust that you will treat my daughter well, so you are forcing me to arrange other protection and comfort for her.

From his small smile, she saw that Ananda, too, understood this; and Anuruddha's lips were twitching in amusement.

"Bhāta," she replied, also too-loud.

A palanquin waited for them in the front courtyard of the women's quarters and, once she was seated in it, they set off, her cousins walking beside her. She kept the curtains open so she might gaze out at the world they were passing and chat.

They meandered through the Vessa Quarter and then suddenly Ananda gestured to the palanquin bearers to stop. Before Yasodhara was a dark, narrow passageway between two houses that looked like it led to a scraggly backyard or rickety artisan's workshop.

Ananda gestured for Yasodhara to get out. She could see that both cousins were amused at her bewilderment.

"This way, bhagini," Ananda said. He took her by the elbow and guided her down the passageway, which was so narrow they had to go single file.

When she reached the end, Yasodhara gasped. There before her was a lovely little park with flowering trees, a fountain and benches, a bird feeder with grains that attracted songbirds. The trills and coos of bulbuls and babblers and doves mingled with the plashing of the fountain.

"It's maintained by Vimala, ñātiké, so her clients will have a pleasant entry into her house." Anuruddha gestured and she saw, on the other side of the park, a high wattle and daub parapet wall beyond which she could glimpse the second and third storeys and the thatched roof of the ganikā's house.

They crossed the park to the door and clanged the bell. When the maid came to the door, Ananda said, "Your mistress, please."

The maid bowed. "You are expected, sāmi, let me just get the keys to the private entrance." Then, noticing Anuruddha, she cried out with a grin, "Ah, the god Vayu pays us an unexpected visit!"

"No, no," Anuruddha demurred and gestured to Yasodhara. "I am accompanying my cousin."

The maid held the door open. "But while you wait, beautiful god . . . ?"

He shook his head, laughed sheepishly.

The maid left the door a little ajar and went to get the key. To Yasodhara's inquiring look, Ananda answered, "We don't go in, bhagini. We must walk around the wall to a door that leads up to Vimala's private quarters."

"Ah!" she cried. "So I don't get to see the ganikās? The house?" Before they could reply, she boldly pushed open the door and went in. It was her one chance to enter this glamorous, mysterious world; she was not going to let it pass.

And now, inside, she stared agog at the sight before her:

On the verandahs that spanned three sides of the house (the fourth side the parapet wall), the voluptuous ganikās, like apsaras in heaven, sunned themselves, sewed their clothes for the evening and gossiped. The house itself was beautifully maintained, the first floor's wattle and daub walls decorated with elegant chalk designs, the upper wooden floors painted in bright colours. One of the ganikās was practising on her veena, a music master seated cross-legged before her, calling out the beat by clapping; another ganikā used a mortar to crush seeds and dried flowers, preparing a beautifying potion, the grinding releasing a scent of fennel and cardamom into the air.

The women now noticed Yasodhara and nodded to her in a friendly manner. But when Anuruddha came in to retrieve her, they cried out, "Oh, god Vayu is among us! You honour us at this odd hour!" Two ganikās stepped off the verandah and started towards them, but Anuruddha, with a grin, waved them away, took a reluctant Yasodhara by the arm and guided her back out.

The maid soon joined them and led them around to a side door in the parapet wall. As the woman unlocked the door, Ananda said to Yasodhara, "This is where we leave you, bhagini." He gestured to the park. "We will wait for you here."

She nodded and followed the servant up the dark staircase, enclosed in wood to maintain the privacy of the visitor, and also to keep hidden the women's living quarters on the second floor.

When she arrived at the receiving room on the third floor, she took a moment to let her eyes adjust to the dimness. And then there she was, the courtesan Vimala, seated cross-legged on a charpoy in a ray of sunshine coming through the window: lovely, with her enchanting heart-shaped face and rounded hips, breasts straining against her bodice cloth, which she wore secured around her neck in an elaborate knot. She beckoned Yasodhara forward with a dimpled smile and said sweetly, "Come, daharé, join me," patting the charpoy and arranging some cushions for her guest. As Yasodhara climbed onto the charpoy and settled herself, she found her-self smiling back shyly under the ganikā's merry gaze, taking in her plump naked arms, the press of her voluptuous thighs against the crisp folds of her dhoti, the scent of jasmine from her hair.

When Yasodhara was properly settled, Vimala took her guest by the chin and examined her face. "So lovely. The entire city speaks of your bridal procession." She turned Yasodhara's face this way and that. "Ambapali would be envious."

Yasodhara blushed at this highest compliment a woman could be paid—to be compared to the great courtesan of Vesali, the most beautiful woman in the Middle Country. "And . . . and have you ever met the great Ambapali?" she asked, to deflect further compliments.

Vimala nodded and mock-grimaced. "No woman—especially someone like me, whose beauty is her career—should meet the great Ambapali. I am nothing but a crow compared to her."

"So, then the stories are true?" Yasodhara asked breathless, for she had always longed to see this legendary beauty.

Vimala laughed and nodded. "They say she is not human, but the daughter of an apsara. And when you see her, you can believe that is true. Her beauty is unearthly." She took Yasodhara's hand. "And now tell me, daharé: Are there any problems in the marital bed? Any questions you want to ask me on how to please your husband? Tell me also how your nights have been this past week."

Yasodhara blushed, but then, seeing the placid, professional interest of the ganikā, she narrated the events of their wedding night, and her relations with Siddhartha since.

Vimala was genuinely happy and, when she was done, declared with the satisfaction of work well accomplished, "Ah then, my ganikā Kusuma trained your husband well. She will be pleased to hear that." She let out a merry laugh, as Yasodhara blushed, embarrassed and also jealous. Vimala took her by the chin again. "So very charming."

Now cries of "Ammé, ammé!" made them turn, and Yasodhara saw a little girl running towards the charpoy, her heavy nurse lumbering after her. An open door behind them showed stairs that led down to the private quarters.

The girl was holding out a garland of violet flowers and, when she reached the charpoy, she cried, "Ammé, see what I made you." Then, noticing Yasodhara, she pressed shyly against Vimala.

The ganikā lifted the child onto her lap and kissed her all over, crying, "Ah, jewel of my eye!"

Holding the child close, she looked across at Yasodhara. "Isn't my Visaka lovely?" She kissed the child again, lowered her to the ground and gently patted her behind, gesturing towards the nurse. The girl went obediently and let the nurse lead her back towards the door.

"Her parents, Brahmin farmers, died in a plague last year that destroyed their village. Poor thing, left orphaned at three. So I've adopted her. The true love of my life." Sensing Yasodhara's unasked question, she added, "Her future is assured, daharé. When she is thirteen, I will secure a great position for her." She nodded to confirm that Yasodhara had understood what she meant by "position," then laughed merrily at her guest's barely concealed dismay. "But this is who we are, daharé!" She reached out and gently pinched her chin. Then she rang a bell and, when the maid arrived, she nodded, gesturing to the stairs, at the same time pressing Yasodhara's knee to say this was not a signal she should leave.

After they had chatted for a few moments more, Yasodhara heard footsteps and soon Ananda appeared at the top of the stairs. Yasodhara looked from Vimala to him, noting immediately the casual intimacy between them, in the way neither greeted the other. Vimala took a key from under her cushion and held it out to Ananda. "Have a look and see if it suits you. If it doesn't, we can think of something else."

He nodded, turning the key in his hand contemplatively.

"You remember the cross-street?"

"Yes. And I'm sure it will suit me well."

They gave each other a long look, then Vimala became merry again. "Your ñātiké is lovely, Siddhartha is indeed a lucky man"—now patting Yasodhara's knee to say the meeting was indeed over.

The moment they were out the street door, Yasodhara grabbed Ananda's arm. "Bhāta, you and the ganikā are lovers!"

A surprised shout of laughter escaped Ananda, his habitually solemn expression fracturing open. "I couldn't afford Vimala! Anyway, she's contracted right now to the Setthi of the silversmiths."

"But then what is your relation to her, bhāta?"

He took her elbow and began to lead her across the park. "A good question." He gave her a teasing glance. "Would you like a short answer, the way a messenger might tell a raja? Or would you like it told in the way merchants tell stories on their long caravan journeys?"

"The latter, of course!" They were almost at the other end of the park when she remembered and cried, "But where is Anuruddha?"

Ananda grimaced and pointed to the ganikā's house. "I'm afraid we've lost him for today." Seeing Yasodhara's concern, he added, "Don't worry, I have an arrangement with Vimala as to how much my half-brother can bid. And now for your story."

⚘

It begins, bhagini, about a year after I had arrived in Kapilavastu. That morning, I was summoned by my father. I already knew the reasons for this summons and, as I made my way through the interconnected courtyards towards his receiving room, I was filled with gloominess. "Ah," I cried to myself, "how impossible it is to believe that just a year ago, I had a different life, a life of happiness in Takkasila." Even saying the city's name to myself brought back the memory of that busy merchants' street I'd lived on, the dust and heat of commerce, the merry cries and laughter of the sellers seated outside their shops; myself on a stool beside my master Mendaka, the two of us whisking flies off our goods with dried palms. *How have I come to this?* I kept asking myself, as if I didn't already know the answer. When I arrived in the main courtyard, I went up the verandah steps with a sigh and knocked on the door of my father's receiving room.

"Enter," my father called out.

I came in to find my father and my half-brother Mahanama lounging on cushions, a fug of maleness and pipe smoke filling the room because of the shuttered windows.

"Come." My father crooked his finger, then snorted to clear the mucus in his throat, in that disgusting way of his. I studied them as I approached, my contempt hidden beneath a blank expression. For I truly have only contempt for them: Mahanama, with his merry smile of a bully, banned from the courtesan houses because of cruelty; my father, who, despite the air of superiority he gives himself, is largely broke, living high off his borrowings from setthis, and paying their exorbitant interest. And of course, there was Anuruddha, the cause of my summons, like a schoolboy whipped, giving me furtive, frightened glances.

When I reached him, my father pushed a clay tablet across the floor. "Pick it up."

I did so, and read the sums of Anuruddha's gambling debts, incurred at
Vimala's house, counting with disbelief the strokes and symbols denoting
the huge amounts spent, Anuruddha's seal pressed next to each to acknowledge the debt. As I read, I glanced at Anuruddha, who kept his gaze in the
distance, too nervous now to meet my eye.

"How did this come about, Ananda?" my father demanded. And
Mahanama added, as he dug a morsel from between his teeth with his ivory
toothpick, "We trusted you to keep an eye on my brother. It's the only thing
we've asked of you in return for our kindness in taking you in."

Before I could speak, Anuruddha said, "The debt is mine. Incurred by
me. I take responsibility for it, you cannot blame Ananda."

My father waved his fly whisk at Anuruddha. "A donkey brays and is a
pack animal. It's not a horse. It will never be a horse."

Anuruddha winced at the insult, then went back to staring into the distance.

"But I expected better from you." My father glared at me. "That woman
is threatening to take up a case against Anuruddha. A case she says she will
bring before my brother Suddhodana. The humiliation! A case before the
raja! I will have to listen to her disputations before the whole court. No, no,
Ananda, you must go see that ganikā and resolve this."

"We trusted you." Mahanama plumped a cushion pettishly and shoved
it under his armpit. "We took you destitute into our house. This is a poor
way to repay us."

A rage rose in me at his words. I wanted to say to him that the position
of first son, with all its privileges, should be mine, not his; that if I wished,
I too could take up a case against them both, using the Vedas to assert my
birthright. But there was no point in saying any of this. I bowed to say I
would take care of the problem.

Anuruddha followed me out and, as we went down the verandah steps,
he grabbed my arm. "I'm sorry, bhāta, I truly am."

"What good is your penitence, Anuruddha? Our father and brother
blame me! Even though I have done nothing wrong."

"I'll go see Vimala. It's my debt, I am responsible for it."

"Yes, yes, I can see how that visit will go. You will present this tablet,
Vimala will take it away from you, laugh, tease, flirt, call on her women for

reinforcements. Next thing, the dice board will be spread out and a game in progress, new notations added to the tablet. And you in foolish bliss. That ganikā hasn't got where she has without knowing how to play the feckless sons of the nobility."

Anuruddha blanched at my damning assessment of him but, not caring, I waved him away and set off with that tablet.

When I got to the ganikā's house and told the maid my business, she ushered me inside and left me waiting while she went to tell her mistress. I had, of course, been in here often to keep an eye on Anuruddha, though lately, resenting my role as my brother's nursemaid, I had avoided coming. The ganikās went about their business, ignoring me because they knew they would get no trade from me.

The maid soon returned and, much to my surprise, told me her mistress would see me in her private quarters—an honour usually only given to one man, the Setthi of the Silversmiths, to whom Vimala was currently contracted.

When I reached the top of the stairs, there was Vimala seated on her charpoy. She beckoned me forward with that famous dimpled smile of hers and gestured for me to sit on the charpoy with her, saying, "Come, mitta, join me." I had fully expected to sit on the rug before her.

As I climbed onto the charpoy and seated myself, arranging the folds of my dhoti, my resentment began to melt under her merry gaze. She seemed to have sussed out my mood and its cause. Take care, Ananda, I told myself, these are ganikās' tricks, the woman is trying to disarm you.

"Ah, it's been a while since you last visited us, mitta," Vimala said with a teasing laugh. "Tired of being your brother's guard and nursemaid?"

I blushed, but couldn't help smiling at how well she had guessed the truth.

"I've missed you, mitta. One of the few intelligent men who visit here." I glanced at her and saw she was sincere. Many a time our eyes had met as we watched some dissolute nobleman fritter away his money on the dice board, a small nod passing between us.

I said nothing, and placed the tablet before her.

"Ah." With a flirtatious laugh, she pushed it back to me. "What use do I have for it? I know well the sums."

"My brother honours your house, mitta. Having someone from our family, the royal family, in your house, as you know, increases your standing. So, I am asking you, forgive the debt."

"But my standing is very good already, mitta." She gave me a winning smile, clasping her knees. "And it's the rich Vessas that bring the true money, not the sons of noblemen."

"But the sons of noblemen, particularly the sons of the royal family, bring in the rich Vessas. My brother's presence here gives a shine to your house. Which the other houses lack. If he was, let us say, to take his business to the house of the ganikā Kalika, drawing along with him his friends—also of the best families—in no time many of your rich Vessa clients would also be going to Kalika's."

Vimala gave me a shrewd look, then dropped her coquettishness and sat up straight, businesslike. "I have a house to run, mitta, and my future, and my daughter's too, to protect. I won't be beautiful forever." She picked up the tablet and read it carefully. I knew she was just playing for time and suppressed my smile. It had been a while since I'd bargained for anything and I was thrilled at how easily the old trading skills came back to me.

Finally, she pushed the tablet back to me. "This is my offer: I will forgive the debts in exchange for the paddy land your family owns, ten yojana from the city. As well as the orchard adjoining it."

"A quarter of the paddy land. The orchard is not negotiable."

"A quarter?" She gestured angrily to the tablet. "Look at the amount of the debt, mitta. Can't you read?"

Yet I knew she was not truly angry; she had called me "mitta." This was just a counter-offer. "Half the paddy land, then."

She promptly took her seal, wet the clay with a silver dipper and pressed the seal over the final amount to cancel the debt.

Business done, we sat back smiling at each other. She made me a wad of betel using her own special blend of spices and aromatic herbs from a teak box. After she held it out to me on a little silver tray, she made one for herself. We chewed our betel in silence, listening to a ganikā on a veena singing a song of lost love in the courtyard below. "Tell me," she finally said, "why do you stick by Anuruddha?"

"He is my brother and—"

"Half-brother."

"—and you could say I've become fond of him, since coming here. Besides, I don't have a choice. You don't know my circumstances and—"

"I do. I know them well." She nodded at my surprise. "Anuruddha told me. You are a talented negotiator, mitta. Hardly anyone gets one up on the ganikā Vimala." She laughed. "So, set up on your own, make yourself independent."

"On what would I set myself up?" I scoffed. "A man needs capital to start."

"I will give you the capital."

"What?" I gasped.

She laughed at my astonishment. "At a high rate of interest, of course, or a portion of your profits."

I examined her, still astonished. "Why would you trust me? What if I cheat you?"

"Ah, but you won't. You're a man of honour. I have watched you here. You resist all the charms of my ganikās. I've used them to test you."

I started to laugh. It was such a ridiculous, but such a brilliant, offer. She laughed too, smacking her hands together. "Well, it's sealed?"

I nodded. "But not a word to my family, please."

She took a square of yellow silk cloth, dipped her seal in red dye and pressed it to the cloth. She held the cloth out to me. "Go and see Jatila the Mahasetthi. You need his blessings and patronage before you start any commerce in our Vessa quarters. He is a good man, a friend. His wife was a former ganikā, you know. A friend of mine."

When I told my father and Mahanama of the deal I'd struck to erase the debt, they were furious—but had to accept it, as they didn't want the humiliation of Vimala taking up a case against them. I also lied and told them that Vimala and I had settled on three quarters of the paddy land, rather than half. The woman deserved the extra.

☙

Yasodhara had been listening so intently to the story that now, when Ananda broke off his tale and called out to the palanquin bearers to stop, she let out a sigh. "Ah, bhāta, it's cruel to stop there."

He laughed, pleased she had been so engrossed. "Bhagini, now you get to *see* the next part of the story." Hopping out, he held out his hand to help her dismount.

She saw, from the shops on the street, that they were still in the Vessa Quarter.

Ananda gestured across the street to a shabby house, its wattle and daub boundary wall in a bad state, tufts of weeds growing in the broken crevices. The thatched roof, peeking above the wall, was also dishevelled with weeds, and a family of herons was nesting in the thatch.

"Mine if I want it. A gift from Vimala for quadrupling the amount she initially invested." He smiled with quiet pride and Yasodhara smiled back, truly happy for him.

Once they had entered through the cracked street door, grey with age and lack of paint, they stood taking in the courtyard, its earthen floor rutted with anthills and littered with leaves. A large neem tree grew in the centre, and the warped bench wrapping around it was spattered with bird droppings. The single-storey building along three sides of the courtyard was also in a poor state, its wattle and daub walls cracked. When they went into the receiving room, they found a large hole in the thatch. Something rustled underneath the debris on the floor—a mouse, a snake?

"Will you take it, bhāta?" Yasodhara asked, looking around skeptically.

"Yes, because it will finally allow us freedom from our father and Mahanama."

"'Us,' bhāta?"

He laughed. "Anuruddha will come with me. Despite his feckless ways, he is a good man, in love with the world, and generous—too generous. Some of his debts, you know, are incurred for his friends." He led her out onto the verandah and they went to inspect another room. "When I first came here, Anuruddha was the only one who was kind to me. Bringing me gifts, making sure I ate, just sitting patiently with me while I wept at my losses. No, no, I won't abandon him to my father and Mahanama. And I have an arrangement with Vimala now, which controls his betting."

"You are a good man, bhāta," Yasodhara said, with fond admiration for her new friend.

⚬

Yasodhara had been married a fortnight when Siddhartha, as her mother had predicted, received his posting. Governor of the Northern Province. When he told her, she gazed at him appalled. "But that's so far away," she whispered. "We . . . we will be on our own. When will I ever see my family again?"

"But we will only be there for a few years, Ushas." He took her hands and kissed her forehead, trying to reassure her. "I can't refuse the posting, unfortunately. My pita's order . . ." He shrugged. They both knew, without having to say a word, that this position was Suddhodana's way of negating his son's success in Savatthi. He was sending Siddhartha so far away that he, Siddhartha, would become irrelevant.

"Oh, Surya." Yasodhara sat down shakily on the edge of their bed.

Her parents and brother were still in Kapilavastu, staying in the palace guest apartment, visiting relatives and making sure she was well settled before they left—her father also using the opportunity to firm up relations between the two kingdoms. Later that day, when Pamita came to the marriage suite, Yasodhara told her mother the news. Pamita blanched, but then gathered herself together. "Ushas, this is your first real challenge as a wife." She took Yasodhara by the shoulders. "You must meet it with courage and vigour. Because a woman's life brings great challenges. So, come, let us now think about this future in the north and make plans for it."

Yasodhara was silent for moment, struggling to rise to this test. Finally, she smiled wanly and nodded.

In the days that followed, as she and her mother prepared for her new life, buying warm shawls and woollen blankets and furred slippers, she noticed that Siddhartha had become excited about this posting, returning with a glitter in his eyes from meeting various officials about his duties, or from speaking with former rashtrikas of the Northern Province. He tried to suppress his excitement around her, but she was not fooled. Once, when in their marriage suite, she happened to hear his voice and, looking down through a louvred window, saw that he was talking to her father, both men having strolled over together.

"And there, mātula," Siddhartha was enthusing to Dandapani, rubbing his hands together, "I will be useful, challenged. It's a rough province, beset with many problems. I can do much good there. Help many people. Keep busy. There are the cheating tax officials, the vana-dasa raids on our crops, highway robbers. All interesting problems to solve."

Her father laughed. "You are truly a strange man, daharā. But I'm happy this posting suits you."

Looking down at her husband, Yasodhara felt for the first time a distaste. There was something false and exaggerated, off-putting, about his enthusiasm.

By the time he came up to her, she was kneeling before a trunk, unloading all her wedding gifts because none of them could come with her—the gold pots and brassware, the filigreed lamps, too heavy for the two barges they were allotted for the journey. She turned to him and gestured to her gifts. "You didn't tell me the voyage would be by river. *And* that we would only have two barges. I found out through ammé!" She thrust a brass wine jug at him. "Did *you* know that hardly any merchants come up that far? I will have nothing, nothing. No cosmetics, no wine, no—"

"I'm sorry, Ushas." He squatted beside her and rested an arm on her shoulder. "I just found out too about the voyage."

But she was not fooled by his attempt to be downcast. "It's all very well for you, you're excited by this new posting." He started to protest but she cut him short. "Yes, yes, I just heard you talking to my pita."

He looked at her, guilty.

"Whereas, for me, this is exile. Exile from Ramagama, from my ammé, my pita, Devadatta, the civilized world." She waved her hand to encompass their suite. "Soon, soon, I will not know any of this. I would never have chosen the Northern Province, if *I'd* been given a choice."

"But I had no choice either, my pita—"

"No, but you've got something that excites you. Don't you dare pretend otherwise."

Siddhartha was silenced. "Well," he said after a moment, rather sullen, "would you like me to turn the position down?"

"Oh, don't be silly!"

"Then what? What would you like, Ushas?"

She gave a massive shrug and turned away from him. "An empty seed-pod, that's all I am, an empty seedpod carried along by any river current. Why, a ganikā has more say in her life than I do. Yes, yes, a ganikā!" she cried at his look of bewilderment.

She turned from him again and began to put her wedding gifts away in another larger trunk that would go back to her parents' home, making a mighty clatter as she did so, aware that this was the first time they were quarrelling.

With a loud, irritated *ttttch*, Siddhartha grabbed his bathing things and stalked off to wash before the midday sacrifice.

After he was gone, she sat back on her haunches, twisting her hands in her lap, feeling bad about her outbursts, yet at the same time believing stubbornly in the truth of what she'd said.

Of course, they soon made up and, that afternoon, after the sacrifices and meal, back in their suite, they kissed and hugged urgently, then fell across the bed to make furious love. Yet a residue of the quarrel remained, because Siddhartha knew she was unhappy about going.

The next time she was alone with her mother, both of them packing another trunk with heavy blankets, fur-lined shoes and other necessities for the cold north, she confessed to the quarrel. Pamita nodded, taking it in as she continued to pack the trunk.

"And well, Siddhartha, he's so excited about going now, so distracted by the prospect. I can't help myself, I'm irritated by his enthusiasm, irritated by how he tries to keep his enthusiasm from me now, and then his—" She broke off because her mother's shoulders were shaking with silent laughter. Yet when Pamita lifted her gaze, there was bitterness in her mirth.

"My dear Ushas, what you're truly upset about is that, for the first time, you've come up against the limits of our women's lot. Because it is our lot to follow our men. To be carried along by their needs and ambitions, their plans and schemes."

"But with pita, *you* led in your life together, you planned—"

"I did what I could within the bounds of being his wife. And no marriage is perfect. How could you think otherwise, dhītā? Your pita and I too are human, with our annoyances and failures just like everyone else. And you discover those annoyances and failures very soon after marriage. Your pita's vacillation can truly irritate me. And I know he thinks I push him too hard sometimes, thinks I emasculate him. To be honest, I've sometimes wondered if he resents me for canvassing to get him on the throne. Perhaps he would have been happier in a lower administrative position."

Yasodhara picked up a blanket and began to fold it, thoughtful. Of course she didn't think her parents' marriage perfect, but she'd never imagined her father might have been happier not being raja, or might have felt pushed into it by her ambitious mother.

"And your analogy of an empty seedpod carried by a river current is wrong. A seedpod isn't empty. It travels full of seeds to propagate itself in some unknown place."

For a while they were silent.

"There is something else."

Yasodhara looked up from folding a blanket, alarmed by her mother's tone.

"Your bhāta has been offered a position here. By Suddhodana. In the palace guards."

"Oh."

"You knew!"

After a moment's pause, Yasodhara confessed that she had suggested to Devadatta that he find a position here. "But that was when I thought I would be here too, ammé, to look out for him."

Pamita nodded sadly. "Well, perhaps this will be the making of him."

When next Yasodhara saw her brother, he strutted towards her, so handsome with his shaved, oiled head and palace guard uniform, its brass-studded leather breastplate sitting well on his broad chest. She slipped her hand around his bicep as they walked towards the sacrificial courtyard and said teasingly, "Look, look, bhāta, those girls are glancing over at you."

Devadatta blushed and snorted, shaking his head. "Those twittering sparrows?"

Yet she could tell he was pleased. *Yes, this might be the making of him.*

She hadn't seen Ananda and Anuruddha since she'd heard the news, as they had been busy with their new house. But finally they came to see her one morning at the women's quarters. As she went down to the courtyard to greet them, she felt torn between her loyalty to Siddhartha and her wish to not hide her unhappiness from her friends. The moment she saw their sympathetic faces, however, she knew she didn't have to put on a brave front. As she hugged Anuruddha, her tears wet his chest. How she would miss them—particularly Ananda, whom she had begun to think of as a brother.

Time passed swiftly and, sooner than she could have imagined, it was the last night before she left for the Northern Province. Knowing they wouldn't sleep, she and her mother passed the night sewing a quilt they'd started after they learned Yasodhara would be going away. It was a lovely dark-orange cotton, with a heavy woollen blanket serving as batting within. They had already sewn squares of red and blue cloth onto the orange cover and now they began to stitch in a pattern of vines and flowers on the squares, using red or blue thread. They spoke little as they worked, relishing the companionable silence of mother and daughter, both of them thinking of the numerous other times they'd performed similar tasks in silence. Yet, as the night passed, Yasodhara felt a heaviness growing and growing within her, increasing with each changing of the guards—the clink of spears, the gruff murmurs of the men floating up from the courtyard below. Occasionally an owl hooted, a rodent squeaked. She kept glancing at Pamita, bent over her work. She couldn't quite comprehend that this was the last time she would be with her mother for a very long time; could only feel this reality as a growing weight inside her. "We'll never get this done in time," Pamita said with a sigh, after the third change of guards.

"Then we'll just have to save it for when I return."

"No, no, I want you to take it, dhītā. Finish it up north. It will remind you of me."

Yasodhara said nothing.

It was still dark outside when a servant woman, after a brief knock, put her head inside and said, "Sāmini, it's time to rise and dress." Yasodhara nodded to dismiss her. The moment the woman was gone, she snatched up a pair of scissors and started to cut through the quilt. "Ushas!" Pamita gasped in dismay, but Yasodhara continued her cutting and soon the quilt fell apart in two halves. She held on to one section and pushed the other towards her mother. "We will each finish our own half and then, when we meet again, we'll join them together."

Pamita started to cry helplessly, clutching her half, and soon Yasodhara was crying too, mother and daughter clinging to each other.

The two carts had been loaded the previous night but Yasodhara and Pamita bustled about making sure everything was in place, if only to avoid being still. Then, it was time. Yasodhara's brother and father arrived to see her off. After she had embraced her father and touched his feet, she and her brother stood for a long moment regarding each other. "I will come and see you, bhagini," Devadatta promised gruffly.

"Be good to our parents, bhāta," she whispered as she touched his face. "You are all they have now." He nodded, lips pressed together, but would not meet her eyes.

Before she got into her cart, Yasodhara held her mother's hands and studied her face. "Ushas, dhītā," Pamita said, memorizing Yasodhara's face in turn, "don't forget me." She swallowed hard. "If, in our absence from each other, I am taken by Yama, know that I will watch you from the Land of the Fathers."

"Ah, ammé!"

"But these things happen, dhītā. None of us know when Yama will come for us with his noose."

Yasodhara's tears started to flow then and she brushed them away angrily. She turned and climbed the steps into the cart where Siddhartha waited for her. Ignoring his outstretched hand, she knelt at the edge of the vehicle and stared at her mother, neither woman breaking gaze. As the convoy began to trundle forward, Yasodhara kept her eyes on her mother, so small, so lost in the group that had gathered to say goodbye.

5

The Acacia Tree

"USHAS, USHAS."

She startled awake to find Siddhartha bent over her in the rapidly descending gloom. "We're here, Ushas. We've reached Mudgala."

It took Yasodhara a moment to orient herself—to the thrust of the barge's logs under her thick blanket, the rocking boat, the faint smell of ash used to cure the oxhide tent. She sat up, pushing the blanket off, and struggled to rise, Siddhartha clutching her arm to help her up. "Are we . . . really here?"

Seeing that he was examining her with concern, she eased her arm from his grip and began to groggily re-plait her hair. She was depleted, exhausted, from the arduous three-day journey by river. The rocking of the barge had made her so nauseated she was unable to keep food down. Even when they stopped for the night, their two barges tied to trees on the bank, and Siddhartha had carried her to the shore and fed her the simple meal of rice and lentil gruel the guards had prepared for them, she could only tolerate a few mouthfuls. Then there were the terrifying treks through jungle at the points where the river turned into rapids, their barges and luggage carried by the four guards and the local vana-dasas who acted as guides and porters for river traffic. She had been petrified at the sounds from the jungle, the rumble of tigers and leopards. Once, a rhinoceros came crashing through the undergrowth, barely missing them as it lumbered past to the river. There was also a close shave with a viper that suddenly dropped from a tree into her path. The vana-dasas were so quick, she had barely registered the snake before one of them had pinioned it with a long-handled fork and sliced its head off.

When her hair was done, Siddhartha gestured for her to turn around. "Your bodice cloth, it's hanging loose." He untied the knot at the back of her neck, lifting the two ends of cloth to bring her breasts up firmer, before retying it. She could smell her own fetidness—a faint odour of vomit and the slightly rancid coconut oil in her hair. She knew that her illness these last three days had frightened him because she'd heard him one night, when he thought she was asleep, confessing his worries to the senior guard. The old man, a veteran of river journeys, had assured him she'd survive the sickness. Until that moment, she had not thought of her own mortality. She had certainly not assumed, when she said goodbye to her family, that it might be her whom Yama came for with his noose. Siddhartha's fear made her grimly determined to survive, and she forced herself to eat and drink after that, whenever they were off the barge. Recalling that determination now, she drew her shawl tighter around her shoulders and signalled to Siddhartha that she was ready. They went out together and stood on the barge, gazing towards the shore. In the descending dusk, she could see numerous flaring torches held up by the villagers who had gathered to welcome them, alerted by a boatman posted at the bend in the river. Beyond the villagers was a steep bank. She couldn't see anything at the top in the gloom, except occasional tufts of smoke from the hearths of the homes that made up the village of Mudgala.

As the barge drew closer to the shore, she clutched instinctively at Siddhartha's hand and he squeezed her hand back. This was their new life. The thought sent a throb of homesickness through her for her family, for Ramagama. *No, no, I mustn't cry, I am the rashtrika's wife.* She straightened her back. She would not shame herself before these strangers.

Once the barges had hit the sandy bottom, they were in knee-deep water. The villagers, whom she could see more clearly now, made no move to come forward. She and Siddhartha glanced at each other. They would have to wade through the water to the shore.

The moment they stepped off the raft, splashing themselves, they both gasped, the frigid water clutching at their knees and shins as they hurriedly floundered their way to land. The villagers surged forward to greet them, nodding and smiling. The welcome was genuine but to Yasodhara the faces and smiles looked grotesque in the flickering torches. An old Brahmin with a long beard and grey hair pulled up in a tight knot came forward. He bowed to Siddhartha. "I am Vagantha, the gambojaka, sāmi." He gestured to an old woman who also came forward, bearing a tray woven from river rushes. The gambojaka took a clay jug of water from the tray and began to perform the rituals of welcome, offering Siddhartha the water to wash his feet, then curds mixed with spices and honey, both men chanting the verses of host and guest from the Vedas. As the rituals went on, the old woman nodded to Yasodhara, her motherly twinkle saying she knew what she must be feeling. Yasodhara smiled back, comforted by this kindness, liking and trusting the woman immediately. The couple were village Brahmins and had the hard, lithe muscles of people who worked the fields. A few of their teeth were missing, and their hair was greyer and sparser than that of their city counterparts. With soft, melodic voices and unhurried, discreet move-ments, they had the refinement of village gentry.

When the rituals were over, Vagantha said, "Sāmi, sāmini, it's a pleasure to finally have you here. Let me introduce my wife, Rupasiri." The woman bowed, then signalled to two villagers, who came forward with thick wool-len shawls. Yasodhara and Siddhartha took those gratefully, shivering now from wading through the river and from the cool evening air. The gambo-jaka introduced the other village officials and their wives and, as he did so, Yasodhara felt better and better, her sickness and nausea dissipating now that she was on firm ground. The air had a crisp, astringent odour to it that was invigorating. "Let us proceed to your home." Vagantha gestured, indicating that they must scramble up a path cut into the steep riverbank to reach the level ground above. The villagers followed, some of them helping the guards carry the trunks.

When they reached the top of the bank, Rupasiri took Yasodhara's arm. "Look, sāmini." Yasodhara turned in the direction the woman was point-ing, and gasped. The foothills of the Himalayas—layer upon layer of peaks disappearing into the distance, each taller than the last until finally the mountains were lost in a haze. The closer ones were black in the dusk, but the further back the peaks went, the lighter and lighter blue they became, the sky above fading upwards from red to orange to pink to blue, to grey.

A single hawk soared and dipped over the mountains as if monarch of
them all. The villagers watched the newcomers, grinning with delight to
see these city folks' awe.

As they made their way towards the village, Yasodhara, feeling better
by the moment, looked around with great curiosity at the vegetable gardens they passed, beanpoles heavy with pods, the large splayed leaves of
various gourds. Beyond, she could see terraced paddy fields on the hillsides,
barely visible now. Rupasiri walked beside her in companionable silence.
Whenever Yasodhara happened to meet her eye, the old woman nodded
and smiled as if to say, "Everything will be well, you are among friends."

Soon they came to a thorana that led into the village. Yasodhara passed
under it into the central square with its floor of beaten earth. In the middle
of the square was a massive banyan tree, its aerial prop roots forming a
many-chambered abode in which she could see a shrine to the Yaksha and
Yakshi of the village, housed in a mud hut, as well as a large communal
well. The square was bounded on all sides by residences—some simple
one-room huts, others proper houses. Between these dwellings were lanes
that led away from the square, lined with houses and huts. Where the
lanes ended, Yasodhara could glimpse fields and, beyond these, the dark
blur of jungle.

Yasodhara had certainly been in similar villages before, yet she felt like
she was seeing everything with new eyes because this was now her home.
Aware of the villagers staring, she turned her gaze to them, and they immediately ducked their heads in respect. Then it struck her: as the rashtrika's
wife, she was first among the women, even higher than Rupasiri. But she
was just sixteen, younger than most; how was she supposed to act, what
were they expecting her to be? She straightened her shoulders and drew her
shawl more tightly about herself, trying to look the part.

Rupasiri and Vagantha were gesturing towards a lane between two
houses and Yasodhara and Siddhartha followed. Once they had passed the
last building along the lane, there was scrub on either side and then ahead
stood a house. *My house.* Yasodhara peered through the dusk at the single-
storey wattle and daub structure. She was reassured to see that the boundary wall was in good condition, the thatch neat. She entered the compound
through a wooden door in the boundary wall and paused to take in the

courtyard, also neat and tidy, as were the buildings on three sides and the verandah wrapping around them. An Ashoka tree stood in the middle of the courtyard and Yasodhara thought of the Ashoka tree in the women's quarters of her childhood home, the way she and her mother would often sit in its shade, smelling the sweet flowers as they worked on embroidering a shawl or threading a garland. At the thought of her diminutive mother, full of vitality and good humour, the tears pushed themselves up. She bit her lip. *No, no, I am the rashtrika's wife.*

While Vagantha and Siddhartha stood in the courtyard, talking about a meeting with the village committee tomorrow, Rupasiri led Yasodhara through a door on the verandah into the main bedroom. She bustled about lighting lamps, the room revealing itself with each lit lamp as Yasodhara looked around. A large brazier filled with hot coals occupied a central place in the bedroom, providing some relief from the damp chill, which gave the air a smell like clotted river weeds, slimy and greenish. There was a large bed, a few trunks for storage, some shelves and a couple of stools. That was it. No divans and comfortable chairs, no tapestries or murals on the clay walls, no statues in nooks, no garlands and smoking incense and elegant rugs. The floor had been reconditioned with a new layer of clay mixed with wood-fired cow dung to disinfect it, and a faint leafy odour rose from the floor. Thickly furred mountain-goat and sheep rugs were scattered about.

Rupasiri beckoned Yasodhara over to the bed with an apologetic smile. "I'm afraid the rope of the webbing is only two strings thick, sāmini. It's not the six-stringed ropes of your palace beds." She smiled ruefully. "You will get used to it. Soon you won't remember you slept in any other bed." Yasodhara tested the bed with her hand and, seeing how much it sagged, struggled to hide her dismay. How lumpy the mattress was, too. Rupasiri clucked in commiseration, then reached for a dowel with spiral threads and a handle. "The ropes can be tightened for some comfort." She demonstrated, then held out the instrument to Yasodhara. "You try, sāmini." Yasodhara accepted the instrument reluctantly and tried to tighten a rope, but she was so clumsy that Rupasiri took it back from her with a smile. "Never mind, you are tired and it's dark. I'll come and show you properly tomorrow." Now Rupasiri gestured to some bathing cloths on a trunk.

"It's only going to get colder. You and your husband should bathe soon. Unfortunately, unlike the bathing ponds you're used to, here there is only a well in a corner of the courtyard."

Rupasiri left her to change and Yasodhara could hear her murmuring the same bathing instructions to Siddhartha. A moment later, he entered. "Well, Ushas, what do you think?" he asked with a large smile, rubbing his hands together.

"Change, please, Surya. I don't think I could stand bathing if it got any colder."

He was hurt at her rebuff but she turned away crossly, annoyed at his hurt, and began to remove her bodice cloth and unravel her dhoti. He began pulling apart his dhoti as well. Once she had tied her bathing cloth above her breasts, she turned around and found him also changed, bathing cloth wrapped around his waist. "It's a well, not a bathing pond. I suppose you didn't know about that either when you accepted this position, as you didn't know about this awful bed." Then, as the realization came to her: "We're expected to draw our own water! There are no servants."

"What fun!" Siddhartha grinned, with a look of appeal. But she would not agree, and went out ahead of him, chin high, taking a lamp with her.

The well was surrounded by thatched screens for privacy. Siddhartha drew up water and offered the leather bucket to her. She poured it over herself, gasping at the cold. As she rapidly soaped herself with a perfumed ball of clay, teeth chattering, he drew out another bucketful and dunked it over himself, letting out a merry shout. He was trying to make an adventure of it, but she was too sour with fear and worry to do anything but glare at him. She grabbed the rope from him and, with much grunting, drew up her own water, pouring a couple of buckets over herself. She left him to finish and scurried back to their bedroom.

Yet, once she had dried herself and was sitting by the brazier tying her bodice cloth, her skin tingling, she suddenly felt better, clean. She smelled a fragrant strand of her hair, comforted by its odour, its soft dampness against her face. Siddhartha came in and caught her doing this. She frowned petulantly and dropped the strand of hair. He was careful to keep his expression respectful and contrite, but she could tell he was relieved at her changed mood.

They dressed and entered the receiving room. A fire had been prepared in its large hearth and Rupasiri knelt before a low table, laying out dinner on banana leaves. It was simple fare: boiled rice, curd, some cured venison and a fried leaf Yasodhara had never seen before. As they sat down to eat, she realized that, for the first time in three days, she was ravenous. She ate with zest, and both Siddhartha and Rupasiri watched her, smiling. The headman's wife was seated cross-legged on a cushion a short distance from them, mending a shawl. "Mmm, what's this delicious leaf?" Yasodhara asked between mouthfuls.

"It's sanjeevani, sāmini, and, apart from being delicious, has many medicinal properties, according to the local people here."

"My wife's had a terrible journey." Siddhartha glanced sympathetically at Yasodhara. "Sick most of the time."

"Ah yes, the hellish journey from the south. I remember it well." Rupasiri smiled and nodded at Yasodhara's inquiring look. "I too come from the south, like you, sāmini. Came here as a young bride too. Yes," she continued as she passed a new thread through the eye of her needle, "life here has proved to be more satisfying than I expected." She gave Yasodhara a reassuring nod.

But then, just as Yasodhara was feeling soothed, Rupasiri added, "Now, about tomorrow morning: I have left some lentils to soak and there is rice in a box in the kitchen which I will show you. For your gruel." Yasodhara gawked at her. Rupasiri laughed. "Never mind. I'll come and show you how to make gruel tomorrow, then." With a keen glance, she added, "Yes, yes, I should have thought about it. You don't know domestic work."

"But can't someone be hired?" Siddhartha pleaded. "I'm willing to pay anything."

Rupasiri smiled and shook her head. "We're all Brahmins or Khattiyas in this village, sāmi. All with our own lives to take care of."

Yasodhara pushed her plate away, appetite gone. There was the verandah and courtyard that would have to be swept twice a day, the fire lit in this room (she'd never lit a fire in her life!), the hot coals prepared for the brazier in the bedroom, the drawing of water for cooking and washing, the meals to be prepared. How was she to do all this work that she'd never done before? Work that required knowledge she didn't have.

After Rupasiri departed, the guards took their positions in the sentry hut outside the gate. As Yasodhara and Siddhartha put out the fire in the receiving room and clumsily washed the plates and dishes by the well, they were silent. Finally, he whispered, "Ushas—"

"What?" she hissed back. He fell silent again, the quiet broken only by her ill-natured scrubbing of a pot.

When they had done their chores and were in bed, they lay in the dark, still silent. "Ushas," he eventually whispered again, "do you notice anything?"

She could hear his desperation to make up. After a moment, she said in a more pleasant tone, "Yes, I have noticed. No noise."

He snuggled up to her. "No horses' hooves. No cart wheels. No human voices."

"No revellers raucously singing or bellowing for more drink," she added, her lips inches from his, suddenly wanting more than ever this physical release, this temporary oblivion from her cares.

"Do you remember the stories our grandmothers told us of the world when they were children? We are back in that time." He slid his hand over her naked breasts and she sighed, pulling his face down to them.

The next morning, she awoke ahead of Siddhartha and gasped softly at the sight out the window. She crept from the bed and went to stand with both hands on the sill, gazing at the mighty mountains in the distance. They were clearer now in the morning light, which lay in a haze over the snow-covered peaks, rays of sun striping the slopes. "Home of the gods," she murmured and, as if the gods had spoken, a voice within her said, "Start your new life well."

She let herself out quietly and stood on the verandah, hugging herself under her shawl because of the cold, contemplating these words. A pale-pink light lay over the beaten earth of the courtyard floor, from which tufts of mist rose. The smell in the air was sharp and sweet and after a moment she noticed the acacia tree spilling its branches and lovely yellow blossoms over the boundary wall, nodding in the breeze like a friendly, curious neighbour. Once again, she was aware of the absence of city noises. The only sound here was the breeze in the trees, her own breath, and of course the dawn chorus, of a variety and intensity she'd never heard before.

She spotted a broom leaning against the side of the verandah and, remembering that voice within, she picked it up and began to sweep. This she could do. Used to love to do as a child, joining the slaves as they swept the courtyards. Her father had even gifted her a little broom. That memory of her home and childhood was with her as she set about her task, drawing the love of her parents about her as if it were the shawl around her shoulders. Soon she was smiling at how easily the motion of sweeping came back to her, those little tricks and tips the slave women had taught her. She felt lulled by the rhythm of her work, lost in it, tranquil—unaware that Siddhartha, awakened by the scrape of the broom's ekels, had come out to watch her from the verandah; and that Rupasiri had slipped in through the boundary door and was watching her too. When she finally did notice, she laughed and gestured mockingly to the pile of leaves she'd amassed. "You are learning, sāmini," Rupasiri said with a smile.

Yasodhara nodded and laughed again, then transferred her friendly gaze to Siddhartha. She must not merely start her life well, but seize hold of it. That was what the voice was telling her. And she was sure now that voice wasn't a god's but a local deity's, perhaps a devata who might live in that very acacia tree, or even the yakshi of the village. She was being welcomed here; and she must honour the spirit's welcome, submit to its command. A peace stole over her. It was time to lay aside her resentment at Siddhartha. This was her life, and there was no point pining for another one. She held on to this thought as she went to put away the broom, tenderly touching Siddhartha's face as she passed him; and she held on to it later as she squatted before the kitchen fire, Rupasiri hovering over her as she tried repeatedly to get it going, coughing at the smoky mess she was making yet refusing to give in or let the gambojaka's wife do it for her. Finally, she made a decent enough flame and squatted back on her haunches, watching with satisfaction and pleasure as the gruel began to bubble.

As the porridge simmered, Rupasiri took her to see the storeroom off the kitchen. It was dark in there, the one wooden window closed to keep out animals. Rupasiri bustled over and opened the window, and in the light that poured through, Yasodhara saw that the room was small, nothing like the many-chambered granaries of her parents' palace. Clay jars of rice and pulses were elevated from the ground on wooden stands and there was a dusty smell in the air from grain and mouse droppings. As Yasodhara opened the tops of jars to peer in at the supplies, Rupasiri said, "You must know, sāmini, that the share of grain tax the rashtrika keeps is very little. Most of the grain tax goes to Kapilavastu. See, our yields are much smaller than fields in the southern states, yet we must pay the same grain tax to Kapilavastu as the southern states."

Yasodhara frowned. "But then, how will I manage?"

"I'm afraid you must cultivate your own fields." Rupasiri nodded sympathetically at Yasodhara's shock. "There is also, you should know, sāmini, a vegetable garden behind the house that you must tend . . . it's the only place you will get your vegetables. We, alas, don't have markets here. There is some occasional bartering between us village women, but one must have something to barter, you understand?"

"But . . ." Yasodhara sat down on a stool, her legs shaking. "I . . . I've never done cultivation. I mean, I . . . I've been with my mother to see our fields, but she only supervised from the bunds. And—and we had, *have*, a Manager of the Fields."

"You will learn, sāmini. I will teach you."

"But I have to feed us! Siddhartha and me. *Now*. We have to eat!" She jumped up and went from jar to jar, looking in each. How long would this last? Was she to start rationing? How was she to go about managing?

"We will teach you. In fact, today, the women are meeting to weed the paddy fields. Go and change into an old dhoti and bodice cloth, then we must join the women."

"No, no, first I must see this vegetable garden. I—I must see how much food we have."

Rupasiri regarded her gravely. "You won't starve, daharé."

Yasodhara flapped out of the storeroom. "But no, I must, I must, see this garden," she insisted, barely registering that the gambojaka's wife had called her "daharé" instead of "sāmini."

Rupasiri took her out the kitchen door, beyond which there were no steps but a direct hop down to the back garden. Once there, Yasodhara looked around her. The beds were neatly laid out and weeded; probably Rupasiri had kept them up. She began to go down the rows, hands folded tightly under her shawl, fingers shredding a tassel as she looked at the various plants. She had no idea what most of them were. Seeing her bewilderment, Rupasiri pointed to each row as they passed, saying, "Eggplant, garlic, bitter gourd, onion, taro, calabash." Then for the first time she touched Yasodhara, taking the hand that was shredding the tassel and pressing it in her own. "You remind me so much of myself when I first came here, daharé."

"But you came from a village, Rupasiri," Yasodhara whispered. "You already knew everything that I must now learn. Or we starve."

Rupasiri laughed. "We, the village, will not let you starve."

Yasodhara frowned, shaking her head. She and Siddhartha were the rashtrika and his wife. They couldn't be dependent on the village. It would be a loss of face.

She went to her room and changed into an old dhoti. Then she sat on the edge of her bed, twisting her interlaced fingers. *Every time I find some equilibrium, another thing comes along to pull me back into uncertainty.* After a moment, she stood with a sigh and a small moan. *Well, if I can't find equilibrium, I must pretend.*

Rupasiri was waiting in the courtyard, smiling gently. Yasodhara stepped off the verandah, chin high.

As she followed Rupasiri along the lane that led to the square, other women came out of their houses and joined them, nodding shyly to Yasodhara, lagging behind out of respect, whispering in conversation with each other. She noticed that they wore old cloths wrapped around their waists and thighs, rather than dhotis. She must remember to do the same next time. In the square, even more women waited, and they too fell into step behind her and Rupasiri. They passed through the square and headed in the direction of the river, then veered off to walk single file through vegetable gardens towards terraced paddy fields on a hillside. By now, the chill had disappeared and the air was warm without being hot. It had a fresh smell of earth and grass and manure. In the vegetable gardens, Yasodhara saw young girls and boys at work, squatted over their family plots. *Family. Yet another thing I don't have.* She would have to manage everything on her own.

When they were at the base of the hill, Rupasiri pointed out the terraces that belonged to the rashtrika. As the groups of women made their way up the incline, they broke apart, picked up woven baskets lying at the edges of plots and splashed into the ankle-high mud of their own fields. At the rashtrika's plots, Rupasiri, with a wry glance at Yasodhara, laid aside her shawl, hitched up and knotted her cloth, took a basket and strode into the muddy field. Seeing that the village women were watching with little smiles, Yasodhara laid aside her own slippers and shawl, rolled up her dhoti, grabbed a basket and followed the older woman into the field, her toes curling with disgust at the slimy mud. The wiggle of a worm beneath her foot made her gasp and hurriedly splash forward. The women let out a small cheer and one of them cried, "You are one of us now, sāmini." She nodded and grinned, trying to keep the revulsion from her face.

Rupasiri bent from her waist to the paddy shoots, gesturing for Yasodhara to do the same. "Note, daharé, here is a weed, not a sapling. See, the weed is a close mimicry of the paddy shoot, but is minutely furred around the edges." Yasodhara stooped close, studying the difference intently.

Rupasiri led the way, going along the first row of saplings and picking out a few weeds, but leaving others so that Yasodhara could practise learning to identify and pluck them out. She stayed very close to Yasodhara, stilling her pupil's hand whenever she was about to pick out a paddy sapling. Yasodhara was slow at first, teeth gritted, determined to learn, and even more determined not to lose face in front of the other women. The sun beat down on her back, but the weather was still very pleasant, a cool wind stirring her hair, drying the sweat on her back and brow. Soon she found that she'd caught on and was moving at quite a good pace, not making any more mistakes in identifying the weeds. "You're doing well, daharé," Rupasiri said softly, patting her shoulder. Yasodhara nodded, pleased. Rupasiri stood back and let her go on by herself, row by row, hand shading her eyes from the sun as she watched. A woman started a call-and-response song. The other women picked it up, moving in rhythm to the melody. "Sing, daharé," Rupasiri whispered, "it really does make the work easier, faster. And the women will be delighted." Yasodhara listened and picked up the tune. She began to sing along with the women, soon taken with how the song lulled her into a tempo of picking and tossing into the basket, picking, tossing.

After they had worked for a while, Rupasiri glanced up at the sun and called out that they should rest. Yasodhara had worked all this while with her back bent and now, as she straightened up, she gasped, the muscles of her lower back stiff and seized up. Rupasiri patted her shoulder. "You will soon get used to it, daharé. Other rashtrikas' wives have, and they weren't as young as you."

The women made their way to sit in a glade of trees at the top of the hill. The vista of the surrounding valleys and mountains was magnificent from here. Yasodhara, exhilarated by her success, stood taking the view in, tranquility stealing over her as she breathed in the earthy smell of paddy and the crisp tang of the air, and watched a hawk once again soaring, dipping, soaring, dipping over the mountains. She sighed with pleasure and turned to the women. "Do you simply get used to this after a while?"

"Like anything else, sāmini," a woman with a jolly expression replied. "Our husbands, our bunions." The other women cackled and murmured in agreement.

One of them gestured for Yasodhara to sit with them and, once she had joined them, another woman offered her a clay pitcher. She drank thirstily, smacking her lips because the water was sweetened. Once she passed the pitcher back, still another woman offered her some betel and a small piece of areca nut. She chewed, enjoying the zest of the leaf and nut, her mouth coming alive at the astringent taste. "It's nice that you're trying to be one of us," the woman said, "we appreciate that. Another city lady wouldn't have drunk from our pitcher or enjoyed our simple betel."

"You mean the former rashtrika's wife," a plump woman added with a cackle. "A harsh and haughty one, sāmini." The others tried to hush her up, but she declared, "I am plain-speaking. And that is the truth."

When her companions saw that Yasodhara was pleased at the compliment rather than offended on behalf of her predecessor, another woman added, "We are glad you and your husband are here, sāmini. We have heard great things about him."

Any exhilaration and pride Yasodhara felt at her accomplishments in the field wore out by mid-afternoon. Mastering the weeding lost its pleasure and she was aware of her aching calves, her throbbing back when she straightened up, a cut on her finger that stung constantly. As she limped home later, she was numb with tiredness, looking forward to rest and bathing. But when she entered the courtyard and found it silent and deserted, it came to her freshly that she had no servants or slaves—so used was she to their presence that she had instinctively looked around expecting someone to come scurrying to meet her needs. She glared at the well. She must draw her own water to wash her hands and legs, then begin to prepare the evening meal. She hobbled over to the well and took up the bucket, lowering it in, her arms and shoulders so stiff and painful she gasped as she pulled the bucket back. She sat on a stone by the well, washed her face, hands and feet, then rested back against the well wall, waiting to dry off in the sun.

She fell asleep seated there and was woken sometime later by a soft, "Sāmini, sāmini." She opened her eyes blearily then let out a small shriek. Dangling before her was a dead hare. The guard who was holding the hare smiled hesitantly. "For your evening meal, sāmini. The sāmi instructed us to hunt for something to give you for dinner." She regarded the animal, its fur bloody where the arrow had pierced its side. Her disgust deepened to horror as it dawned on her that she was expected to skin and disembowel the creature, and chop and cook it. Feeling the man's keen gaze on her and knowing she must not lose face, she nodded and scrambled up, taking the hare gingerly from him.

In the kitchen, she flung the hare down on the chopping stone and stared at it for a while. "Well," she finally declared harshly, "gawking won't make a meal." She picked up the knife and held it a moment, wondering where to start. And now a memory came back: her brother Devadatta, skinning and gutting a hare he had caught. In fact, she'd seen her brother skin and gut animals many times. Often, they'd ride off together into the forest to spend the day, galloping through the undergrowth, then swimming in a pond or stream. Her brother would shoot a hare or squirrel or bird with his bow and arrow, then make a fire to roast his kill. "Bhāta, guide my hand." She grabbed the hare's skin at its neck and with a moan cut across the neck. She paused a moment, breathing deeply to prevent herself from vomiting; then took a large gulp of water from a jug and rubbed an arm across her face to wipe away the sweat. She closed her eyes, recalling her brother's tanned, handsome face frowning with concentration, his burly frame squatted over an animal, strong hands at work. She flipped the hare over; cut its skin from throat to tail; then began to pull the skin off. Once that was done, she chopped off the paws and then the tail. The hare splayed on its back, she made an incision in its belly, her brother murmuring, "Gently, bhagini, you don't want to pierce the innards." She cut up to the neck, laying the creature open. Reaching inside, gasping and near retching, she tore its innards out. She took the innards, skin, head and paw and threw them out the back door, knowing they would soon be taken by the crows perched on the garden fence. For a moment she stood at the door, breathing in the cool air. Then she washed her hands from a bucket of water, using a dried-gourd dipper. "Yes, yes, I have done it," she thought, and felt the satisfaction and relief of enduring an ordeal. Cooking the hare would be easy because there was already a spit in place above the kitchen fire.

Later, when Yasodhara served the meal to Siddhartha, she did so with a smile of pride. He ate heartily, nodding. "Yes, it's delicious."

Sitting across from him, she took her first bite of the hare and rice and lentils, then shrugged. "It's edible, but not in the least tasty."

"But you will get better with time, Ushas."

"Yes, Surya. I will."

They ate in peaceable silence, nodding and smiling whenever they happened to catch each other's eyes. A sense of companionship stole over them; and the silence reminded Yasodhara of that quiet between her parents when the family would gather each evening in her mother's room. She recalled, with both longing and pleasure, Pamita and Dandapani reclining on the bed in tranquil amity, passing the pipe between them, the sweet smell of ganja and clove powder perfuming the air while she and her brother played a game of chaturanga on the floor. "Start your new life well," the devata had told her—because by now she was convinced there was indeed a devata, and that he lived in the acacia tree beyond her boundary wall, a tree that was blooming out of season precisely because of this spirit's presence.

6

Yama's Noose

OVER THE NEXT decade, life passed tranquilly in Mudgala for Yasodhara, who was so busy that she often fell into bed happy with fatigue and
was immediately asleep. The yields from her paddy fields and vegetable
garden increased each year and the admiring women told her that she was
blessed with the gift of fecundity.

The one area in which she was not fruitful was children. A few times
she got pregnant and miscarried within three months. "But what if I'm
cursed, Surya?" she would say in tears to Siddhartha each time this happened. And each time, he would reassure her, pointing out that their own
mothers and their aunt Prajapati all gave birth late in their twenties, to
healthy children—reminding her that, for some reason known only to the
gods, this was the lot of their Gotama Gotra. But she knew too about all
the miscarriages and stillborn babies their mothers and aunts had endured
before the healthy children came; and about the women of their gotra who
remained barren. "It doesn't bear thinking of," she'd tell herself after each
miscarriage. "There's nothing to do but keep going, to hope I conceive and
finally bear a child."

In one thing she knew she was lucky: she had married a good, talented man—she had, in effect, married her father. As the years passed,
Siddhartha gained the admiration and respect of Vagantha, the village
committee and the entire province. He was soon completely in control
of his jurisdiction, able to make decisions and act on problems with the
wisdom of a man much older and more experienced. He quickly took

in hand the issue of the corrupt village officials who had colluded with
the previous rashtrika to rob grain taxes and exploit the villagers. They
were fined and removed from their positions, and the more troublesome
banished from the province. Two years after his arrival, he embarked on
an ambitious road-building and -widening scheme, which opened up the
distant villages to each other, allowing for greater trade and prosperity.
Within a year, the taxes were up and the tax collectors who came from
Kapilavastu reported that the sangha was very pleased. Siddhartha also
brought under control the raiding of crops by the vana-dasa tribes. The
four guards they'd brought with them from Kapilavastu had been selected
for their prowess and experience. They set about training young village
men across the province in combat, and the vana-dasa tribes soon found it
difficult to raid the fields.

Yasodhara often found herself studying her husband with interest as he
talked about what he had done that day, or after she learned of his actions
from the village women. She'd known of his intelligence and political acuity before, but the extent of his talent was a revelation to her. He also had
charisma, which was a surprise to her. In Kapilavastu and Ramagama, he
had always been a loner lost in his lofty thoughts. Yet now, when there
were ceremonial occasions—a marriage, a funeral, a harvest festival—and
she went with him to various villages, the inhabitants lined the road to
greet them, calling out, "Hail Siddhartha! Hail our beloved rashtrika!" They
would take the bridle of his horse and lead him into the village, women
throwing flower petals over him. Siddhartha lacked the burliness that made
a man conventionally handsome, like her brother. Yet now she observed
that village women looked at him with desire. If he'd wanted, he could
have had some of these women and, in the more remote villages, this
would have been considered an honour bestowed on the family. But he was
not that kind of man.

Siddhartha, of course, had his peculiarities, his faults, which revealed
themselves in the first year of their marriage. He had a penchant for melancholy—a strange moodiness and brooding that would come over him
almost always in response to the philosophy of the Nigantha and Ajivaka
ascetics. Yasodhara found his ongoing interest in these philosophies bewildering, given that he was an energetic and talented administrator, a person

happy to go out into the world, to fix problems, ambitious to improve his province—in other words a man who, in his daily life, was the very opposite of those world-renouncing, world-despising ascetics. In fact, he was happiest, she'd noticed, when he was doing the work of saving a village, or halting a raid on crops by vana-dasas, or dealing with a water problem, or getting roads broadened to distant villages. She had come to predict when the melancholy would rise up in him—usually when he was worried or upset about something. But also, inexplicably, after some success, such as visiting a village where he was hailed and feted, or after the grain tax had been particularly good and the Kapilavastu tax collector brought praise from the sangha. This was truly a mystery to her. But she soon came to accept this melancholy as part of him, and was comforted that it was such a minor flaw compared with those of other husbands. And she was always able to tease him out of his moods, to jolly him along, calling him "my miserable macaque" after the monkey with its mournful, worried-looking face. She could tell he was grateful when she rescued him from his brooding.

"Yes, yes, I am lucky," she told herself. But she also knew that she had made her own luck. Like her mother, she had guided her marriage to a tranquil harbour. She was no longer that girl who felt as if she were a seedpod carried by any river current. She had found what she was good at: things grew easily for her, she had the touch. And she was never more at peace than when she was bending over her rows of paddy or squatting at her garden beds or pruning her flowering bushes around the courtyard.

Then one evening, in their eleventh year in Mudgala, Siddhartha said, with a little laugh, as he and Yasodhara took their places by the fire after the evening meal, "The tax collector from Kapilavastu brought the strangest news today. The emperor Maha Kosala has abdicated his throne to his son Pasénadi and taken up the ascetic path of the Niganthas. Disappeared from the world." He laughed again. "I never thought the old man would do it. No matter what he said to me, I never thought he would."

Yasodhara was stoking the fire, barely paying attention, because the world outside Mudgala now always felt distant, ephemeral, to her. Yet seeing he was waiting for some response, she said, "Oh dear, that is a shame.

He was a good maharaja." Then added, because he seemed to want more from her, "This must be quite a scandal!"

"Hmm, yes," he replied, still seeming dissatisfied by her response.

Rupasiri and Vagantha dropped by that evening, joining Yasodhara and Siddhartha in the receiving room, as they occasionally did, to tell stories and discuss the goings-on in the village and the province. No sooner were they seated than the subject of the maharaja came up.

"I am disappointed in our maharaja," Vagantha said, and Rupasiri also shook her head. "These new philosophies are dangerous, sāmi-sāmini. The world of our gods and the world of us humans exist in a delicate balance. They are strong and powerful because we offer sacrifices to them. If we, and our young, stop offering sacrifices, the gods will then grow weak and the world will slide into chaos. Yes, yes, I am disappointed. The old maharaja shouldn't have set such a bad example."

"But," Siddhartha said lightly, poking at the fire, "is there not something about the Nigantha theory of karma that makes sense? How else to explain the numerous instances where a person does everything correctly and virtuously, and yet misfortune rains on them? To simply say they have displeased the gods makes little sense, because often they have been scrupulous in the sacrifices yet are still brought low. In such a case, wouldn't it make more sense to say that their misfortune is the result of bad karma from a previous act, in this life or in an earlier life?"

The old Brahmin couple smiled at him indulgently, shaking their heads to show they understood he was being provocative to start a friendly argument.

"A man can serve his family, his people, his world, with scrupulous honesty and still do poorly in life," Siddhartha continued, smiling, but now with an edge to his voice. "While another man who is dishonest, vain, petty, who doesn't have half the talent of this other man, prospers. Couldn't that be because of their karma?"

The old couple looked at him askance, seeing he was serious. Siddhartha poked moodily at the fire, not meeting their gaze.

"Now, now, ayyé," Yasodhara said with a laugh. "You are forgetting the gods, the devatas of the air and water, all of whom will punish the feckless man . . . at some point."

"Indeed, daharé," Rupasiri added, nodding vigorously.

Siddhartha grinned sheepishly. He changed the subject and soon seemed himself as they discussed a vana-dasa raid that had happened yesterday.

Yet, a few days later, Yasodhara came home from the fields early to find Siddhartha seated on their bed, leaning back on his elbows, gazing into the distance. He started at her entry, so lost in his thoughts that he hadn't heard her footsteps on the verandah.

"Surya?"

She glimpsed his guilt before his features settled into a mild smile. But under her scrutiny, his smile faded and he said, in a choked voice, "I had to punish some highway robbers today."

She went and crouched before him, pressing his knee. "Oh, I'm sorry, Surya." She knew that he hated having to pass that particular sentence of flogging with thorny whips, nostrils slit, an ear cut off; that each time he had to steel himself to do it and each time he came home and vomited. She could, this close, catch a faint whiff of vomit.

"The six men were brought to the village square. When they saw me, they wailed, holding out their bound hands, crying, 'Sāmi, be merciful, banish us. But not this punishment.'" He got up and began to pace. "Their backs and limbs were already ragged and bleeding, strips of skin torn off from the whips. But what choice did I have? The sentence had to be carried out, I had to sit there with a stony face and watch: each man held on the ground like a sacrificial goat by our soldiers, his limbs thrashing; the men screaming as their nostrils were slit, their ears cut off."

"But Surya, what is to be done? It's for the protection of everyone else. And look at all the good you have done in this province."

"But what is the point of all the good I have done! What is the point of this punishment! The place of those thieves will simply be taken by others. And there, there, a long line of thieves stretching behind them. Because such is human greed and evil. And I, as rashtrika, in this province, or someday another province, will have to keep meting out these punishments."

He fell on the bed and rolled over on his side, curled up. "How ridiculous to believe I was actually making progress here, that someday, through my efforts, this province would arrive in a golden era of peace and prosperity."

He was in one of his melancholy moods. The thing as always was to bear with him through it. "Ah, Surya," she said softly, stroking his back, "but the province *has* arrived in an age of great prosperity, great peace."

He got up and went to stand at the window, looking out. Then he turned to her. "I . . . I'm not happy being here, Ushas. Everything is meaningless. I . . . I just keep on doing and doing and . . . and . . ."

"But our life *is* happy here," she said firmly. "We *are* happy, Surya." Her voice began to rise. "You're just upset at having to administer this punishment. But it's not the same as being unhappy with your life."

"No, no, beloved." He came and took her hand. "You are right. I don't want to be gone from here." He met her scrutiny with a smile. "I think I'm just a little bored; perhaps I need a new challenge. Something to look forward to, something that will keep me busy and happy."

Yasodhara went to the washstand and began to scrub the mud off her arms. Despite his reassurance, she could tell Siddhartha truly was dissatisfied with his life. "You're twenty-seven and look at all you've accomplished, Surya. Most men haven't achieved a tenth of what you have at your age. And we're so happy here. So settled, so lucky this is our home."

"But, beloved, this life, this happiness we have, it's temporary." He tried to mask the impatience in his voice, but she heard it. "No rashtrika remains in his position for life. We are nobles, not villagers. It is our lot, as senior administrators, to move around in these positions. Yes, yes, all of us stuck in this—"

"No! Do not say 'honeypot of power'! I don't want to hear that ridiculous phrase!"

He went back to stand at the window, hands clutching the sill, gazing out unseeing.

She watched him, drying herself off. A taint was spreading across her lovely life, like a chamber pot flung into a pond. He had spoken a truth she hadn't considered: their life here was temporary. Though why, why hadn't she considered this?

She let out a little sob. "I don't want to leave Mudgala. I don't."

He came, took her in his arms and kissed her head. "But you speak as if we're leaving tomorrow, beloved."

"But still . . ."

"Look, Ushas, we might yet have many years here."

"But then, at some point it will end, it will all end. And I will lose the life I love."

He held her tighter and kissed her head and wet cheeks over and over again, murmuring, "Oh my love, my love."

It was time to take the paddy saplings from their nursery bed and replant them in the waterlogged fields—one of Yasodhara's favourite moments in the cycle of cultivation. There was tenderness in the act of taking these budding, fragile shoots and introducing them to the deeper fields, and she always felt a sense of accomplishment that she had nursed them from seed. Over the past decade, the work had given her great satisfaction—the feel of the earth in her hands, the sense of power in growing the food they ate; a satisfaction that compensated for the ache in her limbs and back, the heat of the sun on her head, her callused hands and feet. But this year, as they replanted the paddy, the women's chatter during breaks irritated her. She felt scorn at their simplicity, found their problems suddenly naïve and silly. It took all her effort to hide these feelings from the others, to laugh at their rustic humour, to act interested and concerned over their troubles. She had been given the role of leader in the call-and-response singing they did to keep themselves moving in rhythm as they replanted the saplings. In previous years, she had relished the role, loved how song, through the force of its melody, kept the human body in action, pushing it beyond tiredness. Now she didn't want to lead and made the excuse that her throat was sore. The women weren't fooled. Thinking she might be grieving yet another miscarriage, they beckoned in a motherly fashion for her to sit between their legs on breaks so they could comb the mud out of her hair and re-plait it, insisting she eat the sweets they'd brought. Their kindness and sympathy only irritated her further.

As the days went on, Yasodhara felt increasingly infected by a feeling of temporariness, the sense of everything being conditional and on unstable ground; she was pulled into a mire of uncertainty, unable to take joy in her work, frightened to care too much about it because she didn't know when it would be snatched from her. And now she saw that part of Siddhartha's melancholy too probably came from his being infected by this same sense of temporariness.

In the evenings now, instead of their animated fireside chats, she and Siddhartha sat mostly in silence, exchanging desultory conversation, gazing at the fire. During the day, they were busy with work and duties, surrounded by people who loved and admired them, so it was easier to push aside their unhappiness. But in the evenings, they had to face it—and they faced it in each other, both caught and thrashing around in their own nets of uncertainty. During the time between the evening meal and bed, they busied themselves with various tasks. He took up whittling as a way to keep himself distracted. She had various sewing projects, and moved from one to the next restlessly.

The rains arrived, ushering in the Vassa season, and soon the air was so humid that breathing was hard. Once again, bed legs had to be put in buckets of water because snakes and scorpions, flushed out of their holes and taking refuge in houses, might climb up and burrow into sheets and blankets. A ceiling of muslin had to be hung up again, to catch the creatures if they fell out of rafters. The constantly dark, looming sky deepened Yasodhara's despondency, which was not helped by the fact that Siddhartha went about his duties with grim weariness and distaste. The committee and the villagers were aware of the change in him. They had, she noticed, slowly started to avoid him, as if no longer trusting him. At the same time, the women drew a tighter circle around her, more solicitous of her welfare, as if they feared Siddhartha was cruel to her when the two of them were alone.

They were thrown even more than usual into each other's company because the rains kept them often indoors. Most cultivation was impossible, and the roads were washed out, so Siddhartha couldn't go far on inspection. He took up more woodcarving projects and, just like when he was a boy, he visited the artisans of the village, squatting with the potter, the carpenter, the cane weaver, to learn their art—any chance to be away from the house. Yasodhara resented him going, but was also glad to have the home to herself, falling back with relief into her private self, like entering a cool pond on a hot day. One day he gave her a gift: a sandalwood bangle that he had carved with a design of acacia flowers. She thanked him, blushing prettily as if she were a young girl again and he was courting her in Ramagama. But the bangle was a proxy. She often removed it when he was away from home.

One year later, after the rainy season had passed, Yasodhara was in her back garden, turning over the soil of a vegetable plot with a hoe, mixing in buffalo dung before she sowed her seeds, when she heard her name being called and turned to find Siddhartha standing in the back doorway. He stepped into the garden and came towards her. Leaning on her hoe, she watched him approach, apprehensive. She could tell he brought bad news. When he reached her, he said, his face twisting with sorrow, "Oh, Ushas, it's your ammé. You must return immediately to see her before she is Yama's."

"But . . ." Yasodhara went back to mixing the dung, then stopped. "How . . . do you know?"

"Your pita has sent guards, and a barge."

Only then was it real, and she started to weep loudly, standing in the mud, clutching the handle of her hoe. He took her in his arms, kissing her hair, whispering, "Oh, Ushas, oh Ushas." She let go of the hoe and clung to him.

He led her back to the house, an arm around her waist because she was trembling; then guided her to the well and made her sit on a large stone while he washed her hands and feet tenderly, gazing up at her all the while.

"What is her illness?" she finally asked, her voice dull.

"The wasting, panting disease. She's been ailing for a while, but kept the news from us to avoid troubling you."

"Oh, why did she do that? Why?" she cried plaintively, wringing her hands. "I could have gone and nursed her back to health."

He gave her his shawl to dry herself. "All the rituals were done to propitiate the disease demon, all potions and ointments tried by the Royal Bisaj, so the chief guard told me."

She wiped her arms and legs. "Can she really be dying? . . . I can't believe it is so."

Though Yasodhara hadn't seen her mother in twelve years, Pamita had been in her thoughts and memories each day. She had always imagined there'd be many visits to come.

Then a new thought struck her. "Oh, Surya, I'll see ammé, pita. Devadatta too. I'll see Ramagama!"

Siddhartha sighed, squatting back on his haunches. "I wish I could come too."

Seeing his despondency, she said passionately, "Oh, but why can't you come? Why?"

"And leave all my wretched duties?" He grimaced and waved his hand to encompass their surroundings. "Unfortunately, I am chained to all this."

"I . . . I should go pack a small trunk." As she stood and started to walk away, she reached out, intending to pat his back, but then retracted her hand.

She was kneeling before the trunk, hurriedly putting away some clothes, when Siddhartha came to stand over her. She could see from his face that he was working up to something and she sat back, waiting. Finally, he blurted, "Tell your pita that, if he offers me a position, I will take it. Any position."

She nodded slowly, not taking her eyes off him. His face fractured with annoyance at her solemnity. "But surely you'd be willing to leave Mudgala for Ramagama?"

She went back to packing. "I've already thought about asking," she lied, after a moment.

"You have?"

"Yes. Of course." She leaned into the trunk to press things down so he couldn't see her expression. It was unlikely her father had the power to free Siddhartha. When she finally sat back, her face wore a gentle expression. "And I *would* exchange Mudgala for Ramagama, Surya." She gave him a loving smile. He smiled back, happy. So easily fooled, so easily placated.

Once she was ready, she sent the trunk ahead to the barge and went to quickly pay her respects to the devata of the ever-blooming acacia tree. As she knelt before the shrine, she offered some grain to the spirit and whispered, "Be well and strong in my absence, mitta"—because "friend" was how she had come to think of him. "Bless my home, and most of all bless and protect my husband while I am away." She kissed the tree trunk, stroked it, then got up, bowed and left.

When she and Siddhartha reached the river, they stood on the beach holding hands and gazing at each other.

"Oh, Surya," she whispered. "I do wish you were coming." Because now, she really did wish this. It might be just the tonic he needed—getting away from Mudgala, even for a short time.

He shrugged, lips pressed together. "Give my loving wishes to your parents." Then he added, "And try and enjoy Ramagama, Ushas, despite your sorrow. Our sorrow," he added with a sad nod to acknowledge the impending death of Pamita, whom he too loved.

She embraced him once more, then hastily splashed out to the barge, where four guards waited, alongside her trunk.

After the barge had set off, she stood watching Siddhartha alone on the beach, a forlorn figure. He lifted his hand, then turned and began to trudge up the steep bank. As she watched him growing smaller and smaller, hunched forward from the effort of climbing, she felt a premonition of danger take hold of her. *No, no, he will be fine.* She twisted away, shaking this feeling off.

The barge soon rounded a bend in the river and the steep banks of Mudgala disappeared from view. They were now in Moriya territory. Looking around at the forest on both shores, she felt a softening within. She was escaping Siddhartha, escaping their marriage; could feel herself expanding inside, realizing only now how small she had shrunk herself over the last year to fit his unhappiness. *Yes, yes*, she thought, folding her arms under her shawl, shredding a tassel. *The world rasps at a marriage, like a knife at a rope.* How true that old adage had proven to be. In the last year, Siddhartha had grown even more discontented with his work, short with the village council, brusque and brooding with her. Worse, though, was his attempt to recompense for his brusqueness—there was something so desperately forced about it, as if he were a prisoner behind bars stretching out a hand, begging for freedom. The council members were still respectful of Siddhartha, but even more distant. She was sure they had by now discerned that he didn't want to be in Mudgala.

The feeling that everything was conditional and on unstable ground should have subsided within her by now—after all, every rashtrika's wife must be aware of the temporariness of her posting, mustn't she?—but

Siddhartha's ongoing unhappiness, his sharp melancholy, had prevented her from letting it go. Glancing at her wrist, she realized she had left behind that sandalwood bangle he'd made for her.

The three-day journey was a blur of river and treks through the jungle and meals eaten on banks. All of Yasodhara's energy and attention went into getting through this hostile landscape. There was also her river sickness that kept her nauseated and always with a slight headache. It was much milder than the last time, however. Her life in Mudgala had toughened her; and they were riding with the current, not against it, so the voyage was less choppy. The long periods on the barge, the boredom of it, for some reason kept at bay her worries about what she had left behind and what she was going to. She felt a great numbness within her; this in-between state was like being in the Mansions of the Moon—that liminal place where one's spirit dwelt for a while before rising up to the Land of the Fathers.

They finally arrived at the end of the journey and there, as the raft pulled towards the docking station, Yasodhara saw her brother waiting on the pier. A roiling panic rushed up: now she was truly aware that she was going to her mother's death. As she drew ever closer to Devadatta, neither of them waving, she felt a throb of sorrow that was like homesickness, aware from the physical changes in him of all the years of his life she had missed. Devadatta had grown broader and his limbs fuller and stronger—he was truly a man at twenty-nine. Her brother was swarthier than ever from all the soldiering, and his gold earrings, chain and brass bracelet lay stark and shining against his skin—Devadatta handsome and virile with his shaved head, leather breastplate, arm and leg guards.

As the raft bumped against the dock, Yasodhara searched his face for news but he deliberately kept his expression impassive. Once the barge was secured, he reached out his hand and she took it, stepping up onto the dock and into his arms. "Oh, tell me I haven't arrived too late, bhāta," she whispered.

He kissed the top of her head, whispering back, "No, no, bhagini, you haven't."

"Is she really dying? I . . . I can't still believe it is so." Now her tears flowed and she nuzzled into him, comforted by his smell of leather and faint sweat. "Oh bhāta, what will happen to us without her? Even in all these years apart, I've counted on her being here. Never a day goes by when I don't think of her."

Devadatta patted her back awkwardly. "Come, come, we must hurry," he said gruffly, frightened by her tears.

She examined her brother and he, aware of her scrutiny, looked away with a twist of a smile. She couldn't tell if their mother's dying had softened him towards their parents or not.

Devadatta had brought two bullock carts with him and, once Yasodhara was settled in the first, the guards and trunk in the one behind, their party set off. Devadatta rode his horse alongside Yasodhara's cart so he could talk to her. She had heard, in recent years, about his success in Kapilavastu through the tax collectors who came for the grain tax, and now she was eager to learn the news directly from him and be distracted from her grief. Devadatta had risen to become the head of the palace guards and was much valued by the ruling triad of Suddhodana, Amitodhana and Mahanama. He spoke of his work with the glow of success and Yasodhara was truly happy for him.

"But still not married?" she chided, trying to inject some levity into their conversation, to connect with him again through this sisterly ribbing.

He laughed and waved a hand. "A soldier should never marry."

"Yet many do." She gave him a cheeky smile.

He waved this away with a mock groan. Yet something about his laugh, his groan, his prideful lack of worry, told her that, although he was unmarried at twenty-nine, he had a woman whom he loved, and who loved him back. She didn't probe, suspecting she wouldn't be happy to know who it was—probably a ganikā, hopefully not a vesiyā. She noticed now that he wore a chain partially concealed under his breastplate—a leather thong with animal teeth as pendants. A gift from his beloved?

"And what of Ananda and Anuruddha?" she asked to change the subject. "I hear from the Kapilavastu tax collector that Ananda is now a member of the Bankers' Guild, so successful has he been as a merchant." She made a wry face. "But Anuruddha, the tax collector tells me, continues his vices."

"Oh Ananda, yes." Devadatta gave the exaggerated groan of someone feigning reluctance to reveal a piece of gossip. "Well I warn you, he has some ugly news. But I'm sure he will tell you himself when he arrives."

"Ananda is coming to Ramagama?"

Devadatta looked stern. "Yes, ammé has sent a messenger for him."
He scowled. "I don't understand why he should be here. He's a disgrace.
A traitor to Mahanama and his father, who he has humiliated and disgraced
by—"

"Yes, yes, bhāta," she said, cutting him off, not wanting to hear some
accusation about Ananda which she already knew she would disagree
with. Whatever Ananda had supposedly done to Mahanama and his father,
he was justified in doing it, she was sure; and she didn't want to argue
with her brother and spoil this reunion with Devadatta. "But tell me more
about your duties as Head Guard. The Kapilavastu tax inspector always
has nothing but praise for you."

Devadatta glowed at this, and began to talk about his work. She listened to him, nodding, but all the while brooding on her mother's reason
for sending for Ananda. Pamita somehow already knew that Devadatta
would fail Yasodhara at the moment of their mother's death. She would
need Ananda then. Or so her mother felt.

They had been travelling for some time when suddenly they came
around a bend in the road, and there were the fortifications of Ramagama.
Yasodhara cried out involuntarily, gazing with wonder at the massive
wooden stocks, the large brass-studded gate, as if she had never seen
them before.

Once they had passed through the city gates, she peered out of the cart
with awe, as if she'd entered a mythical kingdom. In her mind, she had
walked these beloved streets almost daily for the past twelve years; they'd
been part of her dreams. How captivating it was to see the clean, neatly
ordered beaten-earth streets in the poorer section they were passing, the
drainage that her father had built so people weren't throwing their chamber
pots into the street, the wells dug at regular intervals, around which women
clustered to draw water, gossip and laugh. The carts soon left this section
behind and the houses got larger, the beaten-earth roads wider. These were
the streets of her childhood, where she'd walked with her nurse, where
she'd run and played with her cousins. The road travelled through numerous squares and, as they crossed them, she gazed at the children playing
the same games she had played—games of marbles or throwing a cloth

ball or riding broomsticks as if they were horses. Little girls crouched in circles with their dolls. The well in one square reminded her of a time when Devadatta had climbed down into it, using the bucket's rope, and fetched out a doll she had accidentally dropped in there. A raised, roofed platform in another square reminded her of a wine merchant from the Yavana city state of Athens who had always set up his wares there and who, fluent in their language, would treat her and her companions to tales of the Yavana gods, narrated in his odd accent.

Soon she saw the palace ahead, with its high wattle and daub boundary wall, its large gates. A great happiness took hold of her. *I am home, I am home,* she cried within, forgetting for a moment her mother's imminent death. But then, once they had gone around the wall to the side entrance of the women's quarters, fear clutched her chest. Her elderly aunt and the other women were gathered, waiting to greet her with mournful expressions. Before the cart had properly stopped she jumped out, crying, "Am I too late? Oh, tell me I'm not!"

"No, no, daharé," her aunt said, kissing her.

The women made as if to lead the way inside, but she hurried past them through the gates, drawing her shawl tightly about her. She strode across the courtyard, glancing cursorily at the lovely flowering bushes, the pond edged with pretty rocks, the tamhan tree in the centre of the courtyard with its beautiful purple blossoms, the swing, attached to its branches, that had been installed for her as a child. No time for nostalgia. She wanted only to see her mother now. She hurried up the stairs to the second floor, then down the corridor to Pamita's room.

Before she entered, she took a moment to prepare herself, closing her eyes and breathing deeply. Then she passed through the doorway with a smile. Despite this preparation, her jaw dropped as she gazed at her mother in bed. Pamita was so impossibly old and shrunken, her eyes huge in her small face as she gazed back at her daughter, as if from a distant place. Despite the lit incense, the flowers in bowls of water, the room had a sour smell of vomit and old sweat, the sweet-rot odour of a dying body. Yasodhara moved to the bed in a daze and stood, saying nothing. Her mother was now so thin the skin on her face was creased and sagging, cheeks caved in. She panted as she breathed. Pamita held out her hands and

Yasodhara took them, kneeling as she kissed the wrinkled fingers over and over, wetting them with her tears. "Ushas," her mother said, and Yasodhara wept harder knowing that soon she would never hear her mother speak her nickname again.

When Yasodhara was finally calm and seated on the edge of the bed, Pamita gazed at her for a long time, her eyes so full of love, so full of regret to be saying goodbye. She was propped up high by bolsters and pillows—the only way she could breathe, given her congested lungs. Pamita turned up her palms in her lap, in a small but oh-so-poignant gesture of submission, a tiny, sad shrug. "How fortunate that you have come, Ushas . . . that I am seeing you before Yama takes me." Then she did a thing the very old or very sick do—an infant-like pursing and sucking that helped her control her tongue and facial muscles so she could continue the effort of speaking. "You are not happy, dhītā. You think no one sees it, but I do."

Yasodhara was taken aback. "No, no, ammé, I am happy," she said, determined not to trouble her mother.

Pamita shook her head. "You are lucky. You've caught me on a good day. Tomorrow, or even in a little while, I might not be like this. So, tell me now. Let us use this time well. I know you long to tell me."

Yasodhara began to weep again and soon she was unburdening herself, telling Pamita about Siddhartha's discontent and how it affected her own happiness; about this disease of temporariness that had infected her life; about the distance that seemed to have permanently come between her and Siddhartha, even while they continued all the outward customs and rituals of their marriage; how she could not settle into her life anymore and summon up the enthusiasm and pleasure she'd felt before. When she was done, she cried, "What is to be done, ammé?"

For a long time Pamita was silent. Then she shook her head to say she had no idea and closed her eyes wearily. "And has there always been this melancholy in him? Or is it something new?"

"It has always been there." She told Pamita how, even during their courtship, Siddhartha had quoted the ascetic sects on the meaninglessness of life and the ever-present reality of suffering—though she was realizing, even as she spoke, that Siddhartha had stopped mentioning the sects in the last year. How odd that she hadn't noticed this change. What did it mean?

"And there's nothing that Siddhartha can find to inspire and excite him in Mudgala?"

Yasodhara shook her head. "It's a small village, ammé. A simple province."

"And Siddhartha too large for it." Pamita said this decisively, nodding. "A great intelligence like that, unless challenged, goes sour, rots. Is he cruel to you, daharé?"

"No . . . no . . ."

Pamita gestured for her to go on.

"When I'm in the fields, I forget our troubles. But then . . . as I walk towards my house, a house I used to love, I feel . . . this constriction of my entire being."

Pamita nodded, squeezing Yasodhara's hand. "I wish I had a solution to offer you, daharé." Then she smiled sadly, painfully, regretfully, and turned up her palms again in that gesture of submission. "Ah, ah," she said, her voice cracking as she remembered something. She pointed to a parcel on a table. "I had that put aside for you."

Yasodhara went to the table and frowned at the parcel wrapped in rough cotton. She brought it back to the bed and Pamita gestured for her to open it. She untied the string and the cotton fell back to reveal half a blanket—the one they'd worked on during their last night together, twelve years ago. "Oh, ammé," she whispered and shook it out, seeing that the orange and blue had faded with time. "I . . . I should have brought my half."

"Why, child?" Mother and daughter looked at each other for a long moment, eyes filling with tears. Yasodhara was the one who would live; this half now belonged in her life at Mudgala.

Pamita closed her eyes with a long, tired sigh and pressed further into the stacked pillows. Then almost immediately she fell asleep, head turned to one side, snoring gently, exhausted. Yasodhara watched her mother hungrily. Every moment counted now.

After some time, Pamita opened her eyes again. "Ushas," she said, "understand this: I have now passed to another world in which pain and death are my greatest reality. The life I lived, the people I loved, have grown faint. Pain absorbs me completely, dhītā."

"Oh, ammé."

There was a shuffling sound at the doorway, and Yasodhara turned to find Devadatta there, frowning and nervous.

Pamita held out a hand to him and he came forward reluctantly and took it.

"Have you eaten, puthā?"

He nodded, and said gruffly, "Ammé, don't concern yourself about me. Get well."

Yasodhara gazed from mother to son. There had been some reconciliation, though perhaps not as much as her mother would have desired. At least he's come home, she thought. At least he's being kind to her.

Later, once she had changed, Yasodhara went to visit her father. When she came into his private receiving room, he rose to meet her and, for a long moment, they stood looking at each other. His hair was now completely white, face elongated and hollowed with grief, eyes sunken and deeply hooded. Why, she thought as she bent to touch his feet, he looks just as unwell as ammé. He took her shoulders and raised her up and they stood examining each other once more, as if trying to find the missing years between them. Finally he let her go and beckoned her to sit—not beside him on the low divan or on his lap as in the old days, but cross-legged on the floor, a low table between them, as befitted her status as a twenty-eight-year-old married woman. He inquired about her journey, her life in the Northern Province, if she was happy with Siddhartha. She told her story again, gaining comfort from recounting it once more.

"Pita, can't you . . . can't you help us? Help Siddhartha? Give him a position?"

Her father stared ahead, silent. After a moment, he picked up a tablet of accounts, put it down, then shoved it aside, peevishly. "You know what must happen now that your mother is dying."

His tone was ominous, angry. Yasodhara frowned, not understanding.

"I don't have a second wife," he said impatiently, irritated that she hadn't grasped his meaning.

"Ah, no!" Her eyes widened with repulsion. He was the raja; it was his duty to perform the role of householder in the thrice-daily sacrifices.

Without a wife, a marital fire, he could not perform the rituals. He would have to take a second wife immediately.

"Oh, pita," she said softly, horrified for him, for herself.

His sternness softened to sorrow. "No, no, I will not do it. You cannot imagine I would."

"Then?"

He shrugged to say the answer was obvious. She was silent as she absorbed his meaning: he would step down as raja.

"I've already informed the Council of Amicis and they will, in the next days, propose successors for the sangha to discuss and vote on." He grimaced. "But then there is your bhata. I am sure Devadatta still expects to be raja after me, despite everything. You must talk to him, dhītā. I don't have it in me to face his anger and accusations."

She nodded distractedly because a new thought had come to her as she gazed at her father. He would not long survive his wife. He knew this somewhere within himself, which was the other reason he wanted to step down. She closed her eyes for a moment, overwhelmed.

Once she left her father, Yasodhara went swiftly to her room. She sat in the window well, taking in the familiar view of the royal square below with its inhabitants coming and going, some slaves at the well drawing water, one of them singing a song in a language she didn't understand. In the santagara, a few statesmen were seated cross-legged in a corner, shoulders hunched as they discussed a matter of importance.

This was her home. She had always imagined returning here, to this palace, to this room, to this view. Always imagined this room being here for her, and for her children too. But the moment her father stepped down, her family would have to give up the palace to the new raja and his family. Impossible to imagine anyone else in this room, but that was how it would be soon. She looked around at the familiar objects from her first sixteen years of life—the rag dolls with their painted terracotta heads, a silver box crammed to overflowing with her childhood necklaces and bangles, earrings and rings, the set of bells that tinkled in the window, the magenta quilt with its aquamarine rhombuses stitched on diagonals. Where would all this go? And where would her father go? There was their mansion in the city, rented out currently, and which she had only ever seen from the outside. Then there was their estate, a day's journey from the city, where her father had been born and spent his early years. Her instincts told her that this was where he would go, like an old elephant returning to the herd's graveyard to die. *And then what will become of me? Soon, soon, I will be exiled from all this.* How provisional her life had truly become, how unfixed. In the last year, as she had allowed herself to contemplate, even to accept, that her life in Mudgala would have to end and would do so abruptly one day, she'd offered herself the comfort of this home. She had made it, in her mind, the stable place that she could always return to, would return to when she had finally carried a child to term. But now it too had become as temporary as Mudgala. She would be rendered truly homeless. *Ah, no, these thoughts must stop!* She clapped her hands, to summon her stronger self. There was so little time left with her mother; whatever time Yama granted them must be used well.

In the days that followed, Yasodhara devoted herself to being her mother's nurse, refusing to leave her side for very long, spending nights on a divan by her bedside, wanting to return all the love and care Pamita had given her; wanting also to get as much of her mother as she could before her departure to the Land of the Fathers.

Pamita was now mostly unconscious, and caring for her inert body and making it comfortable was a steady chore. When she was conscious, Pamita used all her strength to drink sips of water, a sweat breaking out on her face from the effort. She was always restless in her sleep, always uncomfortable, no matter what position Yasodhara and her widowed aunt placed her in. She kept up a steady whispered muttering night and day. Occasionally she called out, "Hurting, hurting" or "Sssh, sssh, quiet, quiet," even when the room was silent. Or "Turn out the lamps, my eyes," even when it was dark. Occasionally, as she lay there breathing hard, she would suddenly open her eyes and ask, "How is your father?" or "Is your brother well? Has he eaten?"

Devadatta, fearful of illness and death, seldom visited their mother and, when he did, he stayed only briefly, standing by the door gazing stricken at Pamita's unconscious form. From her widowed aunt—who was the de facto head of the women's quarters and would no doubt go with her father to tend his house wherever he moved—Yasodhara learned that, in the past twelve years, Devadatta had rarely visited his parents. He had come only when his duties as head of the palace guards meant he must accompany their uncle Suddhodana on a royal visit. On these occasions, he paid his respect to his parents, but chose to eat with the royal convoy from Kapilavastu, and never dropped by Pamita's room, of an evening, to visit.

Remembering her father's request, she tore herself away from the sick-bed one morning and went looking for her brother at the stables. She didn't find him there. The grooms told her he didn't come there anymore, but instead was always with the palace guards in their barracks. She could tell they were hurt at this desertion by their old friend. Yasodhara sent a mes-sage for him and waited in the third-floor receiving room, seated on the charpoy where her mother had once entertained visitors, filled with sorrow and anguish that she would have to wound her brother. When Devadatta arrived, he stood in the dimness at the entrance for a moment, surveying her before he came forward, face hidden in shadow. She beckoned him to sit on the charpoy, her smile forced. He was immediately alerted and stood by the charpoy, arms folded protectively over his stomach.

"Bhāta." She gave him a look of appeal, begging him not to be angry with her. "Our pita wants me to inform you that he is abdicating. He doesn't wish to marry again in order to keep the marital fire burning for the sacrifice."

Devadatta stepped forward, breathless, and seeing his vulnerable hope, she quailed inwardly. "The fact is . . . well, he has asked the Council of Amicis to suggest nominees." She raised her eyebrows to say he was not one of the candidates and watched as the truth darkened his face.

"I see." Then he cried, "Why not me? Why not? Have I not proven myself in Kapilavastu?"

"Bhāta." She took his elbow, but he broke away, clutching his elbow as if she had wounded him. "You, too," he whispered, then leaned in to examine her, breathing hard, unable to believe this was so. "You didn't even ask our pita to nominate me? And I trusted you, I love you. I thought you loved me too! Ah, Ushas!" He turned and rushed towards the door.

"Bhāta!"

Yasodhara sat there, her head thrown back in exhaustion, listening to his footsteps clatter down the stairs; she understood now why her mother had sent for Ananda. Pamita had anticipated this rift between her and Devadatta. How was she to bear this? How was she to keep enduring one thing after another? "Oh, when will Ananda come? When?" she cried quietly, longing for her cousin.

One evening, Pamita, who had been asleep all day, opened her eyes and glanced at Yasodhara, then moved her gaze to her husband, looking at him with much love. "Is it time for the morning sacrifice, beloved?" she asked, then closed her eyes. After a moment, the death rattle started.

"What is that sound?" Dandapani jumped up, his eyes begging Yasodhara to tell him this wasn't the end.

"Oh, pita." Her own eyes filled with tears.

He sat down, got up again, sat down once more, then with a throttled cry he covered his face and rocked back and forth.

"Pita, pita," Yasodhara whispered, going to him, removing his hands, kissing his wet cheeks. "Let her go in peace. The ancestors have come to take her, they are all around us. Let her go in peace."

Dandapani nodded briefly and sat back in his chair, shoulders slumped. Yasodhara perched on the edge of the bed and took one of Pamita's hands, gesturing for her father to do the same. After a moment, he took his wife's other hand. "It's warm," he whispered, looking wide-eyed at Yasodhara, no longer a parent but a child needing comfort.

She nodded. "Sssh," she said, staring at her mother, willing her to go, telling her silently that she should go, that the ancestors had come, there was nothing to be frightened of. How calm I am, she thought, viewing herself from a great distance. How strangely calm. Is this how it's supposed to be?

The laboured breathing continued a little while longer and then Pamita's breath stopped. Yasodhara and her father looked at each other in terror. Yasodhara leaned quickly over her mother's face. All was still. Then Pamita breathed one final, quiet exhalation. Another long silence. "She's gone," Yasodhara whispered with disbelief. She turned to Dandapani. "Oh, pita, she's gone! She's gone!" She threw her arms around her father and they clung to each other, sobbing. Then they broke apart to touch and kiss Pamita's lifeless body.

Devadatta, who had been summoned, arrived now. He stood at the door, hands pressed behind him against the door frame, staring aghast at Pamita. Yasodhara knew it was taking all of his will to stay in the room.

They did not have long for their grief. The funeral duties and rituals had to be performed right away. Dandapani and Devadatta left to inform the priests that a pit needed to be dug. The area for the rituals had already been identified and cleared on the south-facing side of the forest, an old cow already found to be the anustarani. Yasodhara and the women of the quarters set about preparing Pamita's body, cutting off her hair, shaving her head and body. Then they dressed her in new garments and scented her well so that she would last the night. They laid her out and arranged her hands so they were cupped together for carrying the entrails of the anustarani cow to the afterlife. Through all this, Yasodhara was still calm, removed, watching herself from somewhere else in the room.

The next day, the female members of the Chandala caste, whose occupation it was to carry female corpses, arrived with a bier made of bamboo and deer skin. They lifted Pamita's body gently onto the pallet. Yasodhara put Pamita's sacrificial implements by her—the noose with which Dandapani had yoked her waist thrice a day during the sacrifices, the spoon she had used to ladle ghee into the sacrificial fire, the brass pot from which she had scattered seed into the flames.

The Chandala women carried the pallet down the stairs. The funeral procession awaited them in the women's courtyard. Yasodhara went to join her father and brother at the front. Devadatta appeared still stunned, as if just awoken to this new reality; Dandapani was shrunken, shoulders stooped. With trembling hands he carried the marital fire in a small brazier, to be extinguished at the grave. The flame had already been snuffed out in the sacrificial enclosure. As Yasodhara took her place beside her family, she felt empty inside, wrung out. Was it natural to feel no sadness? For her only emotion to be vigilance that every detail of the funeral was properly carried out? Just one thing to be done, and then the next thing to be done?

The Chandala women lined up behind the family. Following them were the priests leading the anustarani cow and carrying the skin of an anustarani goat they'd slaughtered that morning, flies buzzing around the hide. With the priests were three slaughterers. The other relatives and members of their gotra, along with the palace officials, made up the rear.

As the funeral procession left the palace, Yasodhara saw that the janata had come out to bid farewell to their devi, lining either side of the street. Yasodhara felt for the first time that day the sting of tears at the corners of her eyes as she saw their sad faces. Her nose began to run and she wiped it hurriedly on the edge of her shawl.

The janata fell in behind the relatives, a river of people snaking through the city, so beloved was Pamita among the populace. They departed at the border of the forest. From there, only the relatives could follow. When the procession reached the cremation pit, lined with kusa grass over a layer of wood, Pamita was lowered in. The priests chanted verses from the Vedas and then it was time to slaughter the old cow. All the male relatives gathered to help and once the cow was dead, the slaughterers worked quickly and efficiently. The parts of the cow were laid in the grave around Pamita, the steaming entrails in her hands, so that the pain of her cremation would be lessened by the cow having taken on that pain. The goat's hide was laid over her body. The family and relatives came forward to scatter grain and sesame seed on the body, while the priests chanted suttas inviting the spirits of dead ancestors to sit on the southern side of the pit. Before kindling could be laid over Pamita's body, Dandapani stepped forward with the marital fire and, using a brass bowl, extinguished it. At this, Yasodhara began to wail—more out of fear than sorrow, panicked like a child in the market who'd lost sight of her mother. Soon others around her were weeping aloud too.

The brazier was laid in the pit, wood piled on top of the corpse. The priests lit the wood, starting at the head of the corpse and working their way down to the feet. As the fire rose, the priests poured streams of ghee into it, offering prayers to the ancestors, asking that they welcome and guide Pamita to the Mansions of the Moon and then to the Land of the Fathers; and offering prayers, rice cakes, milk, meat, whey, honey and water to various gods, asking them to ensure long life and prosperity for all the living relatives. Then everyone gathered there joined the priests in reciting the funeral hymn.

The fire was roaring now, and Pamita's corpse was consumed in flames. Yasodhara and the other mourners circled the pit, left to right, and departed without looking back.

That night, Yasodhara and Dandapani were in the receiving room, picking desultorily through the evening meal, when a slave came with a message from Devadatta. He had left and wished them to know. After the slave was gone, they continued to eat in silence for a while.

"I have failed Devadatta, but I don't know what I could have done differently." Dandapani sighed, then said in a choked voice, "I wish your ammé was here."

"Devadatta has failed himself, pita," Yasodhara replied, angry with her brother for deserting her and her father at this moment when they most needed each other. "There is nothing you could have done differently."

Dandapani pushed his food away and indicated for a servant to bring him water for his hands. "Devadatta's anger has been hard to bear, all these years. There was an emptiness in us, as if he had died. Yes, yes, our lives were never truly happy after he moved to Kapilavastu, and you to Mudgala."

As Yasodhara watched her father wash his hands, a thought rose, sorrowful and bitter and unbidden: But you still bore it together, you were united in your sorrow. How lucky.

7

Siddhartha and the Truth of Truths

IN THE DAYS immediately after Yasodhara's departure, Siddhartha deeply missed her, especially in the evenings. He stared morosely into the fire, his whittling tools laid aside, truly regretting the way he had kept her at such a distance, asking himself over and over, "Ah, what has come over me, why have I become this person?" Yet, after a few days, to his surprise, his mind began to lighten and his thoughts loosen, as if ventilated. At first, he was puzzled at this change. Then, slowly, it came to him that before, during their evenings together, his mind had raced guiltily as he'd stared at the fire or whittled away, aware of Yasodhara's anxiety as she watched him. Now, in her absence, his mind was finally still. And in that stillness, he found himself reviewing the string of circumstances that had brought him to this point in his life: how he'd met the Nigantha ascetic in Maha Kosala's palace; how he'd hoped to subdue this defect in himself, first by marrying Yasodhara and later by taking up the challenges of Mudgala with vigour. But the news of Maha Kosala's abdication had made a lie of everything he'd achieved. Suddenly the reins of the chariot he'd been guiding with such care, such effort, had slipped from his hands and he felt himself trapped in a rickety contraption that jounced and bounced along of its own will.

As Siddhartha sat gazing at the fire, he was also mourning Maha Kosala, who surely must have starved himself to death by now; and he also recalled his time at the Savatthi Court, the kindness of the old man towards him, his soft, gravelly voice, his chuckle. He was thinking too of his old friend Pasénadi. He'd heard from the tax collectors who came to collect the grain tax that, when Pasénadi ascended the throne, succeeding his father Maha Kosala, he had made another strategic marriage, this time to the Moriya raja's two sisters. These new wives didn't wince at his touch like his first wife Ubbiri, but they were avaricious. No better than vesiyās or ganikās, Pasénadi had apparently described them to other members of the court, because in exchange for sexual relations, they always had some favour to ask for the corps of relatives they'd brought with them to the Savatthi Court. What a strange and terrible life his old friend now led—his private relations so public that even a mere tax collector knew the details of them. Pasénadi, the second-most-powerful man in the Middle Country after the Maharaja Bimbisara, was nothing but a beast in a cage, with his pacing, snarling, eating, defecating, mating viewed from all sides by avid spectators. Was that the reward of power and prestige?

Siddhartha was also sure, from having watched his own father, that Pasénadi probably trusted nobody and was thus searingly alone. His old friend had also turned notoriously cruel—coming down hard on any vassal state that dared oppose him, his soldiers confiscating all the grain in a rebel village and leaving the villagers to die of starvation. But then, Siddhartha mused, he couldn't claim to be much better himself, inflicting such pain and suffering on those he sentenced. And the sheer futility of his actions! For, no matter how many men he punished or fined or reprimanded or sacked, behind them was a whole line of men waiting to take their place; and each time he meted out punishments, he was reminded that this was his lot in life, that he would keep on executing these punishments not just here, but in whatever other position he was sent to, without ever really fixing the problem at its root—because what could fix the inherent evil and greed in the hearts of so many men?

One evening, about a week after Yasodhara's departure, Siddhartha came home from his day's work to be met at the street door by Rupasiri, who was looking after his household needs until his wife returned. "Sāmi," she said, giving him a quizzical look, "a samana claiming to know you is waiting for you." She gestured towards the receiving room across the courtyard and left, shutting the street door behind her.

Siddhartha rushed into the room, breathless with premonition, to find a man seated cross-legged on the floor, watching him approach with bright alertness. He knelt and peered at the samana's face. "Sāmi, is it you?" he whispered. For the Maha Kosala he knew had been fat, his cheeks bloated, and this man before him, while not gaunt, was certainly on the edge of it.

"Yes, it is I, daharā." The old emperor smiled.

With a cry of joy, Siddhartha prostrated himself, touching the old man's feet.

"Siddhartha, Siddhartha!" Maha Kosala said, laughing. "I am no longer your maharaja."

Siddhartha squatted back on his haunches, hands dangling over his knees, and regarded Maha Kosala in wonder. "I do not worship you because you used to be my maharaja, sāmi. I worship you because, unknown even to me, I called for you and you heard and answered."

Maha Kosala chuckled, and Siddhartha wasn't sure if he was dismissing such a fancy or agreeing with it. Now, for the first time, he took in Maha Kosala's clean robes; the older man was neither naked nor wearing a loin cloth like the ascetics. "Are you no longer a Nigantha, sāmi?"

"It's been a year since I abdicated, daharā. I would be dead by now if I'd followed that path. No, no, I have returned to the ways of our forefathers, to the sacrifices. Though," Maha Kosala raised a hand briefly, "with some new thoughts and ideas, which enhance our rituals."

Siddhartha eased himself into a cross-legged position, settling in to hear the former maharaja's story.

For many months after his abdication, Maha Kosala told him, he had followed faithfully the practices of the Niganthas, travelling with a group of fellow ascetics all over the Middle Country. Their travels finally brought them to Kashi, that great city of intellectual ferment, the place where young Brahmins went to study. Maha Kosala and the Niganthas took up residence in a forested park close to the city. By now, the old emperor had witnessed a few of his fellow ascetics die, starving themselves to death. The first such death had filled him with fervour to do the same, but then, after witnessing the third or fourth, he had begun to doubt the path he'd chosen. He started to question not just the terrible suffering and self-punishment, but the very idea that this was the right way.

Now, residing in that park were also some young Brahmins. The Niganthas used the same water hole as the Brahmins. And since, in their desire to not create any new karma, they avoided action if possible, they would ask the Brahmins to draw water for them. One of the young Brahmins, a student in Kashi, was always willing to help Maha Kosala. As he drew his water, they would talk, exchanging ideas. The former maharaja soon learned that this Brahmin was part of a movement that was advocating a new formulation of the old ways—new insights into the Vedas which changed and deepened the way one practised the Vedic rituals and sacrifices. These new thoughts came from the kingdom of Videha in the Kuru-Panchala district, further east, where they had been known for some time, taught by a famous sage, Yajnavalkya, in the time of King Janaka. By now the old maharaja was hungry for a new way of thinking and he soon found himself listening with interest and gratitude to this philosophy.

Maha Kosala smiled at how intently Siddhartha was listening to his tale. He drew a breath and continued, explaining the tenets of this new doctrine, the Truth of Truths:

"Each person, daharā, has in them an Atman, a soul, that is eternal and unchanging because it is part of a universal soul called Brahman, the Supreme Self. The highest bliss a person can achieve is to be reunited with that universal soul, because then a person is united with that which is eternal and unchanging inside them. In the old way it was believed that, after death, everyone went to the Land of the Fathers and lived there, returning occasionally to be reborn in their family or gotra. In the new beliefs, however, three possible things can happen to a person after death. The best people's souls—those Brahmins practising austerities and sacrifices in the forest— pass from the fires of cremation into the air, rising to the moon where they dwell for six months in its mansions. Then their Atmans continue upwards into the world of the gods and from there into the Land of the Fathers. Yet their journey does not end there, daharā. Soon a person who consists entirely of mind comes to lead them to the world of Brahman, where they live in eternal bliss.

"Now, the Atmans of the second group of people—us Khattiyas and also Brahmins practising the Vedic ways—follow the same route as the first group of people, from the Mansions of the Moon to the Land of the Fathers. But, instead of us going up further to reunite with Brahman, we return to earth. And the womb we enter is determined by the life we have led before. It is not of our own choice, like an ancestor choosing to return and inhabit a relative's womb. No, rather, it is the laws of karma that determine our new birth. So, people who observed correctly and earnestly the sacrifices, who gave to forest Brahmins and priests and practised well the austerities, who lived an ethical life, enter a pleasant womb like that of a Brahmin or Khattiya. But those Khattiyas and Brahmins and priests who did not honour and perform well the sacrifices, who did not honour and treat well forest Brahmins and priests, who practised no austerities, who lived a violent, cruel life, can expect to enter a foul womb like that of a dog or pig or a Dasa woman.

"Then finally there is the third category of people: Vessas, Suddas and Dasas who do not practise the sacrifices, who do not know the Vedas. They, upon death, because they are not cremated with our proper Vedic rites, are born over and over again on this earth as snakes, insects, worms and animals, or at best born again as Suddas or Dasas."

When Maha Kosala was done, he waited, watching Siddhartha with twinkling eyes.

Siddhartha was silent awhile, staring at the ground, thinking. Then he said, "Since Vessas, Suddas and the Dasas can never obtain eternal bliss, a person, by their birth, is already fated for eternal bliss or the life of a worm."

Maha Kosala nodded.

"But many of them are good people who lead honourable lives. The path offered by the Ajivaka and the Nigantha is harsh, but at least it is open to all. Aren't even our old Vedic ways better, because then all that is sought through the sacrifices is to keep the balance of the cosmos and strengthen the gods?"

"But this is the true path, daharā. There is no other."

Siddhartha was silent again, picking at a fold of his dhoti. "It is interesting, though, what you say about karma. Because I too have been thinking about how our actions, or even our thoughts, produce results that then lead to other thoughts and actions, and other results, and so on and on."

Maha Kosala nodded, gesturing for him to continue. "Tell me what is in your unhappy heart, daharā."

And so, Siddhartha told him of how that long-ago visit to the ascetic in the palace garden had made him aware of the suffering of the world, the futility of all action; how he'd struggled with this futility, suppressed it by working hard, taking on all his challenges in Mudgala with zest. But then, news of Maha Kosala's abdication had slackened something in him, so that he found all his duties now distasteful and pointless. And now this sense of meaninglessness was growing and growing in him.

"Ah," Maha Kosala said softly, "then you understand how it was for me too."

"You felt the same way, sāmi!"

Maha Kosala laughed. "Of course! Long before the visit with that ascetic."

Siddhartha turned this over in his mind. Yes, of course, the old man would have felt the same way, felt it so strongly that he finally gave up his empire to follow an ascetic path. "And . . . and these others you've encountered, the Niganthas, the followers of the Truth of Truths, they feel the same as us?"

Maha Kosala nodded merrily.

"I am not alone in my feelings. This thing I've been calling a flaw, a defect, it isn't so—correct, sāmi?"

"Yes, daharā."

Siddhartha stared into the empty fireplace, hardly able to speak for the joy of this discovery. "But I, but we, what we feel, surely it isn't normal? I . . . I've asked myself over and over again in the last year, Why can't I be happy in my life? After all, many other rashtrikas, even maharajas and rajas, must feel their lives, their work, often dull and quotidian. And yet they bear this with equanimity, aren't as ripped and shredded within because of this understanding, as we are."

The old man nodded. "We are indeed ripped and shredded." Then he added, "But these other people, though they form the vast majority, aren't right or correct to ignore the futility of existence. No, no, daharā, the vast majority are wrong to avoid the chasm—and I say this as someone who's truly seen the world and its people in all their multiplicities. You and I, we're right to look into the chasm. Whereas this vast majority run around frantically, grabbing for more and more, as a way to avoid looking into the chasm.

"Know this also, daharā: people are unhappy and act from that unhappiness, because they see themselves as separate from others. If, however, we accept that we are all part of Brahman and we learn to dissolve this illusion of separation through meditation, we lose our unhappiness and grief by being united with the Supreme Self. This delusion of duality and separation—I versus everyone else—is like froth on the river. It is only an illusion of solidity, one that disappears when we understand the truth. And by understanding that there is no duality, no I versus everyone else, we become peaceful, accepting that we are one with everything else and everyone else, because all of us are one with the Supreme Self."

"Then teach me what you know, sāmi."

The old man explained to Siddhartha that the Truth of Truths took the old rituals and meditations—chanting the syllable Om, reciting various suttas, auspicious days of fasting and half fasting—and deepened them. The practitioner, under the instruction of the teacher, learned to see the eternal that lay behind these practices; learned to do the rituals and chanting in a deeper contemplative manner, temporarily letting go of worldly attachments and glimpsing their Atman within. "Thus," Maha Kosala promised him, "we experience, for a time, the peace and bliss of the eternal, which is both within and without us, just like space is inside an empty pot and also outside it."

As an example, Maha Kosala picked the Gayatri Sutta, well known from being recited at every sacrifice, and explained to Siddhartha how the sutta represented the eternal Brahman, and so also the Atman within a person; how, by concentrating on this deeper meaning in the sutta, one achieved an inner quiet and tranquility—one's Atman uniting, albeit temporarily, with Brahman, and enjoying for a short time that eternal bliss. He led Siddhartha in chanting the sutta in the new way, showing him how to be aware of its deeper meaning, how to open himself within so he could see that empty clarity which was his Atman.

As he followed Maha Kosala's instructions, Siddhartha was astonished by how quickly the burdens of his life fell away from him, how quickly he reached this state of tranquility and inner quiet. When he opened his eyes after the meditation, Maha Kosala, seeing his wonder, laughed and clapped his hands. "Siddhartha of the Gotama Gotra, I knew you would achieve this quickly. That is why I came to you . . . and also, knowing that you are one of us."

Siddhartha was quiet for a moment, afraid he would weep, so great was his relief, his joy at the discovery of this peace within.

In the weeks that followed, he began to long for the end of his day so that he might return to Maha Kosala and practise further under his guidance, going to deeper and deeper levels of stillness within. As he made for home after long hours at work, his heart quickened at the pleasure that awaited him and his whole being was filled with love for the old man who would be watching quietly for him on the verandah or in the receiving room.

He had experienced this calm and tranquility before: following some exertion and then a cold river bath; or after he and Yasodhara had made love and, her head resting on his chest, he played with her hair; or standing alone on the ramparts of Kapilavastu, watching the sunset turn the Rohini River golden. But now he saw with wonder that such tranquility could always be his, whenever he wanted it, just by meditating on the deeper meaning of the suttas—by opening himself up to an awareness of his Atman, allowing the borders of himself to grow porous and flow outwards, dissolving into the world around him, which was Brahman. And this was bliss. Maha Kosala taught Siddhartha to see the eternal in the sacrificial fire, too, which was also Brahman; and taught him that, when reciting the names of the gods, when praying to them at the sacrifices, he should be aware that they were not separate from him but also part of Brahman, to which he belonged, they and he one.

For a few weeks Maha Kosala and Siddhartha practised together in this way. Then, one evening, when they were finished their meditation, the old man said, "My work is done here, daharā."

"Ah, no, my guru, that is not possible!" Siddhartha cried in dismay. "I am not yet properly conversant in the philosophy. No, no, you must stay, at least until after the rains."

Maha Kosala laughed. "Froth on the river," he said. Then he rose and stretched himself. "Tomorrow I depart, to spread the word further."

Siddhartha bowed his head in acceptance. Knowing that the old man would want to slip away without a proper goodbye, he rose very early the next morning. With great love and gratitude, and tears in his eyes, he saluted Maha Kosala and watched him go.

8

The Empire of Faith

IN THE WEEKS after her mother's death, whenever she could spare the time from helping her widowed aunt pack up for Dandapani's move to their family estate, Yasodhara walked the streets of Ramagama, mourning the loss of Pamita but also mourning her beloved city. Her time here was drawing to a close and soon, too soon, the city would know her no more.

Returning one afternoon from such a walk, she saw a caravan of carts loaded with goods waiting outside the entrance to the women's quarters, a merchant standing by them. She hastened her footsteps, wondering why her aunt was considering anything new when already there was so much to pack up. But as she drew closer, the merchant raised his hand and smiled. Crying out in pleasure, she ran to greet Ananda. She took both his hands and examined him, tears running down her cheeks even as she laughed. Her cousin appeared much the same as before, except for his yellow turban, shawl and waist sash.

"Vessa colours, bhāta?" she cried, as she gestured to his clothes.

"Other merchants would cheat me if they knew I was a Khattiya, bhag-ini," Ananda said, grinning, his face transforming for a moment into cheer-iness before it returned to its usual long-nosed melancholy. But no, not melancholy anymore, she saw; just introspection. "I was travelling and only arrived home a few days ago." He gestured to the caravan, his drivers and assistant. "It took me a little while to renew my supplies. A merchant never travels anywhere without some commerce in mind."

He beckoned her to the carts and she followed him, looking in as he raised the flaps to show her the pottery, textiles and even jars of honey he hoped to sell.

"And where will your travels take you now?" she asked wistfully. "Through the great Lavanasagara Desert?"

He smiled to acknowledge the memory of the story he had told her the first time they'd met. "No, I go south to Rajagaha."

"The capital of the Magadha Empire." She sighed. "Another city I will never see. How lucky you are, bhāta, to be a man."

He took her arm. "But come, tell me how things have been with you." He gestured to the entrance to the women's quarters, but she shook her head.

"No, let us go to a park."

Once they were walking among the trees, Yasodhara told him of her mother's last days and how she had died, and also of Devadatta's desertion. Ananda expressed his sorrow at Pamita's death, his regret he had missed seeing her while she was alive, shaking his head gravely over Devadatta's behaviour. "And now my pita," she said, "I . . . I know I won't ever see him again. He won't survive my ammé long. I just know he won't." But then, suddenly weary of her troubles, she waved her hand to push them away and cried, "Now tell me about yourself. I want to hear of your success." And so Ananda related how he had become a prosperous merchant, a good friend of the Mahasetthi, Jatila, and a member of the Bankers' Guild. "And Anuruddha?" she asked, grimacing to say she already knew her cousin was still addicted to the dice board.

Ananda was sombre for a moment, then shrugged. "I've managed to curtail Anuruddha's gambling by that arrangement I have with Vimala. But I can't stop him from going to other ganikā houses or even street gambling."

"Does he really street gamble?" she asked, alarmed to think of Anuruddha in the dangerous areas of Kapilavastu, being cheated by ruthless men who set up their dice boards on tables along streets and who, she had heard, would knife you for a few coins.

"I don't know, I've only heard rumours . . . I'm too frightened to ask him." Ananda was quiet, brooding. "The truth is, I don't know what I can do to divert my bhāta from his habit. Can't, oddly, picture who Anuruddha would be without it." He turned to her. "And you, bhagini? We've heard scandalous rumours that you cultivate your own fields? Have you turned into a peasant?"

She laughed and began to tell him about her enjoyment and satisfaction growing things, her friendship with the women of Mudgala. She barely mentioned Siddhartha, and Ananda didn't ask. Out of loyalty to her marriage, to her husband, she couldn't tell him the truth and she was grateful he had guessed she was unhappy; his discretion was one of the things she loved about her cousin.

"Bhāta," she said, when he had finally walked her back to the women's quarters. "I keep dawdling and dawdling in this city because I don't have the courage to leave my pita . . . to say this last goodbye." She twisted her hands together in distress. "Meanwhile he and my aunt wait on my departure so they can finally go to our family estate. But now you're here . . . Promise me you will accompany me as far as Lumbini. Because then I will have the courage to leave, and return to Mudgala."

"Ah, then I will have some use! And your mother in the Land of the Fathers will be happy. How wise she was to summon me."

The night before she left, Yasodhara went to see her father one last time in his receiving room. It was empty now except for some cushions on the floor. A dread built and built in Yasodhara as she and her father made desultory conversation, seated on those cushions. When she finally got up to leave, she bent to touch Dandapani's feet. Once he'd lifted her up by the shoulders, they gazed at each other hungrily, both knowing they'd probably never see each other again. "Pita, if I bear a child, I will bring him or her to see you."

Her father nodded. "I hold you to that promise, dhītā."

She left quietly before dawn, seated beside Ananda in one of his carts, her own following at the back of his caravan. For a while she wept quietly over the loss of her mother, her city, and more freshly the loss of her father. Yet, once they had halted to do a makeshift version of the morning sacrifices, she realized that she must stopper up her sadness. Otherwise, she would simply not be able to make the arduous trip home.

When they had set off again, she said to Ananda, "Devadatta tells me you have disgraced and humiliated your father and Mahanama. Amuse me, bhata, with the story."

"Ah," he said with a little smile, and began to tell her his tale.

⚓

My story begins on a morning two years ago, bhagini, when I returned from a meeting of the Bankers' Guild to find my servant waiting for me outside the street door, peering anxiously down the road. Seeing me, he gestured excitedly and, when I had hurried up to him, he whispered, "You have a visitor, sāmi," but then stood blocking my way in as if he feared for me.

I pushed past the man and hurried in to find a woman seated on the bench that wrapped around the neem tree in the middle of my courtyard. She rose and bowed silently and it took me a moment to recognize her: the slave Nagamunda from my father's house, who ran the women's quarters. I hadn't seen her in ten years, not since I'd left my father's home. She was older now, probably in her mid-thirties like me, but still beautiful in an eerie way, her transparent pale skin with a bluish undertone, the veins visible on her neck and hands ("Gecko" was her unkind nickname by the other servants). Her hair was that dark auburn common to people from the northern part of the Parthian Empire.

In the time I'd lived in my father's house, the woman had eaten every day with me and the senior household servants, but I'd had nothing to say to her. Rather, I'd chatted with the other senior servants, whom I'd known in my boyhood, before my mother and I were banished, and who were always kind to me.

There was a movement now behind the woman and a girl in her early teens stood up from the section of the bench hidden by the tree trunk. A beautiful child, with a heart-shaped face, skin the colour of damp river sand, auburn tints in her dark-brown hair. Her daughter, I thought, then immediately caught myself. Daughter? I hadn't even known the woman had a child!

The slave came forward silently and bent to touch my feet. I tried to move back, feeling she didn't owe me this obeisance, but she firmly grasped my foot, held it for a moment, patted it gently and then rose again. Her face was impassive, as if unaware she had flustered me. "My daughter." She beckoned the girl forward, who dimpled a smile as she bent to touch my feet. When she straightened up, her gaze was shy but also frank and friendly, even slightly mischievous, as if saying, "Well, that's my mother, but don't take offence." I found myself smiling back. But then, as the thought came to me, I blurted out, "My pita? Has something happened?"

Nagamunda shook her head and then stood, head lowered. After a moment of examining her, puzzled, I gestured for them to follow me to the receiving room. She signalled her daughter to remain on the bench, then stroked her shoulder because the girl suddenly looked frightened. I called for my servant and when he came, I said, "Give the young lady something to drink."

As we entered my receiving room, I saw the slave woman's eyes move, appraising, admiring, over the walls with their fresh coat of mud and new chalk designs, the fluffy yak-skin rugs on the clay floor, cushions and bolsters scattered about, comfortable divans, statues and knick-knacks from my various travels. She gave me a small nod to say, "Congratulations, you have done well," and I bowed slightly to acknowledge this. But now I was truly nervous because I knew something bad was coming. Any interaction with my father or half-brother or their household could only bring trouble.

Once we were seated—Nagamunda cross-legged on a rug, I across from her on another rug, a low table between us—I said, "What can I help you with?" keeping my voice pleasant but businesslike.

"I come seeking your kindness, mitta." Her accent was slightly guttural, but she was fluent in our language. "You have always been an upright man. Treated me, a mere slave, with respect and kindness."

Her wheedling tone made me even more nervous; I knew a sale when I heard one. "I made no special effort in the way I treated you."

"But that's just it, mitta. Kindness, goodness, come naturally to you . . . unlike your half-brother, Mahanama."

I frowned, a notion beginning to sprout. Nagamunda, seeing my knitted brows, nodded to say I'd guessed correctly. "My daughter Vasabha is his." She grimaced and her grimace told me more: the union with Mahanama was forced. "One of those well-kept secrets of the women's quarters, mitta." She let out a bitter laugh. "So well-kept that even Mahanama's wife could pretend not to know of it. Until now." She straightened her back. "My Vasabha is fourteen. I have her future to think about. So, I've told Mahanama that I'm taking up a case against him in court, unless he gives her an inheritance."

"Oh." I sat back, examining the woman, who tilted her chin defiantly. I could put the rest together: Nagamunda had made her threat, set the household in an uproar and been thrown out into the street with her daughter.

"I'm glad I threatened him, no matter that it's led to this. My Vasabha will not be denied her rights." She smiled bravely. "I remember your kindness, mitta. Know also of your reputation, your success, as a merchant. So, I'm hoping you will be kind." She clasped her hands, suddenly close to tears. "If you won't take us both in, then at least take my Vasabha."

I was silent, leaning forward, looking into the distance as I stroked my cheek. I couldn't also throw them onto the street like Mahanama but, at the same time, I didn't want them here.

In the ten years prior, I'd had little contact with my father or half-brother. A few times, I had run into them in the street and then there'd been some awkward staring and bowing, but that was it. I didn't want to now bring my family's troubles and acrimony into my own house. I sighed, clapped my hands loudly and called out for my servant. The man immediately appeared; he'd probably been listening on the verandah. I told him that he was to take Nagamunda and her daughter to the spare bedroom in a corner of the verandah. She started to thank me, but I waved my hand and gave her a stern look to say this was temporary.

Once they were gone, I continued to sit, stroking my cheek, feeling resentful but also guilty over my resentment. They truly were destitute. And that girl was young and beautiful, a deadly combination in a beggar's life. "No, no," I murmured to myself with a little shiver, thinking of her fate. "I couldn't live with myself if that happened. I simply couldn't."

I decided to talk it over with Anuruddha. Once I'd knocked on the door to his room, I entered to find the room still dark, even though it was well past midday, and permeated by a sour fug of alcohol and old sweat.

When I called to him, Anuruddha groaned and struggled into a sitting position, looking blearily through the gloom. I opened the shutters of a window, letting in bands of light, then went and sat on the bed. I told Anuruddha what had happened, taking in, as if seeing him anew, just how dissipated he looked, a good ten years older than his twenty-eight years. Yes, yes, I must do something about this, I said to myself, as I had numerous times. But I knew I wouldn't.

When I was done telling him my news, I said, "Did you know any of this?"

Anuruddha shook his head. "How strange that the child remained a secret until now." He grinned sleepily. "Yes, yes, a scandal. Especially when people find out you've taken in the woman and her daughter."

I sighed and pushed back my turban. I'd forgotten about the world with its gossip.

Still not sure what to do, I went to see Vimala for her advice. When I was finished telling her, the ganika nodded thoughtfully, chewing on a wad of betel. "Are they beautiful?" I frowned, not liking her businesslike expression. "Exotic as well, no doubt," Vimala added. "Do they both have that strange transparent skin, that red hair of their people?"

"Ah, no!"

She let out a peal of laughter. "But of course I am thinking of them for my house, mitta! Isn't that what you've come to me about?"

"Certainly not!" I cried, appalled. "How could you think that!"

"But then, mitta, what is their future, if you cannot have them in your house? They must make a living somehow. No noble home will take them in. Not even a Vessa household. What wife would agree to have that woman in her house, with her illegitimate child?" She cocked her head and pursed her lips, eyes twinkling. After a moment, I grinned and wagged a finger at her. She had been testing me; helping me to discover what I must do, by offering the alternative.

When I returned to my house, I found the girl, Vasabha, sweeping the courtyard. She nodded in a friendly manner but then ducked her head shyly and turned away to continue her task. "You don't need to do that," I said, going up to her. Then added, "daharé," wanting to make sure there was not even the slightest hint I might be amorously interested in her.

"But then what, sāmi?" She gave me a sidelong merry look and I laughed. The girl was smart. Despite her quietness, her shyness, she saw things clearly and had a sense of humour. Another girl would be agitated, upset, at this expulsion from Mahanama's home, but she took it calmly. She had, I saw now, one of those easygoing natures, like a river reed that bends with the current but stays firmly rooted.

"Yes, yes," I said, shaking my head, smiling. "I see your point. You cannot sit in your room all day, doing nothing. Have you," I added as the thought came to me, "have you had any schooling?"

She laughed shyly and shook her head. "How could that be possible, sāmi?"

"No, no, I suppose not."

I turned at the sound of a door opening onto the verandah. Nagamunda was coming out of Anuruddha's room, bearing a brass tray with the remains of a meal. She smiled, nodded to me and bustled towards the kitchen. I felt suddenly dispirited. My eyes rested for a moment on the well in a corner of the courtyard. I would have to get a coconut-frond privacy screen erected around it so the women could also bathe there. The girl was examining me, as if she'd read my mind. "Well, well, I will leave you to your task." I started to walk away but then turned and added, "And, for as long as you are here, you will call me 'mātula.'"

She smiled, genuinely pleased. "Mātula."

The next day, Nagamunda told me at the midday meal that she had made good on her threat. She had gone that very morning to the palace and officially taken up a case against Mahanama, suing him for her daughter's inheritance. I gawked at her and Anuruddha chortled, hand over mouth to prevent his food flying out. Vasabha smiled at his amusement, her eyes darting from me to him, to check our reactions.

"You will not win," I said after a moment. "My uncle Suddhodanna, the raja, will be hearing the case."

"There is winning and there is winning, mitta." She dished out food for me, kneeling behind me like a good wife to ensure all my needs were met. "The threat of the case alone, the shame of it, might be enough."

"There won't even be standing room!" Anuruddha cried, still laughing. "The entire city will come to hear it."

"Yes, precisely." Nagamunda smiled indulgently at Anuruddha as if he were a roguish but charming boy. "I haven't lived in that household without learning that reputation and status are everything. Your half-brother and father course along on their status, borrowing, borrowing. But the Setthis wait like jackals for a sign of weakness. Then they'll go in for the kill."

I regarded Nagamunda, half-admiring, half-wary. When she came to me, she'd already had this plan. My home was the secure base she needed to launch her campaign. Even I, a man, who had broken away from my family, my caste, didn't have her nerve.

A soft laugh from Vasabha made me glance up. She was studying my morose face, had guessed my thoughts again. "You frighten him, ammé."

Nagamunda looked genuinely embarrassed. "I'm sorry, mitta, I never..."

"No, no," I said diplomatically, "I am only impressed."

"In my position, you would have done the same, mitta. Have you never seen a doe take on a wild dog to defend her fawn, a pigeon take on a hawk, a she-elephant a pride of lions?"

"Yes, but none of them have taken on the ruling triad," I joked, to quell my unease. Then I wagged my finger at Vasabha, mock-admonishing. "And you, daharé. I've been thinking about your education. There must be a Brahmin somewhere who can be hired to teach you."

"Ah, you are truly a good man," Nagamunda cried.

In the end, Mahanama did settle out of court, mostly because his wife and mother pressured him to do so, furious that they would be humiliated by a public case. He bequeathed to Nagamunda a piece of paddy land and its adjoining mango orchard. He granted her freedom, but not that of her daughter: a threat that he still had power over her. Nagamunda took this with a shrug, saying to me, "He will have to acknowledge her officially first, in order to claim and sell her. And Mahanama aspires to be raja one day." She chuckled harshly. "Reputation and status."

His story over, Ananda twitched the reins of his cart, clucking for the oxen to go faster. For a while he stared ahead, nodding as if in conversation with himself.

Yasodhara examined him, sensing he wished to say something else.

"Nagamunda is not her real name," he finally blurted out. "A slave merchant gave it to her when he bought her from a soldier, whose spoil of war she was." He hissed "spoil" and then Yasodhara understood. He and the slave were lovers.

"Ah poor woman, I'm glad she found a refuge with you," she murmured diplomatically to say she comprehended.

"But I am not like the slave trader or Mahanama," he added sharply. "It was she, she who came to me of her own free will."

"Then I am truly happy for you, bhāta."

Ananda nodded but continued to brood, his face returning to its old melancholy. There was some trouble in the relationship but he would not tell her out of loyalty to the woman—any more than she would speak to him of her own troubled marriage.

They finally reached Lumbini. As Yasodhara got down from his cart, she said to Ananda, "Bhāta, I cannot bear another farewell. I will go visit the Yakshi and please be gone when I return."

He nodded. "We will meet again, bhagini, I know that." He smiled. "There is great profit to be made, evidently, on that river ride up north to Mudgala."

She nodded, took one last look at him, then turned abruptly and set off across the park, lifting a hand backwards in farewell. She would not look back, no she would not.

As she made her way through the grass towards the path that led to the shrine, she gazed around at the other women pilgrims, resting under tamhan and akash trees laden with gorgeous lilac and white flowers. The women ate snacks, braided garlands for the Yakshi, gazed wistfully at the river with knees drawn to chest; in the river itself, other women immersed themselves in the water with great gasps, as if drowning. She studied the women's faces, seeing in them her own worries and fears—some barren like her, some struggling with adulterous or cruel husbands, or worse, abandoned by them. Then there were the wives of soldiers and hunters and men in other dangerous professions, come to beg for protection for their husbands, to beg the Yakshi not to make them widows.

Once in the temple, she prostrated herself before the image, stretched out fully on the floor. In a long, murmured whisper, she unburdened her concerns about Siddhartha and their marriage. She told the Yakshi about her sorrow at her mother's death, and her fear and sadness that she would probably never see her father again, her worry about him in his widowed state of grief; also confessed her worry about Devadatta, whom she still loved, despite being angry with him. And she also begged for an end to her barrenness.

When she finally left the mud hut, she felt lighter from confessing her cares, and more able to continue on her journey. Two of the prettily painted terracotta beads on her necklace were crushed from the act of prostrating herself on the ground. The Yakshi had left her fingerprints on Yasodhara as a promise of protection.

The morning Yasodhara arrived at Mudgala, she waded to the shore with no one to greet her; she had sent no messenger ahead. The two guards who had accompanied her tied up the barge, took her trunk and followed as she led the way up the bank. It was the harvesting season and, as she walked towards the village, she could see the women and men in the distant fields cutting tall stalks, their clothes specks of colour against the golden paddy. They were nearing the end of Vasanta and she was a little surprised at how hot it was for spring; she had to wipe her face a couple of times on the journey along the road. When she reached the deserted village square, she stood gazing at the shrine for the Yaksha and Yakshi of Mudgala, at the well, the banyan tree, the surrounding houses, seeing everything anew after her time away; she inhaled anew the odour of wood-fired dung, of manure piled in a corner, of dust and earth. How simple, how rustic everything seemed. How shabby. And how quiet compared with Ramagama, a quiet that, in her new state of grief, filled her with desolation. She turned her eyes towards the foothills where the buzzards circled above the peaks, and a feeling of distaste and panic rose in her. She was back in her life, in her marriage; already shrivelling within, already returning to that state of constriction she'd grown used to. She was sharp with sorrow and longing for Ramagama, for her ailing father; how she regretted leaving, even though she knew she'd had no other choice.

When she arrived at her house, she stood for a long moment looking around the courtyard, listening to a dove tutting in the eaves. The guards put her trunk in the bedroom, saluted her and left. She went to the street door and watched them walking down the lane, the last remnants of her other life in Ramagama disappearing. She finally went back inside, shut the door and stood against it, arms behind her back, aware of a bottomless darkness in her, like gazing into a very deep well. *But no, I am already in that well. If I don't scrabble up to the light . . .*

She walked slowly to the kitchen, passed through it with a cursory glance and entered the storeroom. From one of the large clay pots, she took a handful of grain and went out to the acacia tree. She was glad to see that someone had kept up the shrine for her. She knelt before the little clay abode, placed the grain in the shrine and touched her forehead to the earth. "Mitta," she whispered, "I am back. Help me to take up my old life, I am struggling. Help me find some way to love my life here." Then silently she poured out her homesickness and sadness to the devata.

She was so lost in her outpouring that she didn't hear Siddhartha approach. Only when he'd squatted by her and whispered "Ushas" did she look up with a sharp breath to find him gently smiling at her. They regarded each other for a moment. He reached out and pushed back a strand of her hair. "I looked after the shrine for you, beloved." She didn't respond, staring at him. He had changed, she could tell it right away: Siddhartha was gazing at her with great love, in a way he hadn't for a long time. She rose quickly to her feet. He took her face in his hands. "Ah, my poor Ushas." He drew her to him and she felt comforted by the familiarity of his body, his smell. She wrapped her arms tightly around him, still bewildered by this change in him.

Once they broke apart, he took her hand. As they walked around the perimeter wall towards the street door, he asked about Pamita's death, about her father. She told him about her parents and also about Ananda; about Devadatta and how he left without saying goodbye on the very night after their mother's funeral. By the time she was done, they were seated on the bed in their room. All the while she'd been talking, she was aware that Siddhartha was simmering with some news, and when she was finished, she said, "You've listened patiently to me, Surya. What is this thing you are dying to tell me?"

He laughed.

"Yes, yes, I can tell something has changed," she urged. "I'm keen to know. Because I see that you're happy."

"Ah Ushas, I *am* happy," he said softly, eyes shining. "After a very long time." He gave her a meaningful look that was an apology for the way he had treated her in the last year.

He told her then about Maha Kosala's visit and conversion to the Truth of Truths.

Yasodhara watched him, full of wonder as he jumped up to pace while he talked, hands behind his back, rubbing his nose periodically, a tic when he was excited. She suspected there were things that he and Maha Kosala had discussed that he wasn't telling her, but she put this thought aside.

"And the best thing, Ushas, is that once the village heard I was learning this philosophy, they asked to be enlightened too. All the villagers are now practising the Truth of Truths! This philosophy has the potential to unite Brahmins and Khattiyas—within a kingdom, but also across kingdoms. An empire of faith!"

The thing she had longed for, but given up expecting, had come to pass. Siddhartha had found a new project, a new goal, and by doing so, it was possible that their marriage might also be renewed. Yet then, much to her surprise as she watched him lean against the windowsill, back to the Himalayas, and talk on, she felt resentment building within her at his enthusiasm. She wanted to continue grieving over what she had lost, not leap to considering the new. She shook her head to dismiss this resentment and leaned forward to ask him a question about how the Gayatri Sutta was to be said in the new way. Listening intently to his answers, she said to herself, echoing her mother, "If you want your marriage to be happy, then you must make it so."

"An empire of faith, Ushas!" Siddhartha repeated, opening his hands wide with a laugh. "My next plan is to send emissaries to the Moriya across the river. Perhaps, the Truth of Truths will make us better neighbours."

"Oh, a wonderful idea, Surya! Maybe you'll make a convert of the Moriya rashtrika and his wife!" They both laughed. Despite repeated invitations, the Moriya rashtrika and his wife had never visited, nor invited them to visit. The Moriya were touchy about river rights because the Kali Gandak River passed first through Mudgala before reaching Moriya territory further south.

Following dinner, they sat on the verandah, since it was too hot to sit inside, and continued to talk about Yasodhara's time in Ramagama and her sorrow, and then again of Siddhartha's passion for the Truth of Truths. But after awhile, Siddhartha picked up the statue he was whittling and bent over it intently.

"What is it, Surya?" Yashodhara asked. She frowned at how brooding and silent he had suddenly become.

He waved his hand to say it was nothing. "So, tell me again about Ananda and his success."

She gave his shoulder a little shake. "Surya, you can either tell me what troubles you, or suffer unnecessarily with it."

He sighed deeply, then gave her an apologetic look. "I . . . I meditate at this time, after the evening meal."

"Well then, go and do it! We can talk later, when we're in bed."

"But are you sure, Ushas? I could do it tomorrow or—" She pushed him to go, with a teasing laugh. He laughed too, leapt up, bent to kiss her fervently and left. She watched him go along the verandah and disappear into their bedroom. Then she gazed out into the dark courtyard, trying to stifle her hurt at being abandoned.

The daily sacrifices in Mudgala had changed. Instead of each household doing their own rituals, Siddhartha and the villagers had constructed a sacrificial enclosure not far from the village square, where everyone gathered to do the rituals together. The next morning, as they prepared to go to the enclosure, Yasodhara also learned that her and Siddhartha's marital fire had been moved there because they were the chief sacrificers in the ritual. "I'm glad to hear that, Surya," she said. She was determined to make this work, determined that she would give herself wholeheartedly to his new passion.

When they reached the enclosure, the village women cried out and flocked to Yasodhara, touching her arms, her face, saying, "We missed you, daharé . . ." "Our times in the field are just not the same . . ." "We harvested your plot, you must come and see the yield, even greater than last year." "Yes, sāmini, you are indeed blessed with the fecund touch . . ." "Have you noticed this heat, sāmini? And Gimha hasn't yet even begun!" Surrounded by them, Yasodhara finally felt happy, truly home.

She entered the sacrificial courtyard through the southern women's entrance, while Siddhartha and the men entered through the eastern men's entrance.

The Brahmin who knew the Vedas best was serving as the priest. He had preceded everyone else and the three fires in the compound were crackling away. Siddhartha took his designated place to the left of the ahavaniya hearth and Yasodhara sat before the domestic fire. Someone had laid out her sacrificial utensils by her seat, along with the cord of munja grass with which her husband would yoke her waist.

As the Gayatri Sutta chant began, Yasodhara observed the fervency with which the villagers recited it, their eyes closed, each trying to find the Atman within them, to connect through it to Brahman. The person she scrutinized most sharply was Siddhartha, seated across the sacrificial enclosure from her, cross-legged, back straight, head held high, nostrils dilated with concentration. She finally closed her eyes and tried to give herself over to the chant, to lose herself in it, just as she had often lost herself in song when in the fields. But the words were just words; she could not sink beyond them, could not enter the chant. She opened her eyes again and studied the men across from her, the women beside her. She studied the new focus and passion with which they were reciting the suttas, the way they watched intently the feeding of the fires, the love with which they called out the names of the gods, seeing themselves as one with the gods—gods who were no longer separate, impersonal forces. These sacrifices used to be a chore to be got through; now Yasodhara was witnessing a new dedication, a fervency (particularly in her husband) that only made her feel profoundly alienated.

As Yasodhara went about her day—accompanying the women to look at her yield, arranging for the grain to be threshed by the vana-dasas who emerged from the forest tri-annually to help with the harvesting—she remained lost in thought. If she wanted her marriage to be successful, she needed to engage deeper with this new philosophy. No matter her own contrary thoughts, she must put them away and work alongside Siddhartha. Because it was clear he did truly experience this bliss and oneness, was truly made tranquil by the Truth of Truths.

The next day at the sacrifices, she tried but, once again, could not enter into the state of tranquility the others seemed to share. As she worked in her back garden that day, it came to her why she couldn't: her grief was out of step with this notion of inner bliss, with the idea of uniting joyfully with her Atman and with Brahman. There was no place for grief in this new philosophy.

That evening she told Siddhartha her reason for being unable to enter the state of tranquility. After she was done, he was silent, nodding. "Such dark feelings are caused by wrong thinking, Ushas, by clinging to the falseness of duality. By clinging to the notion of oneself as separate from the rest of the world."

Yasodhara put down her sewing. "I . . . I don't understand."

"You must accept that your ammé is not gone, but dissolved into the Supreme Self like a lump of salt in water. Then you, who are also part of Brahman, can dissolve this illusion of separation through meditation. You can lose your grief by being united with Brahman, and hence with your ammé."

"But my grief is not an illusion! My ammé *is* gone. I will never see her again, never hear her beloved voice. No one will ever look at me again with that love only a mother has for a child." She got up, agitated and angry at the philosophy for calling her grief an illusion, and most of all resenting Siddhartha for advising her to see it thus.

"Sssh, Ushas." He took her hand. "Give yourself time. There is no hurry to—"

She snatched her hand away. "No, no, it's not an illusion. How could you say that?"

After a moment, she sat back down, picked up her cloth and continued mending the tear in it.

After that, Yasodhara was relieved in the evenings when Siddhartha went away to their bedroom to meditate. Left alone, she was free to experience her grief fully: her anguished longing for her mother, her bitter distaste for everything in her life. She often awoke in the middle of the night in a panic, thinking she must go urgently to her mother, that she had already delayed too long and Pamita was dying in pain and discomfort because of her lack of vigilance. In the daytime, the panic was also with her, formless and sloshing about in her stomach.

Eventually, she realized something paradoxical had happened: a part of her seemed to have broken off and drifted away, leaving her incomplete; yet, at the same time, her mother's spirit, her mother's way of being, had come to live in Yasodhara. She gave this spirit space, and purposely started to use her mother's phrases, her mother's pithy sayings, purposely allowed her voice to develop that exclamatory crack of Pamita's when excited or disbelieving. None of this, she knew with a pang of guilt, was in keeping with the Truth of Truths, which insisted she abandon the idea of duality and see her mother as a lump of salt melted into Brahman; and that she melt herself, her grief, into Brahman too, and thereby find a connection with her departed mother.

One morning, as she was walking back from the fields with Rupasiri, the old woman said, "Yes-yes, the Moriya rashtrika's reaction to your husband's offer to teach the Truth of Truths is unfortunate."

The day before, Vagantha had returned from a visit to the Moriya rashtrika, bringing a message: the Moriya rashtrika wished Siddhartha to know that he was already a convert to the Truth of Truths, because Maha Kosala had passed through their village too. He wished Siddhartha to know that he had no intention of preaching the Truth of Truths to all Khattiyas and Brahmins in his province, nor even his village. This philosophy had been given to him by the former maharaja and therefore the rashtrika believed it was meant only for nobles like him. He forbade Siddhartha to send any missionaries to his province.

"Ah, unfortunate indeed," Yasodhara replied. Both women shook their heads at the foolishness of the Moriya.

"Unfortunate indeed," Rupasiri repeated after a moment.

Yasodhara gave her a quick look. This repetition was an invitation to something else. "Tell me, pitucché," she said tentatively, "and do you experience this oneness with Brahman?"

Rupasiri let out a little huff of a laugh. "No more than you, daharé."

Their eyes met and they smiled at each other. They walked along in silence for a few steps, wiping their faces with their old shawls. It was truly hot now—Gimha had definitely arrived, earlier than usual.

"And the other women?" ventured Yasodhara.

"I think not. Though they say nothing."

A stone-curlew in a tree let out a sharp whistling, *pick-pick-pick-pick*, descending to *pick-wick*, *pick-wick*.

"And does your husband know you don't experience this oneness?" Yasodhara asked.

Rupasiri laughed and shrugged to say, "Why not?"

"And he's not troubled by this?"

"No, daharé. He enjoys practising the philosophy, but it's not *important*." She gave Yasodhara a meaningful glance.

All at once, Yasodhara understood. Rupasiri was telling her that Siddhartha was alone in his keenness for the Truth of Truths. The villagers were pleased to go along with it, happy to be united as a village in doing the rituals, and some of them probably experienced a bit of tranquility within. But none of them shared Siddhartha's fervour. He, who was usually so acute, had been fooled by the villagers' pretense of zeal. Or rather, Yasodhara worried, he had let himself be fooled.

9

Gnats

YASODHARA WAS EXAMINING her paddy saplings one morning, worried for their state because of the drought that had persisted in the months since her return, when she happened to look up and see, through a blur of sweat, a strange procession wending its way down below, along the road that led to the village. She hastily wiped her face on the shawl wrapped around her waist, then, hands on hips, took a better look at the procession: a group of elderly men with the dignity that suggested they were headmen or members of village councils, some walking, others riding asses, one pulling along a cow on a rope, the beast garlanded as a gift. The other women nearby had straightened up too, and were also watching the procession. She turned and called to Rupasiri, "Do you know these men, pitucché?"

Rupasiri shook her head. "It's too far to see their faces, daharé, but I am guessing officials from distant villages."

This had to do with the drought; of that Yasodhara was sure.

She squinted against the sun, looking at the Kali Gandak in the distance. How greatly it had shrunk, the exposed riverbed cracked and rutted so the channels weren't bringing enough water. Beyond the fields, the grass was brown, the earth crumbling, a smell of dust in the air. And here they were, at the end of the month of Kattika, well into Sarada, when the autumn coolness should have started. At first, everyone had hoped the rains were just late, as they sometimes could be. Rituals had been performed to Rudra, the rain god, to the Yaksha and Yakshi of the village. Similar rites had been done in villages across the province. Gradually, however, news began to trickle in, brought by the occasional trader, that the rains had failed far south, which always got the rain first before it travelled up here to the Northern Province. The gathering of the Sarada harvest a week ago had been a subdued affair, partly because the ongoing heat made the work exhausting, partly because the villagers knew that there would be a very small winter crop to come. By diverting water from the Kali Gandak, they had been able to keep the saplings growing in their beds these last fifty days, for the winter crop. Yet they would only be able to replant half of them. There simply wasn't enough water for anything more. Yasodhara looked with anguish at the half of her saplings that she couldn't water. They were yellow and shrivelling; some had collapsed and were just brown squiggles on the earth.

By the time Yasodhara and the women reached the square, the entire village had gathered to see who the visitors were. Because she was the rashtrika's wife, the crowd parted to allow her and Rupasiri through. She saw Siddhartha seated on a stool, Vagantha and the village council around him, grave. The visitors sat before them in a semicircle, their faces mournful, paddy stalks on the ground by their feet. The stalks looked burned. Siddhartha beckoned her closer. She bowed cursorily to the visitors, then squatted to examine the paddy, picking it up and turning it over. "A blight," Rupasiri whispered behind her, eyes round with fear.

Yasodhara turned to the men. "How did this happen, mitto?"

"A disease brought by a hot wind, sāmini," one of the men said, his eyes haunted. "Our entire crop destroyed in days." She and Rupasiri glanced at each other again. They could be next.

"What help can I offer you?" Siddhartha leaned forward, elbows on knees, hands clasped.

The visitors looked at each other significantly. Then their spokesman said, "We ask that you exempt us from paying paddy tax this season."

Siddhartha sat back, surprised. A murmur rose from the village council. The tax was non-negotiable. The council members glanced at each other, shaking their heads subtly to say this was not a good idea.

Yasodhara watched Siddhartha, who was frowning. They must be truly desperate to ask this.

"By rationing our granaries, we should be able to manage until the next rains," one of the visitors added. "But we will be hungry. And if the rains fail again . . ." The man lifted his hands in a helpless gesture to say that then they would starve.

Siddhartha's frown deepened. "Kapilavastu will not be pleased."

"But sāmi, we know *you'll* be merciful," another man cried. "We know *you* cherish our welfare."

"Sāmi, you've performed wonders for our province since coming here."

"We consider you our true raja."

"A benevolent monarch."

"We're all part of Brahman, so you've taught us. All united together, no separation between us. Are we not, therefore, the same, *equal*, to those in Kapilavastu?"

Siddhartha was silent, pondering on this. Yasodhara watched him, apprehensive. She noted Vagantha's concern too.

After a moment, Siddhartha nodded. "Yes, I'll exempt you."

There was a shocked silence among the village council; she and Rupasiri glanced at each other.

"Why should you starve while they eat in Kapilavastu?" Siddhartha continued. "And you're right, we're all one in Brahman."

The visitors were joyful. "We knew you wouldn't let us down, guru," one of the men cried. Another rushed to touch Siddhartha's feet, and a third brought forward the cow and offered it to Siddhartha, who, Yasodhara could see, was already beginning to wonder what he'd done.

The moment she and Siddhartha were settled on mats on the verandah that evening, palm leaf fans in hand, Yasodhara said, "Surya, are you sure you've done the right thing? Your pita, our mātula Amitodhana, Mahanama, the sangha, they will all be angry."

"No doubt, Ushas." Siddhartha waved his fan. "But it's not fair that these poor people should starve so the nobles can sit there in luxury and comfort. These peasants are my subjects after all, I owe them—"

"They aren't *your* subjects, they're your pita's. Surya, you can't make a decision like this. It's breaking royal law. Taxation is decided by Kapilavastu, not us."

"When that man said that all of us are one in Brahman, I simply couldn't refuse him. Because he reminded me of the truth. We are all one. And so, I should, I *must*, treat them as if they are one with me. Treat them in the same way I would treat you, or anyone else I love."

"But, Surya." She rapped her fan against her thigh. "You can't flout the law. If you do it, then everyone else will do it too. Your Truth of Truths is fine when it's about you, but not when it's about matters of state. The two are separate."

"Ah, but then it wouldn't be the Truth of Truths, in which there is no such separation." He waggled his fan at her. "I know what you think of the Truth of Truths, Ushas. I know that the villagers have stopped believing in it the way I do." He nodded at her surprise. "But I still believe in it. It has saved me from myself. So I can't, now when I am tested, back away from its principles. Don't ask me to. I . . . I simply cannot do that." He jumped up and began to pace. "It is not right, it is not moral, that these poor peasants should starve—because they *will* starve—to feed the nobles in Kapilavastu. This oneness that I feel—that you don't believe in—is real. We *are* all one, all part of Brahman, I have felt that unity when meditating. So I must act as if we are all one." He rubbed the tip of his nose with two fingers. "The starvation of those people is not some figment of imagination. Look at your own fields. Imagine if a blight destroyed them."

"But Surya, you will be punished, your pita—"

"I can't! I can't let these people starve." He waved his hand in agitation. "Why do you ask this of me? Why? I . . . I know you speak out of worry for me. But it isn't fanaticism. I am truly acting out of compassion for these peasants, truly do see them as one with me."

She nodded after a moment to acknowledge the truth of this. In the last months, this sense of oneness had been his guide in his duties, and she had seen the consideration with which he treated not just other people, but her too. Despite knowing that she didn't believe in his philosophy, he had never resented her for this, but had left her to her grief when he went quietly each evening to meditate. In bed at night, he was gentle and loving with her. After a long period when their intimacy had been inconsistent, they were making love on a regular basis; no longer was it some duty they both felt they needed to perform to validate their marriage. Yasodhara had watched and waited for his brooding to return, but it hadn't. He was truly changed by the philosophy, she couldn't deny that. And yet, she feared for him. His idealism was a fragile, dangerous thing in this complicated world, a world that didn't often return a person's love and compassion.

Usually the process of moving the seedlings from their beds to the flooded fields was a joyful time, with much singing among the women as they worked. But now their voices rose in a parched, subdued chanting, as if at a funeral. There was something terrible about abandoning half of the saplings they had nurtured these last fifty days to shrivel and die in the drained plots. The other half were moved to the fields that had been flooded by diverting water from the river. The village held further rituals and fire sacrifices to Rudra, slaughtering two water buffalo for him, hoping he would favour them with rain, even this late.

Yasodhara was heavy with worry. Fortunately, the fall yield was strong in Mudgala and so, with some austerity, they could get through this year and part of the next. But what would they do if the rains failed again next year? And meanwhile, the days were unbearably hot, the air stifling, even the birds and insects subdued. The only thing that thrived were clouds of gnats who, attracted to hot, sweating bodies, hovered over Yasodhara and the women while they worked, getting in their eyes and mouths, sticking to any exposed skin. When she bathed at the well, Yasodhara even found dead ones in her belly button. "Everything is dying, except these things I want to die," she muttered.

When the tax collector came with his barges to collect the fall harvest taxes, Yasodhara made sure to be present to support her husband. Vagantha and the village council stayed away, having come up with various excuses. None of them wanted to be implicated in Siddhartha's decision.

After the man had come ashore, Siddhartha led him to the sacks of grain piled on the beach. The collector frowned. "Sāmi, but where is the rest?"

"Ah, yes." Siddhartha clasped his hands behind his back. "I'm afraid this is it. There's been a blight in some of the villages, and so their fall harvest is destroyed. What remains in their granaries must be conserved to last until the rains come again."

The man's eyes widened in alarm. "But nonetheless, the tax must be paid. The villagers' situation is none of my concern."

"I'm sorry, but my people will not starve."

"The royal taxation law says—"

"I know exactly what the law says."

The man was silent, shaking his head. Siddhartha stood there with a small, pleasant smile, but Yasodhara could tell he was uneasy, confronted now with the reality of what he'd put in motion.

The collector raised his eyebrows. "The raja will not be pleased."

"So, what can be done?" Siddhartha demanded impatiently. He gestured to the drying Kali Gandak, its exposed riverbed stinking of mud, decayed fish and rotting river plants, the barges beached where the river had once flowed.

"But it's not my decision, sāmi. The sangha in Kapilavastu, the amicis, your father, will be unhappy. It is I who will be summoned to explain this to the treasurer." He raised an eyebrow. "Your cousin Mahanama. I will have to face his wrath."

"Surely the other provinces must be suffering because of the drought too? Haven't any of them reduced their taxes?"

"All have paid as usual, sāmi."

Siddhartha raised an eyebrow to express polite skepticism. "And there was no revolt? There should be a revolt against such greed and cruelty."

"Yes, of course there were revolts. But they were quickly and decisively put down. A few burnt villages, a few gambojakas executed or exiled, has sent the message very quickly." The collector nodded, then addressed Yasodhara with a dry smile. "Your brother, as head of the palace guards, was most assiduous in all this. Yes, yes, he enforced executions and suppressed revolts with great finesse. We're all very grateful to Devadatta." He turned to regard the stock of paddy, mouth twisted, stroking his chin. Then he said again, softly, "The raja will not be pleased with you."

Siddhartha shrugged. "It . . . it can't be helped. I will not make my people starve to feed those fat gullets in Kapilavastu."

"'Fat gullets in Kapilavastu,'" the man murmured with a little snort—no doubt, thought Yasodhara, storing that phrase to share with his fellow collectors.

The man left, and Yasodhara and Siddhartha stood watching his barges go down the river, one of them empty. After he had gone around the bend, Siddhartha turned to her with a small smile and shrugged. "And well, Ushas, you see your worry was all for nothing. We are too far north. There is nothing they can do to us."

"Yes, you're probably right, Surya," she murmured, glancing away.

As the drought persisted, the Moriya began to protest that the Sakiya were taking too much water. The Kali Gandak flowed first through Sakiya territory before it rounded a bend and entered Moriya lands further south. By helping themselves to the river water first, the Sakiya were greatly reducing the water that reached the Moriya, and the Moriya claimed they didn't have enough to irrigate their fields. The Moriya rashtrika sent a message to Siddhartha demanding that the Sakiya cease all diversion—a ridiculous request that was unnecessarily provocative and impossible to observe.

During previous droughts, there had been much conflict, even war, between the Moriya and Sakiya, so Siddhartha invited the rashtrika and his gambojakas to visit and discuss what could be done to reach an agreeable solution to their mutual problem. The rashtrika sent no reply. But, the next day, when Siddhartha and the villagers were on the river shore, digging deeper the channel to the fields, Moriya rafts appeared on the Sakiya loop of the river. The boats sat out in the middle of the water, the Moriya guards surveying the villagers on the beach from this distance, legs apart, spears firmly planted next to them. Siddhartha, ignoring that these guards had entered Sakiya territory without paying a toll, sent a boat with his own four guards to invite the men to shore. The Moriya leader refused with a wave of his hand. Siddhartha decided to ignore them. Along with the villagers, he continued to dig the river channel deeper. The Moriya boats left that evening.

Yasodhara and the women had watched the whole thing from their terraced fields on the hillside. The women around her, and indeed the other villagers later, were full of praise for Siddhartha, saying that he had acted with much restraint and tact, but still got what he wanted, which was to dig the channel deeper. The villagers chortled over Siddhartha sending his guards like that to invite the Moriya guards, already knowing the invitation would be rebuffed. And yet, through this graciousness, he had put himself in the higher position and made the Moriya guards look silly. "I mean," one woman chuckled to the others, "what were they planning to do out there in the middle of the river? Yes-yes, they truly looked foolish, like children who have left home in a huff, but now grow hungry as mealtime approaches and come to loiter at the gate."

Yasodhara, listening to them, felt admiration for Siddhartha, despite her reservations about his recent choices. Later that evening when they were seated on the verandah, he told her that he'd talked this provocation over with Vagantha and the village council and had decided to send another invitation to the Moriya rashtrika, in a few days. Meanwhile, they would work at night to dig the channel. In the daytime, they would stay away from the river so that the Moriya guards, if they returned, would find the beach deserted and take this as a sign of cowardice, of capitulation.

Siddhartha was right. When he did send the invitation to the Moriya rashtrika a few days later, it was accepted immediately.

On the day of the Moriyas' arrival, the villagers were alerted by the toll collector's assistant, sent ahead to inform them that the rashtrika and his entourage had arrived at the point where the Kali Gandak became Sakiya. Siddhartha and Yasodhara, along with the village council, went to greet the visitors. When the barge hit the sand, a chair was sent in and the rashtrika was carried to the shore, as the rest of the delegation waded after him. They reached the beach and Siddhartha went forward to perform the guest rituals, bowing humbly. The rashtrika was thin and tall, with a weak chin and an exhausted look because of a lung disease that shortened his breath. There was something ascetic and predatory about him, Yasodhara thought; he reminded her of a heron stooped forward, hunting for fish in mud. The rashtrika remained cold and aloof throughout the rituals, yet she saw there was a suppressed excitement under this coldness. He believed, foolishly, that he had already won this battle.

Yasodhara had to feed the delegation and so was witness to most of the negotiations. As she moved around discreetly, face inscrutable, ensuring that the men were well fed, she watched her husband's skill as a negotiator. The rashtrika and his council were intractable and soon tempers became frayed on all sides. Yet Siddhartha never lost his temper, smiling meekly throughout, appearing to offer spontaneous compromises that, she could tell, he had come prepared to offer anyway. He was careful not to appear confident but rather played the vacillating and hapless young administrator, turning often to Vagantha and the council, who played along with this tactic; turning also to the rashtrika and his officers, asking what should be done. By keeping calm, he didn't exhaust himself.

Yasodhara had rarely seen her husband negotiate before—and never with such high stakes. She was fascinated by his skill and intelligence, which kept him a few steps ahead of everyone else. Because of his seemingly conciliatory attitude, and his appeal to the rashtrika's wisdom as the older man, the rashtrika gradually began to melt and, as is always the case with those who come in anger and then have their anger softened, the rashtrika's relief at this release made him eager to reach a compromise. Also, Siddhartha had discerned his enemy's weakness, which was the man's shortness of breath. By calling on the rashtrika so many times to express his opinions and thoughts, he exhausted his guest to a point where the man could not think very well.

By the end of the meal, Siddhartha had worked everyone to silence, this silence an assent to his solution, even if it was not posed as *his* solution but one they had all agreed on. Siddhartha had already dug the channel to the depth he wanted; there was nothing to be done about that. The compromise was a sluice gate that would be constructed to limit the amount of water taken from the river. A Moriya inspector would come to live in Mudgala and make sure the Sakiya were only opening the channel on the agreed three days a week.

The next day, the Moriya inspector arrived. From the moment he stepped off the boat and was greeted by Yasodhara and Siddhartha with the guest rituals, it was clear to Yasodhara that he was going to be disagreeable. He reminded her of the rashtrika: that same embattled expression, ready to take offence easily; ascetic-looking despite the numerous rings on his fingers, the chains clinking on his chest. The man had a goitre which moved up and down his neck as he spoke.

When Yasodhara showed him his accommodation—the sentry's hut just outside the boundary wall of their home—the inspector's nose flared with dismay. "Surely not here, sāmini."

"I am afraid so," she replied coldly, feeling no need to placate the man, already sure that, whatever she did, he would not be pleased. "There is no room in our home." He tried on a sneer of disbelief but she looked at him steadily and the sneer faded. To insult the Sakiya rashtrika's wife would result in his immediate return. And she was subtly egging him on to do so.

10

The Python

TWO MONTHS AFTER the inspector's arrival, Siddhartha and Yasodhara were at their meal on the verandah one morning when they heard
the door crashing open in the hut outside and a shout of "Help" from the
inspector. Siddhartha dashed across the courtyard, signalling Yasodhara to
stay where she was, but she ignored his command and went after him.

As she rushed out of the street door, she cried out, for there was
Devadatta, sword in hand, towering over the kneeling inspector. His hand
was wrapped around the man's hair, which had come undone from its
topknot, head jerked back, goitre bobbing up and down. With Devadatta
were six palace guards from Kapilavastu, who kept Siddhartha at bay with
their swords and shields, even as Siddhartha cried out, "I order you to leave
the man alone! I order you as rashtrika!"

"Bhāta!"

At the sound of her voice, Devadatta spun around and his fierceness,
his grip, slackened for a moment. Then he turned to the inspector with a
shout and twisted his head back even further. Yasodhara rushed towards
him, skirting the guards, and grabbed his arm. "Bhāta, please. Why are you
doing this?"

For a moment, they locked gazes and Yasodhara was truly frightened
by the wild blood lust in his eyes. Then Devadatta threw the inspector to
the ground, turned savagely and, with a roar, brought his sword down
over and over on the door of the hut. As Yasodhara watched her brother,

unrecognizable to her in his savagery, she was recalling what the tax collector had told them about Devadatta's cruelty to those who refused to pay taxes.

Devadatta, his blood lust satiated, went limp. Then, with a shake of his head, he regained himself. "Bhagini," he said gruffly and wiped a hand across his mouth.

"What are you doing here, bhāta?" she whispered, even though she knew the answer. "Why have you come to disrupt our lives?"

"Disrupt? I've come to save your honour, to save—"

She cut him off with a wave of her hand and went over to the inspector, to try to help him up.

By now, other villagers, having heard the commotion, were running up the lane. But seeing Devadatta and the palace guards, they hung back, frightened, knowing here was the retribution for those unpaid taxes. Soon Vagantha and Rupasiri arrived, and Yasodhara signalled the headman's wife to help get the inspector to his feet. Between them, they guided the man towards the street door. Before they went in, she glanced back to see her brother and Siddhartha arguing. Devadatta's sword, she was relieved to see, was sheathed.

Yasodhara led the inspector to the well, brought over a stool and sat him down. All the while, the man uttered whining threats, but she barely paid attention to his words, listening instead to the unintelligible sounds of Siddhartha and Devadatta quarrelling. After examining the inspector's knees, which were scratched and bleeding from where he had been forced down on the gravel, Yasodhara went to get rags and some ground herbs she'd made into a healing balm, still straining to hear the argument continuing outside.

She was dressing the inspector's abrasions when Siddhartha strode in, furious. He gave her a desperate glance as he hurried across the courtyard towards their bedroom. She signalled Rupasiri to finish the dressing and rushed after him.

In their room, Siddhartha went to the window and for a moment stood gripping its frame. Then, with a plangent cry, he grabbed the water jug from its stand and threw it to the ground, shards of red pottery scattering in all directions, water darkening the clay floor.

"Surya!"

"I am overridden! Yes, yes," he said, nodding at her silent shock. "Your brother is to take charge of the taxation and deal with the Moriya."

He sat on the bed, clutching his head. After a moment, he looked up at her. "The triad and the sangha . . . they believe that the lower grain taxes I sent was because of these negotiations. They say I've been too soft with the Moriya and it's cost them taxes. According to your bhata, they say I shouldn't have compromised. That I should have diverted the entire Kali Gandak River, if needed, so I could pay the whole tax to Kapilavastu. And there is to be a war with the Moriya! A war!" He looked at her desperately as if begging her to stop this from happening.

"A war?" Yasodhara folded her arms against her stomach. "But how . . . that doesn't make any sense. There's just Devadatta and his six palace guards against the Moriya. He cannot win."

Siddhartha gave her a long, pained look to say there was more. She shakily lowered herself down on a bench and waited. "Ah, Ushas, how to tell you?" He looked at his hands, miserable. "Your bhata, as you know, has always loved and been admired by the vana-dasa tribes. But what we didn't know, and I've just found out, is . . . well, he's married to a chieftain's daughter from a tribe further south."

"Married?" She ran a hand across her face. "Are you sure? . . . Married?"

"Wedded in their terms, but not, certainly, in ours, as the union is not consecrated by the Vedas. And, you see, the tribe Devadatta has married into is related to the one that lives in the forest here, outside Mudgala. Devadatta arrived with his father-in-law, who went into the forest to seek an alliance with his kinsmen. Your brother can count on the tribe here to back him in this conflict. That's how he'll win the war. These tribes don't acknowledge our territorial boundaries. Moriya and Sakiya mean nothing to them. They have their own loyalties. And if the tribe on our side goes to war with the Moriya, they will have the support of tribal kinsmen in Moriya territory."

In her shock, Yasodhara barely heard any of this. She couldn't think of any man she knew who'd even had a vana-dasa mistress; and here her brother was married to a vana-dasa woman. She recalled now that moment when she and Devadatta were riding to Ramagama and she'd asked him about marriage, and guessed from his blush of pride that he had a woman he loved. That chain Devadatta always wore—animal teeth on a leather cord . . . it was his marriage necklace, not a gift from his beloved.

She got up, sat down, got up again. After a moment, she let out a strangled groan. "My pita, my poor pita, how will he bear this?"

Leaving the bedroom, she went to look for Devadatta.

Rupasiri was still soothing the inspector by the well and Yasodhara gave her an agonized look as she went past. The lane outside the street door was deserted, but she knew by instinct where she'd find Devadatta. She hurried along, bubbling with anger and shame.

Scrambling down the riverbank, she saw that the entire village had gathered to watch Devadatta at work. She made her way through the crowd, not looking at anyone, not wanting to see their worry. Only when she reached the front did she stop, watching Devadatta and his six palace guards hacking away at the sluice gate, throwing the amputated pieces of wood in the sand. Her lips curled with contempt at his stupidity, at this heedless action that would lead to nothing.

The water was finally freed and it rushed forward along the channel. Devadatta turned to the villagers, arms lifted, as if expecting a cheer, but they gazed back at him with silent hostility. He noticed Yasodhara then, and saw her contempt. Hurt flickered across his face, then he scowled and spat. He pushed through the crowd and made his way up the bank.

Yasodhara followed him up and along the road that led to the village. When the road turned a corner and the villagers could no longer see them, she called out his name harshly. He waited for her, head bent, pouting. When she came up to him, she hissed, "You've made an idiot, a spectacle, of yourself."

"Ah, bhagini," he cried, "have you no gratitude? I came out of love for you, to protect you. It's an insult that the Moriya sent a man to inspect the water we take, as if we are a Moriya vassal state. They have the audacity to dictate how much water we can use? And your husband accepts this like a coward."

She laughed harshly, a sound like a smashed pot. "It was an agreement. A compromise. We're getting what we want from it, you fool." She gestured towards the channel that was surging along not far from them. "There is another sluice gate at the other end of the channel which will not let the water through. You can't simply flood and flood a field. It will kill the winter rice. Any simpleton knows that."

"A point had to be made." He folded his arms across his chest.

"And what is this point, exactly?" She regarded him, hands on hips. "You say you did it out of love for me, but what you do to Siddhartha affects me too. And then this marriage to a vana-dasa woman?" She watched his features set obstinately. "Ammé, in the Land of the Fathers, must be weeping to see what you've come to. And as for pita, I worry for him when he finds out. Because he will find out now. Everyone will know how you've fought this war, why the vana-dasas helped you, why—"

"Pita is dead."

"What?"

"Pita is dead." Devadatta nodded at her shock. "I . . . I was going to tell you. It happened about a month ago, a disease ravaged the estate and—"

She slapped him.

For a long moment, they stood staring at each other, he clutching his cheek, she grasping her tingling hand. A terrible thought came to her now, rattled into existence by her slap. She leaned forward. "What reward did our uncles and cousin offer you for defeating the Moriya?" He looked away but she saw the truth. "Rashtrika of the Northern Province! Bhāta!" He glowered at her defiantly.

She turned and rushed away. After she had gone some distance, though, she abruptly changed direction and went to her fields. When she reached her plot, she waded in and began to go along the rows, checking the saplings that were growing rapidly now in their new environment, relishing the cool feel of the mud between her toes, the smell of manure and green growing things. A breeze, hot though it was, dried her sweat and she began to hum a cultivating song. She didn't want this moment to end—didn't know what she would do, who she would become, when it did end.

She lost track of time, letting herself sink into the trancelike state that came over her whenever she was in her fields or garden, going down row after row, checking the saplings, pulling out weeds, crushing the occasional insect between her fingers. Finally, she heard her name being called and looked up to see Siddhartha coming along the bund towards her. "Aaah," she murmured, irritated. "Leave me alone, leave me alone."

"Ushas, Ushas!" His voice cracked with agitation. He splashed through the waterlogged fields and she stood watching him approach, clutching weeds in each hand. When he reached her, they stared at each other for a long moment.

"It's really true, then."

He nodded glumly.

Slowly she sank on her knees in the mud.

"Ushas, I'm sorry. So sorry."

"I warned you," she said under her breath. "But you didn't listen," she continued, her voice rising as she stood up. "You didn't listen to me."

"Ah, Ushas, I did what was best for the people who—"

"Best? But look what your actions have caused. A war! You have caused a war!"

His face fissured with shock and hurt, but she couldn't stop herself from pressing on because he had robbed her of her life. "For the sake of those villagers who might, in the end, have survived somehow until the next rains, you are bringing such death and destruction. Many will die because of your actions. There will be widows, children without fathers. Burning homes."

"Ushas, stop, stop."

"For the sake of your Truth of Truths, to prove your Truth of Truths right, you have caused this. And now what do you think of your philosophy? Are you still feeling that oneness with Brahman?"

She turned away and went back to examining her crop, shaking hands reaching out to pluck a weed, to remove an insect. After a little while, she heard Siddhartha leave, his feet plodding heavily through the water and mud.

The moment he was out of the fields, she straightened up and watched him, torn between bitterness and guilt. She looked around at the beloved Himalayas in the distance, the valley laid out below her, the thatched roofs of the village, the children at work in the vegetable plots, the Kali Gandak.

Soon, very soon, I will not know any of this. She felt like she had stepped over the edge of a cliff and was falling through the air, clutching at branches, rocks, ledges, each thing slipping out of her grip.

By the time Yasodhara got home that evening, she was truly exhausted. She entered the courtyard to find her brother and Siddhartha seated at opposite ends of the verandah. They turned to regard her through the gloom, eyes glittering as they stood up. She shook her head as she went across the courtyard towards the bedroom to get her bathing things, wanting only to be left alone. "Tired, tired, need to bathe," she croaked, waving them away, refusing to glance at these men she still loved, but who, driven by their ambitions, had ruined her life—because, yes, Siddhartha's adherence to his philosophy was also a form of ambition.

Back in her room after her bath, dressed in a fresh dhoti and bodice cloth, she lay back on the bed for a moment's rest. The next thing she knew, it was morning and light was pealing in through the open window. She got up with a hiss, rubbed her face to summon up some energy and then went out. Neither Siddhartha nor Devadatta were anywhere to be seen. In the kitchen, she found some gruel in a pot and knew that Rupasiri or one of the women had come and prepared it. With each mouthful, she felt her strength return.

Once she was done, she was suddenly aware that it was eerily quiet both within her house and outside. She went through the street door and made her way down the deserted lane to the village. When she got to the square, she found it was bustling with silent, grim-faced villagers rushing about, loading boxes and baskets onto carts, goats and asses. One of the women saw her, left her work and hurried up to Yasodhara. "I'm not sure if anyone has told you, sāmini, but we're going into the forests to hide. There will be war today."

She nodded, unsurprised. "Do you know where my husband is?"

"Gone with Vagantha and the village council to scout out a place for us in the forest. The Moriya inspector was sent back and Moriya boats have crossed over into our part of the river. Full of armed men. But the lack of any guards on our banks makes them wary to land, thinking they'll be ambushed. So, they just wait out there."

She nodded again. The woman returned to her packing and Yasodhara stood watching everyone busily at work, feeling like a ghost. After a while, she turned and slowly went back up the lane to her home.

Siddhartha returned at midday to find her seated against a verandah pillar, legs straight out, ankles crossed. She watched him come towards her. "Why didn't you go with the others?" he asked wearily, when he reached her. "I told the villagers to take you with them."

She shrugged. "I will not have long in my home. I don't want to leave it."

His face had changed overnight: a great hollowing out, his eyes haunted. "Ushas, believe me, I didn't think it would come to this."

"No, no, I dare say you didn't. But that's the thing, isn't it?" She looked at him steadily. "Out of curiosity, what did you think would happen? Surely you must have expected some consequence for disobeying your pita?"

He was silent for a moment, scuffing his toe in the dirt. "I assumed, being this far up north . . . and I believed, *believe*, that if you act from the truth that we are all one in Brahman, everything . . ." He trailed off feebly. Then added more forcefully: "No matter what happens with this war, Ushas, we have the happiness of loving each other."

She waved away his attempt at reconciliation, then said, quietly, "We'll probably win because of my bhata."

She had heard in the village that Devadatta and his six palace guards, along with her and Siddhartha's own four guards, had long since disappeared into the forest. They had gone to join the tribe. Though she didn't trust her brother with many things, she trusted him as a soldier.

"Yes," Siddhartha said grudgingly, "I think he will succeed."

"There is nothing to be done." She shrugged. "It's all out of our hands."

Later, they went together through the deserted village to the top of the riverbank, each keeping to a side of the path. As they walked along, she told him of her father's death. "Oh, Ushas," he murmured sadly, but made no attempt to cross the path and embrace her, probably guessing from her cold, dull tone that she wanted to be left alone.

Crouching behind bushes, Yasodhara and Siddhartha watched the Moriya soldiers on their rafts. The day progressed and, in the eighth part, when the

Sun was heading home to his beloved Dawn, a new Moriya boat arrived, its men rowing furiously. There were panicked shouts between the newcomers and the others, before all the boats left together, the Moriya shooting their rafts along at a desperate speed.

Siddhartha and Yasodhara exchanged glances. There must have been an ambush.

Later, at the beginning of the second part of the night, when it was completely dark, they saw in the distance a glow of fire above the treetops to the south. Bhogagama, the Moriya village, was in flames.

Soon their own villagers trickled back, coming to sit on the bank as they watched the lit-up sky. There was no jubilation among them. Rupasiri, seated beside Yasodhara, said softly, "It is an empty victory, daharé. For years to come, even generations, the Moriya will never forget this."

Yasodhara nodded. She glanced at Siddhartha and saw he had heard this too. It was taking all his will to keep that mild expression on his face.

When they finally retired, she and Siddhartha lay apart on their bed, hands behind heads, looking at the ceiling. At the first light of dawn, they got up and did the sacrifices with the rest of the village, Yasodhara feeling that there was something heartbreaking and forlorn about this routine now.

Sometime later, hearing the bell clang, she went to the street door, Siddhartha right behind her. They stepped out to find Devadatta, his guards, and two vana-dasa chieftains, all on horses. The chieftains were lean and wrinkled, and wore nothing but loincloths, many rings on their noses and ears, and many necklaces of shell and animal teeth around their necks. She examined her brother, too: he was scarred and dishevelled from the battle, his body grimy and sweat-streaked; yet his chin was thrust out, his back straight, a successful warrior. Devadatta gruffly introduced the chieftains—one the leader of the local tribe, the other Devadatta's father-in-law. Yasodhara looked at the latter closely and saw that he was dignified and stately—no different, really, from Vagantha. She'd never really studied a vana-dasa in this way before, never thought of them as fathers, brothers, mothers, sisters, husbands, wives.

Siddhartha didn't ask these warriors to dismount and enter, nor did he thank them. He just stood in silence once the introductions were over.

The men grinned and nodded at the insult. Then, with a bow to Devadatta, the new rashtrika, the chieftains turned their horses and rode away.

Devadatta dismounted, his face stern. He tied his horse to a nearby tree, then signalled Siddhartha to follow him into the compound. With a hollow laugh, Siddhartha trailed after him—and Yasodhara followed too, wondering what would happen next. Devadatta led them to the receiving room. When he entered, he stopped, startled at the sight of open trunks that were half-filled with objects. "But what is this?" he demanded, truly surprised. "There is no need to leave so soon." He turned to Siddhartha. "I . . . I expected you to stay and hand over the administration."

Siddhartha picked up a clay pot and examined it as if he had never seen the object before.

Devadatta turned to Yasodhara. "I . . . I'd hoped we might have some time together, bhagini."

"How can we stay, bhāta? My husband's authority has been superseded by you. The only thing to do, the only proper and dignified thing, is to leave right away." And to make her point, she went back to packing, gloating bitterly at her brother's fear. The reality of what he had taken on was sinking in.

"Our matalas, Mahanama, the ministers, will be unhappy. They want Siddhartha to hand over his duties properly."

"The village council will advise and guide you, as they did me." Siddhartha put the pot down, gave Devadatta a wan smile and left the room.

That evening, Vagantha began Devadatta's tutoring. Yasodhara was witness to the meeting, alongside Siddhartha. She watched her brother poring over the tablets of survey records and tax figures under a lamp. He frowned sternly as he asked the gambojaka questions, sitting on his hands so no one could see their tremor. Vagantha answered politely but obliquely.

Here was the thing her brother had always wanted—an appointment worthy of a prince. But, now that he had got it, he was up against what he'd been able to ignore so far: lack of intelligence and understanding about how to administer a land. And then suddenly, despite everything her brother had done to her, she felt sorry for him. Because he was her brother and their ties went back to the beginning of their lives. She'd loved him for a long time. With this acknowledgement, she also felt that her parents, watching from the Land of the Fathers, wished her to be kind to their misguided son, to forgive him; she felt the pressure of her parents' will, an obligation to forgive.

So Yasodhara took up a lamp and, leaving the men alone, went to her granary. She scooped up a handful of seeds, let herself out the street door and made her way cautiously to the shrine under the acacia tree, holding the lamp before her so she could see any possible dangers in the dark. When she got to the tree, she put the lamp on the ground and knelt before the shrine. She placed the grain inside, then bent over, forehead resting on the earth. "Mitta, I have come to say goodbye." And now she began to weep, finally understanding that she was going away, that she would never worship at this shrine again, whispering how difficult it was to forgive her brother, begging the devata to help her forgive him; telling the devata also of her sorrow at her father's death, how his dying had permanently sealed shut that part of her; how Ramagama was truly no longer her home, and she nobody's daughter. Finally, she became quiet, forehead still pressed to the earth, listening to the sound of cicadas, the distant hoot of an owl. Then suddenly there was a rustle of leaves in the tree above and she sat up, startled. Something was moving through the branches. With a gasp, she grabbed her lamp and scuttled back, away from the tree, holding up the light. At first, she couldn't see anything but then, with a thump, a python dropped from the tree. Uncoiling itself, the snake, without even a glance in her direction, began to majestically slither away. She held the lamp higher to watch the snake depart. It was a sign, a command from the devata to reconcile with her brother. No, more than a sign. It was the devata himself, in the guise of a snake, leaving the acacia tree because tomorrow she would be gone too, and there would be no one to worship him. She was filled with wonder, with peace, and with sadness.

Yasodhara told Siddhartha that she wanted to leave the next morning well before dawn. That way, they could travel far enough to reach a place where they'd dock the rafts and do a makeshift version of the morning sacrifice, using their sacred marital fire, which would be carried back with them in a brazier. But her real reason for the early departure was that she didn't want to say goodbye to the villagers, the women in particular—nor to see Mudgala, where she had been so happy, recede from her, lost forever.

Before they left, Yasodhara went to her brother's room to say goodbye. She stood a moment in the doorway gazing at Devadatta, who slept lying on his back, one arm flung out, the other behind his head. She recalled all the times as a little girl when she would creep into his room, afraid of the dark or a nightmare, and find him sleeping thus; how she would crawl into his bed and he would put his arm around her, still half-asleep as he murmured, "It's nothing, bhagini, you're safe now." She went up to the bed and gently shook him. He opened his eyes and stared at her unseeing at first, then with recognition.

"Bhagini?"

She sat on the edge of the bed. "Bhāta, we go now." He made to sit up, but she gently pushed him back. "There is no need to come and see us off." She was silent a moment, looking at her hands. "I've been thinking much more about your marriage. The vana-dasa are so foreign to me, to most of us. But they too are mothers and fathers, brothers and sisters, husbands and wives. They too love no different from us. I recall Ananda once telling me of their hospitality and kindness to merchants who lose their way in the forest or break a wheel, or are caught in the rains." She reached out and pressed his arm. "Our parents only ever wanted our happiness. They would have struggled to accept this union, as I have. I remember how, when I used to ask you about marriage in the past, you avoided the question. Yet, I could tell you loved someone. So, I . . . I see that she makes you happy. And our parents in the Land of the Fathers also see this, I am sure." She touched his cheek. "But be worthy of that love, bhāta. Allow her love to make you a better man."

Now he did push himself into a sitting position. "Must you go, Ushas?"

She nodded and her eyes welled with tears. "We are all that's left now of our family, bhāta. Let us love each other, no matter what the circumstances." Then she kissed his forehead and hastily left the room.

Despite her and Siddhartha's attempt to depart in secret, word had spread, and when they came down to the river, the villagers had gathered silently to see them off, faces flickering and elongated in the light of the torches they carried. Vagantha and Rupasiri performed the formal farewell rituals, reciting mantras for a safe journey, and the villagers picked up the refrain—a murmuring swell, like wind through leaves. Yasodhara could not tear her eyes away from the women who also looked back at her, eyes begging her not to go, knowing their pleas were futile. When the rituals were done, Rupasiri came forward to embrace Yasodhara. Before she could do so, Yasodhara fell to her knees and kissed Rupasiri's feet. "Pitucché, bless me in my life to come," she cried in a strangled voice, wanting to acknowledge her debt to this woman. A murmur of wonder went out among the villagers that she, the rashtrika's wife, had prostrated herself before the gambojaka's wife. This action released something in the villagers, and they began to weep. Rupasiri placed both hands on Yasodhara's head to bless her, then raised Yasodhara up. They gazed at each other, touching each other's cheeks as they wept. Then Rupasiri unknotted a fold in her dhoti with shaking hands and held something out. A chain made of acacia seeds. Yasodhara gasped as she examined it. "When . . . ?"

Rupasiri smiled. "Yesterday, daharé. The women helped me, too. Plucked from your tree."

Yasodhara moved her gaze to the women, nodding and smiling her thanks through her tears. She slipped the chain over her head.

Siddhartha touched her arm. "Ushas, we should go." He pointed to the two rafts waiting for them. The four guards they had come with all those years ago were already on board.

Yasodhara took one last look at the villagers. Then, with a nod, she turned and followed Siddhartha out to a raft. Siddhartha gave a signal to the guards, who thrust their long poles in the water. The raft glided forward. It struck her then that she had forgotten to tell Rupasiri about the python in the tree. Ah, never mind, I'll tell her tomorrow, she thought—and immediately a hollow cry echoed within her.

There would be no tomorrow.

DUKKHA II

IN THE WEEKS that follow Siddhartha's resurfacing, messengers bring Yasodhara further news of his philosophy; and slowly she begins to understand more about this Middle Way. He, the Awakened One, now claims there is no such thing as an Atman, a permanent entity in every being. Nor, by extension, does there exist a permanent force that is the universe, called Brahman. Instead, everything is in flux and changing all the time, including each person, including the world, the stars, the planets. Including the gods. Everything is on fire—burning itself out, being reborn, burning itself out again, only to then be reborn once more and burn out once more, an endless cycle.

Siddhartha offers a way out of this eternal cycle through comprehending the truth of existence, at the centre of which is understanding dukkha. Though what he means by this, Yasodhara still doesn't understand. The word is so vague. "Dukkha" covers so many states of negative feeling: dissatisfaction, irritation, annoyance, great suffering, etc.

As the days pass and messengers come and go, her anger towards him increases. Thanks to his growing fame, she can't go anywhere in Kapilavastu without people studying her with avid curiosity to see how she is taking this news of his resurfacing. Unable to bear their glances and smirks, she stops going out on foot, instead using the quarter's palanquin, its curtains drawn as the bearers jog through the streets, so she won't have to meet the janata's stares. Women of her gotra and other noble women pay visits to the quarters, hoping to see her. But she keeps to her room during the visits, refusing to go down to meet them; or if she happens to return from an errand and encounters them in the courtyard, she nods pleasantly, then claims tiredness or some chore and escapes.

Often at night now, when her son is asleep in the antechamber, Yasodhara quietly drags forward a wooden chest, one normally kept hidden
behind other chests and draped with a quilt. Kneeling before it, she takes
a deep breath, then stealthily opens the lid and peers inside. There in the
centre of the trunk lies Siddhartha's shorn hair, his jewels, and that yellow
shawl he sent back to her through the charioteer Channa, in whose chariot
he made his escape ten years ago, disguised as a Vessa. The coils of hair, a
symbol of his renunciation, are dried and discoloured, and look like a nest
of snakes, giving off a sickly-sweet odour of rot. Resting her chin on the
edge of the chest, she recalls her shock and disbelief when her uncle and
brother came rushing into her bedroom that morning with the news that
Siddhartha was gone. "Go after him, send your soldiers," she'd screamed
at her uncle with a fierceness she wouldn't have dared use before. "Send
your spies into the jungle after him!" But Suddhodana stood motionless
and looked at her helplessly. Siddhartha had already crossed over into
Moriya territory, and couldn't be captured.

She doesn't remember much of what happened after that, or rather she
remembers only brief moments: Devadatta's sweat-streaked face, grim
with defeat when he came to tell her that he and some palace guards had
set out nonetheless but failed to catch Siddhartha in time; the charioteer
Channa coming towards her across the gloom of the receiving room, bearing in his arms a yellow bundle, which he presented to her nervously—and
her horror when she unknotted the shawl with trembling fingers to find
Siddhartha's hair and jewels. She had demanded to know how Siddhartha
had seemed when the charioteer left him on the banks of the Anoma River.
"Happy, sāmini, happy," the man had replied with an apologetic wince.

After that, she lost track of time and herself. To this day, she has almost
no memory of what she did and said in the months that followed; and still
wouldn't know, if not for her aunt and some of the women who told her,
later on, that she'd wandered the city barefoot and draped in Siddhartha's
yellow shawl, looking for her husband.

Only one moment from that lost period has stayed with her: she comes
to herself in her bedroom, hearing her name called loudly by her aunt
as the other women shriek. One of them leaps across her room towards
the window where, turning now, she sees Rahula, wailing with hunger, on

the edge of the windowsill, where she has left him. And then she becomes aware that she is naked and seated before her mirror, face fully made up. Later the women told her that she had said, with a high laugh, as if nothing dangerous had happened, "But is it already time for the sacrifices?" After that, her aunt and the women took over Rahula's welfare, and a wet nurse was hired to feed him.

In the chest are also items Yasodhara has no memory of buying in the Vessa Quarter: a pair of slippers for Siddhartha, a vase for a window in their new house, a yak-skin rug for their new bedroom, woollen blankets, a chain of amber beads she evidently made for Siddhartha—all in preparation for his return and their move to a new home. This was something, so her aunt told her later, she was convinced would happen. Most of the items have been eaten by silverfish, disintegrated or faded in these past ten years, and yet she can't bring herself to throw them away.

Even now, ten years on, she asks herself how such a thing could have happened. How could she have just slipped through the cracks of sanity into another reality in which she believed, fiercely, in an illusion? This period of madness has meant that she has lost her authority in the women's quarters. Any excessive show of emotion by her, any decision the other women don't agree with, is seen as a trace of that madness.

And now she is worried again about her stability. Recently she's started to have that dream she hasn't dreamt in a long time; a dream whose meaning is so obvious she doesn't need a medicine woman or priest to interpret it.

In it, she is wandering in a forest, gathering firewood, when suddenly she sees an elephant in a thicket ahead. For a moment they are still, regarding each other, then with a bellow the elephant rushes at her, trunk raised. Dropping her firewood, she plunges through the trees, the tusker crashing after her. As she runs, she can hear the thunder of its feet, the shattering and crunching of undergrowth, can taste the dust stirred up as it gains on her. At the edge of the forest is a well, into which a nearby tree has pushed its roots through the brick lining. She clambers down one of the roots into the well and hangs there in the gloom waiting for the elephant to give up and go away. But then, hearing a rustle, she glances down and sees a cobra winding its way up that very root towards her. She searches around frantically for another root she might swing to but sees that on the other four roots are four more snakes, their red eyes glowing in the dim-ness. And now, to her horror, smoke is seeping into the well and she hears the crackle of burning brush. A forest fire has started around the well and soon the smoke spirals in, choking her.

She first had that dream on the night of her return to Kapilavastu from Mudgala. And now, as then, when she wakes the following morning there are welts on her arms where she has furiously scratched herself in her sleep.

A Woman Eaten
and Eaten

1

In the Realm of Ghosts

KAPILAVASTU: MASSIVE WOODEN fortifications in the distance, flares blazing at guard posts along the ramparts, brass-studded gates fifteen times the height of a man. As Yasodhara gazed at the approaching city, panic trembled through her body, indistinguishable from the juddering of the cart in which she and Siddhartha travelled. Her new life was now real; the women's quarters awaited her, with her aunt Prajapati as her new mother-in-law— yes, *new* was how it felt, as if she were not a long-married woman, but a young bride arriving at her future home.

As the chariot rumbled across the drawbridge, she rested a hand against her forehead. "Ushas." Siddhartha touched her shoulder gingerly, but she shrugged away from him. She would not conceal her misery from him; why should she? Let him pickle in what he'd done to her.

When their cart pulled up to the toll booth, the Keeper of the Gates came to examine their chariot, to see what goods they'd brought and tax them accordingly. He lifted up the back flap and his stern expression softened to astonishment. "Dahara, why are you here?" he cried, forgetting himself, for he had known Siddhartha ever since he'd been an inquisitive child who passed many segments of the day with the Keeper, watching him work.

"My term in the north is over, Sonanda." The gatekeeper, his eyes widening at Siddhartha's grave tone, seemed to understand that Siddhartha was, for some reason, in disgrace.

As their cart rumbled on past the toll booth, Yasodhara gazed out at the city, as if seeing it for the first time, noting how, even at this time when the stars were out, the streets were as busy as they would be during the day in Ramagama. The wavering torches and lanterns carried by pedestrians, the flares in brackets before shops, made the people of Kapilavastu look as if they were inhabitants of an underwater kingdom. And now she recalled that she had thought the same thing the night she had arrived here as a new bride—truly another lifetime ago.

Here in this city the heat was thicker, and so it concentrated the stink of clogged drains, horse and bullock dung, the cooking smells of roasting grain and charring meat—all mingling pungently with the ever-present tang of urine. As she pressed her shawl to her face, she noticed cows and goats nosing through a pile of refuse. How emaciated and filthy they were compared with the animals in Mudgala, and sickly yellow under the lights of the torches. In Mudgala, at this time of the evening, she would be sitting on her verandah fanning herself, legs stretched out and crossed at the ankles in contentment as she watched fireflies dance in the courtyard.

Siddhartha was regarding her intently, his eyes luminescent in the flares. She turned once more from his appeal.

They were approaching the palace and the road broadened, the poverty falling away, the thatched roofs of mansions rising grandly around them. Finally, they reached the royal square with its great pillared santagara in one corner, where issues of the kingdom were decided by the sangha. A royal audience platform stood in the centre of the square, mounted from all sides by vertiginous steps. At the far end of the royal square was the high wattle and daub perimeter wall of the palace, its large wooden gates studded with brass knobs. They made their way along the wall and, as they turned the corner into a side street, Yasodhara saw her aunt Prajapati and a few serving maids (alerted by a rider sent by the gatekeeper) waiting to greet them before the street doors in the side wall that led into the women's quarters. Her aunt—lit by flickering torches the maids held up—carried a tray with incense and water for the homecoming rituals.

As Yasodhara alighted shakily from the cart, she examined her aunt, who stared back at her, face inscrutable, unsurprised. Prajapati had probably expected they would be sent back once Devadatta was established in his position as rashtrika; she might even know by now of the war with the Moriya. Once Prajapati had performed the cleansing rituals on Siddhartha, he stepped over the small, circular brass mandala embedded in the street and was in home territory. Yasodhara stood before the mandala with its embossed svastika smeared in red saffron paste and looked numbly at her aunt, longing for comfort but knowing she wouldn't get any from this woman. Her aunt, thin and tall, her bony face handsomely austere, had the inwardly turned expression of someone in pain, eyelids half-lowered as if nursing a perpetual headache from the cares thrust on her by her husband, and his neglect and cruelty. Her elaborate hairstyle weighed down her head, like a large flower on a fragile stem.

Prajapati began the ritual, waving incense over Yasodhara to chase away any evil spirits who had travelled in the folds of her clothes and might try to enter the home. Yasodhara reached across the mandala and took, with faintly trembling hands, the small water pot, washing her feet to purify herself. When she finally stepped over the threshold of the mandala, her aunt's embrace was perfunctory, formal.

Prajapati led her and Siddhartha silently into the women's courtyard and up a flight of stairs to the second floor, the wooden steps creaking and sighing under their feet. She guided them along a corridor towards the suite they would occupy, the polished wooden walls of the passage glowing from lamps in brackets. The women of the quarters came to the doors of their rooms to watch them pass, spectral under the corridor lamps. Yasodhara had met most of them on previous visits with her mother and also during the first weeks of her marriage, but she didn't know them well: her uncle's two concubines Sumana and Upasama, the two widowed relatives Tissa and Utara, the orphaned spinster cousin Mitta. Yasodhara saw that there were two new young women in the quarters, and her eyes rested momentarily on their lovely faces, wondering who they were and what their role was here. All of these women returned her gaze, some with looks of sympathy or curiosity, others with stares of contempt or malicious pleasure at her and Siddhartha's fall. Here too, because of the heat, smells were intense— the suffocating odour of women's perfumes and unguents, the cloying heaviness of sesame oil from the lamps, and, beneath it all, a sourness that reminded her of unwashed hair. "This is my life, among these women," she thought, light-headed.

Siddhartha's half-sister, Sundari Nanda, was waiting in their suite, perfuming the room with incense, ordering around the servants and slaves who had carried their trunks up and were lighting lamps. Sundari Nanda, twenty-seven and still unmarried, had the sharp, flustered movements of a spinster. Her beauty had faded, a dryness to it. Her voice, when she greeted them, was harsh with delight. "Bhāta! Bhagini! How joyful to see you after all these years!" Yasodhara could not tell if she was being genuine or was gloating. Perhaps Sundari Nanda, disappointed by life, might not know herself what her motives were, what emotions shaded her tone.

"Tell my pita I am too tired to come to him tonight," Siddhartha said to Prajapati. "I will present myself tomorrow morning." His tone was formal as if addressing her as the devi, the queen, and not as his stepmother. Yasodhara knew this formality came from holding back his emotions. Prajapati examined him a moment, then nodded. As she turned to leave, her eyes rested for a moment on Yasodhara, appraising. Yasodhara turned away wearily from her gaze.

That night she could not sleep, her body slick with sweat from the heat. The city's noises came to her through the window: *clip-clop* of horse hooves, dogs barking, the susurration of sandalled feet. Siddhartha was motionless beside her, but she knew he was not asleep—his breath was uneven and shallow. Finally, not caring that he knew she was awake, she crept from the bed, wrapped a shawl about her naked body and went into the antechamber, a dark, windowless room, where, by the moonlight coming in from the bedroom window, she groped her way to a low divan and sat, knees drawn up, back resting against the cool wooden wall.

After a moment, her fingers began to rip absent-mindedly at a tassel on her shawl. Siddhartha stirred in bed and she stiffened, afraid he would call to her, or worse, come and join her. When he continued to remain in bed, she was relieved. *What a place we've come to that I dread his company.* It was as if, in coming to Kapilavastu, she found herself in a new marriage, the river a birth canal through which she had passed to this new life.

She finally fell asleep in the antechamber and dreamt for the first time of being chased by the elephant, waking to welts on her arms.

The next morning, after the sacrifice, Siddhartha ate in their room while Yasodhara served him. Both of them were silent, withdrawn into their own thoughts and fears. Then, with a desperate, pleading glance at her, like a child being sent off to his first day of fencing and riding lessons, Siddhartha tied his sash tight, set his turban on his head and went to see his father. Wearily, Yasodhara watched him go; she had no comfort to offer.

After she had eaten, she sat on the edge of a divan, watching a maid clear up the dishes and stack them in a reed basket to be taken down and washed. Through the window, she could hear the women in the courtyard below, their muffled chatter, the sound of water being drawn from the pond, someone practising a song. The light coming in was already a heavy gold, like hot ghee. She noted that the window frame needed a coat of paint and was rotting in places. A few wooden slats on the louvred windows were broken. A fly buzzed around her face evading the swat of her palm fan.

There was a discreet knock on the door. Sundari Nanda put her head in and grimaced apologetically. "In the morning, all the women gather in the courtyard."

Yasodhara nodded, slowly uncurled her limbs and rose from the divan. Here it was, the moment she must truly face her new life.

When she entered the courtyard, she paused for a moment, taking in the eight women on reed mats around Prajapati, who was seated cross-legged on a charpoy. A fretful irritation flickered across her aunt's face at seeing her, before her expression settled into guarded blankness. She beckoned Yasodhara to come and take her place among the women. There was a swollen silence as Yasodhara made her way towards the circle. Not looking at the women, she picked her way to an empty spot between her aunt Utara and the old concubine Sumana. "Here, daharé," the old concubine said, once she was seated, and held out a bowl of rice to be de-stoned, a twinkle in her eyes. Yasodhara bent over it, close to tears at this kindness.

Around her, the poor relatives were busy shelling peas, picking stones out of rice or pulses, mending torn shawls or turbans—none of these tasks expected of them by their devi, but done to give themselves some dignity and worth. Sumana, long passed over by Suddhodana, worked alongside the relatives. But Upasama, the other concubine, still enjoyed the raja's favour and felt no such obligation. She sat on a swing in a corner, the two new young women at her feet. Seeing them grouped thus, Yasodhara realized with a sickening lurch that the girls, both teenagers, were not relatives; they were her uncle's latest concubines. She gazed at their lovely faces, horrified. One of them was learning the veena from a musician, the other was trying to teach her parrot an off-colour verse. There was in their faces, their gestures, that forced ripening one sees in beggar children. Sundari Nanda, who seemed to belong somewhere between the two groups, had taken up her bowl of rice to be de-stoned and gone to sit with the concubines, giggling and chortling along with them at the parrot's attempts to learn the verse.

Yasodhara noticed that her aunt had seen her abhorrence at the new concubines. Their eyes met for a moment, then Yasodhara hastily bent over her task.

As she worked away, she studied the women, weighing what she knew of them. Their weaknesses and temperaments had not mattered to her in the past, but now she had to consider each one carefully, judge if they were friend or foe.

She looked first at Tissa, who was the eldest, even older than Prajapati— a country cousin of her mother and aunt's, who had lost her entire family in a sweating-fever epidemic and been rendered dumb by the shock. She was a bent-over stick of a woman who looked frail but had surprising energy and stamina, always busy as if to keep her past at bay. Now, even as the other women sat around at their various tasks, Tissa had snatched a broom from a slave and was vigorously sweeping the leaves in the courtyard. Seeing Yasodhara examining her, she nodded, smiled and winked as if to say, "I see your fear, I am watching out for you." She was a friend. A woman whose tragedy had made her kind.

The other older relative, Utara, who sat beside Yasodhara, was also Prajapati's cousin. Her husband had been a compulsive gambler and, on his death, she had been reduced to penury. Childless, and without anyone to look after her, she would have had to sell herself into domestic bondage as a slave, like many noblewomen in her position, if Prajapati had not heard of her plight and invited Utara into her home. Since her arrival, she had developed a mysterious pain in her legs which persisted, despite various balms and potions brought by medicine women. She was red-eyed and haggard, with the preoccupied look of one in chronic pain. A friend, thought Yasodhara—if only because she was too absorbed by her pain for any malice or spite.

The old concubine Sumana had already proved she was a friend. In her mid-fifties, she still had a sweet, heart-shaped face that was always merry, and her laugh sounded like little clinking cymbals. She was willing to see the good in anyone—a quality that might have served her well as a courtesan, except that Sumana was gullible to any story of misfortune. When admonished for allowing herself to be tricked she always stuck out her tongue in self-mockery and declared with a giggle, "Nothing to be done." The endowment Prajapati had settled on her, once Suddhodana had tired of the woman and wanted her gone, had been cheated from Sumana years ago by various relatives. When the devi heard that Sumana had lost her house, duped out of it by a nephew, she'd visited Sumana, fallen by now to the prostitutes' quarter, and found her living in a room among vesiyās. Sumana had burst into tears when she saw Prajapati, but soon found something to laugh about and sent out for sweets she could not afford. Prajapati had invited Sumana back to the women's quarters, where she was much loved by all the others.

Yasodhara watched Prajapati, bent over an accounts tablet, lips moving as she did the additions, her elaborate hairstyle weighing down her head. "You have to make allowances for your pitucché, Ushas," her mother had always said, reminding her that Suddhodana had never loved Prajapati; reminding her that when Prajapati's sister Maya died in childbirth, Prajapati had to nurse Siddhartha as well as her own daughter; that Prajapati had to further bear the brunt of her husband's anger and sorrow as Suddhodana went around saying that the wrong sister had died. "It takes courage to bear such contempt, Ushas," her mother had always said, "to bear the humiliation of the concubines my brother installs in that women's quarters. Try to understand, Ushas, and be kind." But Yasodhara wasn't able to be kind back then. Perhaps, she realized now, this was because she saw in her aunt's plight the true powerlessness of women.

She turned her eyes next to her cousin Mitta—and saw that Mitta had been waiting to trap her gaze. Her cousin smiled with cruel amusement as she tossed a shelled pea into a bowl, her expression saying, "Yes, I see your fear." About Yasodhara's age, Mitta had been orphaned at ten when she lost her family to a fever that had disfigured and scarred her skin, leaving pimples all over her face and body. These had now grown red and pustular in the hot season. Yasodhara knew her cousin was feared and hated by the other women. How funny, she thought, that Mitta's name meant "friend," but the woman herself was like a malevolent house ghost, attacking for no reason. The other women never knew when they might discover a dead mouse in their bed, a favourite shawl ripped, a vase they'd received as a gift shattered. They feared Mitta because there was something implacable about her hatred, her spiteful presence flitting about the quarters, hugging the walls of the corridors when anyone passed her as if she feared contagion, refusing to fraternize with the others and staying in her room when not busy. The other women periodically petitioned Prajapati to get rid of her, but she never did because she was oddly dependent on Mitta. The palace household was frightened of her in a way they weren't of their devi. If Prajapati had a troublesome worker, she only had to mention them to Mitta and the problem was dealt with.

Yasodhara heard a sudden harsh laugh and turned to take in Upasama, the other older concubine, a haughty woman with a hooked nose on which she wore a sparkling jewel. Seeing Yasodhara considering her, she gave her a baleful look under hooded eyes, as if she were the raja's wife and Yasodhara an extra mouth to feed. In her early forties, she was still beautiful, which was the reason Suddhodana had not ordered that she should go. She was also willing to service any guest whom the raja wanted to please or flatter. It was rumoured that she, rather than the city's courtesans, had initiated many of the young men of the court into the art of love.

Finally, Yasodhara turned to study her cousin. Sundari Nanda was unmarried at twenty-eight. In her younger years, no man had been good enough for her and she'd turned down many proposals, some from very worthy candidates. Gradually the offers trickled away as she aged and her beauty began to fade. Now, the only men who would have her were much older widowers. Yasodhara could not tell if she was friend or foe.

The other women were eyeing Yasodhara as she regarded them, and finally Sumana the old concubine asked, with a merry smile, "Is it true, daharé, that you did your own field work in Mudgala? We heard rumours it was so."

Forcing herself to sound cordial, Yasodhara said, "Yes, I did learn to do it." Then, with great feeling: "I enjoyed doing it, the work brought me peace."

Some of the women murmured in sympathy mixed with wonder that she, a raja's daughter, had done such menial work.

"You aren't the only one here to do field work." Mitta ripped open a pod and tossed the peas into her bowl. "Tissa, being from the country, also tended her own fields." Tissa nodded vigorously to say yes, she certainly had, and whisked her broom briskly, nodding and smiling at Yasodhara to stay brave.

Yasodhara smiled vaguely as she bent over her bowl, not wishing to engage with Mitta.

"Well I think it's vile. I would never work the fields." Mitta gestured with disgust at Yasodhara's feet. "Your soles, they're cracked. There's still dirt in your toenails."

"Then it's a good thing our aunt took you in, Mitta," Yasodhara fired back before she could stop herself. "Otherwise you would have been lucky to get field work. Most likely you would have ended up a slave or become a ganikā. Though," and she gestured to Mitta's face, "the latter is unlikely."

For a moment she and Mitta stared at each other, neither backing down.

Prajapati said nothing, and bent even further over her accounts tablet. Avoiding her duty, Yasodhara thought bitterly. I am her daughter-in-law; I should be seated on that charpoy with her. My mother must be weeping in the Land of the Fathers to see this.

Yasodhara returned to de-stoning the rice in her bowl, making sure to keep her expression contemptuous so Mitta wouldn't think she'd surrendered. And all the while a heavy misery was rising in her. In Mudgala right now, the women would be in their fields working in rhythm as they sang a song. A pang went through her to think of her own plots untended, abandoned; to think of her friends who would soon be sitting under a tree at the top of the slope, sipping on sweetened water and chewing betel, gossiping and laughing. She knew they would be thinking of her and missing her, as she did them. She wiped a hand across her sweaty brow. No, no, she mustn't think of all that. If she let such thoughts in, she would not be able to keep going.

"Yes," Utara, the widow of the gambler, said, finally breaking the tense silence, "the things we take for granted when we have our health. I would happily do field work or even dig roads if it would rid me of this terrible pain." She moaned and rubbed her thighs and knees.

"I have done field work," one of the young concubines offered in a small voice. "My parents, though shopkeepers in our village, did have their own fields."

The other women remained silent, glancing at Prajapati, who pretended not to hear. Then Upasama, the older concubine, added languorously, "This conversation is exceedingly dull. The croaking of the parrot interests me more."

Another strained silence descended on the courtyard. Yasodhara bent over her bowl, biting on her lower lip so she wouldn't start crying. Occasionally, she glanced up at the buildings surrounding the courtyard, noting how sadly shabby they were, not from poverty but from neglect. The wattle and daub walls of the ground floor were in need of a new coating of mud, the wooden walls of the upper two floors in need of a good lacquering, the varnish so worn in places that the wood was exposed and had moss growing on it. The thatch was dishevelled, sprouting weeds, the courtyard absent of any flowering bushes or pretty plants. Through an archway, she could see a walled garden full of weeds, the soil broken and dry.

It felt impossible, unreal, that this was her life.

After a while, Prajapati looked up and held out a tablet to Sundari Nanda. "Take this to the Manager of the Granaries, dhītā."

As Sundari Nanda went to get the tablet, Yasodhara stood up, eager for escape. "I will go with you, ñātiké. I'd like to see the granaries."

She and her cousin left the quarters and walked in silence for a while, crossing the busy main palace courtyard with its intricately carved and painted wooden pillars that held up the verandahs running around the four sides. Doors led off the verandahs into palace offices, from which streams of people came and went.

After they'd passed through an archway into the granary courtyard, Yasodhara turned to her cousin, raised an eyebrow and murmured, "Those new girls . . ."

Sundari Nanda giggled, but seeing that Yasodhara remained grave, she shook her head mournfully. "Yes, yes, it's terrible. And my pita now sixty-five."

"Who are they, these unfortunate creatures, ñātiké?"

"The one teaching the parrot is Sanga. A simple village girl whose parents, shopkeepers, fell on bad times. On one of my pita's tours of the villages, the girl caught his eye and the parents, with other children to feed, were happy to sell her. After all, it's a privilege to be honoured thus by the raja." Sundari Nanda giggled again to say she was being ironic.

"How . . . how old is she?"

"Seventeen."

"And how long has she been here?"

"Four years."

"She was thirteen," Yasodhara murmured sadly.

"She sends whatever money or gifts my pita gives her back to her family," Sundari Nanda offered, as if this justified the girl's plight.

"And the other girl?"

"Ah, Visaka. Now she's truly a trained courtesan. From a Brahmin family, she was orphaned at three when her entire village was destroyed in an epidemic. The ganikā Vimala adopted and groomed her and, at the age of thirteen, auctioned her off to the highest bidder. My pita of course had to have such a jewel and—"

She broke off because Yasodhara was staring at her, aghast. "Why I . . . I've met the girl as a child! When I went to visit the ganikā after my marriage."

Unbidden, an image rose in Yasodhara's mind of Suddhodana's hairy, sagging body pressed on the girl's delicate frame. "This is my life," she thought again, horrified. "This is the home in which I will have to live the rest of my days."

When she returned to the courtyard, she felt suddenly as if the women had transformed in her absence, in the way a traveller in a ghost tale might become aware that his fellow travellers are not humans, but ghosts who have a deadly purpose for him.

2

Siddhartha and His Mentors

AS SIDDHARTHA WALKED towards the palace receiving hall for his audience with his father, he recalled the numerous times Suddhodana had beaten or humiliated him before a gathering for not succeeding in the manly sports, accusing Siddhartha of deliberately failing in order to spite him. He recalled, too, his father's anger and hurt when the Senapati of Kapilavastu had chosen Siddhartha over Mahanama for the Savatthi Court. To revenge that perceived slight, his father had tried to humble him with that inconsequential posting in Mudgala. He could only imagine his father's frustration when Siddhartha had thrived in his post, turning the Northern Province into a success. *And this is the dance I am entering into* he thought bitterly.

The entrance to the receiving hall was crowded with jostling petitioners, kept at bay by guards. A palace official went among the petitioners selecting (no doubt for a bribe) who went in and who was kept out. When the official saw Siddhartha, he barked at the petitioners, "Clear the way for the raja's son." Siddhartha made his way through the crowd, conscious of the petitioners' hungry eyes on him, their desperation to have their cases heard like heat rising from their bodies.

At the front of the hall, Suddhodana sat on his throne, talking in a low, worried voice to his brother Amitodhana and his nephew Mahanama, who stood on either side of him, their heads bent towards him. They were deep in conversation, no doubt, about what had happened in Mudgala. None of the triad had noticed Siddhartha yet and so he was free to study them.

In the twelve years that had passed, the muscles of his father's powerful chest, arms and torso had blurred into plumpness. His skin, which had
always seemed to absorb light, now had a dull sheen like unpolished brass,
and his hair was not only greyer but dryer, like coconut husk—a peevish lift
to one corner of his mouth now, as he talked to his brother and nephew.

Siddhartha's uncle Amitodhana had always had the pettish, desiccated
manner of an old man—and Siddhartha had often thought that his uncle's act
of taking a younger second wife was akin to acquiring, after careful thought,
a good tract of forest land for timber. In his early sixties, like Suddhodana,
Amitodhana had simply grown more into who he'd been all along.

Mahanama noticed Siddhartha's approach, and his face broke into a
bullying grin. He gave his cousin a quick bow, neck craning forward to
peer at Siddhartha because he was a little short-sighted. "Ah, here is our
Siddhartha!"

Suddhodana looked up quickly.

"Our illustrious rashtrika!" Mahanama added loudly, for the entire court
to hear.

For a moment Siddhartha and Suddhodana stared at each other, before
the older man's features settled into petulant severity.

"Pita, I present myself to you." Siddhartha came forward and touched
his father's feet.

Suddhodana nodded grimly, then gestured for him to stand to one side.
He beckoned an amici forward and began to talk to him as if Siddhartha
wasn't there.

Siddhartha had prepared himself for this humiliation. It had happened
before, when he was sixteen and returned from his success at the Savatthi
Court. He stood now with his face impassive, looking out over the gathered
amicis, nobles, administrators and clerks. He studied particularly the petitioners who came forward to bow and flatter his father, to beg for favours.
So great was their effort to fawn that they often bared their upper teeth
when they smiled, like dogs snarling. He observed, too, the way the higher
nobles—all from the Gotama Gotra, of course, as they only promoted their
own—did not deign to notice the toadying glances of those less important.
What an effort it must take to avoid their eyes, Siddhartha thought in wonder. What a crowding and bumping of desires and aspirations.

Yet he was also a participant in this great parody of life that was being enacted—and his part in this show, in this distortion of living, was to stand here and enact the humiliated, defeated son. It was a role that he *had* to play, a role thrust on him by his father, thrust on him by the very fact that here he stood, facing the court, who eyed him with sly glances of delight or worry or pity. No matter his will, his desires, his thoughts, he must play this role. Just like he would have to act out whatever position was finally given to him—rashtrika, administrator, high clerk?—once his father had satisfied his urge to humiliate him.

"Siddhartha!"

He looked up quickly to see, striding towards him, the Senapati of Kapilavastu—his old friend and mentor, who had chosen him all those years ago to go to the Savatthi Court. "Siddhartha!" the senapati cried again as he stood before the younger man, smiling with pleasure. The general had aged, but was still sharp and virile in the way of a soldier-scholar. Siddhartha quickly bent to touch his feet, and the senapati raised him by the shoulders and examined him, head cocked to one side. "You have come into yourself. I've heard of your excellent work up north. I am not surprised."

Suddhodana cleared his throat, and Siddhartha became aware that his father, uncle and cousin were observing this interaction with annoyance.

The senapati let go of Siddhartha and turned towards the raja, his expression hardening.

Siddhartha watched keenly. The senapati had no doubt arrived to deliver a reprimand on behalf of the maharaja. By destroying the Moriya village, his father, uncle and cousin had made two enemies: the Moriya, but also Pasénadi. The maharaja was, after all, married to the Moriya raja's sisters. He was also overlord of the Moriya kingdom. Invading and destroying the Moriya village was a challenge to his power.

His father turned to Siddhartha and waved a hand at him dismissively— "Yes, yes, thank you for coming to pay your respects, Siddhartha." Clearly he didn't want his son to hear whatever censure might be delivered.

The senapati gave Siddhartha a quick look to say that he should wait for him outside.

Back in the public courtyard, Siddhartha squatted in the shade of a verandah watching petitioners and officials come and go from the receiving hall. Soon the senapati emerged. Siddhartha stood up and the general, see-ing him, gestured him over, face stern and worried. "I'm afraid your father is in a very bad place," the senapati said. "The maharaja is furious." He put an arm around Siddhartha's shoulders and ushered him a little further from the hall, so they could talk more privately. "That attack on the Moriya by the way, was not sanctioned by Suddhodana; he knew nothing about it." He nodded gravely at Siddhartha's astonishment. "Mahanama. He ordered the attack, using Devadatta as his dupe. I am sure Devadatta had no idea he was being used."

"But why, sāmi? Why would Mahanama do that?"

"I think, and Pasénadi believes too, that Mahanama was trying to prove that your father is incompetent and needs to be succeeded by a younger raja—himself." He huffed and shook his head at such stupidity. "Until I told him the truth just now, your father believed Devadatta had organized the attack on his own."

Siddhartha turned to study the entrance to the receiving hall. Petitioners were streaming out, and the officials and guards were shutting the doors. His father was clearly too upset to conduct any further business today.

The senapati cleared his throat to get Siddhartha's attention. "Pasénadi says he will not receive anyone from the Sakiya Court. As far as he's con-cerned, the entire Sakiya race are in his disgrace." He made a face to say the maharaja, too, was a man of hasty passions and actions. "I am sure our beloved maharaja will change his mind in time," he added dryly. "And when that happens, I want you to be prepared." He rested a hand on Siddhartha's shoulder. "I've already told your father: when Pasénadi requests someone, you are the one who must be sent, because of your boyhood friendship with him."

"But sāmi . . ." Siddhartha shook his head to say he didn't want this task.

"No, Siddhartha, you must go. No matter what your feelings are towards your father and cousin, you must put them aside for the sake of the state. For the sake of your people." The senapati gave him a keen look. "For your own future." By which the senapati was telling him that he believed, as he had always believed, that Siddhartha would be raja one day.

He smiled quizzically. "But of course, I told your father, one cannot send a man who isn't a high official. It would be an insult to the maharaja." He patted Siddhartha's shoulder again. "Expect a good position soon."

Siddhartha returned to the women's quarters, pondering all the senapati had told him. He stood for a moment, watching Yasodhara helping the old concubine Sumana sew a rent in a quilt. The women noticed him and fell silent. Yasodhara now looked up quickly, saw him and rose to her feet. He nodded for her to follow and went upstairs, his feet plodding up each wooden step.

When he got to their bedroom, he threw himself on a rug and stretched out, ankles crossed, hands cupping his neck as he stared at the ceiling.

"Surya?" Yasodhara shut the door and came to him. "What's happened, Surya?"

He told her everything and, when he was done, she frowned, puzzled at his dejection. "All this is good for you, isn't it?"

"But don't you see? I don't want to go!" He jumped up and paced the room. "Why should I get involved in all this . . . this charade, this ridiculous jostling for . . . I want none of it!"

"Surya, what are you saying? This might be our escape from here! My escape from this realm of ghosts. You simply must go, if the maharaja asks for someone. And, when you're there, you must ask Pasénadi to give us a posting somewhere else."

"Don't be ridiculous! That old friendship is now dead, it's been dead for years. The maharaja will offer me nothing. If Pasénadi had given any thought to me these last years, don't you think he would have asked for me?" He threw himself back on the rug and covered his eyes with his arm. "No, no, I don't want to go. I can't."

"Surya, why can't you? Why?"

Siddhartha curled up on his side, away from her.

The next day, Mahanama came to the women's quarters looking for Siddhartha—an unusual action because normally, if he'd needed to speak to Siddhartha, he would have sent a messenger to summon him.

Siddhartha climbed the short flight of stairs from the second-floor living quarters to the third-floor receiving room, feeling as if he were a goat being led to slaughter.

He found Mahanama perched on the edge of the charpoy where Prajapati usually received guests, the high-raftered room striped with sunlight coming in through shuttered windows. His cousin jumped up, hands behind his back, expression calculating. Siddhartha eyed him with dread. Mahanama gave a forced smile. "Siddhartha, your father sent me. He has appointed you judge for the Vessas' district, since it seems you are so fond of them."

For a moment, Siddhartha was taken aback; he had thought he would be given some official position in the palace. "Judge." He nodded dully.

"Jatila, the Mahasetthi, is pleased at this appointment as he holds you in high esteem. The Merchants' Council is happy too." Mahanama grimaced sarcastically. "Yes, it seems you're quite the little protegé among them. We didn't know you were on such *intimate* terms with Jatila when you were a boy." Siddhartha gestured impatiently for him to finish. "Well, what more can be said? You will take up your position tomorrow."

Siddhartha nodded. Then, with a little laugh, he turned and went back towards the stairs.

"I don't agree with this appointment," Mahanama called out after him. "I would rather you be given rashtrika of a province. But it seems that your father wants you here."

Siddhartha spun around, surprised.

"Yes, yes, evidently he has great plans for you. Or so he says." He scrutinized Siddhartha's face as if to discover what he might know of these plans.

Siddhartha laughed again and shook his head. His father was playing him off against Mahanama, but his cousin was so blinded by his ambitions and fears, he couldn't see this simple thing.

In the bedroom, he found Yasodhara waiting for him anxiously. He told her of his new position. "Judge," she breathed out and slumped down on the bed. "I was hoping for rashtrika of another province . . . anywhere but here."

Siddhartha pulled off his dhoti, letting it fall in a puddle around his feet. He would have to go see the Mahasetthi now and get his formal blessings for the position. He stepped over the fallen dhoti, shook out a fresh one and began to pleat and drape it.

"Surya, do you think there's any possibility this posting comes with a house?" Her fingers were shredding a tassel on her shawl. "Could you ask Jatila, please? Even in the Vessa Quarter. I wouldn't think it an insult to live there."

"Why do you ask me for what can't be?" Siddhartha cried in anguish. "You think I want this position?" He turned away guiltily from Yasodhara's hurt face and continued pleating and draping his dhoti with trembling fingers. "You think I will be happy in it?" He stabbed at himself. "It is I, I, who will have to go out there every day and be this judge. I who will have to interact with the world and all its crimes. Pass sentences, watch those floggings and slitting of noses and cutting off of ears. Even sentence men to death. *I* will have to listen to men beg for mercy. A mercy I can't grant because I must follow the law. Because I must be what I am told to be—a judge." He broke off. Unable to bear the numb misery on Yasodhara's face, he grabbed his jewellery from a table and rushed to the door. Out in the corridor, he leaned against the wooden wall, eyes closed. Then he wearily slipped on his chain, attached his earrings and bracelets and went softly down the stairs.

At the Mahasetthi's house, Siddhartha was told that Jatila awaited him in the square that contained the Vessas' courthouse. He walked through a narrow lane into the square, and he saw to his surprise that not only Jatila but the entire Merchants' Council had assembled to greet him, standing before the courthouse with its open clay platform, its carved wooden pillars holding up its thatched roof.

"Uparaja!" Jatila called out as Siddhartha crossed the square towards them.

The rest of the Council laughed at this old nickname they'd given Siddhartha when he was a boy, sure even then that he would succeed his father. He grinned, momentarily a boy once more.

He bent to touch Jatila's feet—and heard a murmur of approval from the other setthis at this gesture of respect that broke caste hierarchies. Jatila raised him up by the shoulders and examined him; he had known

Siddhartha from the time he was an inquisitive boy wandering the Vessa Quarter. In turn, Siddhartha gazed back at his old friend and mentor— in his sixties now, greyer, his face more lined, but still with that polished, restrained air of a man entirely successful in the world. "We have, over these last twelve years, heard great things about you, Siddhartha," Jatila said gravely. "And no matter what the world thinks now, we hold you highly." The other setthis murmured in agreement. "And," he continued with a glint of mischief, "no matter the rest of the world, we still call you 'Uparaja.'"

"Hear, hear." "Well said," the other setthis cried.

Siddhartha blushed, suddenly near tears at the affection from these older men, each so successful; it was an affection he did not deserve.

"Daharā."

He turned to find before him the old Brahmin Rakkha, whom he had often visited when a boy. He glanced at Jatila, who nodded with a smile to say that Siddhartha had guessed correctly the reason for the Brahmin's presence. The Mahasetthi, knowing of their previous bond, had invited the Brahmin to be the reciter of law, the person Siddhartha could turn to if he needed clarification on a ruling. Siddhartha smiled and touched the old Brahmin's feet.

"Come, come." Jatila gestured towards the courthouse and now Siddhartha saw that a welcome feast had been laid out for him on the plat- form floor.

As the feast proceeded, Siddhartha, seated cross-legged among his old friends, smiled and nodded, asked questions, pretended to listen with admiration to their tales of travel and success—but all the while, he felt a profound alienation from these friends and mentors of his childhood. As he looked around at them, he could think only of that conversation with Maha Kosala in Mudgala, how the former maharaja had described the way most people ran around frantically, doing, grabbing for more and more, all as a way to avoid looking into the chasm of their own mortality. He now saw this same frantic doing and grabbing behind the laughter and tales of success of his old friends.

The feast went on late into the night. When it was finally over, Sidd- hartha declined the setthis' offers of a palanquin or even a slave to carry a torch and light his way. Instead, waving to his old friends, he set out by whatever little light came from the sleeping homes and closed shops he passed, drawing his shawl about him with a shiver of relief at finally being alone.

After he had walked through a few streets, he realized his feet were taking him towards that platform on the ramparts from which, as a boy, he had liked watching the sun set over the surrounding countryside and the comings and goings of people beyond the fort. The guards recognized him and let him pass up the ladder to the wooden platform, one of them holding up a torch so Siddhartha could see the rungs clearly. Once there, he rested his arms on top of a stockade log, chin on fist, looking over the scene lit by a three-quarter moon. Not far from the ramparts was the sprawl of Dasa hovels, a few meagre lights still burning in homes. Closer to the fort, just beyond the city drawbridge, was the guest house for those who arrived after the gates were shut and needed a place to spend the night—a simple clay platform with wooden pillars and thatched roof, open on all sides, lit well with lamps. He watched with longing the merchants and travellers in there, seated cross-legged or lounging on bolsters, no doubt exchanging travellers' tales, served by a few Dasas who made a little money providing food, water and even bedding for these late visitors. How he wished he was out there with them.

"What will become of me?" he said aloud, moving his head from side to side, the stubble on his chin rasping against his clenched fist.

3

The Lotus

A MONTH AFTER her arrival in Kapilavastu, Yasodhara heard that Ananda had finally returned from a long journey to Bactria, that great marketplace of the world. She went the next morning to see him.

Her palanquin stopped outside his home in the Vessa Quarter, and for a moment she sat gazing at it in wonder. What a derelict state the house had been in the last time she'd seen it, twelve years ago. Now the boundary wall was strong and smooth, with a fresh coating of mud. A family of herons was nesting in the thatched roof and she remembered that, the last time she'd seen the house, there'd been herons nesting in the roof too. Ananda had allowed the birds to return each year, it seemed, and their presence gave the house a hospitable feeling. "What luck to be born a man," she thought, wistful, bitter, "and to be able to change your destiny."

She got out and clanged the bell and, after a moment, a woman opened the door. The slave Nagamunda. Yasodhara examined her with interest, taking in her pale skin with its bluish undertone, her dark auburn hair, fascinated that here before her was Ananda's lover.

The woman stared back at Yasodhara in the haughty, inquiring way of the lady of the household, surveying her finery. "How can I help you, sāmini?"

"I am here to see my ñātaka, Ananda. I am Yasodhara, his ñātiké." She was suddenly nervous, worried. If Ananda had no solution to her predicament, she was at the end of her rope.

"Ah yes!" Nagamunda smiled broadly and bowed, ushering her in. "We heard of your arrival a month ago." The "we" was proprietary.

Once Yasodhara had entered, she looked around enviously at the neat courtyard with its flowering bushes, the neem tree with its wraparound bench. The walls were newly coated in lime, the doors freshly varnished, the thatch neat. Even the sunlight in here didn't seem a heavy gold but sparkled and rippled through the leaves of the tree. A goat tied in a corner gave a rustic smell to the courtyard and Yasodhara felt a pang of homesickness for her own courtyard in Mudgala.

Nagamunda led Yasodhara across to the receiving room, chatting away, asking how she found Kapilavastu changed, expressing surprise that Yasodhara didn't find it much altered, inquiring after Prajapati as if she knew her and was a fellow noblewoman, saying "that lovely lady" rather than "her honour, the devi." Yasodhara had come intending to like the slave woman, sorry for her already because of her sad story, yet now she found the woman's overfamiliar manner off-putting. She recalled Ananda's story about Nagamunda's strength and cunning in her fight against Mahanama; but Yasodhara also recalled Ananda's brooding expression back then, which told her there was some trouble in the relationship.

Once Nagamunda had ushered her to the receiving room, she bustled off to fetch Ananda. Yasodhara remained standing as she took in the simple but well-appointed room, a few fluffy yak-skin rugs on the floor, vases and statues on tables and in nooks, brought no doubt from Ananda's various travels. There was the smell of some foreign incense in the air, sweet and citric like lemons. Through a window, she could hear the goat bleating, the merry tinkle of the clapper around its neck. She picked up an odd foreign figurine that seemed to be a double horse, heads at both ends; on closer examination she saw that the creature, while having horses' manes, was eagle-faced. She was scrutinizing it so intently that she didn't notice Ananda's arrival until, feeling his gaze, she turned and found him standing in the doorway. Because he was backlit, she could not see his face until he came forward to greet her, arms held out, saying "Bhagini" with resonant pleasure.

"Bhāta."

They grasped hands and stood a moment examining each other, smiling. For the first time since her arrival in Kapilavastu, she felt the melancholy lifting in her.

"Ah, I see you've picked up my latest trinket from Bactria."

"Is it a god, bhāta?"

He laughed and shrugged. "The language of trade is mostly gesture, a few words here and there."

He indicated a rug for her to sit on, then sat across from her, a low table between them. "I am very happy to see you, bhagini." He looked at her, head cocked. "Though I imagine you don't want to be here."

She nodded slowly, now fingering a clay statue on the table.

"A goddess. Got off a Yavana merchant from Athens. Isn't it lovely?"

She gave him a sad, wistful look. "You've made your luck, bhāta, I am happy for you."

He nodded, then said kindly, "I'm sorry your luck has changed, bhagini. In all aspects of your life."

Ananda had discerned she was unhappy once again in her marriage. She bent over the statue, hiding the grateful tears that threatened to fall.

Nagamunda bustled in bearing a tray with two clay cups of buttermilk and a plate of sweets made from pulses. Yasodhara watched her kneel by Ananda in the way of a wife and begin to put out the cups and plate.

Yasodhara's gaze shifted to Ananda and she noticed, much to her surprise, a great change in him. He was looking down at his hands, simmering with anger. As Nagamunda leaned forward to push a clay cup towards Yasodhara, she brushed against Ananda. He shrank away, his lips briefly curling in distaste before, aware of Yasodhara's gaze, his features settled into a forced smile.

The freshness of his anger, and Nagamunda's irritated way of ignoring it, told her there'd been a recent quarrel between them.

"I was asking your lovely ñātiké what she thought of our city after all these years away, if she saw any great changes, and she told me she finds it very much the same." Nagamunda grimaced in comic dismay. "Oh dear, we are a dull city. No one would go to Savatthi or Vesali, after a twelve-year absence, and say those places looked the same."

"You've never visited either city," Ananda said icily. "Savatthi and Vesali *haven't* changed much. *I* know. I *have* visited them."

Yasodhara was taken aback at his harsh tone; she had never imagined him even capable of speaking thus. Seeing that both of her hosts were aware of her surprise, she bent again to examine the statue with a polite smile.

"Your ñātaka is a good man. If anyone can help you, he can. As he has helped me." Nagamunda looked close to tears. She rose to her feet, picked up the tray with a trembling hand and left.

"Send Vasabha to replenish the cups in a short while," Ananda called after. "I would like my ñātiké to meet her." Nagamunda nodded, but did not glance back.

After she left, Yasodhara was silent, sipping the sweetened buttermilk.

"Tell me," Ananda finally said, and gave her a smile to say he had regained himself, "how bad is your situation?"

"Oh, bhāta." She sighed, and spread her arms wide to convey her unhappiness. "And those two new concubines. Unbearable, unbearable. Like living in a ganikā's house."

"Yes," he nodded sympathetically, "it must feel so. I am sorry for you, bhagini."

"I am trapped there, bhāta, trapped," she continued, relieved to be able to express herself freely, if not about her marriage, then at least about other things. "Trapped in that palace with all those women in their various forms of anguish, like the cursed in the underworld. I . . . I fear for myself." She held out her arms so he could see the scratch marks there, and nodded at his appalled expression. "And the worst thing is I don't have any awareness of doing it," she whispered.

He took a long sip of his drink, then turned the cup around in his hand, frowning as he pondered her lot.

"Bhagini," he said after a moment, "do you know that the young concubine Visaka is the ganikā Vimala's daughter?"

Yasodhara nodded. Where was her cousin going with this?

"Those music lessons that she gets—our matala doesn't pay for them." He smiled at Yasodhara's surprise. "Vimala might have sold her girl at thirteen, but Visaka is still her daughter. Whom she adores. The lotus, bhagini, is a thing of beauty, yet it grows out of the slime and filth of mud. So good things can grow in bad situations. I know that in Mudgala you were free and independent, that you had a life you loved. But now you must accept that you can never have that life again." She cried out in protest, and Ananda held up his hand to say he wasn't diminishing her loss. "On one of my visits to your mother in Ramagama, she told me how distressed you were when you left here, all those years ago. And yet, you made something of your life, something of yourself. Your mother and I, we admired you for this. So, I know you can make something of your life again. It's perhaps your greatest strength, ñātiké. Your ability to adapt."

Yasodhara was silent, picking at a tassel on her shawl. No one had ever told her she had this strength. "I didn't know you and my mother discussed me."

"With pride and admiration." He laughed. "Your mother said, and I agree with her, that you're really a peasant trapped in the role of a noble-woman, and that in Mudgala you found your true self."

She nodded again slowly.

Their conversation was interrupted once more, but this time by the arrival of the girl Vasabha bearing a clay jug. She came and knelt by Ananda with a dimpled smile at him and a shy glance at Yasodhara. Sixteen now, she was exquisite, her skin the colour of river sand, her hair a glistening black with auburn highlights. As she replenished their cups, Ananda watched her, his face lit with love. Whatever her cousin's troubles with Nagamunda, Yasodhara thought, this child provided relief from them.

"Thank you, dhītā," Ananda said when the girl was done and he touched her arm. Vasabha gave him a smile as she rose. She picked up her tray, bowed to Yasodhara and left.

Once she was gone, Ananda said to Yasodhara, "Isn't she lovely? She has brought such joy into my life. She goes each morning to the ganikā Vimala, who is teaching her all the finer domestic and feminine arts that will make her a suitable wife. I wish to also adopt her, to raise her status." He made a disgusted, angry sound. "But Mahanama blocks this, threatening to adopt her himself. He is trying to get me to pay him for the right to adopt the child he rejected! Can you imagine? But I will do it. Oh yes I will!" he said, his voice rising in anger. "I want the best for my girl. I am saving money to buy off Mahanama, but also biding my time, like a good merchant, waiting for the price to drop. And, oh-ho, it soon will, when Pasénadi's wrath descends on my half-brother." He gave a bitter laugh and sipped on his buttermilk, not looking at Yasodhara.

She examined him, worried. He was like a stranger, this man who was bitter, angry, as if with failure and disappointment.

Trying to guess the cause of his unhappiness, she asked tentatively, "And Anuruddha . . . how is his gambling?"

Ananda gave her a tired, ironic smile. "Still in love with the dice board. What more can be said about him?"

And, as if these words had summoned him, Anuruddha entered, crying, "You're back among us!" He stretched sleepily, grinning at Yasodhara. She stared at him in shock, then quickly laughed to hide her dismay. How dissolute he looked, his face drawn and haggard, already growing jowls, his lean, long frame now flabby; white in his hair even though he was just twenty-nine.

He started to sit next to Ananda but then, catching his sour gaze, he went and sat closer to her. "The city is brighter now because you're here, ñātiké."

"Our Anuruddha does you a favour, bhagini, being up at this time. Isn't that so, Anuruddha?"

Anuruddha grinned and nodded, ignoring Ananda's harsh tone. "I would even rise at dawn to see you, ñātiké."

Ananda made a scoffing sound. "But dawn is when you return home, isn't it, bhāta? So you would be up then anyway."

Anuruddha's grin faltered; he gave Ananda a cowed look.

At the end of her visit, Ananda walked Yasodhara to the street door. Outside, she said to him, "I am sorry to find you so burdened, bhāta. Because I know you are. You don't hide it very well."

He gave her a long, evaluating look, then made a decision. "I will tell you, bhagini. Yes, yes, it will be a relief to talk about it." He took her arm and gestured for the palanquin bearers to follow them.

After they had strolled for a bit, he said, "I am still supposed to be on my travels." He fell silent, struggling over what he wanted to say. "But I returned early. Yesterday. To find Anuruddha entertaining his friends, Bhaddiya and Kimbila. Do you know them?"

"Of course." She had met them many times because they'd been close friends of Anuruddha's since childhood. Kimbila was a cousin, Bhaddiya the son of the dowager Kaligodha, whose late husband was the former raja. Charming young men, but dissolute like Anuruddha.

"Of course, Anuruddha is free to have his friends in my home. But . . ." Again he struggled. "But, there between them sat my Vasabha, being entertained by them. No, no, not entertained, courted. That Bhaddiya had her hand in his. And Nagamunda was up on the verandah watching, happy." He turned to face her, anguished. "She wishes Vasabha to marry a noble Khattiya, and it doesn't matter who. And, of course, the only type of noble Khattiya who will have someone like Vasabha is a dissolute like Bhaddiya. It seems—well, it seems Nagamunda has promised him the orchard and field she got from Mahanama. And I have no power to stop this, no right over my girl. That's why I want to adopt her, so that I will have some rights over her, some say in her fate."

"And Vasabha?"

He shook his head. "She has a pliable nature. Will bend whatever direction she is asked. Which I suspect she learned early, to survive." He scratched under his turban, pushing it askew. "And Anuruddha, how dare he support this. How could he, after all I've done for him? He has betrayed me. I barely know him. And yesterday I found out that Nagamunda has been giving him money to gamble. My money, taken from the household accounts. She is bribing him. I noticed the household sums had gone up, but didn't really think why. No, no," he cried, distraught, "Vasabha must marry a decent, hard-working Vessa. My friends in the Bankers' Guild have promised to help me with this."

Yasodhara nodded supportively, but she knew Ananda had no power to determine anything. *We are all changed, changed,* she thought sadly. *Impossible to believe we were once happy, with all life's goodness before us.*

Back at the women's quarters, Yasodhara was crossing the deserted courtyard when her eyes rested for a moment on the archway that led into the abandoned walled garden. Changing course, she went to stand in the entranceway, examining the rutted earth, the weeds mostly dead because of the heat.

That night, she went to her aunt's room and knocked on her door. When Prajapati called out, "Enter," Yasodhara stuck her head in and said, "Pitucché, may I speak to you?"

Prajapati, who was seated cross-legged on her bed, gave her a keen look, then nodded, putting down a shawl she was embroidering, folding her hands in her lap.

Yasodhara came in and stood by the bed, resting a hand on one of its posts. "Pitucché, that walled garden. I was wondering . . ." She forced a smile. "If you have no use for it, might I grow flowers, perhaps even some vegetables there?"

Prajapati studied her for a moment, then nodded. "No, no, I have no use for it." She picked up the shawl and continued embroidering it. After a moment, seeing she was dismissed, Yasodhara went softly towards the door. Before she had opened it, though, Prajapati called out, "I will send for the head gardener. You can discuss with him what plants you would like."

The next morning the women were in the courtyard, going about their tasks, when Prajapati called out, "Yasodhara," from her charpoy. Yasodhara looked up from her sewing to find her aunt holding out an accounts tablet. "Here. You are your mother's daughter, better with figures than me, I am sure. Help me put these accounts of the fields in order." Yasodhara, astonished, got up off her mat and took the tablet. Her aunt patted the charpoy. "Come, sit by me so you can ask any questions you might have about the accounts." As Yasodhara climbed onto the cot, she saw that Mitta and the concubine Upasama were scowling, but Tissa, Sumana, Utara and even Sundari Nanda were exchanging pleased looks, smiling. The young concubines pretended not to notice, in the way of the lowly—paying close attention only to their music lesson.

All morning, Yasodhara bent over the accounts, moistening the tablets to change the numbers and then pressing Prajapati's royal seal next to the changes. From time to time she snuck a glance at her aunt, who pretended to be absorbed in embroidering that shawl.

That afternoon, when they were in the storeroom, her aunt suddenly said, "I wish your mother was here, I miss her more than you can imagine." She sighed. "There is no one who remembers the person I was before coming here. Did your mother ever tell you that, on a dare, when I was thirteen,

I got our royal elephant to carry me through the streets of Ramagama, held aloft in her trunk?" She smiled wryly at Yasodhara's surprise. "Yes, Ushas, we all have many selves, and some of them are lost from the world but remain within us." This was the first time her aunt had used her nickname and Yasodhara smiled back tentatively, acknowledging this.

After that, they worked in silence, listening to a mouse rustling in the thatch above. Yasodhara squatted beside her aunt, measuring the required grains for the night meal, and the kitchen servants shuffled forward to take the rations. She then used a thick needle to scratch the amount taken into the side of the massive grain pot, wetting the clay so the royal seal could be affixed next to this new marking. As happy as Yasodhara was about this change in her aunt, she still missed Mudgala with a searing pain in her chest.

4

Netted Birds

AS THE PALANQUIN turned down an unprepossessing alleyway, Yasodhara cried, "This can't really be the way to Jatila's house?"

"It is." Siddhartha pointed ahead and now she saw the great gates of polished wood at the end of the lane, studded with brass rivets. She had expected that the entrance to the Mahasetthi's house—the richest man in Kapilavastu, president of the Bankers' Guild and Merchants' Guild—would rival the entrance to the palace.

The gatemen let them in; and then Yasodhara was wonderstruck by the vast courtyard before her, larger than the palace's, with its surrounding span of buildings. Past the furthest boundary, she could see an expanse of sky unmarked by curls of smoke from other home hearths. "Why, the property stretches all the way to the city walls," she murmured, more to herself than Siddhartha. "That's the river beyond it."

"The discreet entrance is to avoid giving affront to the raja and our ruling nobles." Siddhartha's tone mocked the pretentions of their Khattiya caste.

Their palanquin, now escorted by an armed guard, jogged across the main courtyard, which contained the stables and chariots, towards one that held the banking offices. As they went along, Yasodhara noted other discreet entrances from the city into this complex. This was a world she had never entered before; she had never, in fact, dined with or been entertained by a Vessa. She leaned back in the palanquin so as to study her husband better, pulling her shawl around her shoulders because finally the weather had cooled and they were in Hemanta.

Though Siddhartha had been judge of the Vessa Quarter for five months now, this was her first visit to the area with him, and she'd been surprised at how he was hailed as if he were the raja himself. Along the way, their palanquin had stopped many times because various merchants, from small shop owners to heads of guilds and bankers, wanted to clasp Siddhartha's hands, to discuss briefly with him various matters of business. All of these men were delighted to meet the wife of the "Uparaja," as they called him, as if sure he would be the next king. One of them, a very old merchant who told her he had known Siddhartha since he was a boy, had insisted they stop and have a hot herbal drink. Once they were seated under his shop's awning, he'd said to her, "And sāmini, breathe deeply." She'd done as he instructed. "Now tell me, do you miss some smell in the air?" It took her a moment to understand—the ever-present tang of urine was gone. "Your husband's good work," the man cried. "No, no," Siddhartha had demurred, "*your* people's good work. I didn't pay for it, nor provide the labour." "But you ruled, sāmi, that the drainage must be unclogged and dug deeper. Then made sure it was implemented." The man turned to her. "You must be proud of your husband." "Indeed, indeed," she had murmured back, looking slantwise at Siddhartha, who kept his eyes down modestly. Yet the moment the merchant turned away to replenish their cups, she saw a frizzle of irritation cross his face before he returned to his mild, pleasant smile, that smile by which he kept her and the world at a distance.

Now they had left the courtyard of offices behind and were entering a smaller, private square. There, Jatila and his wife Sirima waited to greet them. Yasodhara examined them keenly as they drew nearer, these people of whom she'd heard so much because of their wealth and power.

The bearers lowered the palanquin and Siddhartha stepped out, then turned to take Yasodhara's hand and helped her out. As she went forward to bow, Yasodhara glanced curiously at the Mahasetthi, a man in his sixties, refined and sparse. How strange that she had never met this man who, besides the raja, was really the most important person in the city. She turned her gaze to his wife, Sirima, studying her style. The Mahasetthi's wife wore simple silks, but the yellow dye of her dhoti, sash and shawl was of a depth and intensity that could only be found in the most expensive silk houses of Kashi. Yasodhara was also intrigued by the single motif that wove through all of Sirima's jewellery: this was something new, snakes with inlaid rubies and emeralds for scales, flowing in multiple curves, jaw opened wide to hold rubies. These snakes, a sign of prosperity and fertility, hung down from Sirima's ears. Around her neck, two snakes met in the cleavage of Sirima's breasts, holding in their jaws a larger ruby; they met in the same way on her armbands, anklets and girdle.

The guest rituals over, Sirima took Yasodhara by the shoulders and examined her with an expert eye. "My dear, you are beautiful," she murmured, "the great Ambapali would be jealous."

Yasodhara flushed at this supreme compliment of being called equal in beauty to the famous courtesan of Vesali. "Thank you for inviting me, I am honoured."

"No, my dear, you grace our household. An honour to finally meet the wife of Siddhartha. We've asked so many times and now finally he has granted us this pleasure." Sirima laughed, a tinkle of bells.

Yasodhara smiled and bowed again, wondering what the woman might have guessed about their fraying marriage. She knew that Sirima, before marrying Jatila, had been the most famous courtesan in Kapilavastu. The Mahasetthi's wife understood more than a few things about men and their marriages.

"We shouldn't have even performed the guest rituals for Siddhartha," Sirima added, turning to her husband with that tinkle of a laugh. "He has come so often, he feels like family."

"Indeed," Jatila replied, also with a laugh, placing a hand on Siddhartha's shoulder. He smiled at Yasodhara. "We are very lucky Siddhartha is with us now, here in Kapilavastu, where we can benefit from his wisdom."

Yasodhara, with a quick glance at Siddhartha, whose expression was unreadable, bowed and smiled to say she agreed with the Mahasetthi's assessment of her husband.

How odd this visit to the Vessa Quarter was proving to be. Siddhartha's growing moodiness and irritation over the last few months, combined with the number of nights he stayed in the room assigned to him in the men's quarters, and his guilty silence and fatigue when he did visit her bedroom, had made her believe that he hated his work and probably only did the minimum required. Yet he had, it appeared, brought the same assiduous energy to this job as to the one in Mudgala. Why then the irritation, the fatigue, the moodiness?

With a fluid wave of her hand, the Mahasetthi's wife gestured the way, keeping pace with Yasodhara. Siddhartha and Jatila followed, immediately falling into a murmured conversation about official business.

Though in her fifties, Sirima walked with the light, quick steps of a dancer and Yasodhara felt clumsy as she tried to keep up. Sirima, with a ganikā's skill, glided her effortlessly along a river of intelligent conversation that was not empty chatter but not deep and personal either. As she kept up her end, Yasodhara subtly glanced behind at Siddhartha, noticing that he was overplaying his jollity and charm; this was something not discernible to anyone except her, who knew him well.

Later that evening, once the visit was over and they were back in their palanquin, Siddhartha withdrew into a corner and folded his arms, depleted. After a moment, Yasodhara said tentatively, "They are nice people, kind."

"Of course, Ushas. Why should they be otherwise?"

"It's just an observation, that's all," she snapped, annoyed at his patient tone. "Polite conversation. Which you seem to have forgotten how to—"

"Oh come, come, ayyé." He made a dismissive gesture and chuckled nastily.

She felt a hardness rise in her throat, but she would not cry, would not give him that satisfaction. "Yes, yes, polite conversation. But what a place we've come to that we have 'polite conversations.' Remember that tale of the wise quails who always outwitted the fowler by rising up together to lift his net away? We have ended up where those quails did—unable to agree on lifting the net together, and so become the fowler's prey."

"What a thing to say!"

They travelled on in silence and when they reached the women's quarters, Yasodhara climbed down from the palanquin without glancing at him.

"I won't come tonight, Ushas," Siddhartha said.

"Yes, yes, Surya, I'm tired too." She pretended to be distracted, pulling a gold thread from her red sash and breaking it so she wouldn't have to see the earnest, fixed way he was regarding her—as if he indeed did come by all the time and was making this night an exception.

She turned and went towards the street doors, not looking back.

Inside, she took a lantern from atop a low wall and passed through the short passageway that led to the women's private courtyard. It was deserted at this time, trickles of light spilling out from the rooms above creating patterns on the clay floor, glistening on the pond. She held up her lamp, looking at the new shrubs along the edge of the courtyard, shrubs she had planted in the last four months. She went to the archway that led into the walled garden and held up her lamp again as she walked along beds of flowers and vegetables. These, too, she'd planted in the last months, turning barren waste into a thriving garden, the air redolent with manure and turned soil. As she walked among the beds, she regarded them with fatigued solemnity. The lamp in her hand shook slightly, casting a wavering light over everything as if she were looking upon a moon-speckled pond.

She bent to examine the first flowers that had appeared on the onions she'd planted; moved closer to smell them, then sighed. Try as she might, this walled garden could not replace her fields in Mudgala, her back garden there. One place simply was not the other. And here her actions were watched by others, here she had to perform her role. The solitude her private self craved could not be found. Impossible to find it among these women who, even though they'd been kinder to her recently, weren't Rupasiri and the village women. Now that she had the support of her aunt, she no longer feared the other women. In fact, from her own prison of misery she'd come to feel sympathy for all of them, with their various sorrows and failures, even for the concubine Upasama and her cousin Mitta, who she saw were the same: beauty's hostage. Upasama feared its loss; Mitta had irretrievably lost it.

She still dreamt often of being in Mudgala, of working her beloved fields, and would wake from these dreams stretching happily before the reality of her surroundings sank in. Then a wave of bereavement would drown her, and she was filled with jealous rage at her brother, living in her home, sleeping in her bed, sitting at the fire in her receiving room—Devadatta taking with heedless entitlement all the things that she longed for but could not have: the view of her beloved Himalayas from her window, the feathery feel of her young paddy saplings through her fingers, the smell of the mountain air fragrant with sweet flowers, the village women under their tree, chewing betel and chatting about their lives.

She put the lamp down beside a bench and sat, leaning back, hand resting heavily on her stomach, contemplating her other predicament: after a long time, she was pregnant. So used was she to not being pregnant, she'd stopped keeping track of her monthly cycles, which were very irregular. Then suddenly, last week, she'd been brought up short, realizing she had missed three of them, distracted by the hardship of adjusting to her new life.

The pregnancy filled her with a tired dullness and irritation as she waited yet again for the miscarriage. It would surely happen soon because she had no nausea—a prime sign that the fetus wouldn't carry to term, as she knew from miserable experience. She hadn't told anyone because she wanted to bear her loss quietly. And she certainly wouldn't tell Siddhartha. "How sad my life has become," she murmured to herself, "how sad." She got up, knelt on the ground and, by the light of the lamp, began to pull out a few weeds.

5

Alara Kalama

SOME DAYS LATER, Yasodhara went for the midday meal to the family dining hall and took her usual place, kneeling behind Siddhartha as her aunt knelt behind Suddhodana and Sundari Nanda. As the dishes were brought and she served him, she found herself watching the diners' hands move in their food, mixing various curries, the smear of it on their fingers. A chill passed through her. She bent forward to dish out some pulses for Siddhartha, hand shaking, then knelt back on her haunches and put down the platter, slightly dizzy. A coldness passed through her again, sweat prickling over her face and body. Swiftly, the bile rose up. She leapt to her feet with a little cry, rushed from the hall into the courtyard and, leaning against the boundary wall, threw up copiously into a drain, filled with amazement.

Her aunt had followed her out and, once Yasodhara was finished vomiting, handed her a cup of water. She took a deep draught, her gaze on her aunt, wide-eyed. Prajapati's eyes now also widened. "Ushas," her aunt breathed out. Hearing sounds behind her, Yasodhara turned to find the rest of the family in the hall's entrance, staring at her. Her eyes went to Siddhartha and she saw understanding and shock break across his face.

Suddhodana frowned at his wife. "Ayyé?" Prajapati nodded. "Ah!" he cried and clapped his hands. "A son! I am sure it is a son. My grandson!"

He came down the steps, arms outstretched, but Yasodhara's eyes were still on Siddhartha, watching to see his reaction. A forced smile flickered across his face. "Is it true, Ushas?"

Everyone turned to Siddhartha, hearing the false note, seeing that he still stood in the hall entrance and hadn't made any move towards his wife, one hand clutching the doorpost.

"Why not more joy, puthā?" Suddhodana cried. He took Yasodhara's hands and kissed the top of her head in blessing.

Sundari Nanda nudged Siddhartha.

"Just . . . surprised, pita." He came down the steps. "No, no—shocked." He took Yasodhara's hands. "A child after all this time, Ushas?" He kissed her forehead tenderly, avoiding her searching eyes. "How long have you known?"

"Three months."

"Three months!" her aunt and uncle cried, and Sundari Nanda murmured in surprise.

"But . . . but . . ." Siddhartha stuttered, "you didn't tell me!"

"And why didn't you at least tell *me*, daharé?" her aunt demanded, worried.

Yasodhara turned to Prajapati, breaking from Siddhartha's hold. "There wasn't any point, pitucché. I didn't have nausea, so I was expecting another miscarriage, but now . . ." Joy, hope, expanded in her, and she whispered, awed, "I might carry the child to term."

"Yes," Prajapati said firmly, putting an arm around her shoulders, as if she were weak and needed guidance. "Especially since you're now past the difficult three months."

"You must take to your bed immediately, I insist on it." Suddhodana rubbed his hands together. "This son must be born."

"That's unnecessary, ayyé," Prajapati countered crossly, "it's good for women to move about, to be active."

"Well, well," Suddhodana muttered, taking a step back, "this is women's work, I leave it to you, ayyé."

Yasodhara watched this exchange with amusement. Ever since she and her aunt had become close, she'd noticed a shift in Prajapati's attitude towards her husband.

"Though there will be no more lifting of heavy things, daharé," Prajapati said briskly. "I will assign a gardener to help you. Or one of us women will be by your side. And no more spending lots of time in that garden."

Yasodhara smiled, touched by Prajapati's motherly bossiness. But her smile hardened as she took in Siddhartha. He was standing there with that fixed, pleasant expression on his face that she so hated.

Prajapati waved at the rest of the family. "Go along, finish your meal, I will take Ushas back to the quarters."

As they left, Yasodhara looked back at Siddhartha and, as if he had been waiting for her to do so, he smiled and mouthed, "I love you." She gave him a long look, then nodded and continued on her way.

The other women were having their meal in the courtyard. When they saw Yasodhara being helped in by Prajapati, they rose, surprised and concerned.

"Oh, it's nothing, nothing." Yasodhara indicated for them to sit and continue their meal.

"Nothing?" Prajapati cried. "My niece is pregnant. Three months!"

Tissa, Utara, Sumana and even the young concubines exclaimed in pleasure and hurried over to offer congratulations, to place their hands on her stomach in blessing. Only Mitta and the concubine Upasama held back haughtily.

Not long after, Siddhartha came to her room and found her lying on a divan, a cloth wetted with an astringent herbal mixture pressed over her mouth and nose to quell the nausea—because now, as if in compensation for the past three months, she was copiously, joyfully, queasy.

She watched him come towards her, her eyes cold, having already decided what she would say to him.

He sat beside her and took her free hand. "I am sorry I wasn't more joyful, Ushas."

She pulled her hand away and examined his face. "But are you joyful now?" she said through the cloth. "Are you?"

"Why wouldn't I be?" he answered earnestly. "I, we, are to be blessed with a child." Then he added, "I understand why you didn't tell me. I haven't deserved to be told."

Finally he was acknowledging that he had been treating her badly. After a moment, she said gruffly, "Well, and so now you know."

They were silent for a moment, glancing at each other then looking away, as if bashful young lovers.

"Surya." She removed the cloth from her mouth, wanting to express her thoughts clearly. "This is the first time, in all the instances I've been pregnant, that I'm nauseated. I am also past the third-month point, which I've never passed before. So, I might very well bear this child. No, no, I *will* have this child." She was quiet a moment, looking ahead, tapping the balled-up cloth against her thigh. "And I *will* love our child the way my amme loved me." She turned solemnly to him. "So, how about you?"

"I don't understand, Ushas."

"Are you going to be like my pita . . . or will you be like your pita?"

"Ah, Ushas, how can you ask—"

"Why? Why shouldn't I ask? Do I not have good reason to ask?" She was soon to be a mother, her status had changed, she was bearing the raja's grandchild; finally she felt free with all the anger she'd suppressed. "No matter." She waved her hand contemptuously. "If you plan to be like your pita, I want you to know—"

"I would never be like him! How can you say—"

"No? Well, not harsh and punishing perhaps, but there are other ways to punish a child. Absence, distraction. A. . . a sense that they're not wanted. Which a child picks up quickly, as you well know. No, no," she cut off the start of another protestation from him, "my child will be loved, in the way I was loved. And if you can't do that, then stay away." She pressed the cloth to her mouth again, her agitation having stoked the nausea. Once it passed, she lowered the cloth.

Siddhartha was massaging the tip of his nose, thoughtful. After a moment, he got up, took her hand and kissed it. "I will love our child as it deserves." He was taking seriously what she had said; and no, she saw now, he did not want to be his father, in any way.

That evening, he returned. Yasodhara rose from the divan where she was lying to perform her duty of washing his feet, but he gently and firmly forced her to sit down. She watched, taken aback, as he went to the washing table, poured water into the clay basin and brought it back.

"Surya." She started to rise again, but he shook his head. He knelt before her; then took each foot in turn, and washed it with loving care, drying and kissing it. She watched him, frightened by his penitent manner. Later when they were in bed, he embraced her gently, stroking her hair while she lay stiff in his arms. Wanting to test him, she closed her eyes and made her breath regular and light. When he thought she was asleep, he gently moved her limbs off him and went to stand at the window, a hand resting against the frame, looking into the courtyard below. He stayed like that for a long time and finally she did fall asleep. When she woke in the last segment of the night, before dawn, he was sleeping beside her.

In the days that followed, Siddhartha continued to be solicitous. He performed his duties in the city with a mild gentleness that had the effect of worrying those who loved him, like the Brahmin Rakkha who recited the law for him; like Prajapati and those women in the quarters who esteemed him and were troubled by this strange placidity when he came to visit his wife. Even Upasama and Mitta regarded him with shame and diffidence, as if they had somehow caused this change in him. Her pregnancy had vanquished him in some way, and Yasodhara could not decide if this was a good or bad thing.

A few weeks later, Siddhartha and Yasodhara received an invitation from Jatila the Mahasetthi and his wife Sirima to come and listen to a new sage who had been making his way through the Middle Country. The man was now their guest in the Nigrodha Grove outside the city walls. His name was Alara Kalama, and when Siddhartha told Yasodhara about him, he said, "The sage passes through the Middle Country like a forest fire. He suggests abandonment of the sacrifices as the only way to know Brahman and discover your Atman within. It should be a stormy evening."

Yasodhara raised her eyebrows and examined him closely. "Surya . . ."

"It's just a passing sage, Ushas." He frowned, irritated.

Her silence was profound as he continued to avoid her eye. "I will come," she finally said. At least she could be there to see the effect of the sage on him, and curtail it. "We will have a child soon, you cannot forget that." He nodded, lips pressed together in a smile, but she knew that he was still annoyed at her.

The controversy around the sage brought out a large crowd. When Yasodhara arrived with Siddhartha, she saw that Anuruddha and his friends were among the gathered, along with other young people from the palace and their gotra. Her cousin raised his hand in greeting, but his grin was sheepish and he made no move towards her. She was sure he must know, or have guessed, that Ananda had told her of his attempt to facilitate a courtship between Vasabha and one of his dissolute friends. This cousin, so beloved in her youth, had not come once to see her in the last five months. He truly was in a bad place. She turned away from him; she had her own troubles, and could not take on anyone else's.

The concubines and Sundari Nanda had also come, and to Yaso-dhara's surprise so had Mitta, who sat apart, that same sour expression on her face, pretending not to notice Yasodhara looking at her. Sirima and Jatila came forward and escorted Siddhartha and Yasodhara to the front of the gathering where woollen carpets and thick reed mats had been laid on the grass, and their other guests were seated cross-legged or sprawled among cushions, bolsters, silver and brass spittoons. Platters of sweets and boxes of betel leaves were being taken around by serving women. When they were almost at the front, Yasodhara felt a hand on her arm. She turned to find Ananda with Vasabha, both of them smiling at her.

"Ah, bhata," she cried, happily, "I was looking for you!'" She had sent a message to him earlier to seek her out. She turned from Siddhartha, as if he was not even there, and studied Vasabha. "Daharé, you are lovely. The great Ambapali would be jealous."

Vasabha bowed and blushed at this supreme compliment.

Jatila, Sirima and Ananda greeted each other, and Jatila asked Ananda if he would be at the next meeting of the Bankers' Guild. Yasodhara had forgotten that they would, of course, know each other.

Ananda now introduced Vasabha to the older couple, and Sirima too complimented her by comparing her to Ambapali. She took the girl by the chin and turned her this way and that appraisingly before nodding at Ananda. The look that passed between them told Yasodhara that Sirima was in league with her cousin to find Vasabha a Vessa husband.

"Ushas . . ." Siddhartha said, gesturing to say they should find a seat.

"No, no, you go ahead and sit with Jatila and Sirima and your other friends, Surya. I will sit with Ananda and Vasabha." She bowed to Jatila and Sirima, then turned with a willing smile to her cousin and his daughter, gesturing to some cushions nearby, ignoring Siddhartha's morose stare. He left after a moment, making his way dispiritedly with the Mahasetthi and his wife.

"And you are well, bhagini?" Ananda said with a subtle smile. Her cousin had noted the tension between her and Siddhartha, had understood the way she had used him to snub her husband.

"I pray I will carry this child to term, bhata."

"What do you hope for, sāmi?" Vasabha asked as they settled themselves on a mat. The girl padded some bolsters behind Yasodhara so she would be comfortable.

"Only a healthy child, daharé. Though the raja is convinced it's a boy." They all laughed.

"An heir, an heir," Ananda said jovially.

"Now tell me," Yasodhara said, leaning back against the cushions, "are you enjoying your classes with Vimala?" Vasabha nodded and dimpled a smile. "And," she continued with a sidelong glance at Ananda, "soon you will marry? A Vessa and a decent man, hopefully?"

Vasabha shrugged and gave a little merry laugh. "My mother wishes a noble Khattiya, decent or not. Your ñātaka here wishes a decent Vessa, rich or not."

"Aaah," Yasodhara said with a chuckle and examined the girl. She truly was surprising; the last thing she had expected from demure Vasabha was this plain statement about the conflict between Ananda and Nagamunda. "And what do you wish for, daharé?"

Vasabha shrugged again and smiled at the mat, as if to say she would accept whatever was given to her. Yasodhara did not know what to make of this docility—politeness, reticence, the passivity of the survivor, or a true acceptance of whatever fate may bring? She glanced at Ananda, but he shrugged and made a grimace to say, "See, I told you, she bends with the wind."

A betel box was passed to them. As they opened it and helped themselves to the leaves and condiments, Yasodhara looked around her.

She had never been before to the Nigrodha Grove, which belonged to Jatila and Sirima. It was a pleasant park with lots of banyan trees, bordering the Rohini River. Water had been diverted through underground channels to fill ponds and create fountains that rose up through hollowed bamboo spouts. In one corner of the park, behind a cluster of shrubs, she glimpsed mud huts and men moving around, the occasional flash of a yellow robe.

After a short while, the mendicants started to emerge from the thicket and the crowd fell silent. They came forward in single file, a few of the men in their twenties, but most in middle age. Because of their robes, it was impossible to tell their varna, but from their bearing she guessed they were of the highest, either Khattiya or Brahmin. Alara Kalama came last, accompanied by an acolyte, on whose arm he leaned for support even as he strode forward vigorously, pushing at the ground with his stick as if it were a barge pole that propelled him forward, his yellow robes flapping like sails. He was clean-shaven and bald, his head and face puckered with furrows like a mango seed, his nose and lips pinched.

In front of the audience was a caned cot. When the sage reached it, he held out his staff to his acolyte and then, with some stiffness, mounted the cot and settled himself cross-legged with a sigh, as if it hurt him to sit thus. All the while, he did not acknowledge the crowd before him, speaking softly only to his disciple. Finally, the young man rang a bell and the audience fell silent.

Alara Kalama closed his eyes. He let the silence grow long, and only then began to recite, starting with the traditional opening phrase of story-tellers and orators, his voice, though reedy, carrying to the back of the crowd. "This I have heard, mitto: the Atman in us is one with Brahman, the Supreme Self, and in the beginning knew itself only as 'I am Brahman.' This is the knowledge that a man who is a sage inhabits, as the sage Vamadeva, who gave us this wisdom, inhabited it. Any man who attains this inhabitation through meditation and austerity enters a state of eternal bliss, becoming one with Brahman—which is to say, one with the universe. He *is* Brahman. Even the gods cannot prevail against such a man, for he has become their selves, who are also a part of Brahman."

"Oh dear," Yasodhara murmured to Ananda with a droll look, "not Atman-Brahman again. I thought we were in for something new." Ananda grinned and shook his head in gentle mockery, and Vasabha let out a soft giggle.

"Now, on the other hand," the sage continued, "the man who worships the gods thinking, 'They are them, and I am another,' is like an animal to the gods. Just as many animals serve man, so do ignorant men serve the gods. A wise man should know this."

"Should one not serve the gods, then, through the sacrifice?" Recognizing the voice, Yasodhara turned to see that the Royal Head Priest had leapt up.

"One should not."

There were murmurs of horror, of dissent. Someone called out, "And you, a Brahmin of a renowned gotra, say this? For shame." Another cried out, "The world will slide into chaos and the gods grow weak if we don't strengthen them through the sacrifice. What do you propose then?" A third thundered, "The gods will curse you for this! They will strike you down!"

The sage waited for silence, then continued unperturbed: "Will the gods impede the attainment of this perfect knowledge of oneness with Brahman? They most certainly will. Just as a king will thwart the freedom of his subjects to maintain his own well-being, so the gods will thwart a man who seeks the ultimate freedom. Since the gods depend on man for the sacrifices, from which they draw their power and strength, wouldn't they hinder man from gaining immortality? Because who then will maintain their power? No, I tell you, man is nothing but an animal. A goat, a cow, fodder for the gods."

The Head Priest rose again: "You say the gods wish us ill?"

"I say the gods wish us to be ignorant of our true selves and so deny us perfect bliss." The sage took a sip of water and continued. "Now, this ignorant man who serves the gods is an object of enjoyment to all beings, not just the gods. He makes daily sacrifices and, by doing so, becomes an object of consumption by the gods. He makes offerings to the ancestors and so becomes an object of consumption by the ancestors. He gives shelter, makes wealth with great effort for his wife, his offspring, his other dependants, and so is eaten daily by other human beings. He is even eaten by the animals in his home who, through *his* toil, *his* effort, he feeds and tends. He is even eaten by the birds and ants that live in his garden. A man is eaten and eaten and eaten every day of his life."

"And what do you propose to stop this eating?"

Yasodhara turned her head quickly. The question had come from Siddhartha. He had not stood up to ask it, but she could see him through the guests ahead, lounging against a bolster, left leg cocked up, left arm on his knee, an amused look on his face, as if engaged in intellectual sport. She wasn't fooled; his question was in earnest.

"A man must get rid of the bondages of duty that makes him an animal. He must seek freedom," the sage replied.

"You would recommend this to every man present?"

The sage smiled and shook his head. "Only a man who is truly disgusted with the things of the world that constantly fetter him, that constantly eat him, is able to cultivate this knowledge of unity with Brahman and achieve eternal bliss. The way is open only to the truly disgusted. Just as it is only a truly thirsty man who knows the value of water."

The sage continued to elaborate on the necessity of abandoning the sacrifices as the way to true freedom and unity with Brahman, returning over and over again to that image of the householder as eaten, cannibalized, by his dependants, by the gods, by the ancestors. Yasodhara barely listened, trying to subtly scrutinize Siddhartha through the guests between them, aware that Ananda was watching her; aware also that Vasabha—truly a perceptive girl—had picked up on something, more from Ananda's alertness than any change in her, for Yasodhara studiously kept her poise, her pleasant smile. Siddhartha was lounging lower on the mat and she could no longer see his face—it was shielded from her by his hand, which rested against his cheek.

As the ascetic continued to speak, many Brahmins, and a few old Khattiya too, rose to challenge him. But he kept his serenity, smiling with the sureness of one who knew the truth.

Once Yasodhara and Siddhartha were in their chariot again and the charioteer had set off, she leaned back against some cushions and said sternly, "Well?"

"Hmm?" Siddhartha turned innocent eyes to her.

"Are you then but a beast of burden consumed? Do I consume you? Have you become the truly thirsty?"

"Ah, Ushas, how silly. It was all just intellectual gamesmanship." He placed a hand on her belly, his face earnest, but she frowned back at him.

"I hope you're not starting up with all that Atman-Brahman nonsense again. I hope I don't need to remind you what happened last time." He started to speak but she cut him off. "Except now there is a child involved. Our child. No, no, Surya, this time I won't be so tolerant. I won't. And . . . and if I need to, I will appeal to your pita."

She nodded at his surprise, confirming that she would betray him thus, even though she really hoped not to. Suddhodana came every evening to see her now, some bisaj or medicine woman or masseur in tow, bringing the latest advice, the most recent potions, the best massage for her relaxation and well-being. Her uncle was wondrously changed towards her—jovial and avuncular, calling her "beloved dhītā," and sometimes, when he was in a particularly sentimental mood, "mother of our Gotama lineage."

Siddhartha sighed, then rubbed his nose energetically. "No, no, you have nothing to fear, beloved. And yes, I've learned my lesson. Besides," he added after a moment's reflection, "what does this Atman-Brahman offer to all my Vessa friends, of whom I've grown so fond?"

She gave him a long look and nodded to say she accepted his words— though she knew both of them were ignoring the lie in what he had said: this new philosophy, because it eschewed the sacrifices, was open to the Vessas too, who didn't do the thrice-daily offerings to the gods.

She hadn't expected that he would come to her room, but he followed her to the quarters from the chariot. And he again insisted on washing her feet. She accepted without protest, watching him. He met her worried gaze with a friendly, reassuring smile.

But the next evening, he didn't come, nor the one after that, and soon she was ragged with worry.

6

Siddhartha and the Sage

THAT FIRST NIGHT when Siddhartha did not go to Yasodhara, he went instead to the Nigrodha Grove. At the entrance, he gestured for his chariot to wait, then walked towards the huts that were hidden behind a cluster of trees. He was nervous, and agitated by the overpowering urge that had forced him here. He came through the thicket and stood for a moment, taking in the scene before him. The samanas were crouched around fires making their evening meal, not speaking, except to exchange an occasional word about the cooking preparations. The pleasant smell of burning wood and boiling pulses mixed with the pungent sweetness of a night jasmine bush nearby.

In one of the huts, lit by lamps, Alara Kalama was seated on a pallet eating, served by his acolyte. Siddhartha walked towards him.

At the sound of his footsteps, the samanas turned. One of them rose and came towards him, lightly but swiftly. The man smiled with goodwill and bowed, barring his way.

"I wish to speak with the sage," Siddhartha said, formal and awkward, gesturing towards the hut. He could see the sage within, continuing to eat, seemingly unaware of him. "Tell him it is Siddhartha, son of the raja." The man gave him a keen look and bowed again.

Siddhartha watched the man go into the hut, prostrate himself and speak to the sage, who nodded and said something in reply.

The man came back to Siddhartha and bowed once more. "Our guru doesn't see people this late." He winced sympathetically at Siddhartha's disappointment. "You may join us at dawn for meditation if you wish, or come in the fourth part of the day, before the midday meal." He shrugged kindly. "It is so with everyone, sāmi. The sage doesn't give audiences in the evenings."

"But I work during the day, I am a judge."

The samana bowed to acknowledge this and, with another sympathetic smile, returned to his fellow ascetics.

Siddhartha stood watching them for a while; yet, in the end, he had no choice but to leave. As he walked away, he recalled what the sage had said about the truly thirsty, the truly disgusted. "I am probably not that," he thought to himself. "The sage suspects this and is testing me."

Yet the next morning, his mind and body, as if they had decided for him, woke him well before dawn. He walked through the deserted streets to the city gates and, once outside, found a cart that would take him to the Nigrodha Grove. He arrived just as the meditation was about to start, the samanas sitting in rows before the sage who was on his caned cot. Siddhartha took his place at the back and followed the sage's instruction, placing a hand on his stomach so he could feel his breath rise and fall, keeping his attention there, acknowledging all thoughts and feelings that arrived and departed. He had done versions of this before, but now, perhaps because he hadn't meditated in a long while, perhaps because of the combined concentration of everyone around him, his thoughts and feelings soon stilled and he broke free of his rushing plans and anxieties. His mind sank to quiet ecstasy, his whole being porous and alive in the radiant present; he was tearful with gratitude, with happiness. *How have I lived without this?* he asked himself over and over again. *How have I lived without this blissful arrival home.*

The meditation went on for a long time, beyond any length he had done before. When the gong finally sounded to indicate the end, he opened his eyes and the first thing his gaze fell on was the position of the sun. He should have been at work a long time ago. The claimants and defendants waited; they must be wondering what had happened to him. And yet he could not get up and go to his duty. He simply could not. "I am one of the truly thirsty," he murmured to himself in wonder but also fear. "I am one of the truly disgusted."

Siddhartha found the samana he had conversed with the day before and asked again for an audience with Alara Kalama. This time, it was granted. He entered the hut and prostrated himself before the sage. Then he sat cross-legged and regarded the old man, who regarded him back. "You have returned, Siddhartha," the sage said in his thin, cracked voice, and nodded to say he had expected this.

The sage gestured for Siddhartha to speak and he found himself telling this Alara Kalama about the arrival of Maha Kosala and the Truth of Truths into his life, and of his journey since then—how the philosophy had failed him at a moment of crisis, its message of bliss and oneness out of sync with the way the world truly was; his enormous difficulty since then of finding any meaning in his existence, the sheer burden of getting through a day; how he felt like he was *playing* Siddhartha and the performance left him wrung out. "And then, sāmi, when it couldn't get any harder, I find that my wife is pregnant."

"And you don't want the child?"

Siddhartha was silent a moment, his face working. Then he said, in a choked voice, "How can I say that, sāmi? How can I even allow myself to think that? Because then, I am my own father. Who, all my childhood, accused me of robbing him of his wife, sometimes even called me a little murderer when he was truly angry with me. How am I any different? Because all the days of my life, I will be looking at my child and thinking, 'You robbed me of my true life, of my freedom, of . . .'" He broke off, weeping softly with relief at being able to express these horrible thoughts to someone, thoughts that had crowded his head in the last weeks. "And that poor child . . . he or she will guess my thoughts, because children do, children know if they're not truly loved."

When Siddhartha was calm, Alara Kalama said, "Yes, mitta, it must seem a heavy burden—your esteemed position, your pregnant wife. I have met many similarly burdened men, some more burdened than you. Most cannot release themselves from the yokes of the chariots they pull behind them. But a few do. A few do walk away free, no matter the consequences of doing so."

"But are you really suggesting I leave my wife, my home, to follow you?" Siddhartha asked, breathless, astonished.

"How can I ask this of any man, mitta? All I am telling you is that what seems exceptional to you has been experienced by other men. And that some of those men, more burdened even than you, as decent as you, left behind their loads to follow me. My path is not necessary. It is not open to all. Only the truly thirsty."

"And how will I know if I am truly thirsty?"

"You will know."

"Well, may I come visit you again at night? I work during the day and it would mean much to me to—"

The sage shook his head to stop him. "We sleep at night, mitta. That is all. You will gain nothing by coming."

When Siddhartha arrived at the courthouse, he found a small, worried crowd waiting for him—the Brahmin Rakkha, the Vessas whose cases needed trying. He apologized, saying he was unwell that morning, and took his place on a stool in the courthouse. Petitioners sat cross-legged on the floor before him, ready to present and argue their cases. He was aware of the Brahmin's gaze on him. He was sure the old man had sent a message to the men's quarters earlier and learned he wasn't there.

The next day he was up well before dawn again, as if his body and mind had once more decided his course for him. This time, he arranged for a message to be sent to the Brahmin saying he would arrive to try cases at midday.

On the third day, though, he wasn't at his post by midday. The petitioners and the Brahmin waited all afternoon without the court sitting. The same thing happened the next day.

On the fifth day, after the morning meditation, the sage asked to speak to Siddhartha. When they were seated under a tree some distance from the others for privacy, he said, "I had a visit from Jatila the Mahasetthi yesterday. About you." He nodded at Siddhartha's surprise, then told him what had happened.

The Brahmin Rakkha, loving Siddhartha and having no affection for the ruling triad, had appealed to Jatila the Mahasetthi after Siddhartha had been absent three days. The Mahasetthi was disturbed by this news and set his spies to find out what they could. These caaras questioned the gateman and learned that Siddhartha had left before dawn that morning in a chariot driven by a man named Channa, who now took Siddhartha each morning to the Nigrodha Grove and stayed with him until he was done. The caaras then went to the Nigrodha Grove to see for themselves—and found Siddhartha among the samanas. Jatila had been truly worried by this information. He didn't tell the ruling triad but instead informed Ananda, the only member of the Gotama Gotra he trusted, telling him that he should speak to Yasodhara. Ananda, however, had replied that his cousin had miscarried many times and it was important that nothing trouble her. So Jatila had gone to see Alara Kalama. The Mahasetthi told Alara Kalama that, while Siddhartha was free to do the morning meditations, the sage must insist he return to work at midday. And the sage must make it clear to Siddhartha that his first priority was the health of his wife and child.

The way Alara Kalama stressed "insist" told Siddhartha that this was a direct command from Jatila to the sage. All gurus and their samana schools were dependent on the patronage of people like Jatila. And this guru was staying in his grove, his samanas fed by the Mahasetthi.

"So, you are free to come in the morning, mitta. But nothing else, I'm afraid."

Siddhartha was silent, tracing a finger through the grass, disappointed at the sage's capitulation. "And what do you think of this, sāmi?" he finally asked, unable to keep the accusation from his voice.

"You have the Truth with you now, Siddhartha. There is no need for hastiness, for impatience." The old man smiled kindly. "We will depart one day to continue our wandering. If it is correct that you join us, then leave your wife with something to live for. This much you owe your wife."

At these words, a great relief took hold of Siddhartha. This was the first time anyone had laid out a plan towards his departure. He trusted the sage. If he did decide to follow him, Alara Kalama would guide him on how to break from his current life.

"I too was a married man with many children, mitta. I know what you go through." The sage gestured to encompass the other samanas in the copse. "No one here left without reluctance and anguish. So, you need to test yourself, to know for sure you are not making an error."

"And how do I do that?"

"You love your wife, your child, with all your heart. Love them without reservation. Then see. You will come to know, as we all came to know, if you are one of the truly thirsty. And if you're not," he added, answering Siddhartha's unasked question, "then do what so many are doing: take the Truth into your life and make it your daily friend."

After that, Siddhartha left the grove at midday to try his cases and continued his work into the evening. But while he worked, he held the morning's meditation within him, concentrating not on his breath alone but also the rising of his words, the way his tongue worked as he spoke; aware of the movement of his hands and legs, the turning of his head, even the blinking of his eyes. He discussed his progress with Alara Kalama, and the sage was astonished he had so quickly achieved this depth of awareness, that he could hold his concentration while working.

After a few weeks, Siddhartha experienced a new sensation: a separation between an action and the intent to perform that action. Now, he was suddenly aware that every action, even breathing, came in two stages—the impulse to draw in a breath and the actual drawing in of a breath, the impulse to move a hand and then the movement of the hand. He saw with awe that this impulse, which was thought, preceded any movement, any action, even the smallest. Before, he had thought that bodily movements were quicker than the mind—particularly the involuntary ones of breathing, or small movements of fingers and toes, or a quick brushing away of an insect. But now, he could see that intention came first, even before these minute, involuntary movements. He shared this insight with the sage, who was even more surprised at this progress, for he himself had not reached such an awareness of separation. And because he hadn't, he urged Siddhartha to abandon this practice, saying it was a delusion of duality, and it would prevent Siddhartha from merging his Atman completely with Brahman. Siddhartha didn't argue with the sage, but he also did not give up this exploration. He felt as if he had taken the first step in a greater realization—which did indeed come to him a week later: nothing was permanent in him, everything arose and passed, starting with his breath, then moving on to his feelings and thoughts. Everything arose and passed, arose and passed. What this meant, he had no idea, but he did see it clearly; he also sensed an emptiness in this arising and passing that frightened him. Yet, despite his fear, he felt driven as never before to pursue his investigation.

Now Siddhartha found he was able to give himself wholeheartedly to this new philosophy because, unlike the Truth of Truths, no caste was excluded from it, and the sacrifices had no place in the creed. He saw clearly now the flaw in the Truth of Truths: of trying to engage with the secular world through the sacrifices. By rejecting the sacrifices—which were tied so closely to the worldly realm of marriage and family and varna and one's place in society, and tied also to money through the expenses of ghee and goats and oxen and priestly fees—salvation could be found. Only in separation from the worldly realm could there be true unity with Brahman.

Several weeks after Siddhartha had started visiting the grove, Prajapati summoned him to her third-floor receiving room. Once he had seated himself on the charpoy with her, she studied him for a long moment under hooded eyes. Siddhartha looked back calmly, understanding already the reason for this summons.

"Siddhartha," she finally said, "the news that you go daily to the Nigrodha Grove is spreading through Kapilavastu." She frowned, irritated at his lack of surprise. "Ananda came to tell me this. Because he, like I, like all the women here, are worried for your wife." She sighed. "Your marriage truly is in trouble. I had hoped this was not so, that the child would cause you to draw close again." She leaned forward. "But how can you be thinking of abandoning Ushas for the ascetic path, of all things?"

"This might not occur, pitucché."

"It definitely must not occur. I called you here to remind you of your duty. We are all very worried about Ushas finding out."

She went on to tell Siddhartha that earlier that day she had called a meeting of the women in the small garden off their private courtyard, while Yasodhara was taken away by Ananda to walk in the palace gardens. The women were unsurprised at her news, having already learned it from city gossip. And they had already decided that Yasodhara must never find out. "We too want the child," Sumana, the old concubine, had said, and all the women, even Mitta, even the concubine Upasama, had murmured and nodded in agreement.

"So you see, Siddhartha," Prajapati concluded, "even the women desperately want this child. And I understand why. Its arrival in their lives will give them someone to pour their stifled love upon. So you may do as you please during the day, but you must come every evening and spend the night with Ushas. I insist on this. And if you don't obey I will talk to your pita and have the samanas banished."

Siddhartha was silent, thinking over how Alara Kalama had said he must love his wife and child with his whole heart to test himself. After a moment, he got up off the charpoy and bowed to his stepmother. "Yes, pitucché, I will do as you ask."

7

Crocodiles in Puddles

AS THE WEEKS passed, Yasodhara found herself increasingly absorbed in the changes happening in her body. The nausea and cravings gradually receded and then, as so many women told her would happen, she passed into a state of bliss. Days of contentment followed, as if her body secreted an intoxicant that buoyed her along, everything seeming ephemeral compared with the reality of her changing body and the child who was beginning to turn and kick inside.

To her surprise, Siddhartha started coming every night to be with her, loving her with a tenderness she had not felt in a long while from him. At first, to test him, she pretended sleep to see if his restlessness returned, but he too slept, or if he didn't, meditated in a corner. Slowly, she began to hope again and, after a month, she felt sure Siddhartha had turned a corner. His tenderness and love hadn't flagged; instead his love felt more like it had during their life in Mudgala: genuine, nothing forced or dutiful about it. "It's as I thought," she said to herself with wonder, "the child heals him, heals us."

Soon he began to visit her during the day as well, slipping back to the palace if he had gaps between his afternoon cases, often bringing a small gift, such as a garland of flowers, or a prettily painted terracotta bangle. On some of these visits, he encountered Suddhodana, who had also started to drop in on her spontaneously to check on how his "grandson" was coming along. Siddhartha, she had noticed, had become kinder, even affectionate, towards his father, sometimes teasing him by saying, "And what if it's a girl, pita? Will you love my child then?" "What an inauspicious thing to say!" Suddhodana would roar. "You curse your own child." But Yasodhara could tell her uncle was both perplexed and touched by this change in his son, by the way Siddhartha would laugh at this admonition like a mischievous boy. "Well, well," Suddhodana would add gruffly, "if she is a girl, so be it. A granddaughter is a precious thing and I shall marry her well."

Her uncle was a lonely man now and Yasodhara felt a little sorry for him. His nephew Mahanama, whom he had loved and groomed for succession, had betrayed him by causing the war in Mudgala. And his brother Amitodhana stood behind his son out of loyalty, even though he knew Mahanama was wrong and foolish, and had made for the Sakiya people two enemies: the Moriya, and also their overlord Pasénadi.

One evening, Yasodhara was in her room when she heard the loud strum of a lute in the courtyard and a chorus of men's voices beginning a love song. Immediately, windows into the courtyard were thrown open. The concubines and Sundari Nanda craned their necks out to see whose admiration they had stirred to song, while the older women leaned against window frames, watching with amusement. Yasodhara went to her window and saw it was Anuruddha and his friends Kimbila and Bhaddiya. The men spied her and shifted their positions, facing her. Anuruddha stretched an arm up and let loose with a song he had composed about pregnant beauty, a melody so maudlin and badly written that Yasodhara couldn't help but laugh, though still puzzled to see him here. When the tune was done, the women clapped and Yasodhara signalled she would come down.

The men cheered as she came out, and she smiled and bowed playfully, slipping back easily into that girlish teasing with which she had always jousted with Anuruddha and his friends. The men gathered around her as she sat on a bench, Anuruddha lying at her feet, Kimbila cross-legged before her, Bhaddiya leaning indolently against a verandah post. They entertained her with tales of their misdeeds, and she exclaimed with mock dismay, "Is that really so, Bhaddiya?" or "I would never have thought such a thing of you, Kimbila," or "For shame, Anuruddha." They chortled in delight, each guilty one grinning sheepishly as he admitted to his crime: singing a drunken love song outside the window of a girl he fancied and setting the dogs in the compound howling, then baying along with the dogs; yelling

"Thief, thief," as they ran along a road, waking up the residents who rushed out with lanterns and swords, only to find the street deserted; pretending to accuse each other of cheating at dice at the courtesan Vimala's house and causing such ruckus, she threatened to have them thrown out.

Yet, even as she teased and mock-admonished them, Yasodhara noted to herself that these were the same sorts of misdemeanours they had committed more than a decade ago, when they were seventeen and eighteen. What had been boyish exuberance then, now seemed feeble and immature in men who were twenty-nine; and yes, even dull—in the way of men who haven't outgrown their boyishness are dull. She glanced at Anuruddha, trying to understand why he had come, why he was asking her to participate in this old teasing and flirting. He smiled back cheerily, but there was a pleading in his eyes.

The next time Ananda came to see her, she told him of this visit. He nodded in understanding at her concern.

"That pleading in his eyes, bhāta . . ."

"Like a prisoner behind bars stretching out his hand."

"Ah, yes!"

Ananda pushed back his turban, irritated. "And yet Anuruddha won't change."

"Perhaps he can't."

He scowled. "Yes, yes, but where does that leave me? I am a stranger in my own house, Nagamunda and Anuruddha in league against me."

Yasodhara could only nod in sympathy.

During this time, Yasodhara also noticed a change among the women of the quarters. Those who had been hostile towards her were softer; and those who had kept their distance before were friendlier. The younger concubines, Visaka and Sanga, now offered up the caned cot they were resting on when she came into the courtyard, and passed her sweets they had bought in the market. Instead of their usual raucous laughter and slightly lewd songs, they sang soft ballads and lullabies of love and motherhood, which they told her they had learned from their mothers. They were delighted when she invited them to touch her stomach, clapping and laughing when the child kicked, and talking to the baby within.

She felt desperately sorry for them, still teenagers and already in this gilded bondage, and she listened more closely to their stories. Sanga talked with such love of her parents, such pride at being able to support them and her brothers and sisters, sending whatever money she received from the raja to her family. When Yasodhara asked her how she could love her family after they'd sold her to the raja, Sanga replied, with a little laugh, "But they have done the best they can, sāmini. What good would have come for me, for all of us, if I still had my virtue intact and we were all starving?"

Visaka told Yasodhara about her poor Brahmin family—or what little she remembered of them after being orphaned at three. Most of all, she talked about her adopted mother, Vimala, speaking of the courtesan with love, and boasting about her mother's business acumen, her wealth. She still went to visit the ganikā and always came back with gifts from her indulgent mother. "But she sold you to the highest bidder," Yasodhara said one day. "How can you love her so?"

"Sāmini, she didn't sell me to anyone. She secured for me the raja!" Visaka smiled and glanced at Sanga. They found Yasodhara's morality quaint.

Both concubines hoped one day to set up their own establishments as ganikās, once the raja was done with them. In Visaka's case, she aspired to take over for her mother when Vimala was old. They shared their ambitions with Yasodhara, and she offered to teach the younger women arithmetic, which would help them manage the finances of their establishments. She showed them how to keep accounts using clay tablets and a counting board; and promised that, once her child was born and she had taken up more of her duties again, she would let them follow her around and learn how to run a household, how to avoid being cheated by merchants and servants. She also urged them to consider how they might marry well one day, like Sirima, Jatila's wife, or be like the famous courtesan Padmavati, whose son by the emperor Bimbisara of Magadha had been made a prince.

One day, Yasodhara was on her bed resting, bolstered by pillows, when there was a knock on her door and Mitta entered. Yasodhara immediately sat up further in bed, regarding her spiteful cousin warily. But after a moment, she cocked her head curiously because, rather than glaring with her habitual look of hatred, Mitta looked uncomfortable. She was working herself up to say something, and finally blurted out, "Ñātiké, is it true you are conversant in the mantras and verses of this Truth of Truths? That you learned them from your husband?"

Yasodhara was taken aback. "Yes, Mitta, yes, I do know some of them."

"Then teach me what you know."

There was such sorrow in this appeal that she felt all the antipathy she'd had towards Mitta disappear. She took in, as if seeing it for the first time, her cousin's pitted skin and pustules. Over the next few days, she coached Mitta in the meditations and mantras, surprised at how much she had absorbed from Siddhartha. She also held back her dislike and criticism of the creed because she could see how much the meditations meant to Mitta.

Upasama, the older concubine, was the only one who kept up her malice. Passing Yasodhara in the corridor she declared, "A son for our raja. Best hope you produce that son to keep our raja's favour."

"I don't need to keep our raja's favour," Yasodhara replied tartly. "I am not his wife, nor his concubine. The only person's favour I need to keep is my husband's."

Upasama made a derisive sound. "And how well you do that."

Yasodhara watched the concubine bustle away, wondering what she meant. Things had never been better between her and Siddhartha.

Then, one evening, Siddhartha didn't come to her room, nor send a messenger to explain his absence. Her old worry and trepidation took hold of her and she paced distractedly, neatening the already tidy room. Finally, with a bitter shrug, she decided to go to bed. She had just undressed and was about to extinguish the lamp and get under the blanket when Siddhartha burst in, his face shattered, banging the door shut behind him. She drew a shawl about her naked body then held up the lamp, watching Siddhartha as he strode the length of the room. He crackled with agitation and, when he spoke, his enunciation was precise in an attempt to control his feelings. "That retaliation we all expected from Pasénadi has happened. Mudgala . . ." His voice fractured. He gathered himself, and when he next spoke, his voice was sad but calm. "Oh, Ushas, Mudgala is burnt to the ground."

Yasodhara cried out and, fearing she would drop the lamp or tip the oil, she hastily put it down on a chest and sat shakily on the edge of her bed. "The villagers? Rupasiri? Vagantha?"

"Safe."

She breathed out in relief.

"They'd been expecting a reprisal for some time, so had a quick escape plan into the forest."

" . . . my house?"

He grimaced sadly to say it was destroyed.

She put her face in her hands, and tears fell through her fingers. Her beloved house in ashes, a final confirmation she would never return to that life.

Siddhartha let her cry for a while then said gently, "Your bhata is wounded."

"Devadatta?" She had momentarily forgotten about him in her shock and grief. She wiped her face with her shawl. "How . . . how badly?"

"He's here. Escorted by Pasénadi's men." Then answering her unasked question, he said bitterly: "Only a broken thigh bone. He will no doubt recover."

She rose to light another lamp in a wall niche by the bed, then got dressed, taking her bodice cloth from a stool and wrapping it around her breasts and neck, pleating her dhoti, tying up her hair, searching for her slippers—all this done automatically, her mind numb with shock. When she was finally dressed, however, the reality of what had happened to Mudgala struck her again and she slumped on the bed. "Oh, Surya!"

He came to sit beside her. She touched his back and, with a shudder, he turned and embraced her tightly. They held each other, united in sorrow.

After a while, Yasodhara pulled back and picked up her shawl. She went towards the door, leaving Siddhartha still seated on the bed and lost in his sadness.

She came down the stairs to find Prajapati waiting for her in the courtyard, also dressed. Her aunt's face said she knew everything. Prajapati gently took the lamp from her and together they walked towards the entrance that led into the rest of the palace. The sentry at the doorway saluted, then signalled his junior to light a torch and go with the women. As they paused for the torch to take fire, she heard footsteps and turned to see Siddhartha hurrying towards them. He took her arm. "Ushas, don't overexert yourself . . . remember the child." She nodded, and they walked across the courtyard in silence. Yasodhara was conscious of her aunt glancing from her to him, though she could not read Prajapati's expression. When they got to the entrance of the men's quarters, Siddhartha stopped, frowning as if he wanted to say something. Then, with a shake of his head, he kissed her forehead and went into the night.

Now the Keeper of the Quarters, alerted by the sentries at the men's entrance, came to lead Yasodhara and Prajapati through a maze of courtyards to a corner room off a small square. They entered the well-lit chamber to find Suddhodana, Amitodhana and Mahanama arguing, crowded around a bewildered Devadatta, who was in bed.

"You are a coward, a feeble old man," Mahanama thundered at Suddhodana. "This is a declaration of war! The maharaja must pay for—"

"Pay?" Suddhodana shouted back. "*You* will pay. Yes, yes, I am sending you to the maharaja as a prisoner, since you started this whole—"

"Take care, bhāta," Amitodhana cried. "If you do that you will have a civil war!"

Suddhodana tried to shout an answer but instead broke into a fit of coughing, bending at the waist. When he had recovered himself, he said hoarsely, "My own bhāta, I never thought you would betray me."

At last the men noticed Yasodhara and Prajapati, and they fell silent. As Yasodhara approached the bed, Devadatta looked at her with boyish fear, his eyes begging her to say he was going to be well. His face and body were bruised, his stubble thick, his hair sprouting in sharp spikes on his shaved head. These past months, Yasodhara had felt only anger towards him for how he'd ruined her life, but now, seeing his state, she felt a pang of pity. She bent to stroke his forehead as if he were a child, saying, "Sssh, sssh, all will be well."

Prajapati came up to the bed now too. She and Yasodhara began to talk in lowered tones about how to treat the patient, as if the others weren't in the room. The triad got the hint and left. Yasodhara pulled back the covering sheet to examine Devadatta's leg and found it held in crude splints of branches, the skin wrapped in leaves, from which there came an odour of rotting flesh. He yelped as she gently lifted his leg to study it. She and her aunt exchanged a quick look, worried at that smell.

Soon, the bonesetter arrived. Yasodhara had to summon guards to hold down her brother, stuffing a roll of rag between his teeth so he wouldn't bite off his tongue. Devadatta's eyes were wild with terror and, when the bone setting began, his muffled bellows of pain as he gripped her hand, his beseeching gaze, made her own eyes luminous with tears. "Sssh, sssh, it will soon be done," she whispered over and over.

The man worked fast and, once he had fixed the bone in place, he covered the wound with fresh leaves that had an astringent poultice applied to their undersides, then strapped the leg between bamboo splints. The bonesetter asked for a length of rope and tied Devadatta's lower body to the bed so he could not move. He then gave Yasodhara a bottle containing a powerful sedative of ground herbs. She was to administer a few drops periodically, as needed. The more inert Devadatta was, the quicker that bone would heal. She gave her brother a few drops right away and he was soon asleep, his face haggard yet at the same time vulnerable, a gentle snore escaping between his slack lips.

Yasodhara and her aunt accompanied the bonesetter outside. She could tell the man was worried. "How completely will my brother heal?"

"I don't think we'll need to amputate."

She breathed out, relieved. This had been her worry.

"But his military days are over. He will have a bad limp, never be able to do hand-to-hand combat again. Even riding a horse, getting up on the beast, will be difficult."

She sat on a nearby step, winded. "Pitucché, how will I ever tell him that?" she whispered to Prajapati.

Her aunt patted her shoulder. "Let's take each thing as it comes, daharé."

Though the splints Devadatta had arrived in were crude, the bonesetter continued, someone in Mudgala had known how to set limbs, applying a poultice under the leaves that staunched the blood and started to mend the skin. "That poultice," he murmured, and all three of them shook their heads in incomprehension: the smell of rotting flesh had come from it, rather than Devadatta's leg. "Those leaves too, which even I don't recognize, must have some healing property to them," the bonesetter added. Yasodhara suspected, but did not say, that this was the work of a vana-dasa medicine man. After the bonesetter left, her aunt joined her on the steps and they regarded each other wide-eyed, like survivors of a disaster.

Yasodhara found a manservant to nurse her brother, then she and Prajapati returned to their quarters, Yasodhara lost in her sad thoughts about Mudgala and its destruction. She'd seen homes destroyed by war before, and could picture her beloved house, its thatch burnt, the rafters blackened and broken, the mud walls cracked, the charred litter of her previous life all over the floor, its ashes caught by the wind and scattered about the courtyard.

Yasodhara nursed her brother in the days that followed, and all the while various uncles, cousins, ministers and members of the sangha came to see him. Devadatta mostly slept through these visits, for she kept him sedated so the bone would heal fast. From these visits, she became aware of the general feeling among the ruling class: Pasénadi's attack was an affront to Sakiya sovereignty and pride. The ministers, the sangha, were choosing, however, to ignore that it was Devadatta, representing the Sakiya and instructed by Mahanama, who had destroyed that Moriya village, making retaliation inevitable; that it was he who had first violated another state's sovereignty. She sensed that, underneath their bravado, they were frightened, waiting with unease to see what Pasénadi's next move would be.

As the weeks passed, the bone began to heal and the bonesetter reduced the sleeping potion so her brother was awake more often. The first time he was truly conscious, Yasodhara asked him to tell her what happened. He was silent for a while, brooding, glancing at her from time to time as if to figure out how he should cast his story.

She raised her eyebrows. "Just tell me the truth, bhāta."

He began haltingly. "Pasénadi's troops . . . they were a combination of the Moriya raja's guards and the maharaja's army. We, my four guards and I, weren't even aware of these troops travelling north towards us. Because, rather than using the Kali Gandak, on which we would have spotted them, they came up the Anoma River and then crossed overland to the Moriyas' village, where reconstruction had begun. When I finally did find out about the troops through my vana-dasa connections, it was too late. The vana-dasas, seeing the size of the army, refused to risk their own warriors in what was sure to be a losing battle. I had just my four guards, and the villagers refused to fight. So I sent my surrender, but it was turned down. The troops landed in Mudgala and . . ." He fell silent for a moment, sullen, picking at his lower lip. "After I was wounded, I don't remember much . . . I fainted from pain and only woke much later, already downriver on a barge."

Yasodhara took all of this in, bitterly. "So our villagers had done nothing and yet the warriors destroyed Mudgala. I never thought Pasénadi capable of such cruelty, such stupidity."

"Why are you surprised, bhagini? This is the reason we must break from the Kosala Empire."

"Ah, bhāta, have you learned nothing!"

Devadatta looked away. After a moment, she took his hand and placed it on her stomach then declared accusingly, with a smile, "And you still haven't noticed!"

He gaped at her stomach, seeing for the first time the swelling. "Bhagini," he breathed. "How long? Are you well? Will you bear the child?" He struggled to sit up, but she pushed him back; he must stay still.

"Five months now, bhāta, and yes I am well. I've never carried a child this far. I will bear it to term."

He pulled her close and rested his head against her stomach. "Hello, little warrior," he whispered and Yasodhara laughed, pleased to see her brother loving the child already. The baby kicked and they both gasped. "He hears me, he hears me!" Devadatta cried, clapping his hands.

"'He'? You're as bad as our uncle, bhāta. What if it's a girl, will you love it still?"

"Of course!" he cried, then gave her a keen look. "I know I should hope it's a boy, bhagini, but you want a daughter. So, I will hope the child is a girl."

She bent down and kissed his cheek.

One evening, as Yasodhara was tending her brother, there was a knock on the door. She called out, "Enter," and Ananda poked his head in and gave her a friendly nod. He opened the door wider and ushered Vasabha ahead of him. "Ah," Yasodhara said, happy to see them both, gesturing them forward.

She could tell from the way Devadatta pulled himself into a sitting position and rubbed his face quickly that he was taken by Vasabha's beauty. When she introduced them, the girl smiled willingly at Devadatta but, seeing his attraction, immediately referred to him as "mātula" to keep a friendly distance between them. She sat on the edge of the bed, as if she knew him well, and said, "Now tell me, mātula, how is your leg? Is it mending well?"

Devadatta nodded. "And you . . . daharé. I hear you take classes with Vimala."

"Yes, but not just me. A group of girls from various Vessa families." She laughed. "We get into a lot of mischief, keep those poor ganikās on their toes."

Yasodhara stood up and handed a bowl to Vasabha. "Would you like to feed my bhāta, daharé, while your pita and I talk?"

Vasabha gave her a dimpled smile and took the bowl.

When they were on the verandah, Ananda said, "Well, well, interesting goings on, these days. Nagamunda brings me all the news, got through slaves in my father's household. Mahanama, it seems, is hot to retaliate against Pasénadi but our uncle will not sanction it. Even my father warns Mahanama against it, so there are many stormy scenes at home. Still, Mahanama knows he has to be careful. Already our uncle has cautioned him that if Pasénadi demands further punishment for the guilty, he might offer up Mahanama and send him to the Kosala Court."

"Yes, I heard him say so." They shook their heads and laughed at the ridiculousness of it all.

In the days that followed, Devadatta, now properly awake, was visited by amicis and members of the sangha. Once Yasodhara entered his room to find a group of young noblemen, including Mahanama, around the bed, her brother in full spate: "So, despite the surprise night attack, I rallied my troops and the villagers, and we fought back. Yes, right to the end, until I was captured, I fought for our Sakiya honour."

"They really attacked at night?" Mahanama cried—pretending outrage, Yasodhara was sure, because he no doubt knew the truth.

Devadatta nodded virtuously. The other young men drew in their breath and looked at each other, shaking their heads angrily at this violation of the rules of war.

She cleared her throat. The men turned quickly and, seeing her at the door, they straightened their shawls and turbans and sashes. "My bhāta needs to rest." She came towards the bed, unsmiling, and they began to shuffle out, some bowing to Devadatta before they left him.

Yasodhara went about plumping the pillows and replenishing her brother's water, a potent silence between them. Finally, he said, "They did attack at night, bhagini."

"You never told me that, bhāta."

"I . . . I must have forgotten."

She sighed. "Oh, bhāta, try to live well."

This story of the night raid soon travelled through the city, arousing the ire of the janata against the maharaja. Pasénadi's soldiers, as they patrolled Kapilavastu, had stones lobbed at them from behind. When they spun around, the street was always deserted. Some merchants started to refuse the soldiers service, particularly those who sold sweet perfumed water in large clay jars at various corners. These merchants were normally well patronized by the thirsty soldiers, and their refusal led to frayed tempers. Soon soldiers were destroying the clay jars and wrestling with the merchants, all the while jeered at by the surrounding public. The senapati began to keep more and more soldiers in their barracks during the day. And young noblemen like Anuruddha and his friends went out before dark and returned home only once the sun had risen, as it was no longer safe to walk in the streets at night.

Finally, the bonesetter told Yasodhara that Devadatta was well enough to get out of bed and hobble around. He had ordered crutches, fashioned out of two sturdy branches, in whose forkings Devadatta could rest his armpits. She asked the bonesetter to delay informing her brother about the crutches, because she wished to prepare him for his life ahead.

How she might tell him the truth obsessed her for a few days but then, accepting that the perfect words didn't exist, she went one morning to see Devadatta.

He watched her fearfully as she came to sit by him on the bed, her face grave.

"Bhāta," she said, taking his hand, "today or tomorrow you will start to use your crutches . . . so you need to be prepared."

"How bad is it, bhagini?" he whispered.

She gave him a long, agonized look, unable to speak.

"What is it, bhagini? What?"

"Oh bhāta, you will never be a warrior again."

"Aaah," he cried and threw himself back on his pillow, eyes closed. After a moment, tears began to trickle out of the corners of his eyes. He brushed them away angrily. "But I can ride a horse, so all is not lost. I can fight from my horse, can't I?" He stared at her, pleading.

"The . . . the bonesetter doesn't think so. He says you will need help getting on and off a horse." It was taking all her will to keep going. "You . . . you will have a bad limp, bhāta."

"Well then! All I need is someone to assist me on and off. I *will* be able to fight from my horse."

She was silent. There was no point in stating the obvious: no army wanted a soldier who needed help getting on and off his horse.

His face became stern. "The bonesetter is wrong. I'll prove that to all of you. I will fight, I will be a warrior again!"

The next day when she came to see Devadatta, he was hobbling back and forth across the courtyard on his crutches, the servant beside him, arms held out, fearing his master would fall at any moment. When Devadatta saw her, he cried, "Look, bhagini! That bonesetter said I'd only be capable of getting around my room for the next few days. But I've already come down the steps on my own. Been walking up and down a good while now."

"I am happy for you, bhāta. Perhaps the bonesetter is wrong."

"Perhaps? He most certainly is wrong. Here is proof of it! The problem with you, bhagini, is that you see crocodiles in every puddle of water. Yes, yes, crocodiles!"

Yasodhara was present the day the bonesetter told Devadatta that he no longer needed his crutches. Handing them grimly to the man, Devadatta began to make his way slowly across the courtyard. He stopped frequently to try and adjust his walk, squaring his shoulders, pulling in his stomach muscles, even once slapping his damaged leg as if to straighten it out. But, no matter what he did, when he started forward again, his body listed to one side, his damaged leg like an oar dragging through water.

"Bhāta," Yasodhara said softly, "give yourself a chance . . ."

He waved her away and made his way towards the entrance of the court-yard, shambling along as fast as he could until he disappeared from her view.

Later Yasodhara learned that he had gone to the stables, where he ordered his horse and tried to mount it. Unable to do so, he'd called for a stool but even after the pitying grooms had rushed about and found one, he still couldn't throw his damaged leg over the beast. Finally, the head groom helped him up, distressed at having to humiliate this great warrior. Devadatta had nodded his thanks sternly, then set off at a clip through the streets of Kapilavastu, the head groom following at a discreet distance to make sure he was okay. According to this man, once Devadatta had left the city behind, he rode at what many would consider a good pace, but far below what he had once been capable of. Devadatta had tried to speed up the horse, but it sensed his lack of balance and wouldn't go faster.

It was Suddhodana who told Yasodhara all this when he came to see her that evening, wincing in sympathy as he spoke. He also related how Devadatta had presented himself to Suddhodana that afternoon, saying he was reporting back for duty. Suddhodana had been forced to tell him that he was not fit for guard duty, nor for combat, and Devadatta had cried, "Mātula, don't put me out like an old elephant who must pass his days ambling along the riverbank."

Now, to Yasodhara, Suddhodana promised that he would find Devadatta something to do—but, as he told her, he didn't yet know what this might be.

⚓

One morning not long after this, Suddhodana was visiting again with Yasodhara, who was resting in bed, when Siddhartha entered the room with a garland of lotuses.

"Ah," Suddhodana said, "just the person I was looking for. I was going to send a messenger for you, but this is even better." His face became grave. "More private."

Siddhartha slipped the garland around Yasodhara's neck, exchanging a glance with her. For a moment, Suddhodana was silent, his breath a faint whistle. In the last few days, both of them had noticed that Suddhodana had begun to wheeze, a condition brought on, no doubt, by the stress he was under.

"Well, no point wavering about like a dancing snake, so here it is: a message came from Pasénadi last night. He is passing through Lumbini in two days, on his way to visit the Licchavi princes in Vesali. He wants you, Siddhartha, to come and visit him in Lumbini."

Yasodhara glanced at Siddhartha. Here it was, the summoning from the maharaja that the senapati had said would happen.

After a moment, Siddhartha laughed softly. "Lumbini is half a day's travel from here, and Savatthi three-quarters of a day. We could have just as easily met at his court. Yet he picks Lumbini. Because, in that park, we will have more privacy than we would in Savatthi." He gave a hollow chuckle. "Yes, yes, such is the state of one of the most powerful men in the Middle Country! He cannot trust anyone. Is completely alone."

"True," Suddhodana said quietly. "Look at me, am I not in the same position, unable to trust anyone, also alone?"

Yasodhara was taken aback at this confession. After a moment, Siddhartha said kindly, "I am sorry that you are, pita."

"Of course Mahanama thinks he should go along with you, 'just in case.'" Suddhodana's guffaw ended in a bark of a cough. He bent over, thumping his chest, before he regained himself. "'In case of what?' I asked him. 'In case Pasénadi might want to take you as his prisoner?'" He shook his head, still wheezing. "What a disappointment he is. But you are wise and loyal, puthā." He cleared his throat, seeming embarrassed by his praise of Siddhartha. "And, well, I am trusting you to do what's best for our kingdom. I want Pasénadi to know that I didn't order that attack, that it was Mahanama. Make sure he knows."

"He already does know, pita. Everyone in our city knows, and I'm sure our senapati has informed him."

"But hearing it from you, his old friend, will make him believe it."

Siddhartha bowed to say he would ensure this happened. Suddhodana looked at the ground, considering. Then he said, "I hear you are doing a good job. Jatila has sent me special word to say so."

Siddhartha nodded to acknowledge this praise—moved, Yasodhara saw, that his father would compliment him, but use Jatila's words to do so. "Pita," he said softly, "hasn't the Royal Bisaj seen you about your cough?"

Suddhodana grunted and waved his hand as if at a fly. "I'm not having that mincing old hen fussing around, insisting on this and that potion."

Siddhartha left on his mission the next day, so that he could spend the night in a village near Lumbini and be there to greet the maharaja when he arrived the following morning. Before he left, he told Yasodhara he would return immediately to Kapilavastu after his visit with Pasénadi. Yasodhara waited, like everyone else, to hear the result of the visit.

The day of the meeting passed, and she awoke that evening from a nap to find Siddhartha standing by her bed, looking down at her. She saw right away that he was in a strange mood, exalted but also frightened. He bent and kissed her brow. "Beloved," he whispered. As she struggled into a sitting position, he bolstered her with pillows, then turned away to remove his turban and set it aside, hands trembling. When he turned back, he had regained his composure. With a smile, he sat on the bed, took her hand.

"Pasénadi wants us to send him a bride from our Gotama Gotra, preferably from our ruling family." He nodded at her astonishment. "This will evidently seal relations between our country and the empire, so he says."

"And?" She could tell there was something more to this.

"But don't you see, Ushas? The demand is a deliberate crushing of our gotra's pride."

"Aah," she murmured, understanding. Since its inception, their Gotama Gotra had only married within itself; part of the gotra lore was that their original ancestors had married their own sisters to keep the line pure.

"And don't forget Pasénadi already has three wives, two of whom are the Moriya raja's sisters."

"Aah," she said again, understanding even more now. Within the court hierarchy as well as the women's quarters, the Sakiya wife would be subordinate to the Moriya queens, who would make sure she felt her inferiority. Further, the Sakiya wife's position would be symbolic of the Sakiyas' position in the empire—below the Moriya.

"So what did you tell him?"

"That I would promise to consider all the eligible women," he said in the mock-formal tone of a diplomat, "and, in consultation with our raja, our amicis, pick one who would be worthy of this honour and whose status would enhance our ties with the Kosala Empire." He chuckled sadly. "Have you ever heard of anything more ridiculous, Ushas? And look at me talking to my old friend in that way. Oh, you should have seen him, Ushas," he continued in a tone of exalted sadness. "Fat like a buffalo, but, at the same time, shrivelled up, his shoulders hunched, dark circles under his eyes. The skin on his face looked as if it was melting downwards, pulled by the weight of his jowls and double chin. Ah, is this all power brings? Of course we tried to revive the past, recalling my years in Savatthi, our pranks, his many loves. Exhausting! A dead fire! What a relief it was when he signalled me that the meeting was done. I had intended to tell him of Maha Kosala's visit to me, but the words wouldn't leave my mouth, so dead was our friendship."

Yasodhara studied Siddhartha, not sure what to make of this exalted sadness. "Well, Surya, I can think of a few women," she said, to shake him out of this mood. "Let us make a list."

"Yes, yes, good." She listed a number of women, and he recited their names to memorize them.

"And there is also Sundari Nanda."

"My stepsister?"

"Yes. At twenty-nine, she might see this marriage as a fortunate chance, despite its drawback."

"But do you really think my stepsister, or the parents of these other women, or the women themselves, will consent to the life of humiliation that awaits them? A husband who will not love them, who sees them only as a symbol of their people's subjugation?"

"Well, if they all say no, you can tell the maharaja with honesty that you've tried your best."

When Siddhartha returned to her chamber later that night, he told her that Suddhodana, Amitodhana and Mahanama, as expected, had been outraged, declaring, "Never! That will never happen."

Siddhartha had tried to reason with them, pointing out that they must comply, that this was, in some sense, a small price to pay for what they'd done. His words enraged Mahanama even further, who now declared the situation was Siddhartha's fault, that if he hadn't capitulated in negotiating water rights with the Moriya, Mahanama wouldn't have had to send in troops to assert Sakiya dominance. Ignoring this taunt, Siddhartha calmly told his father that he'd prepared a list of women and, after a moment, Suddhodana had gestured for him to recite it. When Siddhartha had finished, his father was silent for a while, nodding. Then he had said, "You have missed one name. Mahanama's daughter, Mantani, is also of age. Add her to the list." Mahanama and Amitodhana were apoplectic at this, but Suddhodana had smiled placidly and said, "Is it not right that you and your family should pay the price for what happened? Why should some other innocent family have to offer up their girl? Because some young woman must go. This is an order from the maharaja. And I am still the raja, so my wish will be done."

His story over, Siddhartha sighed and said, almost to himself, "I truly am tired of all this."

As predicted, everyone, including Sundari Nanda, refused the offer, once they understood the price that came with it. Siddhartha reported these refusals to the triad and Suddhodana said, "Then there is only one option. Mahanama will give his daughter. I order it, in the interest of good relations between our kingdoms."

Siddhartha had expected this from his father, but he was surprised when Mahanama, with a glance at Amitodhana, bowed his head humbly. "It is my fault that we are in this predicament. So yes, I offer my Mantani."

When Siddhartha told Yasodhara all this, he spoke again in that same tired, unemotional tone he had used before. She studied him for a moment, then said gently, "You have done your best, Surya. I'm sorry it's tired you out so much."

He smiled softly and pressed her hand.

"But I'm telling you something is not right, Surya. I don't trust Mahanama."

Two weeks later a venerable court peer, dispatched by Pasénadi, arrived to claim the maharaja's Sakiya bride. Mahanama invited him to his home, where the peer was received with great cordiality by Mahanama and his wife. At a grand meal prepared just for him, the peer met Mahanama's daughter. And afterwards, there was a private marriage ceremony, with the peer standing in as proxy for the Maharaja Pasénadi—this being the one condition Mahanama had insisted on. Then Mahanama escorted his daughter in a curtained palanquin outside the city walls, where he handed her over to her new life.

Within a week the truth came out: Mahanama had not given Pasénadi his legitimate daughter Mantani but rather his daughter by the slave woman Nagamunda, having sanctified and legitimized the adoption of the child a short time before, through the necessary Vedic ceremony. He had done as he promised—and now he boasted about how he'd tricked the maharaja, relating how he'd even excused himself during the meal on some urgent business so as not to sully himself by eating with a slave.

It was Prajapati who brought this news to Yasodhara while she was doing some gentle pruning in the walled garden. "But Ananda . . . ?" she cried. "How could he have allowed this to happen?"

Prajapati grimaced. "He's away travelling with a caravan to Ramagama. Returns today."

She wiped her hands against her dhoti. "I must go and be there when he gets the news."

Ananda's frightened servant let Yasodhara in through the street door, informing her his master still hadn't returned. She looked around, trying to decide what to do, and only then remembered Nagamunda. "The slave woman?" she demanded. The man grimaced. "She is gone with her daughter. As her nurse."

Yasodhara nodded and stepped up onto the verandah, a terrible suspicion growing within her. She hurried along the verandah and, not bothering to knock, opened Anuruddha's door and marched in, calling out his name.

Anuruddha sat up with a gasp.

For a moment, they stared at each other in the darkness. Yasodhara took in the fug of unwashed body and old clothes. She strode across the room and opened a window, letting the light in, then came back to stand by the bed.

"How, ñātaka? How is this possible?"

Anuruddha turned away and gulped water from a clay cup on his bed-side table. Then he said slowly, "Mahanama . . . he adopted her, ñātiké. In secret."

She waved her hand impatiently to say she already knew this; knew also that he was playing for time. "But what about you, ñātaka? Didn't you protest? Fight for your bhāta? Or at least inform whoever the maharaja sent of the deception?"

"But what right did I have over the girl, ñātiké?"

She leaned forward to glare at him, and Anuruddha dropped his eyes. "Mahanama has paid your debts!"

Anuruddha opened his mouth to protest but then thought better of it. He smoothed the edge of his sheet.

She let out a high laugh. "Well, well, and now you must tell me every-thing."

Anuruddha nodded meekly, and Yasodhara learned that Mahanama had approached Nagamunda with the proposition to adopt Vasabha and give her in marriage to Pasénadi. At first Nagamunda had hesitated out of fear that the plan would fail and that she and her daughter would look foolish—like jackals parading around in lion skins, Yasodhara thought. The slave woman had also been worried that failure could ruin Vasabha's marriage prospects forever. Yet Mahanama made her see that, once he had legally adopted Vasabha, he was fulfilling his promise to give the maharaja his daughter; and that, whatever Pasénadi's feelings about the ruse might be, he would have no choice but to accept Vasabha as his legitimate wife, because his request for a Sakiya bride of the Gotama Gotra had been met.

After Anuruddha was done telling his tale, Yasodhara said nothing for a long while. She went to sit in the window well, looking out at the house on the other side of the street. She lost track of time until finally she heard Ananda's voice calling out with alarm, "Nagamunda? Vasabha?"

Shooting Anuruddha a look of reproach and dread, she hastily left the room.

Ananda was standing in the middle of his courtyard, dusty and dirty from his trip. Seeing Yasodhara, he frowned. He strode swiftly to the edge of the verandah, alarmed. "What . . . what has happened?"

"Let us go to the receiving room, bhāta."

Dazed, he followed her lead. Once in the room, she gestured to some cushions on the floor but he cried, "No, no!"

So, standing with her hands clasped in front of her, she told him what had happened, including Anuruddha's complicity in it.

When she was done, Ananda put his head in his hands and was still for a moment. "And my Vasabha?" he finally said in a muffled, choked voice. "Did she protest at all?" He dropped his hands and began to pace. "But no, what choice did she have? What choice but to go along with it. I was not here to protect my girl! No one was here to protect my girl!" When she tried to touch him as he passed, he shied away and went to stand at the window, staring out unseeing. Then, hearing a sound, they both turned to see that Anuruddha had come in quietly and was standing by the door.

"Bhāta." Anuruddha came forward cautiously, holding out a package wrapped in cotton. Too frightened to hand it to Ananda, he placed it on a table, then backed away to the door. "From Vasabha . . ."

Ananda grabbed the parcel and unravelled the cloth. Inside was one of her bangles.

"She begs you not to be angry with her."

After a long moment, Ananda gave a small, high laugh. "A river reed, she has bent with the current. Oh, but Pasénadi will find a way to punish us. This is the beginning of the end of the Gotama Gotra." He turned to Yasodhara with another bitter laugh. "See, see, my entire life is ruined."

He started towards the door and Anuruddha shrank aside to let him pass. "Bhāta, do you want me gone? Shall I return to our father's house?"

Ananda contemplated him for a moment, then shrugged and left.

Yasodhara followed her cousin out, across the courtyard and through the street door, not sure whether to keep him company or give him time alone. Once on the street, however, she stood and watched him walk away, passing neighbours and fellow merchants without acknowledging their bows of greeting, blind to the keen way they looked at him, knowing what had happened.

8

Robe, Razor and Begging Bowl

A FEW DAYS later, Yasodhara learned that Ananda had never returned home. He had walked out of the city, past the drawbridge, to the wells where caravans stop to replenish their water supplies. There, he had joined one of them, though no one was sure in what direction he had gone. Different people insisted the caravan was going to Takkasila or Rajagaha or Vesali. When Yasodhara heard this news, she thought, "Yes, this is the best thing for him to do. For now."

One morning not long after Ananda's departure, she was seated in the women's walled garden, threading a garland of flowers, when she looked up to find Devadatta watching her from the entrance. Even at a distance, she could see his excited expression. She put down her garland and waited, feeling pained as she watched him hobbling towards her, sweating with agitation. "Bhagini," he cried breathlessly when he reached her, "I am the only one who truly loves you, because I am the only one who is now telling you a truth that I learned from the grooms. A truth that has been kept from you by everyone—our pitucché, the women here, Ananda, Anuruddha, everyone! Siddhartha spends his mornings with those samanas in the Nigrodha Grove. He only goes to work afterwards."

She picked up her garland and threaded another flower, trying to appear calm although her hands were shaking. "But he comes to me every night, bhāta. He is at peace. If these samanas help him to be at peace, then . . ." She smiled up at him. "And he does love me, he does. Once again, as he did in Mudgala." She threaded another flower. "I know, more than anyone," she continued, her voice rising, despite her effort to maintain her façade, "the trouble these philosophies can get him into, so I will talk to him. We have a child, he *will* understand, he must understand that—"

"But he's thinking of becoming a samana! That's what everyone is worried about, that's why no one has told you. It's not harmless. Jatila himself went and had a talk with that Alara Kalama, telling him he must limit Siddhartha's visits."

She laughed. "A samana? Siddhartha?" Yet a darkness started to seep across her mind.

"Why do you think everyone has conspired to keep this from you?" Devadatta insisted.

Yasodhara threaded a few more flowers with fumbling fingers. After a while, she glanced up at him and frowned. "No, but that's ridiculous. I will talk to Siddhartha tonight." Then she said softly, "Everyone? Even my pitucché knew and she kept this from me?" It was suddenly frightening to think that Prajapati hadn't told her.

She got up, forgetting her garland, and walked quickly towards the garden entrance, Devadatta hobbling after her. In the archway, she stood, hand on a column, and watched the other women. They were in the courtyard going about their usual duties, the concubines getting music lessons, the aunts and cousins picking stones out of rice, Prajapati doing accounts on the charpoy. The normalcy of this scene made Devadatta's words seem suddenly more real. He had come up behind her and she could hear his slight panting, feel his heat.

The women saw her now, and stopped what they were doing to nod and smile. She studied them, recalling their various kindnesses, but also what Upasama had said—about what a poor job she did keeping her husband's favour.

The women started to frown, glancing at each other, concerned.

Sumana, the old concubine, stood up; Prajapati put down her tablet and struggled off the charpoy. "Are you well, daharé?"

Yasodhara nodded. "Just tired, pitucché." She walked past them with a wan smile and hurried upstairs. In her room, she sat down on her bed with a gasp, leaning back, legs spread out, one hand grasping her stomach, the other resting back on the bed for support. She took several deep breaths, eyes closed, feeling a bead of sweat trickling down the side of her cheek. After a moment, she grabbed a corner of her shawl and wiped her face. Various images and moments with Siddhartha crowded her mind—that renewed love with which he gazed at her, the gifts he brought, that way he washed her feet as if it were an act of penitence. None of it made sense.

There was a soft knock and she called out, "Yes?"

Devadatta entered, his face worried. "Bhagini . . . the child?"

She nodded to say all was fine, and wiped her face again. She indicated for him to sit quietly on the divan, then pushed herself back on the bed until she could lie down, hands over her stomach, waiting for her strength to gather. She knew what she had to do next. She gazed towards the window, watching the sunlight change position, the room gradually growing gloomier. A mynah came to perch on the sill, spilling out a burble of rising notes. She could smell her brother nearby, that old stables odour of horses and hay. Her brother no longer went to the guards' barracks, but frequented the stables and his old friends there these days.

Finally, she felt strong enough, and she gestured for Devadatta to come help her out of bed.

"You should rest, bhagini," he whispered as he crept up to her. His righteous anger had long dissipated, and now he was frightened at what he had unleashed. *I should resent him, I should*, she thought, but she felt too apprehensive even for that.

"The men's quarters," she said. She went towards the door and Devadatta followed obediently.

They came down to the courtyard together, and the women, by now alerted that something had happened, watched her, concerned. "Daharé," her aunt said, rising again from the cot.

"No, no, pitucché, I'm not overexerting myself." Gesturing her aunt away, she continued out of the quarters with Devadatta, not looking at any of the women, truly angry with them now for what they had hidden from her.

Devadatta took her to Siddhartha's room, and she stood in the dim chamber, with its drawn shutters, looking at the bed, the chests, the tables and divan. She could smell Siddhartha, the odour of his sweat mixed with camphor coming off the dirty dhotis he'd flung about. It felt like the room of a stranger, a chamber in which she was trespassing. She went to one of the windows and threw it open, then turned back to the room, leaning against the windowsill, rooted in place, momentarily unable to do what she must. She was reminded of her mother's room as it had looked soon after the funeral—that sense of emptiness. It was as if Siddhartha had died and here were all his things, which had taken on new poignancy and significance, but were also inert, as if he would never use them again. She drew in her breath to gather herself, then pushed away from the window. She automatically bent to pick up a dirty dhoti flung over a chair and folded it; then fingered bits of his jewellery on the table, so familiar to her and yet so profoundly alien in this environment. And all the time her fear was building, and a knot grew and grew in her throat.

"Bhagini?"

She turned towards Devadatta who had remained in the doorway, from where he was watching her, alarmed. She studied him, then sighed. Either she had to act now or leave.

She went over to a chest and squatted down with difficulty. After closing her eyes for a moment, she opened the lid and gazed at the contents inside—dhotis and shawls neatly folded and stacked. How familiar this idiosyncrasy of her husband's: keeping things in chests and on shelves so neat, and yet flinging objects he'd used on chairs and floor, divans and tables. The knot tightened in her throat; this was likely the moment of truth. She lifted a pile of dhotis. There, beneath them, was the yellow robe. She reached down with trembling fingers and plucked it out. The length of cloth came unwound as she drew it forth and, once she'd flapped it open, she sat back on her knees, gazing at it spread on the floor, her nostrils dilated. She turned back to the chest. Under a pile of shawls, she found the razor for shaving his head and the begging bowl.

She shut the chest. Picking up the robe, the bowl, the razor, she struggled to her feet and drifted towards the door as if in a dream, passing her brother without glancing at him.

When Siddhartha came to Yasodhara that night, he followed his usual routine—removing his turban and slippers, throwing his shawl on the divan.

When he turned around, however, to get the foot bowl, she had beaten him to it and was pouring water into the bowl from a clay jug. She walked over, put the bowl by a stool, lowered herself awkwardly into a kneeling position, then looked up at him, waiting, her face stubborn. He sat with a sigh, a murmur of "Ushas," and offered his feet reluctantly, nervous. She washed and scrubbed his feet with the harsh efficiency of a mother bathing a squirming child. Once she had dried them with a rag, she sat back and regarded him.

At first, he frowned at her hard stare, not understanding. But then, as she continued to glare at him, he flushed. She saw a flash of fear in his eyes before he glanced away.

"Ushas," he began, but she held up a hand to silence him. She went to the window and threw the water out into the street. "Ushas," he said again.

She spun around. "I don't want to hear about it, I don't want to know. If you're unhappy with me, be like a normal man and go to a ganikā. Yes, yes I wish you would. Why don't you?" she begged.

"Ushas." He tried to embrace her, but she raised her arms in a shrug and moved away.

She went to her bed, took the robe, bowl and razor from under a pillow and flung them on the floor. The bowl cracked as it hit the floor. "When were you going to leave me?" she cried as he stared, stricken. "When? I demand you tell me."

"Ushas, you're upset . . . the child . . . I—"

"Were you going to tell me at all, you coward? Or were you going to just slip away into the night without a word?"

"No . . . I . . ." He composed his face, then he said in an almost matter-of-fact tone, "I was going to leave sometime after the birth of our child."

Yasodhara sat heavily on the bed. Until this moment, she had hoped he would deny his plan. Now it was real.

Soon, she got up and began to ready herself for bed; she didn't know what else to say or do. She slipped under the sheet naked and finally looked at Siddhartha. He was standing in the same place. "Come to bed, Surya," she whispered.

He sighed, began to remove his dhoti, then changed his mind. He walked to the door, shoulders hunched with resignation, taking his shawl and turban. ""Don't leave me, Surya!" Yasodhara called out, panicked. "Please don't leave! Come and talk to me, tell me everything. I promise I'll listen without being angry."

He hesitated, half turned towards her.

"This much you owe me," she pleaded.

He gave her a long look, then nodded. He put his turban and shawl on a table and sat on the edge of the bed. He twisted his hands in his lap. Finally he gave a little laugh. "I . . . I've told you the truth so many times in my head, but now . . ." He shot her a haunted look.

"But you must," she whispered, "you must tell me. If you love me at all."

He nodded. With great effort, and haltingly, he began to speak. He told her how, before their marriage, he had heard a Nigantha speak and felt the words resonate in him; he came to think of this calling as a defect he must master, and he'd indeed tried to master it all those years in Mudgala; how the visit by Maha Kosala had made him realize it was not a defect, but a calling shared by a small minority of other men too; how the Truth of Truths had satisfied him for a while but then failed him; how, once he'd returned to Kapilavastu, he could find no peace until he'd answered the call again through Alara Kalama; and how finally, seeing the state of his old friend Pasénadi, he had come to know that he was truly one of the thirsty.

After he was done, he looked down at his hands. Yasodhara studied him, shattered. Finally, she said in a small voice, "All these years, when I've loved you with all my being, you've been a stranger to me."

"Oh, Ushas," he whispered, his eyes luminescent. Yet he did not deny the truth of this.

"So then," she said softly, "what was all this new love you felt for me, Surya? Because it was real, it is real. I know this *is* real."

"It is, Ushas. Because I do love you, and the loss of you is real to me. And it grew more real when I realized I . . . I would leave you." He suddenly began to sob, face in hands, shoulders shaking. "I don't want to leave, because I . . . I do love you. But I must, I must."

"But why? Why must you?" she begged, tears running down her cheeks too.

"Because there is no choice. I . . . I can't see how to live if I can't follow that path."

They sat like that for a while, crying softly. And later, calmer, they continued to sit in silence, listening to the sounds out on the street, the women moving along the corridor. Finally, Yasodhara whispered, "Stay the night, Surya."

Siddhartha nodded miserably and took off his dhoti, folding it neatly for once. In bed, he looked at her beseechingly, and she held her arms out to him. They burrowed into each other, too wrung out to weep any more.

When Yasodhara woke the next morning, he was gone. She lay sprawled in bed, exhausted, unable to get up. Or rather, she was frightened to get out of her bed, because as long as she stayed in it, she wouldn't have to face the wrecked reality of her life. Finally, there was a knock on the door and her aunt put her head inside. She peered at Yasodhara in the darkness, then tiptoed over. "Are you well, daharé? I was worried."

Yasodhara nodded and gestured wordlessly at the window. Her aunt went and opened it. As the light streamed in, her aunt studied her, truly worried, then came softly to the bed and took Yasodhara's hand. "Tell me, daharé."

"I know. About Siddhartha and Alara Kalama."

Her aunt breathed out. "How?"

Yasodhara told Prajapati everything, and her aunt listened, a frown knitting itself across her forehead. "What am I to do, pitucché?" Yasodhara whispered when she was done.

"You do what any woman in your position must do." Prajapati's voice was harsh with purpose. "You fight for your marriage."

"But how, how?"

"The first thing is that man, Alara Kalama, must be sent on his way. He's a wandering ascetic, isn't he? Well, it's time for him to wander off."

Yasodhara drew strength from her aunt's words. Here was a purpose, a plan. "But how can we order him to—" She broke off. The answer was obvious.

A message was delivered to Suddhodana, asking him to come immediately. Yasodhara sent a message for Devadatta too—resent him though she did, he was completely on her side.

The two men soon arrived, worried at the urgent summons, sure it must concern the child. When they rushed into her room, Yasodhara was propped up in bed, dressed, her hair pinned up. They stood still for a moment, taking her in; taking in Prajapati too, seated cross-legged on the bed. Then Suddhodana, face stern with worry, stepped forward to the foot of the bed, gripping one of its posts. His breath was a high wheezing, and she worried for a moment if she should involve her uncle. Since the debacle with Vasabha, his health had declined further. On hearing that news, he had fainted and been forced to stay in bed for a few days, heart hammering in his chest.

Yet Yasodhara knew she had no choice but to tell him, so she and Prajapati took turns informing Suddhodana about Siddhartha.

As they spoke, his face purpled with rage—a rage that was also fear, because once again, as with Vasabha, he had not known what was going on in his own kingdom. When they were finished, Suddhodana turned to his nephew. "You knew too?" Devadatta nodded. "How?"

"The grooms, mātula."

"Even the grooms!" He turned to his wife. "Ayyé, *how* have you not told me? Because, look what you've done! You've let this thing go on for too long, caused such damage, when, if you'd told me, I—" He broke off, coughing.

"Ayyé, this is not the time for recriminations. It's the moment to act. Your grandson . . ." Prajapati gestured to Yasodhara's swollen belly.

Her uncle gripped the bedpost again to gain control and, once his cough had quieted down, he said, "Yes, yes, my grandson." He set his lips firmly. "So, Siddhartha is no longer happy with being merely a judge. Well, you are his wife. You tell me what would make him happy. What post can I offer him? Rashtrika of another province?"

She stared at him; this was the last thing she had expected.

"Ayyé," Prajapati offered hesitantly, "isn't it possible—very likely—that Siddhartha's attraction to this samana way is genuine?"

"Genuine?" Suddhodana cried. "A prince who has been brought up in luxury, who is well placed in the administration of this land? Who is much loved by the people he serves, who loves his wife and has conceived a child, a son, through her? How can Siddhartha, who has never walked anywhere in his life, walk for miles and miles barefoot, as these samanas do? How can Siddhartha, who eats three, sometimes four, meals a day, who has never known starvation or thirst, tolerate living off leaves or grass or whatever is slopped into his begging bowl? No, no, this is about that old stubbornness of his, about shaming and humiliating me." He began to pace. "This is about making a fool of me before my people and the sangha. How he must be enjoying my humiliation right now. Enjoying that I had no idea what he was up to. Well, I am the raja, and he knows nothing about humiliation yet. I will teach him." This tirade exhausted her uncle and he stood breathing harshly for awhile. Then, forgetting he had asked Yasodhara to suggest a position for his son, he stormed out of the room, commanding a frightened Devadatta to follow him.

The moment they were gone, Yasodhara struggled out of bed. "We shouldn't have told him. Pitucché, call for our palanquin—no, no, a chariot will be faster. I must go to the Nigrodha Grove and warn Siddhartha."

"Ushas, I beg you, stay calm, do not exert yourself. For the sake of the child."

She ignored her aunt and continued putting on her slippers, winding a shawl around her shoulders, licking her fingers and pasting back wisps of hair in front of the mirror. But then, once she was dressed, she stood motionless, looking imploringly at Prajapati, paralyzed and unable to act. In the end, she ceded responsibility for action to her uncle.

Later that morning, Yasodhara and Prajapati were summoned to Suddhodana's private receiving room. They went filled with dread, remembering his rage.

In the shuttered chamber, Suddhodana was seated cross-legged on his caned cot, lower lip pushed out righteously. A dishevelled Devadatta stood by his side, arms folded. A movement in a dim corner of the chamber made the women turn sharply. Siddhartha sat in the gloom, leaning back against the wall, his legs straight out, ankles crossed. His face, upper body and legs were dusty, some of the pleats of his dhoti undone. Devadatta had probably stormed into the copse, guards in tow, startled the samanas at their meditation and seized Siddhartha roughly.

Yet despite this, Siddhartha seemed oddly calm and nodded at Yasodhara with a small smile that said, "Don't be upset on my behalf." But she was not reassured; she felt like he was looking at her from some distant place.

Now Suddhodana gestured to some cushions arranged before him. As Yasodhara sat, her eyes slipped to Siddhartha again, who continued to give her that pleasant, distant smile. She truly regretted telling her uncle now.

"This is a family matter and we must deal with it as a family." Suddhodana regarded the women sternly. "Our son, your husband, has come under the thrall of a bad influence. These things happen to many young men, but I hadn't thought my son would be this foolish. Still, these things happen." Suddhodana took a moment to regain his breath, wheezing. "I have sent a message to Jatila that he is to rid the Nigrodha Grove of these heretics."

"But pita," Siddhartha said gently, "just sending Alara Kalama on his way won't stop me. I will continue to believe in the sage's words, continue to—"

"So, then believe!" Suddhodana cried, a little thrown by Siddhartha's tone. "Many people believe! I hear that even Jatila and Sirima are now doing the meditations." Suddhodana paused significantly. "What I have to say next is unfortunate and it pains me to say it. You are temporarily relieved of your duties as judge. Confined to the palace. Indefinitely, or at least until you come to your senses." Suddhodana pointed at Yasodhara. "Look at your wife's condition. You must teach yourself your duty. Must teach yourself joy at the coming birth of your son. Must acknowledge and love your son. Yes, acknowledge! If you aren't here to claim the legitimacy of your son in the naming ceremony, my grandson will be illegitimate!" He began to cough again. When he had calmed down, he signalled Devadatta to come closer. "Now, since I want to keep this a family matter, Devadatta will be your guard. He is going to move into the room next to yours. Once I feel you're well enough to resume your duties, he will accompany you to work and back."

"So, for the rest of my life, he will accompany me?" Siddhartha said, again gently. "Because, pita, I will continue to practise the—"

"By all means practise! Go to Jatila's daily if you wish to practise." Suddhodana gestured to Devadatta with a laugh and a wink: "Who knows, daharā, you too might find yourself an acolyte, from accompanying my son." Devadatta grinned to say that was not likely. And yet, crude and insensitive as her uncle's words were, Yasodhara saw there was truth in what he said. Siddhartha didn't need to go away with the ascetic; he could follow the teachings here. Something lightened within her and she felt a grudging gratitude towards her uncle. Here was something concrete that could be done.

At a signal from Suddhodana, Devadatta crossed the room. "Come, Siddhartha."

"Am I to not be visited by my husband?" Yasodhara demanded quickly. If she had a chance to influence Siddhartha, perhaps she could convince him he would be happy here.

"Of course." Suddhodana nodded to Devadatta that this should be permitted.

Siddhartha stood up. He smiled, as if he understood something they didn't. Ignoring his cousin's proffered hand, he went towards the door, Devadatta following.

"Bring him tonight," Yasodhara called out to Devadatta. He nodded sternly.

That night, Yasodhara opened her door to let Siddhartha through, but when Devadatta made to follow, she frowned at her brother incredulously. She stepped into the corridor, shut the door so Siddhartha couldn't overhear, and took a moment to smother her irritation.

"Bhāta, I must try to win Siddhartha over. Try to make him understand that he does love me and our child. So, give us our time together."

Devadatta twirled the end of his sash, his expression self-righteous. "This man, your husband, was preparing to follow these samanas without a care for you, for your reputation, the legitimacy of your son." She gave him another appealing look and, after a moment, he nodded. "I will post my own men to guard both entrances to the quarters for the night."

She watched him limp down the corridor for a moment, then came inside to find Siddhartha seated on a stool. She brought a bowl of water, knelt in front of him and began to wash his feet. After some time, he said softly, "You told my pita."

"That man Alara Kalama had to leave."

"But his leaving doesn't change my desire to follow the samana path, Ushas."

"No, I daresay not. But the truth is, Surya, hardly any of us get everything we want. Most of us live with half-wants." She gave him a firm look. "And you and I are going to have to learn to live thus. For the sake of our child."

She finished washing his feet, dried them, then sat back. "There is a lot you can do here in Kapilavastu, Surya. A lot of good. As your pita pointed out, the teachings of Alara Kalama are being taken up by many. You, because I know what you are capable of, have grasped them better than most. So, lead our people, in the way you did in Mudgala. You find meaning helping and leading others. This is another chance to do so. And isn't it a wonderful thing that the Vessas, your favourite people, among whom you now work, can also practise and benefit from these teachings?"

He looked at her for a long moment. "Ah, Ushas, I'm sorry I'm causing you such pain." The apology was genuine, and after a moment, she nodded to say she accepted it. She needed to lead in mending their marriage.

In the middle of the night, she awoke in a panic, expecting to find him gone, but he was lying next to her, asleep. The physical proximity of him, his familiar smell, the rise and fall of his chest, his warmth made all he had said about leaving unreal. "I have to be patient," she told herself. "I just have to hang on, to bear through. And soon there will be the child to love, to fill our life."

Later the next day, she learned that Siddhartha had summoned the Brahmin who recited the law and questioned the man about the latest cases. He had also asked the Brahmin about ones that were upcoming, and asked his advice about the decisions he might make. Suddhodana brought her this news when he came to visit. "As you see, dhītā, now Siddhartha returns to himself." Yasodhara could tell her uncle was very pleased with himself, believing he had mastered the situation, but she was not so convinced by this rapid turnabout.

That night when Siddhartha came to her, he was contrite and sweet. He brought her a garland of flowers, saying playfully, "Do you know to what troubles a prisoner must go to get anything from outside his palace cell?"

She bent her head so he could place the garland around her neck and smiled willingly, but she no longer trusted any loving gestures from him. Perhaps she never would again. He lifted her chin and looked at her face for a long moment, taking in her worry. "My poor Ushas," he murmured, "what trouble I have brought on you."

"Ah," she smiled brightly, to bring cheerfulness to their exchange, "but at least the garland is beautiful. How did you get it?"

"Aha! I have become the curiosity of the men's quarters. All manner of people come to look, to gawk, to ask about this new philosophy."

"Ask what?"

He waved his hand vaguely and indicated for her to sit, then went towards the jug and foot bowl. She watched as he poured the water, his back to her. So men were already coming to seek advice and edification about the new philosophy. This was even better than she had hoped. Perhaps she could trust him to stay after all.

He returned to kneel before her with the bowl and began to wash her feet in a tender, gentle way, as if performing a sacred rite, his face suffused with love and sadness. She watched him, hardly daring to breathe. He was returning to her, to their world.

Since Ananda's departure, Anuruddha had come often to see Yasodhara. They would go walking in the palace garden, her cousin looking even more haggard these days. These were mostly silent walks. Anuruddha had little to say to her—he had done what he had done; and she was too tired, too distracted by her own problems, for recriminations. She found there was something restful about walking in silence with someone preoccupied with their own troubles; something restful in not having to keep up a front, or placate and soothe as she had to in the quarters with the women, who were so worried for her, for the baby. When Anuruddha dropped her off at the end of their walks, she would occasionally ask, "Any word?" and he would shake his head. She asked out of habit more than anything. She knew that if he had heard from Ananda, if Ananda had returned, Anuruddha would have told her right away. She missed her cousin—but then again, he had often gone away on extended trips. This too, she kept telling herself, was an extended trip. One day he would show up suddenly at the quarters' street door, holding out, with a grin, some little gift from his travels.

One evening they were walking in the garden when Anuruddha said softly, "Siddhartha seems well in his confinement."

"I take comfort that time mends everything, ñātaka."

"But be careful, ñātiké. A gambler denied his dice only falls more passionately in love with it." He pushed back his turban with a quiet sigh. "I should know well."

Yasodhara nodded thoughtfully. "Yes. I'll tell our mātula that his son has recovered his senses and should be freed. It is time to test Siddhartha."

The next day she spoke to her uncle and Siddhartha was released. He soon resumed all his duties with mild acquiescence, accompanied everywhere by Devadatta. The story of his wanting to leave with Alara Kalama had spread through the city and gave him a new fame—and the fact that he was now escorted by Devadatta only added to his notoriety.

Yasodhara knew he wasn't really happy, but then, neither was she. "But our child will help us love each other in a different way," she told herself yet again.

In the seventh month of Yasodhara's pregnancy, the Simantonnayana ceremony was performed in the sacrificial enclosure. Suddhodana invited a large gathering to witness it. The rite took place in the fortnight of the waxing moon, when it was in conjunction with an asterism that was male. The hide of a freshly slaughtered bull was laid out to the west of the domestic fire, with its neck to the east and hair combed so it fell beyond the edges of the hide. Yasodhara was escorted to sit on the hide and Siddhartha took her hand while he made eight offerings of ghee to the fire, repeating after the Royal Priest verses from the Vedas. She was aware that the guests were studying her and Siddhartha, trying to discern the state of their relations. They were both quietly affectionate and kept their gazes only on each other, ignoring the prying stares. A plate of boiled rice was brought forward by Prajapati and ghee was poured on it. "What do you see?" Siddhartha asked, and as she had been instructed, Yasodhara said, "I see sons and cattle." Then Siddhartha loosened her hair so it covered her face and parted it down the centre with a porcupine quill that had three white spots on it.

He retraced this parting twice more with the quill. Next, Siddhartha retraced the same parting three times with a bunch of unripe fruit that formed the pendant of a rope necklace. As he did so, the Royal Head Priest chanted verses from the Vedas. The necklace was then placed around her neck. Siddhartha retraced the parting in her hair three times again, but this time with a bunch of kusa grass. A Brahmin woman who had many sons was led forward, and she addressed these auspicious words to Yasodhara: "Be you the mother of a valiant son."

For the rest of the day, until the stars began to appear in the sky, Siddhartha observed a vow of silence. Then he left the palace through its north entrance, touched a male calf that was tethered there, and finally broke his silence by reciting one last verse of the Vedas.

As the time for her delivery grew nearer, Yasodhara found she longed for the presence of her mother. She also missed and mourned her father. Often at night she dreamt of being back in her mother's room in Ramagama, and would wake surprised to take in her current surroundings before falling back on her pillow, heavy with grief.

When she was close to term, the midwife who had delivered two generations of the Gotama Gotra in Kapilavastu came to live in the women's quarters. Once her labour began, the woman would be there to ease her through the birth.

Her water broke a week later and Siddhartha was called upon to perform the final rite before birth. He went down to the Rohini River and dipped a cup in it, drawing water in the direction of the current. He returned with the cup to her chamber. There, he placed a turyanti plant at her feet, then touched her head with both hands and recited mantras the Royal Head Priest had taught him. Next, he sprinkled water on her from the cup, chanting further verses: "Just as the wind moves a lake on all sides, so may thou, fetus, move and come out. Just as the wind, the forest and the sea are in movement, so mayst thou, fetus, now in the ninth month, come out together with the afterbirth. May the male child sleeping nine months inside his mother come out a living being, unharmed, his mother herself alive."

Throughout, Yasodhara had kept up a stoic demeanour but now, the ritual over, she moaned as a contraction gripped her. Siddhartha looked at her full of worry and pity, and his eyes stayed on her as Prajapati hastily ushered him out of the room.

Soon the pain, the commands of the midwife, the immense effort it took to force the child out, became her entire world. Between contractions, her mind was adrift in exhaustion and pain. As the day continued, her contractions grew in intensity until finally, with a great push, a yell, she expelled the child from her body. "A boy, a boy!" her aunt and the midwife cried. She propped herself up shakily, watching the midwife suck out the phlegm from his mouth. The moment the woman was done, the child cried out and Yasodhara felt something tug deep in her, as if realigned within. She held out her hands for the child, but then, remembering she was forbidden to touch him yet, dropped her arms in exasperation.

Prajapati ran to push open the window, to cry down the news to Siddhartha, Devadatta, Suddhodana and the women who were gathered in the courtyard, anxiously waiting.

The moment she was tidied up and ready to receive, Siddhartha came in, followed by his father and five priests. No one, except the midwife, had touched the child; they were waiting on Siddhartha to be the one to touch him next. The midwife handed the baby to Siddhartha and he gestured for the Brahmins to each come forward and breathe over the child. Then he breathed thrice over his son and whispered in his ear three times the word "speech"—a wish that the knowledge and wisdom of the Vedas might come to him when he grew into adulthood. Prajapati next gave Siddhartha a golden spoon on which there was a lump of ghee. He placed it against the infant's mouth, making sure a bit got on his tongue, saying, "Puthā, I give unto thee wisdom and knowledge. Puthā, may you have a long life; puthā, may you live in this world for a hundred years, protected by the gods." Bringing his son's ear close to his mouth, he whispered, "Puthā, may god Savitr bestow on thee intelligence; may the two Asvins, wearing wreaths of lotus, give to thee intelligence." He touched the child's two shoulders. "Be a stone, be an axe, be indestructible gold."

After a moment of examining his son, Siddhartha leaned close again and whispered softly into his ear—saying the child's name so he alone would hear it first and thus claim it as his own. Then Siddhartha handed the child to Yasodhara, saying the final verses from the Vedas: "O mother, O strong one, thou hast given birth to a valiant son, mayst thou be endowed with other valiant sons." The Head Priest came forward to tie a hempen string wound with a gold thread around the infant's wrist.

The rituals over, everyone gathered around the bed, talking excitedly.

Yasodhara held the child, gazing at it in wonder, then looked at Siddhartha and smiled. She watched him closely as he came to sit by her, touching the child with his little finger, his face suffused with love. "It happens as I predicted," she thought. "The reality of our child blows away the rest, like straw in a wind."

The boy began to make a sucking, mewling sound. "He wants to be fed, dhītā," Prajapati said quietly.

Yasodhara exposed her breast and waited for the midwife to come forward and show her how to attach the infant's mouth to her nipple. But, before the woman could do so, the child closed his mouth around her nipple and began to suck. Yasodhara laughed in surprise, and the others laughed too.

"Already wise, my grandson," Suddhodana cried.

Once the child was sated, Suddhodana held out his hands and took him with a chortle of delight. Yasodhara was pleased to see that her uncle seemed much recovered suddenly; even his wheeze had disappeared. He began to cross towards the window, then turned to Siddhartha. "And what is my grandson's name?"

"It's Rahula, pita," Siddhartha said after a moment.

A bewildered silence filled the room at this unusual name. Then the Head Priest said, "Ah, after Rahu, the snake who swallows the Sun during an eclipse?"

Siddhartha nodded.

"A warrior's name!" Suddhodana cried. "May my grandson grow as strong as Rahu, who has the strength to consume even the Sun."

But Yasodhara knew there was another meaning to the word "rahu": fetter, impediment. As she looked around the room, she saw that no one else appeared to have remembered this. She couldn't tell even if Siddhartha recalled it or not.

That night, he came to her room. He lay on the bed, the baby between them, gazing at Yasodhara, at the child, his face luminous with love. Finally, she fell asleep. When Prajapati woke her later to feed the child, Siddhartha was gone.

✻

DUKKHA III:
The Three Fires

1

Osprey

SHEAVES OF PADDY mark at regular intervals the borders of the Harvest Festival arena, the sun-kissed smell of mown hay fragrant in the air. Yasodhara, perched on the edge of her stool in the raja's pavilion, watches for Rahula as the boys come out onto the newly harvested field. She is well aware of the prying gazes of the other spectators, keen to discern how she is taking this news of Siddhartha resurfacing a month ago. When she arrived at the tournament, part of her wanted to sit, to hide, among the palace women on the reed mats around her, but pride wouldn't let her. Nor would her festering anger against Siddhartha, against a world that lauds his accomplishments.

Beside her, Prajapati, also on a stool, touches her arm now and points out Rahula, half-hidden by the older and taller boys who are taking their places in a line for the archery competition. The women of the quarters have also seen Rahula and there is a murmur among them, an "aah" like a little breeze, before they turn to smile and nod at Yasodhara.

Next to the women's mats is her uncle on his throne, also under the pavilion canopy constructed out of branches and leaves, poles at each corner holding it up. Prajapati calls, "Ayyé," and points out Rahula to him at the end of the line. Suddhodana lifts his hand to thank her, and a smile lights his face as he sights his grandson. To either side of Suddhodana, on stools, are Mahanama and Amitodhana. To the outside world, the three men present a united front, but she knows that they are like dogs forced by hunger to share the same charnel ground.

How gracefully her Rahula stands. Unlike the other awkward, restive boys, he is relaxed, with a mature calm well beyond his ten years—his arms easily by his side, one hand holding the bow, his energy contained. Yet she knows how much training with Devadatta has brought him to this place of calm confidence. Already in this tournament he has won in wrestling and spear-throwing in his age category. Archery is the final test that will determine if he'll win the golden arrow.

She spots Devadatta now, skirting the edge of the field, making his way towards the line of boys. Reaching his nephew, he puts an arm around Rahula's shoulder and leans down to whisper last-minute instructions, pointing at the target. Rahula nods gravely and narrows his eyes in cool concentration.

The line inches forward, each boy taking his turn to shoot an arrow at the target: a live osprey, its spread-out wings clipped to a propped-up board, chest marked with concentric circles—this bird of the air that hunts in water an offering of thanks to both Vayu, god of the winds, and Rudra, god of rain.

None of the boys hits the osprey, and with each failing shot there are little murmurs of disappointment from families and gotras.

In the sky, a hoopoe flits back and forth. A sign of luck, thinks Yasodhara—but for whom?

Rahula is the last to try. He steps up to the chalked line and checks the position of his feet, directing a quick, serious glance at Devadatta for approval. Yasodhara leans forward, breathless. Around the arena the gathered courtiers, the wealthy Vessas, are also expectant. Rahula is their favourite to win and many have placed bets on him. For a long moment, Rahula holds his position, arrow in place, bow taut and extended. The hoopoe sweeps just over his head. Then, before Yasodhara can breathe in and out, he has let the arrow fly and it strikes the target perfectly in the centre. The osprey cries out harshly before it grows limp.

Yasodhara jumps up, shrieking, as do the women of the palace, and a roar of approval goes through the crowd. Suddhodana claps and lets out a strangled shout. Even Mahanama and Amitodhana are grudgingly impressed.

Now Devadatta, hiding his pride behind a warrior's stern demeanour, goes to Rahula. He grasps the arm that carries the bow and holds it up, then walks Rahula around the perimeter of the cheering field—something so poignant, thinks Yasodhara, about this shambling, limping man leading such a light-stepping youth. They come finally to the raja, and Devadatta drops Rahula's arm and steps back. Rahula kneels before his grandfather. Suddhodana reaches for the golden arrow on a table beside him, leans forward, and places it in Rahula's quiver. Then, casting aside his dignity, he grabs Rahula's face and kisses him, as a laughing Rahula throws his arms around his grandfather's neck. Once again, a murmur of pleasure and approval ripples through the crowd.

But Rahula is not done yet. He gets to his feet and walks the few paces to where the women are seated, reaching back in his quiver for the golden arrow as he draws near. Yasodhara watches him approach, holding her breath, aware of the gaze of the other women on him, on her, aware that the entire arena is watching. When he is before her, he kneels, and with an impish smile offers her the arrow, holding it out formally with both hands.

The crowd applauds as Yasodhara takes the arrow, her eyes filling with tears. She leans forward and touches the side of her son's face.

Later, as Yasodhara follows the women towards the gathered chariots and palanquins that will conduct everyone back to the city, Devadatta catches up and falls into step beside her.

"Thank you, bhāta," she says, taking his arm, "you've made me happy." A look passes between them to acknowledge her misery these last few weeks.

Devadatta gestures to Rahula, who is walking ahead with Suddhodana. "His winning has very little to do with me, bhagini. The boy is naturally gifted." But Yasodhara knows her brother is pleased with Rahula's success, and with her happiness.

Later that night, once Rahula has changed and is in his bed in the antechamber of Yasodhara's room, she comes to sit with him. For a while, he holds the golden arrow in his hand, enjoying how it glistens as he turns it in the lamplight. How much like Siddhartha he looks, with his slim body and upturned nose, his long neck and expressive clavicle that rises and falls with his breath, that flutters with his speaking. But it's not just in his looks. Like Siddhartha at ten, Rahula has a perspicacity well beyond his years.

He is different from Siddhartha, however, in his temperament—his fits of passion, his stubbornness, she acknowledges come from her.

Yasodhara pushes all these thoughts away and leans in to kiss him on the forehead. "We are all so proud of you, puthā."

Rahula nods, but he is distant, pensive.

She squeezes his hand, head cocked inquiringly.

"Ammé, do you think my father would be proud of me today?"

"Yes, yes," she blurts. Then, composing herself, she adds, trying to keep the quiver out of her voice, "Well, to tell the truth, I don't think he would care much either way." She nods sagely at Rahula's dismay. "He was never good at the manly pursuits. So he pretended disdain for them, pretended they didn't matter." She strokes her boy's hair off his forehead. "Rahula, you are now old enough to know and accept some truths. And one of them is that just because a man is your father doesn't mean he is a good man. Look at the way Nanda, the head groom, whips his son for no crime. So, we have to accept that your pita is a selfish man who doesn't love you and me as much as he loves his futile pursuit of 'freedom.' He deserted us without even saying goodbye." She gathers herself, then takes Rahula's hand and strokes it—more to calm herself than to soothe the boy. "So, there you have it, puthā, the truth." She smiles. "I hope I haven't hurt you too much by telling you this. But you are a man now. Your win today proves you are so. And a man, a future raja, must always look at the truth straight on." She nods at Rahula's exclamation. "Yes, indeed, I do think you could be the raja one day. And I know that your ayyaka is going to suggest you go to the Savatthi Court when you turn thirteen."

She expects Rahula to be delighted at this, but instead, his face grows solemn. "Bahiya, Pandu's son, says that my win means nothing. That it is he, Bahiya, who will be picked for the Savatthi Court when we are all thirteen."

Yasodhara laughs. "Fat, lazy Bahiya? He would be the last to be chosen."

"He says his father has promised him that."

"But you are the grandson of the raja. Why would anyone pick Pandu's son over you? Pandu is nothing. Not even an amici. Just a nobleman with a vote in the sangha." She leans in and kisses Rahula. "Puthā, you must not let yourself be cast down by jealous people. A future raja cannot let himself be swayed so easily by what others say."

⚹

At the end of the month, Yasodhara goes, as always, to Ananda's old home. When she reaches her destination, she draws back the palanquin curtain and sits a moment, examining the house—its ruffled thatch looks rather forlorn because it is not yet nesting season for the herons; the wattle and daub of the perimeter wall is broken in one patch, and weeds grow from seeds embedded in the crack. She sighs, then gets out and clangs the bell. When the servant comes to the door, the man bows and says, "Sāmini," unsurprised to see her as it's the last day of the month.

She follows him across the courtyard, noting how badly swept it is, the plants along the edges in need of a good watering, the beds dry in this hot season, the verandahs dusty. The receiving room is dim in the bristling heat, the shutters closed, faint bars of light filtering in through the slats. In one of these shafts, she sees Anuruddha seated in a window well, tablet in hand, bent over a counting board, concentrating so hard his tongue sticks out. "Ah, ñātiké," he cries. He gives her a gay, self-mocking smile, an exaggerated sigh. "Just in time." He holds out the account tablet and she takes it with a smile, perching in the window well next to him. She leans over the counting board and does his accounts, just as she does at the end of every month, helping him keep up Ananda's business.

"I fear I am being cheated by every merchant in this city." He pushes back his yellow turban with a sigh.

"You're not doing too badly, ñātaka." She raises her eyebrows, teasing. "Though you'd do much better if you weren't gambling some of it away."

"Ah ñātiké, don't deny me my one pleasure," he pleads in an exaggerated manner, and they both laugh.

This is why she likes coming to see him. With Anuruddha, she can slip back into her old self; she never feels he is watching her for signs of madness.

"But have you heard the latest news on our famous ñātaka?" he says.

Yasodhara laughs again, grateful that Ananda refers to Siddhartha as their cousin and not her husband, inviting her to maintain a mocking distance.

"Oh dear, oh dear, yes," she cries. "Famous in Rajagaha! And have you also heard? The Maharaja Bimbisara has donated an extensive area of bamboo forest for setting up a monastery."

"Indeed. The Bamboo Grove!"

"Sounds like the haunt of lovers, not ascetics."

Anuruddha holds out a hand and declaims, "In the Bamboo Grove, my beloved, with her luscious thighs like the trunks of banana trees . . . like . . ."

He signals to her for inspiration and she adds, ". . . thighs like the trunks of banana trees, between which she clenched my heart. Her eyes like . . . like . . ."

"Crescent moons that . . . etcetera, etcetera."

They both laugh again.

"Yes," Anuruddha continues, "Bimbisara, like a besotted lover, goes daily, alighting from his chariot and walking into the grove, to sit on the floor before his beloved and listen to him preach. And where the lion leads, the jackals and buzzards follow. People are evidently vying to feed the three hundred monks, to fill their bowls as they pass through the city on their morning alms round."

"And you should see the royal triad. Puffed up with pride again. Yes, the triad's old arrogance is back."

They grimace wryly at each other.

"You should hear them," she continues. "'Our valiant Siddhartha,' 'Our redeemer.' And the sangha is to soon meet in the santagara to pass a motion making Siddhartha a peer of the city."

For the past ten years, ever since Pasénadi discovered Vasabha's true parentage, the fortunes of the ruling triad have been low. The maharaja, upon realizing he was tricked, immediately appointed a new, harsher senapati to Kapilavastu. The new general no longer follows the protocol of suggesting and advising, but simply informs the triad and the sangha of the wishes and commands of the maharaja. The new senapati has also incorporated the palace guards into the army and appointed a mixture of Sakiya soldiers and the maharaja's soldiers to the palace, thus stripping the Sakiya of their last vestige of military sovereignty.

In these past ten years too, Suddhodana's health has waxed and waned, and he is seldom without his wheeze, occasionally taking to bed, his heart banging in his chest. Yet recently, since hearing of Siddhartha's fame, he is sitting up straighter, his wheeze barely there.

When they are done the accounts and Anuruddha sees Yasodhara to the street door, she asks, as she sometimes still does, "And Ananda?"

He shrugs to say no news, and gives his standard reply: "I keep his business up for him."

Yasodhara nods mildly, but she suspects that Anuruddha doesn't try very hard to get information on the whereabouts of his brother. If nothing else, travelling merchants would surely know what's happened to him. She suspects Anuruddha is frightened of the truth.

"And that poor girl Vasabha."

They shake their heads.

The maharaja, unable to dissolve a marriage sanctified by the Vedas and the gods, nor to claim fraud because she was Mahanama's legitimate daughter, did the next best thing—moved her to a house in the ganikā district, thus returning insult with insult. Vasabha has a nine-year-old son by the maharaja now, Vidudabha, his first male child. Yet the maharaja doesn't acknowledge this son and hasn't even seen him.

"I think about her sometimes," Yasodhara says wistfully, "and wonder if, at twenty-six, she is still so pliable. 'Bending with the wind,' as Ananda used to say." She shrugs. "And Nagamunda, I wonder what she thinks of her decision now."

"Ah, why would she complain, ñātiké? Her daughter is married to the Maharaja of the Kosala Empire."

They kiss farewell. As she gets into the palanquin, she looks back at Anuruddha and catches him in a moment of pensiveness before he gives her a smart salute and a grin. She salutes him back, then settles in among the cushions. How shabby he looks at forty—a settled shabbiness, just like the house. But then, at thirty-nine, she must not look much better—she overheard a visiting relative, the other day, maliciously describe her as having "the twitchiness of a cow that has narrowly escaped death by a tiger."

Yasodhara takes another look at the house before drawing the curtain, remembering the day she first saw it, and how, despite its derelict state, it seemed to burst with possibility.

⚘

One day a month later, as the family eat their midday meal—the *swish-swish* of large palm fans waved by the slaves filling the silence as Yasodhara and Prajapati serve Rahula, Sundari Nanda and Suddhodana—a messenger arrives and bows timidly in the doorway. The man is a spy in the Licchavi Republic. Suddhodana gestures him in. He prostrates himself, then stands to one side respectfully and begins to speak: "Sāmi, I bring strange news." He pauses significantly. "As you know, there is drought everywhere in the Middle Country. But it is raining *only* in the Licchavi Republic. *Only* within its borders."

Everyone murmurs in astonishment.

"A miracle, sāmi. Performed by the Awakened One."

Suddhodana signals for the spy to go on.

"A week ago, the Maharaja Bimbisara, as overlord of the Licchavi Republic, sent the Awakened One to Vesali, to help the Licchavi princes deal with an epidemic of the purging-disease that has come to the city with the drought. The maharaja offered them the Awakened One because of his skill as an administrator. But then, not long after the Awakened One arrived, the rains started in Vesali and the epidemic began to abate. Now the rains have spread to the whole republic. A miracle."

"But," Prajapati demands, "how did he perform this miracle?"

Yasodhara notices Rahula straining forward to listen, fiercely intent.

"In Vesali, the Awakened One taught a sutta called the Jewel Sutta, sāmini. This sutta is now being hailed as having miraculous powers to bring rain. The words of the sutta are spreading throughout the Middle Country."

"And does the Awakened One claim to have performed this miracle?" Yasodhara demands.

"No, sāmini. He denies any control over rain or disease. He says he's against magic, superstition and ritual, which he considers distractions from the Middle Way."

Yasodhara gives a huff of a laugh. Siddhartha's teachings are being interpreted against his will.

The moment the messenger is gone, Rahula turns to her. "But, ammé, is it not possible that my pita has performed such a miracle? It's raining only within the Republic."

"He himself denies it, Rahula. I don't know why the rains are falling only in the Licchavi Republic, but it has nothing to do with your pita."

"But the rain *is* falling in the Republic alone," Sundari Nanda now chimes in. "How can it be only falling there and not anywhere else? It must be a miracle."

Everyone turns to Suddhodana to ask his opinion, and Yasodhara notices for the first time that he has retreated into a sad silence, his shoulders stooped. "Ayyé?" Prajapati rests a hand on his arm.

He shrugs her away and frowns. "And here, our people suffer without any relief."

By the next meal, however, Suddhodana is sitting up straight again and even before the food is served, he declares with purpose, "I am inviting Siddhartha to visit. I have been meaning to do this for some time, and now is the moment to do so. He will come out of love and loyalty to me." He nods at Yasodhara's dismay. "I'm sorry, daharé, I know his visit will be hard for you. But you must put the best interests of your son and our state first. Siddhartha will help turn the fortunes of our Sakiya people and therefore the fortunes of our Rahula. He deserves to be the raja someday."

Yasodhara's hand trembles as she dishes food for Rahula. He looks at her, trying to read her thoughts. "And . . . and how do you know he will come, mātula?" Yasodhara asks.

"He's my son and he has always been dutiful."

"So dutiful that he abandoned his wife and child? No, no, believe me, mātula, he will not come." Suddhodana frowns, annoyed at this contradiction but also, she suspects, because she has confirmed his doubts. She turns to Rahula. "Don't expect that your pita will come, puthā."

A royal delegation is dispatched to Siddhartha. It is led by two retired ministers, venerable and pious old men sent to give Siddhartha his father's greeting and invite him to visit. A month passes, then two, and finally the delegation returns. Yasodhara hears the news and hurries to the official receiving room alongside her aunt and Rahula, who clutches her hand with anxious anticipation.

The room is packed with courtiers and amicis. They make their way to the front where the triad is seated, and stand beside them.

The delegates troop in, dusty and tired. As the crowd clears a path to let them through, Yasodhara sees from their dispirited faces that they have failed. And further, the two old ministers are not with them.

One of the men, Kaludayi, a childhood friend of Siddhartha's, comes forward and prostrates himself before the triad. Then he stands back with the other delegates, his head, like theirs, bent in defeat. "But where is Sukkodana?" Suddhodana demands. "Where is Dhotodana?" He looks towards the door as if he expects the two ministers to appear.

The other members glance at each other. Finally, Kaludayi says, "Sāmi, they have renounced the world and joined Siddhartha's school."

There is a stunned silence, followed by murmurs and little gasps from all those gathered. Yasodhara too is astonished, for these men were ardent practisers of the sacrifices, hosting large ceremonies where they offered up dogs, goats, buffaloes and even horses to the gods, bringing in famous Vedic forest ascetics to officiate.

"And . . . what news do you bring from my son?" Suddhodana demands, even though the truth is already clear. "When is he coming to visit us? I expected you to bring him back."

Again the delegates look at each other. And again, it is Kaludayi who speaks: "He remained silent when we invited him to visit Kapilavastu."

"We begged him to return, sāmi," another adds.

"Sāmi," a third member of the delegation cries, "despite some of us being from his Gotama Gotra, despite some of us knowing him since he was a boy, we had to take our place along with other petitioners. Line up even behind Dasas or Suddas to get an audience with him."

"At first, he refused to even see us, claiming tiredness!" a fourth cries.

A sound from Rahula makes Yasodhara turn to him. He returns her gaze—hurt, astonished; and she sees with sorrow that despite her warning, he was sure Siddhartha would come.

Suddhodana orders the room to clear. As the nobles disperse, Yasodhara hears them mutter, "How dare he!" "Thinks he's above us, now that he's

Bimbisara's favourite." She knows that it's only a matter of time before the entire city turns against Siddhartha.

For herself, though, this news is a relief. She doesn't want Siddhartha back here, disturbing her life; there is nothing to be gained for her by his coming.

After the courtiers have left, Suddhodana rises to leave, then sinks back into his chair with a groan. "Ayyaka!" Rahula rushes to his grandfather, Prajapati right behind him. Suddhodana waves them away, eyes closed, face flushed with sweat.

By that evening, Suddhodana has taken to his bed, heart battering against sternum, muttering confusedly. Yasodhara, Prajapati and Rahula are present when the Royal Bisaj examines him. The man's grave expression tells them it is not good news. Rahula is distraught, clutching Suddhodana's hand and whispering, "Ayyaka, I am here with you, do you hear me?" When Yasodhara tries to guide him away with a gentle "Puthā," he glares and shrugs her arm off his shoulders.

They follow the bisaj out of the room. Once the door is shut behind them, he says, "Sāmini, I fear this attack is more serious than the others."

"How serious?" Prajapati whispers.

"I don't think he will ever properly recover."

Yasodhara and Prajapati look at each other, frightened.

"Sāmini . . . I have warned you all."

They nod to acknowledge that he did warn them. Every time Suddhodana took to his bed, the bisaj implored that he must stop eating and drinking so much, that he must hand over more duties to the other members of the triad. But her uncle is jealous of his duties, fearful that if he hands more of them over, Mahanama and Amitodhana will finally depose him by forcing a vote in the sangha for a new raja, on grounds of his ill health.

Later that evening, Yasodhara returns to her uncle's chamber with her aunt to find Rahula there asleep, seated on a stool by the bed, cheek resting on his grandfather's hand. When she gently awakens him, he opens his eyes, face vulnerable for a moment before it hardens. "Go wash your face," she whispers. "Have something to eat." He leaves reluctantly.

Coming out onto the verandah later, she finds Rahula seated on the steps, staring moodily into the dusk, chewing on a piece of roti—his sullenness giving him an air of a teenager rather than a ten-year-old. She sits beside him and tries to put her arm around him, but he moves away with a drawn-out *"Tttch*, ammé!"

"Puthā, I know that you're angry with your pita, but—"

"My pita has caused ayyaka to fall ill. He is a selfish man who only cares for his own fame. Why," Rahula continues, his voice rising, "he cares for foreigners, for these Licchavi, but not for his own people."

Yasodhara feels sure these are Devadatta's words. "Yes, but puthā, he—"

"Aren't you angry with him, ammé? You are, you are! So, why do you pretend you aren't? He has robbed you of everything."

Again, her brother's words. After a moment she sighs and tries another approach. "Yes, I am angry with him. But, puthā, you cannot allow your pita to ruin your life."

Rahula throws up his arms in an angry, despairing gesture. "Why are we discussing my pita? All I care about is ayyaka. I don't care about anything else right now."

Yasodhara decides to leave the conversation there, for the moment. Her son is clearly unable to listen to her right now. As she walks away, she curses Siddhartha for the trouble he has brought down on her.

The next day, the women are at their midday meal in the courtyard— Rahula, Prajapati and Yasodhara, too, because with Suddhodana ill, there is no need for formal dining—when suddenly Rahula says, "My pita should have come here first when he left the forest. Instead he honours all these foreign kings, rather than ayyaka."

The women glance uncertainly at Yasodhara, and she gives them a look to say, "Be patient with him."

"Daharā," the old concubine Sumana says gently, "perhaps your father has his reasons, which we don't know."

"You defend him?" Rahula cries, immediately furious. "I hate him! I hate him!"

Prajapati, shocked, gives Yasodhara an appealing look to say she must chastise Rahula for speaking to Sumana like that. But, before Yasodhara can say anything, Mitta chimes in. "But Rahula, your pita was on his path, like any samana. And a samana who leaves home doesn't keep contact with his family. Look at what a great truth he has brought back to us, about dukkha and the nature of existence."

Rahula leaps to his feet. "Ah, so you think what he did was right? To abandon my ammé and me?" He gestures in a wide arc to include all the women. "I hear you discussing his Middle Way. Discussing his fame. I see that you admire him." The women murmur in protest, in appeal, but he waves his hand dismissively. "You're happy that he doesn't love us, that he cares more for some useless philosophy than us!"

"Rahula, Rahula." Yasodhara reaches to grab his arm but he twists away from her.

"No, no, I hate him, and I will say so. He is a foul, selfish man. Why should I pretend he isn't? What has he done to deserve my love or even my respect?" He runs out of the courtyard. The women look sympathetically at Yasodhara, shaking their heads to say they're sorry she must deal with this.

That night, Rahula doesn't come to Yasodhara's room at the usual time. She is about to go look for him when there's a soft tap at her door and Visaka, one of the young concubines, puts her head in. "A servant just came from the men's quarters, sāmini. Rahula wants you to know he's spending the night with his mātula Devadatta."

"Ah, well, that's probably a good thing," Yasodhara says with a tired smile.

Soon enough, Mahanama and Amitodhana petition Pasénadi to call an election for a new raja. The maharaja sends back an unexpected reply: even though clearly in decline, Suddhodana should, because of all his service to the Sakiya people, remain raja until his death. In the interim, Amitodhana and Mahanama will rule. But there is more: they are to share the duties of ruling with another nobleman, Pandu.

There is general shock at this news. Pandu is an insignificant noble, not even an amici or high official. And Yasodhara, hearing of the Maharaja's decree, now recalls that Bahiya, Pandu's son, told Rahula that he, rather than Rahula, would be sent to the Kosala Court when the boys turned thirteen. This must mean there have been secret talks between Pandu and the maharaja for a while. Like everyone else, she now takes a closer look at Pandu and his gotra, and sees how, over the years, they have quietly grown influential in the city. In a fashion that is rare for a noble Khattiya family, they engage in trade and do not consider banking, owning shops or socializing with Vessas below them. As a result, they are well regarded by all the city's rich bankers and merchants. They have also married into Moriya noble families, which makes them unusual among the Sakiya gentry. This Moriya alliance, Yasodhara understands, will ensure stable borders on that side of the kingdom if Pandu is raja, and hopefully end hostilities with the Moriya, which have lasted all these years.

The maharaja's motives in not allowing an election yet are now clear to Yasodhara too: Suddhodana has been a powerful ruler helped by his brother, nephew and gotra, and this power has caused Pasénadi much difficulty. He doesn't want another gotra to be completely in power. So, for as long as possible, he will keep Pandu and his gotra destabilized by insisting he share power with Amitodhana and Mahanama.

One evening, while Yasodhara and Prajapati are in the devi's room, working on a quilt, a female slave comes from Mahanama and Amitodhana's house with an invitation—to attend the marriage of Mahanama's daughter, Mantani, in two weeks' time. The bridegroom is the son of the Koliya raja. "A strategic marriage," Prajapati murmurs, once the slave is gone. "And don't forget, Ushas, the Koliya raja's mother is of our Gotama Gotra."

Yasodhara nods, raising her eyebrows at her aunt as she embroiders a square on the quilt. She leans in close to see the stitching because the shuttered windows are drawn to keep out the sunlight, which lies like heated honey over everything these days. This marriage will make it harder for Pandu to win votes in the sangha, when it comes time to choose a raja. Historically, the sangha has always picked a Sakiya raja who has marriage ties to the Koliya raja. This marriage makes Mahanama a strong candidate now.

That evening, Yasodhara is entering the raja's private courtyard when she stops in shock. Rahula is standing at the top of the verandah steps, blocking Pandu's ascent up to Suddhodana's room with a spear.

"Rahula!"

He flicks a glance at her before his eyes return to their target. He is holding his spear so that its metal tip is inches from Pandu's face.

"Sāmini." Pandu turns to her with an amused smile and bows. "It is good to see our raja so well guarded." He is spare and hunched, like a clerk who sits cross-legged all day over his account tablets. "And how is our raja?" Pandu's hooded eyes open and close slowly, the long blink of a lizard.

"As well as can be expected, sāmi," Yasodhara says briskly. She returns his elaborate bow with a curt one. "Very kind of you to pay us a visit, but really not necessary at all."

"Ah, but I must keep coming, sāmini. To check on his progress." Pandu is still smiling, but a steeliness has entered his voice. "The raja's ill health is a matter of state. And, as you know, I am one of the state's temporary rulers."

Yasodhara crosses her arms. After a moment of this awkward contest, Pandu bows and walks away, his smile turned nasty.

The moment he is gone, Yasodhara faces Rahula. "Putha, what were you thinking? This man will be the next raja. You, we, cannot afford to get on his wrong side."

"He will not be the next raja," Rahula hisses back. "We will make sure that never happens."

"And who exactly is this 'we'?" Yasodhara is suddenly afraid.

Rahula throws his spear down, the metal tip clanging against the floor. He starts to push past Yasodhara, but she grabs his arm and swings him around. "Who is this we? My bhāta? Who are you listening to, that you would talk this rubbish?" He tries to pull his arm away but she holds on, truly frightened by his stubbornness, his lack of fear of her. "How will you make sure Pandu doesn't become raja? How?"

With a mighty grunt, he breaks from her and stumbles back. "I'm not going to sit by and watch my future fade away." Devadatta's words, thinks Yasodhara.

Before she can say anything more, Rahula turns and runs out of the courtyard.

Later that day, Yasodhara learns that someone frayed the reins on Pandu's chariots so that, when he set off from the palace, the straps broke and the chariot nearly tipped over. It can't have been Rahula, as he was with her in the courtyard, yet she feels sure he knows who did it. She considers confronting Rahula, but already knows he will deny any knowledge. And soon after, rumour begins to spread that it was Devadatta, under Mahanama's instructions.

The next day she finds her brother in the stables, seated on a barrel before the grooms, holding forth on hunting for boar with the vana-dasas when he was rashtrika of the Northern Province. Devadatta is facing away from the door and so doesn't notice her until the grooms begin to shift uncomfortably. He turns to find her examining him coldly.

"Ah, bhagini." He has the grace to blush.

The grooms leave, bowing to Yasodhara. She comes further into the stables, with their familiar smell of horses and manure and hay. Devadatta picks up a coconut husk and begins to rub down a horse. She goes to stand near him, holding the reins to steady the animal. She can tell by his stubborn expression that he knows why she's come.

"Bhāta," she says, after a moment, "what are you doing to my son? Everyone says that you and Mahanama had something to do with those frayed reins on Pandu's chariot."

He smirks. "And who is this 'everyone'?"

"Rahula is only ten years old, bhāta. If you love him, as you claim to do, then leave him out of all this. He deserves a better future."

"What future will he have if Pandu becomes raja, bhagini?"

Yasodhara is silent, realizing that until this moment, she hasn't considered this question.

He smirks. "So you see, I do love our Rahula. Because I am thinking of his future."

2

Changes

A FEW DAYS later, Yasodhara is in her room, the checkered counting board laid out on her bed, various tokens placed on numeric squares as she verifies the accounts tablets for the newly arrived grain tax, when her aunt slips in with a discreet knock and comes to sit by her. She puts aside the tablets with a sigh, having had to recount a few times already, distracted by worries about Rahula's future.

Prajapati's face is grave as they fan themselves with dried palms, the room shuttered because of the unceasing heat outside. "Ushas, the Royal Bisaj told me today that your uncle is not getting better . . . is, in fact, getting worse. Yama's noose has truly tightened around him."

Yasodhara is still for a moment, then fans herself rapidly. "How long, pitucché?"

"A month at most." Prajapati is silent, studying her hands. "So, we must begin to think of our future."

"Yes, I've already been thinking about that. We should give the tenants of our city mansion notice."

Her aunt's face works for a moment. Then she gives Yasodhara a miserable, pleading look. "Oh, Ushas, the town mansion was sold to Jatila a long time ago." She nods at Yasodhara's shock. "My husband has been so profligate! I had no idea how much he had spent until I finally spoke with the amici who handles palace finances. All our fields and orchards are so heavily mortgaged we have no real equity in them. Your uncle's been able to keep our debtors at bay by offering them the favours and concessions a raja can, by paying the interest from the taxes he receives. But once he's dead . . ."

Yasodhara lowers her trembling fan to her lap. "So, what is left, pitucché?"

"A farm in a distant province . . . whose soil is so poor no setthi was willing to offer a mortgage on it to your uncle. Oh, Ushas, I don't know what to do with all the women here. I can't just turn them out into the street. But how will we support ourselves?"

"We have to tell them right away. They need to know." Yasodhara stands, then slumps down again. "What am I going to do with Rahula? What kind of a life will he have there?"

They look at each other helplessly.

A short while later, they gather the other women in the courtyard. They are nervous at this hasty summons, at the sight of Yasodhara and Prajapati's sombre faces. For once, Prajapati doesn't sit on the charpoy but joins them on the mats, so that all of them are in a circle. She tells them the news, and, as she speaks, shock and fear splinter open their faces. After she is done, there is a long moment of silence. Then Sumana and Utara begin to weep and soon the other women join them, even Yasodhara and Prajapati wiping their eyes with their shawls, their soft keening filling the courtyard.

"This is the end of our life here," Sundari Nanda cries, and the women weep even more, clinging to each other, knowing that soon they will part and not know each other anymore. It comes to Yasodhara that, despite their quarrels and differences, they have lived and known each other a long time, and are a family.

Finally, when everyone has quieted down, Yasodhara says, with a glance at her aunt, "You are all welcome to go with us to that farm. But know that our lives will be lived in isolation, surviving on whatever the stony fields produce, working the fields ourselves."

"We will also then have the humiliation of being a burden on you," Mitta says bitterly.

"Yet the alternative is no better," Upasama adds. "Sell ourselves to a courtesan house or, for those who are too old for that—which most of us are—bond ourselves as slaves in noble households."

And once again the women weep, this time at the futures that await them.

In the days that follow, some of the women snap and rage at each other for minor infringements and annoyances. The more peaceable stay in their rooms as much as possible, or leave the quarters on errands in the city, or go to visit parks and shrines. Yasodhara observes that the heat and drought don't help anyone's temper. It is worrying that even the pond in their quarters, fed by an eternal spring, has started to shrink.

The palace granary is well stocked because of the past season's grain, but if the rains fail—and it looks like they will—there will be austerities. Yet, whenever Yasodhara thinks about this, she reminds herself that soon she and the other women will have no access to the granary at all. As she goes about her day, the very buildings around her, even her room, take on an insubstantial, temporary quality, as if she is already a guest here.

One evening Yasodhara is in her room when there is a timid knock, and Sanga and Visaka put their heads in. She gestures to the young concubines to come and join her on the bed, studying their solemn, sweet expressions as they settle in, cross-legged. "Sāmini," Visaka says, "we want you to know first. Sanga and I will return to my mother, Vimala. She is joyful to have me back in her courtesan house and is already looking around for a rich setthi to contract me to. She has also agreed to take Sanga as a junior ganikā." Seeing Yasodhara's dismay, the girls smile bravely. "Don't worry about us, sāmini," Visaka reassures her, "my mother will look after us well."

"But we will always remember your kindness to us," Sanga adds. At her look of humble gratitude, Yasodhara's eyes fill with tears.

The next day, she is in the walled garden, trying to lose herself in planting and tending the beds—fighting to keep at bay the plangent voice that asks, "Why do you bother with what won't be yours?"—when a discreet cough makes her look up. Mitta stands before her. After a moment, her cousin squats on the other side of the bed and helps her, placing a pumpkin seed where Yasodhara makes a hole. Both women shuffle down either side of the bed. "Ñātiké," Mitta says after a short while, "I want you to be the first to know: on the raja's death, I will join the Niganthas. They allow female ascetics into their movement now."

"And starve yourself to death, Mitta?" Yasodhara asks quietly. "Surely it would be better to live with us?"

"I am tired of the endless suffering of this life, ñātiké." Mitta gestures
to the pustules on her face and body, which are worse this year with the
drought. "It would be a relief to burn off all my previous karma by starving
to death. A relief to never return, a joy to be united with the eternal force."
Yasodhara nods. Yet she cannot help but notice there is something defeated
about the way Mitta says this.

At night, as Yasodhara lies in her bed unable to sleep, she has visions of
herself growing old on that farm, becoming a living ghost. She has seen
these isolated houses with their widows or old women tending decrepit
husbands. The women are often half-insane from the isolation, their voices
harsh like crows', looking at visitors with bitter avidity, as if wishing to
consume their still-vital lives.

For days, Yasodhara has avoided telling Rahula about the new future
that awaits them. But at last she accepts she must do it, and goes looking
for him.

She finds him in the Rohini River, helping the mahout bathe the royal
elephant. She stands on the river beach and calls to him, but he either
doesn't hear or pretends not to. The mahout, noticing her, signals to
Rahula. He turns to regard her for a moment, then wades to shore.

"It's always a nice thing to bathe the royal elephant, isn't it, puthā?" she
says as Rahula comes up to her. "When we were young, my bhāta and
I loved doing it. Such gentle beasts."

He nods curtly as he wipes himself down with his shawl.

She points to a banyan tree at the top of the bank. They walk up to it in
silence and sit on a bench in the shade of its aerial prop roots. Birds rustle
above them, and there is a monkey nursing its baby on a nearby branch.
They watch it for a while, then she turns to Rahula. "Puthā, there is something we must talk about." She twists her hands in her lap, finding it hard to
go on; also, she knows she must respect that he has an acuity well beyond
his age, and speak to him as if to an older teenager. "You see, once your
ayyaka dies, we, us women, are going to have to leave the palace. And we
have nowhere to go in the city."

"I know, ammé." He nods at her astonishment. "Mātula told me everything."

She feels a burst of anger towards Devadatta—but then, almost immediately, relief. "Oh, puthā," she exclaims, "I don't know what to do. It's simply not a life for you on that farm, but what can I—"

"That will never happen, ammé. We have a plan."

Her eyes narrow. "What plan?"

"I . . . I can't tell you."

She grabs him by the shoulders. "What plan?" He regards her silently, obstinate. "I am your ammé." She shakes him. "You're a boy, you know nothing of the world. I insist you tell me. Now!"

Rahula glares at her haughtily, then rises and goes back towards the river, scrambling down the bank.

With the persistent heat and the failure of the rains, the Rohini River is drying. And since the river is shared by the Sakiya and Koliya, soon negotiations must take place around controlling water rights so that each side gets a fair share. In the past, when Yasodhara's father was Koliya raja, this was quickly and amicably done. Even with the new Koliya raja, negotiations have not been difficult because of the shared gotra and good relations with the ruling triad. This time, however, Mahanama and Amitodhana let Pandu negotiate the rights and he, blinded by his desire to prove he is best to succeed as raja, does not question why this task has been ceded to him. The Koliya raja doesn't respond to Pandu's request to meet and negotiate water rights. A second request is sent but still no answer comes. Eventually, Pandu realizes he has been set up; Mahanama's daughter, after all, is now married to the Koliya raja's son.

When she hears of all this, Yasodhara understands that this is part of the "plan" Rahula was talking about. She is frightened for her son. Pandu and his gotra won't give in that easily. There may well be civil strife.

⚕

A few days later, Yasodhara is seated on her bed once again doing the accounts, shutters closed, when a servant woman knocks and enters. "Sāmini," she whispers, "a man wishes to see you. A samana. In red robes." Yasodhara becomes still. Red is the colour that Siddhartha's followers wear. The woman also said "robes," not robe: Siddhartha's followers wear two inner ones for the upper and lower body, and one larger one covering the shoulders and entire body.

"Tell him—" Yasodhara's voice cracks. "Send him up to the receiving room. Yes-yes, the receiving room." As the woman turns to go, she calls out after her, "And not a word to anyone. Once you've let him in at the street door, leave us alone. I don't need to be chaperoned."

She goes up to the third floor, her throat hard with fear. As she seats herself cross-legged on the charpoy in the shuttered room, she can hear the man speaking softly with the servant, then the door that leads to the street closing. Footsteps come up the stairs, echoing in the wooden stairwell. Finally he reaches the top step, and Yasodhara peers at the man through the gloom—head shaven, red robes. She breathes out in relief. It isn't Siddhartha. The man takes a moment to orient himself in the dim room, then, catching sight of her, nods and comes forward. His walk is familiar and, in the moment just before he reaches her, Yasodhara recognizes him, and gasps. "Ananda!"

For a long moment she stares at him. Ananda holds her gaze, smiling gently. Then he clasps his hands and bows. "Bhagini." She nods, unable to speak, and gestures for him to sit on the rug before her. As he does so, she examines his robes and also takes in how un-aged her cousin is, his face barely lined at forty-four. There is something feline to his movements, soft yet alert. Once he is properly settled, robes neatly in place, he looks up at her again, calm but no longer smiling.

Finally she speaks, her voice ringing with bitterness. "Ah, you too, Ananda."

He nods thoughtfully, then gives her a begging look. "It is so, bhagini."

"No, no, don't call me that! You've lost that privilege." She straightens her back. "Why are you here?" He looks at her significantly. "Ah! Tell me it's not what I think!"

"I'm afraid it is, ñātiké."

"But why? Why? He said he wasn't going to visit. He remained silent when he was invited."

Ananda looks at his hands, struggling. "News has come to him that his father is in the last phase of his life. He wishes to see him before he passes to the Land of the Fathers."

She closes her eyes, dizzy. "When does he come?"

"Vesali is a fifteen-day walk from here and he set out yesterday. I was sent ahead to warn—I mean to inform—his father that he is coming."

And now, suddenly, it is real. Siddhartha is coming to Kapilavastu, is already on his way, will be here in fourteen days. A rush of anger seizes her. "Well, I am a mere woman. If the great Awakened One wishes to visit, who am I to stop him?" Yet then, as the full meaning of this comes to her, she cries, "I must tell my son! Oh, Ananda," she whispers, falling into their old intimacy in her distress, "what will I tell him?" But before Ananda can speak, she waves her hand to silence him.

They sit like that for a long moment, hearing the sound of a cart rattling and grinding along on the street outside. Finally she says, caustically, "Well, you might as well tell me how you came to this. Because I know you're bursting to do so."

So Ananda begins, saying, "I will start from when I left Kapilavastu on that day I last saw you.

"On that day, for a while after I left you, ñātiké, I wandered dazed through the city and suddenly found myself at the gates. I passed through them and over the drawbridge and soon came upon a caravan that had stopped at the wells where convoys refilled their leather drums. I went to sit on the rim of a well and was soon helping a merchant draw water up. This familiar action of hauling up water, filling drums, the bustle and shouts of the merchants and their servants and slaves, the dung smell of horses, donkeys and goats, began to soothe me. 'And where do you go, mitta?' I asked the man. 'To Rajagaha, mitta,' the merchant replied. I asked to join his caravan, telling him of my qualifications, and he immediately accepted me. Once the convoy had set off, I didn't look back, because, so I told myself, I would never return to Kapilavastu again.

"Once we had reached the Magadha capital, however, I knew I would go no further with that merchant. I had no desire for more adventure, no desire for anything, really, still numb with grief at the loss of my Vasabha; grieving too the way Anuruddha and Nagamunda, to whom I had given a home, given so much, had betrayed me. Still, one must live. So I found a rich setthi and got employment as his clerk and then, later, became one of his traders. Ten years passed in this way, during which I was neither happy nor unhappy. Whatever work needed doing was a rope that I clutched at, hauling myself from day to day. Travelling, which had always brought me such pleasure, still pleased me well enough, but the enjoyment was muted, in the way that a man who has fallen out of love with his wife can continue in the marriage, taking comfort in the reliability of the domestic rituals she performs for him. I was living, I know now, breath held in, waiting.

"Then one day I heard about the arrival of this Awakened One and the Maharaja Bimbisara's embrace of the Middle Way. At first, I paid little attention, because the maharaja was always taking up with this or that samana school. Siddhartha was not known in Rajagaha as the son of Suddhodana, and so it took me a little while to figure out that it was my cousin the entire city was talking about. I went the very next day to the Bamboo Grove to listen to him preach on the Four Great Realities. And to my surprise, I heard in them the story of my own life.

"Afterwards, as I got up to leave with everybody else, a senior monk, Maha Kassapa, approached me and declared, 'You are Ananda, the cousin of the Awakened One.' I was taken aback, but the monk smiled and gestured to my pockmarked cheeks to say that was how he had identified me. 'The Awakened One asks you stay behind and speak with him.' He gestured for me to sit again. By now, Siddhartha was so surrounded by nobles and officials, I couldn't even glimpse him, so I began instead to look around, studying how, as the crowd gradually left, the serenity of the grove reasserted itself. The monks now went quietly about their chores, cleaning their bowls, washing their robes in a small stream. They did all this silently and, because of the silence, I was conscious of the wind murmuring musically through the bamboo, the *hush-hush* sound made by a troop of monkeys as they swung from shoot to shoot, a smell of rice cooking. Finally, the last clutch of noblemen bowed and left, and I saw Siddhartha seated on the grass before a hut. He lifted a hand and gestured me over, smiling. As I drew near, Siddhartha uncrossed his legs and stood up. Once before him, I hesitated, not knowing how I should greet him, but he reached out and drew me into an embrace, saying, as if my visit had been anticipated all along, 'How good it is to see you, ñātaka.' And then it came to me: Siddhartha now had the gift of foresight. He had known that I was in

Rajagaha, that I would come today and exactly where I would sit in the crowd. He had told his monk to look out for me."

At this, Yasodhara makes a derisive sound. "Ugh, how easily you are taken in, ñātaka. He just saw you in the crowd. You are truly indoctrinated."

"No, no, ñātiké, he does have the gift. Sometimes he'll say to me, 'Today a merchant wearing a blue turban will come to see me, make sure he is admitted to my presence, he is deeply in pain.' Or 'There is a woman driven mad with grief at the death of her son, who will come today for an audience. Make sure to have some robe available, as she will be naked.' Or, in the case of our uncle, 'My pita will pass from this world in the next few weeks. I must teach him the Middle Way and free him to a higher birth in his next life.' He has this gift, ñātiké, but doesn't want it known because he is against magic and superstition and—"

"Stop, stop, I've heard enough!" Yasodhara gets off the charpoy and sharply straightens her shawl around her. "All these ten years, I've hoped for your return. Said to myself, 'One day Ananda will come back, and then I will have a true friend in this world.' But now," she gestures to his robes with disgust, "I am truly abandoned."

"Ah, ñātiké!"

She turns from his appeal and strides towards the door that leads down into the private quarters.

Shortly after Ananda's visit, Yasodhara goes looking for Rahula and is told he is practising his archery in the royal park beyond the city walls. When she arrives at the park by chariot, she stands for a moment, watching him shoot his arrows with such intent, his face stern, eyes narrowed, the target an imagined enemy. Like a warrior preparing for battle, she thinks, then immediately dismisses the thought. She approaches him, smelling the sweet mint in the grass, hearing a family of barbets in a jack tree calling to each other.

Rahula notices her approach and lowers his bow.

"Come, puthā." She walks towards a bench under a sal tree and Rahula follows meekly, no doubt frightened by the gravity of her tone.

She sits on the bench and gently pulls him down beside her. Still holding his arm as if afraid he will bolt, she looks out at the Rohini River that borders the park, watching for a moment the ferryman punting some people

across to the other bank. "Puthā, there is some news . . . about your pita."
She glances at him; he regards her intently. "He is coming to Kapilavastu.
To see your ayyaka before he dies. In fact, he is on his way here already
from Vesali."

Rahula snatches his arm away. For a moment, he twists his fingers in his
lap, then he bursts into tears, burying his head in his hands, sobbing. When
she tries to touch him, he shrinks away from her. Finally, he calms himself,
wipes his cheeks with his shawl, picks up his bow and stands. "I don't want
to greet him, I don't want to see him. He's certainly not coming to help me.
I know that."

"Oh, Rahula." Yasodhara wipes her forehead with her shawl, suddenly
depleted. "Do what you want. I can't keep fighting with you."

"And you, ammé?" His tone is now gentle. "Will you have to see him?
Do you *want* to see him?"

She smiles. "I am a mere woman and he is the Awakened One, the
favourite of Bimbisara and the Vesali princes."

After a moment he frowns, confused and sad, then returns to his archery.

As Yasodhara watches him shoot his arrows, she says to herself over and
over, "Soon, soon, Siddhartha will be here." But the words remain unreal.
Her mind is unable to grasp that she will, after all these years, be in his
presence again.

3

All Is Burning

SOME DAYS LATER, Yasodhara is in her room, when there is a patter of footsteps outside, a quick knock, and Mitta bursts in. "They're here!"

The other women hover in the doorway now too, watching her anxiously—everyone except her aunt, who is away shopping in the cloth merchants' street.

"They arrived too late last night to enter Kapilavastu, and so stayed in the rest-house beyond the city gates," Mitta continues. "This morning, they are out begging for their meal."

"Do you . . ." Yasodhara's voice cracks. "Do we know what part of the city Siddhartha begs in?"

Mitta gives her a significant look. "Not in the city, ñātiké. Beyond. Among the Dasas."

"Indeed," she murmurs, taken aback, and seeing that the other women are bewildered by this too.

She nods to dismiss them. The moment they are gone, she jumps up, goes to a corner and pulls forward the trunk where she keeps Siddhartha's things. Opening it, she snatches up the old yellow shawl he sent back to her, and flaps it open. Discoloured and moth-eaten, it will make her look like a poor Vessa woman, the wife of some petty shopkeeper.

Over the past few days, she has agonized about what she will do when Siddhartha arrives, how she will act; now she finds relief in this instinctive volition that has seized her. She goes down to the front courtyard and finds the women flocked together, chattering excitedly. They fall silent when they see her wrapped in the shawl. They glance at each other, nervous, recalling that period of madness when she had worn this garment. Ignoring their concerned looks, Yasodhara hurries out the street door.

She makes her way down one of the side streets off the royal square and soon spots a samana in red robes, head shaved. She follows him at a distance, observing the way he walks, eyes cast down; the way he stands in silence outside doors, having clanged the bell or knocked; the way the householders who answer the door are puzzled, dismissive or generous— and the way, no matter what their reaction, he bows humbly.

As she continues on through the city, she sees more and more of these samanas, all possessing that same calmness and humility. At street corners, people cluster in groups discussing the arrival of the samanas. She learns that there are about a hundred of them, and hears Siddhartha's name frequently, floating to her as she goes past. She gathers from snatches of conversation that "bhikkhu" is how these samanas wish to be addressed. The janata are sometimes jeering, or bewildered, or admiring that these men of good lineage, with their refined accents, these Brahmins, Khattiyas and Vessas, wish to be called "beggar." She learns also that Jatila and his wife have given the bhikkhus permission to stay in their Nigrodha Grove, though they have not gone out to greet them for fear of offending the new ruling family, the Pandu Gotra. The Senapati of Kapilavastu has already ridden out with his men this morning to inspect the bhikkhus. Siddhartha's arrival is seen by the janata as a political gesture, a way to revive the fortunes of the Gotama Gotra. People are eager to see the outcome of what they are sure is going to be an interesting political battle, remembering well Siddhartha's skill in statecraft. The janata are divided: the majority support the Pandu Gotra; but the rest, especially the old, are loyal to the Gotama Gotra. Yasodhara nods to herself. Now she understands why her former husband begs among the Dasas.

The Dasa slum sprawls beyond the moat. Once Yasodhara has crossed the drawbridge, she makes her way through one of the narrow slum streets where sewage flows in shallow runnels along either side of the road. The houses here are without stoops or steps, and inhabitants jump over the drains to reach the street. She presses her shawl to her nose, the smell nauseating, batting away flies that hover before her face and come to rest on her skin. She barely pays attention to her surroundings, searching for Siddhartha among the inhabitants of this neighbourhood. They look back at her curiously because it is strange to see even a poor Vessa woman here. These emaciated people are so low they exist outside the caste structure; most of the men wear nothing but a loincloth, and the women are without bodice cloths, short wraps around their waists. As Yasodhara passes bhikkhu after bhikkhu, she tries to examine each face—a difficult thing to do because the men keep their eyes on the ground when passing a woman. With looks of gratitude they accept the meanest scraps of food, bowing humbly before the lowliest householder who has been generous with them. These men of good Khattiya, Brahmin and Vessa families are taking food from people who would not be allowed to work in their kitchens. It is bewildering, and Yasodhara feels disoriented, not just by her unfamiliar surroundings but also by seeing the very social structure turned upside down.

She reaches an alley and, spotting a samana, is about to enter the narrow lane and check if this might be Siddhartha when she sees the royal palanquin, curtains drawn, heading towards her. Ananda leads it, walking at a sedate but steady pace, and he too is examining the face of each bhikkhu he passes. She slips into the alley and waits. It must be her uncle inside the palanquin. Since hearing about Siddhartha's imminent return from Ananda some days ago, Suddhodana has forced himself to eat, and insisted on shambling around the courtyard once a day to improve his health. Leaning against her on one of these perambulations, he whispered, "He comes to see me to my death." When she protested, he squeezed her shoulder. "No need to protect me, daharé. I feel Yama's noose growing tighter and tighter."

Once the palanquin has passed, she follows it, drawing her shawl over her head. It is going in the direction from which she just came. Ahead is a bhikkhu standing before a doorway, a man whom she already passed without pausing. But now Ananda stops before the bhikkhu. "Awakened One, here is your father come to see you."

Suddhodana draws the curtain back and, for a long moment, father and son stare at each other. Pushing herself into a doorway, Yasodhara gazes and gazes at Siddhartha, struggling even now to see the man she once knew—in the way one struggles to see the child in a person encountered after a long absence. Siddhartha's features are the same, no thinner, no thicker. Yet, despite this, he is transformed, although how, how, she cannot tell—something luminous and sparse lights his features, making them different in the way a lamp held below or above a face changes its aspect.

"Puthā," Suddhodana finally says, his voice gruff, "why do you shame me in this way, begging in the street? Why have you not come this morning to see your father first and pay him respect?"

Siddhartha is silent for a long moment, and Yasodhara can see that his face is filled with poignant affection. "But I have come back, pita. Out of love for you."

"But you dishonour me, you insult me with this begging," Suddhodana cries, truly hurt.

"Pita," Siddhartha reaches out and touches his father's hand briefly, "I only do what Awakened Ones before me have done. Nothing more or less. It's not to dishonour you. Begging is our custom."

Suddhodana stares at his son, bewildered and speechless.

"Mātula." Ananda gently presses his uncle's shoulder. "Lay people may invite the bhikkhus for the midday meal, which is their last meal for the day."

"Ah . . ." Suddhodana surveys his son. "So then, will you allow me to feed you and all your samanas tomorrow?"

For a moment Siddhartha hesitates, but Ananda catches his eye and raises his eyebrows to say he should accept. Siddhartha finally nods. "And I will come tomorrow morning to see you first, pita, before the meal."

The palanquin leaves, and Siddhartha continues on his begging round. Yasodhara follows him, unable to call out his name. She wants to believe, however, that he is aware she trails him, because there is something purposeful in the way he never looks back. She follows Siddhartha all the way through the Dasa Quarter, studying the easy way he chats with the people who stop him in the street to ask about his samana school and why he begs in these quarters, of all places. She can hear the questions, but cannot hear his answers because he speaks in too soft a murmur. He is friendly and often laughs as he talks; he touches these Dasas on their shoulders or arms, as if equals; once, he allows a little girl to take his hand and swing it as she skips alongside him for a few streets. This is the man she knew in Mudgala, friendly and open to the world, warm towards people. Yasodhara feels a homesick pang to see this old Siddhartha; she is surprised he is so unchanged. From the stories of his fame, she expected him to be like Alara Kalama and other sages she'd encountered—severe and withdrawn from the world.

As she follows Siddhartha, a sorrow grows and grows in her, weighing down her footsteps. She follows him out of the Dasa Quarter and, when he takes the road away from the city, she stands and watches him until he turns down the wooded path that will take him to the Nigrodha Grove. After that, she goes on to the city, weary and bereft.

When she arrives at the palace, the women are waiting. She shakes her head, not meeting their eyes, and goes to her room. There, she lies curled up on her bed, heavy with grief, as if no time has passed since the day Siddhartha left her.

Prajapati returns from her shopping and creeps in to sit by Yasodhara, taking one of her tight fists in her own hands and uncurling it. Haltingly, Yasodhara tells her aunt about the encounter between father and son, and about her failure to recognize Siddhartha, his features altered in a way she cannot explain. As she talks, she sees in her aunt's face the marvel and bewilderment she feels too. "I've seen these bhikkhus," Prajapati murmurs. "How humble and friendly they are, so different from other samanas."

Yasodhara gives a sad laugh. "Ah, so you are also enamoured with them, pitucché."

Prajapati is silent for a moment. Then she says carefully, "What I see is how important this movement is. To *hear* of it is one thing, to *see* it here in our streets is another. Yes, yes, Siddhartha is an important man."

Yasodhara frowns, unsure where her aunt is going with all this.

"Ushas"—Prajapati takes her hand—"no matter your feelings towards Siddhartha, here is an opportunity you cannot let pass. For your son, and for us women."

Yasodhara lets out a small cry of protest and snatches back her hand.

"No matter what he's done to you, dhītā," Prajapati continues, "he's a powerful man now. No matter what he says about being only a samana, and no matter his begging in the Dasa Quarter, he is still the friend of

Bimbisara and the Licchavi princes. To not try for Rahula, to not try for us . . . can you truly face yourself knowing you didn't try?"

Yasodhara is silent for a long moment. Then she shuffles over to sit on the edge of the bed and reties her hair, nodding to say her aunt is right. She must strive to put her anger, her pride, aside.

By the midday sacrifices, news of Siddhartha's arrival, and that he will come to the palace for a meal the next day, has spread. In the sacrificial courtyard, as the priests go around to the three fires that blaze in the centre, feeding ghee and rice and millet to the gods, reciting mantras in the old language known only to them, there is an inattentive buzz from the nobles gathered on all sides, some seated on mats, others standing on the verandahs. The priests call for silence, but soon the murmurs start up again, along with the restless rustle of clothing and jewellery. As Yasodhara watches the crowd she thinks of what her aunt said about Siddhartha having become an important man. She can see the truth of this here, in the excitement of the nobles all around her.

The moment the ceremonies are over, a babble of voices fills the sacrificial enclosure. Soon an argument breaks out between Suddhodana and the Brahmin priests. "I am the raja," Suddhodana roars, "and I declare there will be no midday sacrifice tomorrow." A fit of coughing bends him in two. Once he has recovered, he continues hoarsely, "My son has come to visit me. He will have a meal at midday, and the sacrifices will be cancelled."

"What about the penalty, then, sāmi?" the Head Priest asks icily.

Suddhodana takes a moment of stentorian breathing before he says, "We will see about the penalty, and exactly *who* will pay it." He nods grimly, as if to say that the Head Priest might pay a penalty to the raja himself, if he's not careful.

As Yasodhara makes her way through the crowd towards the entrance, the people she passes fall silent. She can feel their hot, avid stares on her, and keeps her face impassive. Inside, she is twisting with panic at the task she must perform soon, a task she feels almost incapable of doing, so unprepared is she to encounter Siddhartha again.

Beyond the sacrificial enclosure, she finds the women of the quarters gathered around Prajapati, who is issuing orders about preparations for the meal tomorrow. The women scatter to their tasks, such eagerness and hope in their faces and movements. They already know, through Prajapati, that Yasodhara is going to ask Siddhartha for help; and they believe that he, whose fame grows and grows throughout the Middle Country, will save them from rural exile or the courtesan houses or slavery. The task Yasodhara must perform to win a reprieve for all of them feels heavier than ever.

Yasodhara had noticed that Rahula was not at the sacrifices. She goes to Devadatta's room, looking for him. The manservant outside tells her that Rahula hasn't left the room since he heard of his father's arrival. Yasodhara nods, knocks briefly on the door and goes in. The windows are shuttered and it takes a moment for her eyes to adjust. Finally, she sees Rahula seated on Devadatta's unmade bed, knees drawn to his chest, eyes glittering in the dimness as he watches her. She goes to the bed and sits by him.

"I have seen him."

"I don't care." Rahula pulls his knees in even tighter.

"Your pita is certainly an important man."

"So, will he save us?" Rahula demands sarcastically. But Yasodhara glimpses the hope behind his words.

She is quiet a moment, silently cursing whichever woman told him of the plan, guessing it was one of the young concubines, since they are closest in age to him. "I don't know. But it is my duty to ask. For you, for all of us."

He leans forward. "But do you really think he'll help us, ammé?"

She strokes his head. "I hope he will, I truly hope so, puthā." But he hears the doubt in her voice and rolls away from her touch.

Yasodhara sends a message to Ananda asking for an audience with Siddhartha. The next morning, all the women except Yasodhara leave the quarters to help with the preparations for Siddhartha's arrival—and as they go, they give her anxious looks, knowing she is staying behind for the return messenger from Ananda. After a short while, the gate bell tolls. Yasodhara runs to the window, panic pulsing in her throat. She sees two bhikkhus standing before the street door. Hurriedly, she throws a shawl over her shoulders and rushes down to the front courtyard.

The bhikkhus introduce themselves as Sariputta and Moggallana.

"Sāmini," one of them says, "prepare yourself for a visit by the Awakened One shortly. He will come to see you before he visits his father. We will come with him."

She closes her eyes, slightly giddy, then nods her assent, unable to speak.

Back in her room, Yasodhara flings open her trunks, throwing clothes on her bed and divan, trying to decide what she will wear. Yet finally, the ridiculousness of ornamenting herself for the Awakened One strikes her and she sits down with a choked laugh. To adorn herself might make it seem like she hopes to win him back. With this thought, she removes her jewels and scrubs her face clean of all cosmetics. She sends for a serving woman and, her voice quavering, dispatches her to tell Prajapati about the visit and ask that the other women keep away from the quarters.

After tidying up her clothes, she sits on her divan to wait. Soon, however, she cannot contain herself. She jumps up, goes to the window and peers down the street; then sits again, then goes to lie on her bed. Yet in a short while, she is up again, at the window, then back on the divan, then back on the bed, repeating this pattern several times, furious at herself that she is acting like a lovesick girl but unable to control her emotions. "Remember," she says to herself over and over, "you have a task to perform, for Rahula, for the women, for yourself. Don't lose your wits."

Finally, the bell clangs. As already instructed, the serving woman lets the monks in but requests that only Siddhartha come up to Yasodhara's suite. This is an imposition, she knows. It is likely against their rules for a monk to be in a woman's chambers alone. But Yasodhara stubbornly feels he owes her this. She will not meet her husband at the gate, nor in the courtyard. Nor even in the third-floor receiving room. And she wants to meet him alone.

She sits on the divan, eyes closed, trembling hands pressed together. When she hears only two sets of footsteps coming down the corridor, she breathes out in relief. He has acceded to her request.

There is a brief knock and the servant woman ushers in Siddhartha, then shuts the door. Yasodhara stands up and turns to face him. For a long moment, she gazes at him, and he at her. In his face, she reads love and gladness to see her after ten years, and sympathy for what she has suffered. She sees also his own pain at the suffering he has caused her.

Something comes tumbling down inside her and, before she knows it, she is weeping, her body shaking. Appalled, ashamed, she twists away and gropes for the divan to sit. "Ah, Ushas." Siddhartha comes towards her. He has used her nickname! Not called her "sāmini," or "bhagini." Her body, with a volition of its own, goes towards him, arms outstretched. He immediately steps back, alarmed. Yet she cannot hold back this impulse to touch him, and when she reaches him, she falls to her knees, touching his feet, still sobbing. Before she can stop herself, she is kissing them, wetting them with her tears. Siddhartha just stands there, allowing her sorrow to drench his feet. He too is weeping.

Finally, Yasodhara scrambles up and away. "I . . . I'm sorry," she stutters.

"Ah, Ushas," he says gently, drying his eyes on a corner of his outer robe.

Taking her cue from him, she says, "Surya," and gestures to the divan, roughly wiping her cheeks with her shawl. To steady her nerves, she reminds herself that she has asked him here for a reason. She must keep this in mind.

After they have sat in silence for a while, Siddhartha begins to speak, staring ahead, as if telling her a story he has rehearsed: "In that forest where I began a fasting to death, Ushas, determined to burn off all my previous karma and never be born again, I soon came to realize that this punishment of my body was not the way to achieve wisdom. So, I accepted a bowl of rice from a village girl and began a more balanced approach to my search for wisdom, a middle path, a middle way, between extreme asceticism and sensual indulgence. And then, slowly, as I meditated, I saw my own previous births: how I had been born over and over again. And I understood that all beings vanish and come back. That our good or bad acts in previous lives determine our current existence. And seeing my previous lives, I finally broke through to the kernel of the wisdom I sought: our desires are what create dukkha. And this creation of dukkha mars our well-being in this life and the lives to come. I saw also that, once all desire has ceased within us, rebirth is destroyed and we are truly free and at peace. And in those previous births, Ushas, you were often there with me, my spouse, my friend. I'm telling you all this because you too can achieve this freedom. You too can—"

"Aaah!" Yasodhara jumps up from the couch and glares down at him. He is here with the intention of proselytizing! "How could you come here with this? How can you think, after all you did to me, that I would be even slightly interested in your philosophy?" She rushes to the window, then turns to face him, leaning on the sill, breathing rapidly. "And what do I gain from your marvellous insights? Nothing! I have lost and lost and lost."

He opens his mouth to protest, but then bows his head. "Yes, it is so. I am sorry for you that it is so, Ushas . . . sorry also that I've brought you to this."

"Though not sorry that you found your truth, your insights?" Siddhartha remains silent. "No, I didn't think so. I wish you hadn't come here. Why did you come?"

"Ushas," he says, pained.

"If you had thought of me, if you had thought of your son, about whom you have asked nothing, nothing, you would not have come." She comes forward to stand over him. "Are you aware of our plight? That Rahula must go with me to a distant estate, that his future is over, even though he is merely ten? That I and the women of these quarters will soon be forced into rural exile or become bonded slaves or courtesans? Do you know all this?"

After a moment he nods, meeting her eyes pleadingly.

"But then, Surya, what have you to offer us?" she cries. "Did you not think that the reason I asked to see you was because I wanted your help? Will you not help?"

"Ushas . . ." Siddhartha gives her another helpless look.

"You're the friend of Bimbisara, of the Licchavi princes. How is it possible that your fame cannot win us release from these terrible futures that await?"

"But Ushas, if I do a favour for you and Rahula and our women, then I must do it for others too. And then I am back where I started, a statesman dispersing favours, a statesman using my influence to convince, to beg, to wheedle this or that, for this or that person."

She gasps. "But *we* aren't this or that person!"

"I'm sorry, I didn't mean it like that, I—"

"We're your wife, your son!"

"But if I do it for you, then I must do it for others, must do it—"

"No, you need not! We're your family, we're—"

"—must do it for all the bhikkhus in my Order who have also left wives and children and families. Must, at minimum, allow them to seek influence and favours for their families. And then, and then, we're no longer a samana order, but . . . but . . . something else."

"How dare you come back to me, to us, with nothing to offer. Nothing! All I have ever done is love you with all my being. Yes, love and serve you. Is that my crime? In your marvellous new philosophy, yes, I guess that would be considered a crime."

She gestures rudely for him to be gone and goes to stand at the window again, glowering at the courtyard below, trembling from her emotions. After a moment, she hears Siddhartha get up and his footsteps recede. The door opens and shuts. The moment he is gone, she puts her head in her hands and rocks back and forth, whipped by anger and grief and humiliation. Yes, humiliation, because she opened herself to him, wept at his feet, only to be dismissed and dishonoured once again; humiliation because, even after all this time, after all he has done, her love for him is still strong.

Yasodhara decides she will not go for the meal; will not participate in serving the bhikkhus; certainly will not serve Siddhartha. But then the draw of his presence—wanting to see how he is received by the guests, wanting to just gaze at him despite how she hates him—is too great. She goes to his oration, twitching with resentment at her own stupid desire to be there.

In the public courtyard a great crowd has gathered, not just of nobles but of important Vessas too, all invited by Suddhodana so that he might display his son. There, on a wooden dais constructed specially for the occasion, sits Siddhartha. On either side of him are Sariputta and Moggallana, the two senior monks who came to see Yasodhara earlier. The other monks sit on the ground before the dais in rows, facing the audience, and she sees Ananda in the last row. Right behind him is Anuruddha, in the first row of audience members.

As she takes her place at the back, in the shadows of a verandah, half-hidden by a pillar so that no one will see her, Yasodhara regards her cousins sourly. Though she'd already heard the news, Anuruddha came himself to tell her that he had reconciled with his half-brother, that he had fallen at his feet and wept for forgiveness the first time Ananda came to visit. He told her also that Ananda was now staying with him. "Ah, then you are happy," she replied with hard cheerfulness. "That is good to hear." She'd ignored his look of appeal that asked her to also reconcile with Ananda. No, she won't do that. "Yes, I have lost and lost and lost," she says to herself as she sits cross-legged, arranging the pleats of her dhoti.

She has arrived just as the meal is finishing, the entire audience observing silence while the monks eat. Now water is brought for them to wash their hands and their bowls are taken away to be cleaned and returned. She watches the women of the quarters working alongside the servants and slaves, their faces lit with such hope, such grace at this service. How will she tell them that their last hope has failed?

Prajapati alone serves her stepson and his two senior monks, bowing humbly as she takes their bowls, offering them water to wash their hands, glowing all the while with pride. Looking at the serene expression on Siddhartha's face, Yasodhara wonders how he can smile like that, knowing he has condemned his stepmother to a life of rural exile.

Suddhodana sits in a chair in the first row of guests. The Senapati of Kapilavastu, as the maharaja's representative, sits on the floor to one side of him, Mahanama and Amitodhana on the other. Ranged behind Suddhodana and the important guests are rows of Brahmins, come from all over the city. The Royal Head Priest has invited them as reinforcements, truly worried about the cancelling of the midday sacrifices. Siddhartha's influence in other parts of the Middle Country has already led to people giving up the sacrifices there.

The clatter of bowls being cleared finally ceases. The women, their duties done, go to sit on the side. Siddhartha watches until every last one has taken her place, then with a nod, a smile of gratitude for their service, he gazes at the ground in front of him, one finger touching the dais, gathering himself to speak.

"This I have discovered, mitto: all is burning with the three fires."

A murmur of surprise, and of approval from the Brahmins, ripples through the crowd. His first words acknowledge and pay homage to the three fires of the sacrifice—even if they also depart from the traditional "this I have heard" that starts all orations and stories.

"And what are these three fires, mitto? They are the fire of passion, the fire of hatred, the fire of delusion."

A ripple of shock goes through the audience at this skilful oratorical twist of the sacrificial fires. Despite her anger, Yasodhara feels a grudging admiration at his dexterity.

"Everything in us burns with these fires. The eyes are burning, what the eyes see or experience is burning. Whether pleasant or unpleasant, it is burning. But burning with what? What is burning? Not the eye as a physical object, not the forms it gazes on. What is burning is the fires of our craving, fuelled by passion and jealousy, hatred and ambition. Fuelled also by the delusion of believing that objects or people, including ourselves, are solid and lasting. Because the truth is that everything is constantly changing, constantly disintegrating."

Yasodhara leans forward, eyes narrowed, listening intently despite herself.

"Chief among these delusions of permanence is the notion of Brahman, of Atman. This notion of an unchanging eternal spirit within and without ourselves is merely a fantasy that our burning minds clutch at, seeking the permanent in the impermanent. And because we fool ourselves that the things we see are permanent, and because we want them desperately to be permanent, we burn with sorrow, with discontent, with dissatisfaction at their change and inevitable decay. We burn with grief, with despair, because everything we see is impermanent, everything beloved is passing. And most beloved of all, our own forms, are sickening and aging and passing.

"In the same way the ear is burning, sounds are burning. Again, it is not the sounds or the ear that burns but our desire for pleasant sounds, our aversion and hatred of unpleasant sounds, our love of flattering and amorous words, our aversion to cruel and critical words. In the same way the nose and odours are burning. In the same way our tongues and flavours are burning; our bodies and everything we touch are burning. The mind too is burning. Whatever thoughts or sensations the mind believes to be pleasant or painful or neither-pleasant-nor-painful, all those too are burning."

Yasodhara notices that a few people are nodding with understanding but most of the audience is frowning with bewilderment, not sure what the Awakened One is talking about; or glaring at him, as the Brahmins are. "Good," she thinks, "his teachings will not take hold here."

"Mitto," Siddhartha continues, "when a wise follower of the Middle Way has understood this truth within himself, he starts to develop a separation from all his sensory organs. A separation from his eyes and what he sees, a separation from his ears and what he hears, a separation from his nose and what he smells, a separation from his tongue and what he tastes, a separation from his mind and the sensations and thoughts that bloom and fade in it. On hearing a persistent loud sound, for example, he simply says to himself, 'Ah, phenomenon of sound,' and gives his attention to the sound, to the silences between the pulses of the sound. And, as he contemplates the sound more deeply, it begins to break into smaller and smaller components until finally he sees the truth of impermanence in the very sound. He sees the truth that nothing is static or whole, but everything is in flux and changing. And if the sound causes him anger or irritation, he simply says to himself, 'Mind of anger,' or 'Mind of irritation.' And, by doing this, he separates himself from the sound, from his emotions to the sound. So he does with his other senses and what they register.

"And, as he develops and hones this separation, his cravings and urges and clinging cease, just like a fire that is not fed by fuel dies out. And finally, this man, now fully awoken, experiences Nibbana, the Great Extinguishing. He passes to a state where his mind is clear and pure and joyful, as a person passes from a great heat to the coolness of a lotus-covered pond. And with this dying of the fires, he is liberated and says to himself, 'Ah, indeed, I am free.'"

Siddhartha falls silent, looking at the ground in front of him, his oration over.

As Yasodhara looks around to see the audience's reaction, her eyes rest on a distant verandah and she lets out a little "huh" and leans forward. Rahula and Devadatta. Her son has come to hear Siddhartha—no doubt driven, like her, against his own will. She stares at him, not sure if he sees her in the shadow. After a moment, she lifts a hand and he promptly lifts his too. Yet, because his face is indistinct, she cannot tell how he is feeling.

Gazing at Rahula, she is reminded again of Siddhartha's refusal to help. How will she tell her boy this?

The Royal Head Priest stands now to challenge Siddhartha. "Prove to us that there is no Atman or Brahman," he demands. "Prove to us that the gods are impermanent."

Siddhartha nods, letting the priest's words, his anger, die down in silence before responding.

"If the entire universe is the manifestation of a permanent entity called Brahman, if that entity exists in us too, called Atman, why cannot we say to our physical form, which is after all part of this permanent entity, 'Dear Form, be this or that. Don't change.' But we cannot. Rather our form is beyond our control. It sickens, hurts, lusts for things it cannot have, weakens and dies, and we cannot tell it, 'Now, dear Form, come, come, for shame, why this sickening? I order you to be well, be immortal, be beautiful.'"

A titter goes through the crowd.

"In the same way our feelings are not Atman because they too rise and fall as they will, stimulated by sensory impressions. And, while we can be aware of them through contemplation, we cannot control them. In the same way our perceptions are beyond our control. Even our consciousness is not permanent because it too is in constant flux and we cannot say to it, 'Now listen here, Consciousness, why this ridiculous vacillation? I order you to remain thus or thus.' So, mitta, any kind of form, feeling, perception, consciousness, whether past, present or future, must be regarded as 'This is not I. This is not myself. This is not permanent.' And therefore, there is no permanent Atman or Brahman. And also, no permanent gods."

Some of the crowd clap and cheer, but Yasodhara is not sure if they are doing so because of Siddhartha's oratorical gymnastics or because they do believe what he says now. She suspects the former.

That evening, when the women gather in the courtyard for their meal, Yasodhara tells them that Siddhartha has nothing to offer them. "He shrugged and looked helpless when I asked him," she says bitterly. "Then he went on about how, if he did us a favour, he must do favours for everyone else too, as if we are mere strangers, mere petitioners come to beg."

To her surprise, the other women look sad but not surprised. They nod gently as they let her words settle in.

"We already spoke of this on the way back from the oration, daharé," Sumana the old concubine says with a gentle twinkle in her eyes. "Our Siddhartha is a samana now, he cannot embroil himself in our worldly matters."

"Hearing him speak, hearing his wisdom, we know he is beyond our petty concerns," Utara, her aunt, adds.

"But why not?" Yasodhara says, turning to Prajapati. "Doesn't he owe us this much?"

"The women are right, Ushas." Prajapati sighs. "I shouldn't have suggested you even ask him. It was wrong of me to do so."

Before she can respond, there is a sound of running feet and Rahula bursts into the courtyard. "Ammé, have you talked to my pita?" He takes in the women looking back at him sombrely. "Ammé?"

Yasodhara holds out a hand to him. "Puthā, I tried, but your pita . . ."

"What did he say?" Rahula whispers, bewildered.

"He . . . he said that . . ."

Prajapati comes to her rescue: "It's just that your pita is a samana now, puthā, and samanas cannot, must not, get embroiled in worldly matters."

Rahula is still, his face suddenly so sad, so adult. After a moment, he turns without a word and walks slowly out of the courtyard. Yasodhara rises to go after him, but Prajapati gently stays her. "Let him be, Ushas. He needs time to absorb this."

4

Fathers and Sons

SUDDHODANA ASSUMES THAT Siddhartha will have his meals in the palace from now on but, the next day, much to his incomprehension and dismay, his son goes back to begging in the Dasa Quarter. He sends a message demanding to know why Siddhartha spurns his father's hospitality. Ananda is dispatched to the palace to explain again, patiently, that it is the custom of Awakened Ones and their followers to beg for their meals.

Yasodhara hears that the nobles and janata are also bewildered by Siddhartha's actions. They had taken Suddhodana's ostentatious display of his successful son as a sign that Siddhartha was complicit in this display; that Siddhartha would use the exhibition of his oratory skills to launch himself politically, and to resurrect the fortunes of the Gotama Gotra. Instead, there is Siddhartha, begging in the poorest quarters.

Soon, these poorer householders understand that, if they invite him for a meal when he comes to their door, he will always accept. Streets begin to pool their resources to feed him and his bhikkhus. The oration about the three fires, which Suddhodana and the guests at the palace thought an exclusive entertainment for them, can now be heard by anyone who asks for it. And not just the Fire Oration, but other discourses too. That the Dasas and poorer Vessas might be privy to orations the elite aren't, that the lower varnas hear the very orations given to the Maharaja of Magadha and his court, disgruntles the wealthy and powerful of Kapilavastu. Yet they don't open their homes to the bhikkhus, not wanting to offend Pasénadi and the Pandu Gotra.

For her part, Yasodhara continues to dismiss with contempt Siddhartha's explanation that helping her would mean helping everyone who appeals to him. No matter the rest of the world, he owes his wife and child something. He is, after all, the very person who has brought them to where they are.

She wants Siddhartha gone from the city, and longs for his departure. As for the Middle Way, what drivel. Ridiculous, this idea of giving up desire. Is she supposed to stop loving her son? Stop mourning the loss of the life she had in Mudgala? Why should she, when that life contained such happiness? And what will be her compensation if she does give up desire? It will change nothing about her current situation with all its stresses and worries, the bleak future that awaits. As for this idea that everything is forever changing, it's very well for a man like Siddhartha— for most men, really, who are in control of their destiny and can ride out change. But a woman is simply submerged by change, swept away and drowned in it.

Ananda comes often to beg at the women's quarters. And, much to everyone's surprise, with him comes Anuruddha—who hasn't joined the Order but is inseparable from his brother, accompanying him on his daily rounds, inviting Ananda and other monks to have midday meals in his house, walking Ananda back to the Nigrodha Grove so he can spend as much time as possible with him before the monks go into seclusion for the rest of the day. Anuruddha brings levity to these visits, as he is often out of breath and sweating from his walking around in the heat. The women tease and chide Anuruddha, asking him when he will become a bhikkhu, calling him "Bhikkhu Anuruddha," bantering that he will never be able to give up his profligate ways. He grins good-naturedly as he takes the sweetened water he's offered, adding to the humour with his self-deprecating wit, showing the women with mock-pride the new calluses on his feet from following his brother.

After Prajapati has fed Ananda, the women often assail him with questions about the Middle Way. Ananda answers patiently and in detail, seated on a bench near the archway into the walled garden, where Yasodhara works, helped by Rahula. Yasodhara understands from where he sits that he hopes to win her to the Middle Way, but she keeps up a steady, loud conversation with Rahula as they work side by side, to drown out the sermons.

Ever since Siddhartha's arrival, Rahula has started to follow Yasodhara everywhere, offering to help with whatever tasks she does, coming meekly to his bed in their suite and no longer staying with Devadatta. The reason for this is clear to Yasodhara: they are bound in their anger and resentment towards Siddhartha; they alone have been truly failed by him. They don't, however, speak of this. In fact, his name never passes their lips. As Ananda gives his sermon, Rahula is assiduous about keeping up his end of the conversation, also speaking louder than usual to drown out the words drifting their way.

Prajapati is motherly with her nephew, sometimes forgetting he is a bhikkhu and addressing him as "dahara." Once, after listening to the women's eager questions, she says to Ananda, clicking her tongue scoldingly, "It is not right, dahara, that our women must go out to the Nigrodha Grove and sit in such large gatherings of men. Mitta, Sanga, Visaka and Utara," she gestures to the women, "are even going into poorer homes in the Dasa Quarter, to hear the Awakened One speak."

Ananda smiles, amused by her tone. "Yes, pitucché, you are right." Then he adds, "Pitucché, do you know the story of Yasa's mother? Not long after her son became a monk, she invited the Awakened One and his bhikkhus to a meal. On hearing the philosophy preached, she became the first upasika. Since then, she frequently brings food to feed the monks in the Bamboo Grove, when we are in Rajagaha, and invites other women to come and hear them speak too."

Prajapati claps her hands. "Ah! Then tell the Awakened One that, the day after tomorrow, the women of our quarters will feed the bhikkhus in the Nigrodha Grove. Also, it would be a good thing if, on the bhikkhus' alms round tomorrow, they tell other women about this meal."

Once Ananda and Anuruddha have left, Prajapati sidles into the walled garden and comes to crouch by Yasodhara and Rahula. "I know how you both feel, but the women do wish this and soon they will have no true pleasure in their life. So, I must grant it."

"But you want it too, ayyakā," Rahula says, face stern to hide his hurt.

Prajapati sighs. "Yes, it's true, daharā." She presses Yasodhara's arm. "Can you not get past your anger at all, Ushas? Is it not possible to find some comfort in this philosophy?"

Yasodhara smiles sarcastically. "Unfortunately, 'all is burning' in me, pitucché." She shrugs and turns away from her aunt, gesturing for Rahula to hand her a spade.

Later that day, Yasodhara goes with Prajapati to attend on Suddhodana. When they enter his room, he cries petulantly, "I hear you are offering a meal to those . . . those . . . They are not welcome here!"

"I don't offer it here, ayyé. I take the meal to them." Prajapati shakes her head impatiently as she stirs some gruel in a bowl for him.

"I forbid it."

"You forbid me to feed our son?" she demands incredulously. "If," she continues to a dumbfounded Suddhodana, "you wish the samanas to come to the palace, then you must invite them, ayyé. They will not just come."

"Why should I invite them? He is my son, it is his duty to eat in my house."

Prajapati waves her hand. "Well, so it is." She holds out a spoon of gruel, trying to hide her amusement at Suddhodana's crotchety petulance. Since Siddhartha's return, an odd motherly affection seems to have woken in Prajapati towards her dying husband.

The next evening, Yasodhara is attending to Suddhodana, helping him into bed with the aid of two servants, when there is a soft knock on the door. The old man calls out, "Yes?" and Siddhartha slips in, smiling mischievously because he has broken his own rule that bhikkhus must stay in seclusion after midday. Suddhodana, like everyone, knows of this rule, and though he says, "I am too tired to see you now, you must come at a suitable time if you want an audience with the raja," it is clear to Yasodhara that her uncle is delighted his son has flouted the decree for his sake.

Siddhartha comes up to the bed. For a moment Yasodhara meets his gaze before she sternly goes back to arranging her uncle's pillows and covers, pouring water into a clay cup and dissolving some drops in it that the Royal Bisaj prescribed. She is aware that both men are watching her.

"Are you well, pita?" Siddhartha says as he sits on a stool by the bed.

Suddhodana chews on his cheek for a moment. "No, puthā," he finally replies softly. "I feel Yama's reins tightening, feel the call of the Land of the Fathers." Then he laughs. "But I suppose you don't believe in the Land of the Fathers or the Mansions of the Moon."

Siddhartha nods and smiles to say this is so.

"Tell me, then, what you do believe. Give me something that will ease my passage into wherever it is you think I go next."

Siddhartha starts to explain the Four Great Realities but, before he can get far, Yasodhara interrupts him. "I will come tomorrow morning as well to see to you, mātula," she says to Suddhodana. Then she leaves, without a glance at Siddhartha.

After that, Siddhartha comes every evening after dark to visit his father. Word soon spreads about this—spread by Suddhodana, who is puffed up and pleased at this honour and duty shown to him by his son. Soon he declares that he is an upasaka, a lay follower.

Yasodhara is forced to encounter Siddhartha often in her uncle's room. She continues to maintain her cold distance, despite occasionally catching his pleading gaze.

One evening, after she leaves Siddhartha with his father, she is bustling towards the archway out of the raja's private courtyard when she notices a movement in a dark corner of a verandah. She bends down with a "*Tttch,*" as if to remove a stone from inside her slipper—and uses the gesture to sneak a quick glance. As she guessed, it is Rahula squatting in the dark, watching her.

She rises and leaves the courtyard, only to quickly squat herself in a dark corner of the more public square. A small pulse of fear beats in her throat. After some time, she sees Siddhartha come out of his father's private courtyard and make his way across the square towards the palace gates. A moment later, Rahula slips out of Suddhodana's courtyard and follows him. She gives them both sufficient distance and then follows too, staying, like Rahula, in the shadows.

The trio make their way through the city until finally Siddhartha goes through a door in the fortifications at the end of an unprepossessing alley, a door that is used by the Dasa night-soil cleaners to enter and leave the city after the gates are closed. Rahula slips outside too and, after an interval, Yasodhara does the same, keeping in the shadow of the doorway.

Siddhartha, however, has disappeared. He is not, as she expected, on the path that leads along the edge of the moat to the bridge. Rahula has stopped a little ahead, bewildered.

"Puthā."

She turns quickly to see Siddhartha. He has gone the other way, and is now standing in the moonlight, legs apart, arms folded across his chest. She moves even further into the shadow of the doorway.

After a moment, Rahula walks towards Siddhartha, trying to appear nonchalant. He stops a small distance away.

"What would you like to ask me? To know?" Siddhartha asks gently.

Rahula draws his shawl tighter around himself and kicks at the stockade.

Siddhartha waits patiently, not breaking the silence. Finally Rahula says, "Why did you come back here? Why are you here?"

"Your ayyaka is dying."

"Only for my ayyaka, then." Rahula laughs. "I suppose I don't matter to you. Nor my ammé."

"I love your ammé, and I love you, puthā."

"Love us so much that you didn't send a message all these years even though you were alive? I thought you were dead. I wish you were dead. At least then we would have peace."

Siddhartha is silent, then he nods in agreement. "Your accusation is the truth, puthā."

Rahula is taken aback at this admission of wrong-doing delivered in such a soft, sad way. He is used to his uncle, to his grandfather, to men who fight to prove they are right even when they aren't.

"Yes, I did abandon you both. I did not send any message to tell you I was alive because"— Siddhartha struggles with the words—"the nature of the path I took demanded a complete breaking from the old life in order to be reborn." He takes a step towards Rahula, holding out a hand in appeal. "To have kept the old bonds would not have allowed me to find the Truth."

"But what has your Truth, your path, given me?" Rahula asks, suddenly close to tears.

"Puthā, whatever I say will only sound cynical and callous and hurt you further. Because the truth is, Rahula, unless you come to believe too in the Middle Way, you will never accept that its discovery was worth the cost of being fatherless."

"I will never accept that!"

Siddhartha bows to acknowledge this. "Good night, puthā," he says softly. He walks past Rahula and heads towards the bridge.

When Siddhartha is lost in the darkness, Rahula wipes his eyes and kicks at the stockade over and over again. Yasodhara watches for a time, then melts soundlessly away.

A few nights later, Suddhodana has another seizure. The Royal Bisaj informs the family this is truly the end.

As Yasodhara hurries with Rahula towards the men's quarters—Prajapati having gone ahead of them—she takes his hand. "Expect to find your pita there."

He nods to say that he already knows this.

Reaching Suddhodana's room, they pause in the doorway and take in Siddhartha seated on a stool by the bed; take in also that Suddhodana's breathing is shallow now, long gaps between breaths, a sure sign of the end.

Siddhartha's face, as he looks at his father, is filled with genuine sorrow. But unlike Prajapati, who is swabbing her husband's sweaty forehead, there is no rawness to his grief.

Siddhartha sees Yasodhara now and, with a smile that acknowledges the strain between them, he rises from his stool, presses his palms together and bows. She returns his bow grimly.

"Rahula, go and pay your respects to your pita."

Yasodhara is sure the boy will refuse but, to her surprise, he goes forward and sullenly touches his father's feet. Siddhartha leans down and raises Rahula by his shoulders. "Be strong, puthā."

Rahula winces away from Siddhartha with a scowl. He appropriates the stool where his father was seated and takes his grandfather's hand. "Ayyaka," he whispers, "it is Rahula. Come to see you. Can you hear me?" After a brief silence, Suddhodana makes an incomprehensible sound and presses Rahula's hand. Rahula begins to weep, laying his head on his grandfather's chest. Yasodhara goes to him. At first, he shies away from her touch, but then throws his arms about her, sobbing. It takes Yasodhara a while to realize that Siddhartha has slipped out of the room, leaving them to their sorrow. Not long after his departure, Suddhodana breathes his last breath.

As Yasodhara stands at the foot of the bed with weeping Rahula and Prajapati, she looks at this man who has shrunk to less than half his former size, cheeks fallen in, forehead denting greyish and opaque skin, the fine bones of his feet clearly delineated like the claws of a bird. How changed he is from the uncle who greeted her when she first arrived here as a bride: Suddhodana standing in the courtyard waiting to greet the entourage, lit by two flaring torches, his powerful arms, shoulders and chest brawny in the golden light, the hairs on his chest and arms sparkling.

As Dawn is unfolding her pink banners in the sky, the Chandala men arrive in the raja's courtyard, bearing the stretcher for Suddhodana's body. They squat around a tree smoking, waiting to be allowed into the bedroom so they can bring out the body shaved, bathed and scented.

Yasodhara, who has taken over the funeral duties, sends messages summoning the palace Brahmins, the heralds and musicians to the public courtyard. When the Brahmins arrive, she discusses the upcoming rituals with them. They have already found two anustarani cows in expectation of Suddhodana's death and they go off to slaughter the first with all the due rituals. Next she speaks with the musicians and heralds, settling on who will go to what parts of the city and announce the raja's death.

As she deals with these matters, Mahanama and Amitodhana arrive, followed soon after by Pandu and the Senapati of Kapilavastu. The sena-pati is the temporary raja until the sangha votes in a new one, which they will do in a few days. He is discreet about his new role and soon slips away

with a formal bow to deal with some matter of state, leaving the three con-
tenders with nothing to do but observe each other in the rapidly growing
light, like dogs circling. Soon, conches are being blown and drums beaten
all over the city to announce Suddhodana's death.

By late morning the funeral procession is ready to leave. Yasodhara,
her aunt, Siddhartha and Rahula take their places at the front, along with
Sundari Nanda. It feels odd to be standing like this with Siddhartha, as if he
is still her husband. She shoots him a glance to see if he might be feeling
something similar, but his face is calm and unreadable.

The Chandala men walk behind them, carrying the stretcher on which
Suddhodana lies draped in a gold-threaded cloth, his sacrificial implements by his side. Rahula carries the marital fire that will be snuffed out
at the grave. His face is sombre, grim. Yasodhara puts her hand on his
shoulder and he gives her a willing smile—and with a pang of alarm she
is aware there is something too willing about his smile, as if he has done
something bad and is acting innocent. She frowns questioningly. Rahula
shrugs to say he doesn't understand her silent question, then faces reso-
lutely forward.

Behind the bier are the Brahmin priests with the second anustarani cow,
the fresh skin of the first one carried by one of their group, flies buzzing
about the skin despite the ash smeared on its bloody underside. Beyond the
Brahmins, the relatives are gathered, led by Amitodhana and Mahanama.
Yasodhara glimpses the women of the quarters, sees their large-eyed fear
at what awaits them. Ananda and Anuruddha are also among the relatives.
Then, for the first time, she is aware that Devadatta is absent. "Puthā," she
whispers, leaning in to Rahula, "where is your mātula?"

"He's gone off hunting," Rahula replies promptly—a little too
promptly.

She is about to quiz him further, but the procession starts to move
forward with a blowing of conches, a thundering of drums. The royal
elephant awaits them beyond the gates of the palace. It now leads the
procession, guided by its mahout, riderless and unadorned to symbolize
Suddhodana's passing. The palace guards and army line the sides of the
road; as the procession passes, they fall into line behind it.

Yasodhara had expected that a fair portion of the janata wouldn't come out to say goodbye to their raja, given the impending contest for supremacy between Pandu, Mahanama and Amitodhana. Suddhodana had also lost popularity due to his various bunglings in recent years. Yet to her surprise she sees that the Uttarapatha is lined with people. They are not, however, silent, as they usually would be during a funeral procession. Instead, they fervently murmur verses that she has never heard before. Snatches reach her as she goes along: ". . . that cessation, detachment and Nibbana the Awakened One has realized . . . this precious jewel is the Teachings . . . the precious jewel is the Awakened One." The crowd must be reciting the Jewel Sutta. Now, looking closer, she sees that a lot of those gathered are farmers come from the surrounding countryside. They are emaciated, exhausted, desperate—harbingers of the growing disaster beyond the city walls. Clearly, they are hoping that chanting the sutta in the Awakened One's presence will lead to rain coming to the Sakiya Kingdom. Siddhartha's face is impassive and serene, his gaze inwardly turned, not by any gesture or look betraying that he hears the chanting.

When the procession reaches the forest, only the relatives enter the woods while the others fall away. The moment they are among the trees, Siddhartha turns to Yasodhara and Prajapati, bows and walks away into the forest. Ananda does the same. A murmur of surprise and bewilderment rises among the gotra, but her aunt nods to Yasodhara and they continue on. The rest of the procession soon follows.

"It's the sacrifice of the second anustarani cows," someone says. "They want no part in any ritual that involves the cruelty of the sacrifice."

Later, once the funeral rituals are done and the family is walking towards the city, they see a stream of farmers heading towards the Nigrodha Grove to try and persuade the Awakened One to bring the rains. Watching these people, it dawns on Yasodhara that Siddhartha will soon be gone.

As they enter through the city gates, Rahula stops. He gives Yasodhara a solemn stare, as if memorizing her face, then starts to hurry away.

"Rahula!" she yells, frightened.

He ignores her and breaks into a run, then disappears down a side street.

Her aunt and the other women are staring at her. Yasodhara shakes her head. "Nothing, it's nothing," she mutters, uneasiness throbbing inside her.

5

The Price of Water

IT IS MIDDAY by the time they reach the palace. Yasodhara sits down for a meal in the courtyard with the women, but Prajapati retires to her room, exhausted. The women eat in sober silence, but none of them are red-eyed. They did not love Suddhodana, and now are burdened with the result of his excesses. Yasodhara barely touches her food, distracted by her worry for Rahula.

As they eat, they can hear dimly, beyond high mud walls, the sounds of the city: passing carts, chariots and hawkers. Gradually, however, they become aware of a rising clamour of voices, and rushing feet thumping on the dry clay street. They look at each other, puzzled.

A servant woman bursts in crying, "Sāmini, trouble!"

Yasodhara pushes aside her banana leaf and jumps up. Whatever this trouble, Rahula is involved; she knows this in her heart. She gestures for the woman to speak as she washes her shaking hands, a slave pouring cool water over them from a pitcher.

"A skirmish has broken out between the Sakiya and Koliya over rights to the Rohini River."

"But there hasn't been conflict between the Sakiya and Koliya for so long," Sundari Nanda protests, "not for generations."

"It's those farmers, sāmini, who came from the rural areas. They appealed to the Awakened One for a rain miracle, but their wish wasn't granted. Why, he didn't even give them an audience, sāmini! So, they've opened the very sluice gates that Pandu commanded be kept shut until he had negotiated water rights with the Koliya raja. Broke the gates for good measure. The Koliya controllers and guards on the other side of the river, seeing this, sent immediately for reinforcements and soon a band of armed Koliya villagers arrived. Our janata also by now had gathered on our bank. Even as I speak, arrows and spears are flying."

"This is no mere skirmish led by frustrated farmers." Yasodhara straps on her slippers, reaches for her shawl. "It is the fight for succession in our kingdom. I . . . I fear Rahula is involved."

The other women cry out in protest and horror at this.

Now Prajapati, roused by the servant's alarm, comes rapidly down the stairs. Hearing Yasodhara's last words, she hurries forward and grasps her arm. "Rahula? Are you sure?"

"Yes, yes. I was wondering why Devadatta was absent from the funeral. Now I see. They're both involved."

"Oh, Ushas!"

Yasodhara rushes across the courtyard and out the street door, to find the road crowded with people running towards the ramparts, where there is a guard platform from which to view the battle. She joins the stream of people.

The larger scheme is clear to her: to show that Pandu is a weak ruler who cannot control the janata or negotiate water rights with their neighbour. Mahanama and Amitodhana will sit back until the battle becomes almost uncontrollable, then intervene to save the situation. The Koliya raja (whose son, of course, is married to Mahanama's daughter) will then instruct his people to lay down arms. But, before that, men will be killed and wounded. And her son is in the middle of it all.

When she reaches the ramparts, the ladder up to the platform is blocked by soldiers, who push and prod the janata back with their spears. Yasodhara shoves her way to the front and, taking her royal seal from a knot in her dhoti, proffers it to the commander. He recognizes it immediately, bows and makes way for her. As she clambers up the ladder and away from the noise of the crowd below, she begins to hear the sounds of battle beyond the city, the shouts of men. She reaches the platform and the guards there signal her to crouch in case an arrow comes her way. They make room for her to look through a peephole between the wooden palings.

The battle is bigger than she had imagined: Koliya and Sakiya warriors on either side of the river yell insults at each other, firing arrows which sometimes hit their mark. She searches desperately among the Sakiya for Rahula, but it's impossible to spot any one person in the great throng of people, much less a boy.

Men are dropping on both sides, the wounded and dead dragged up the riverbanks by their comrades. Particularly vulnerable are those who have gone out on barges into the middle of the river. Their bodies fall into the water, where the corpses are immediately submerged, only to pop up a while later as the river sweeps them along, tangling in weeds, snagging against the jagged ends of rocks, a few drifting towards the shore where they bob in the shallows. Already vultures are circling above, and crows are gathering in trees at the tops of the banks. A pack of dogs slide their way down the embankment further along the river, where a corpse has reached the shore.

The city gates were shut when the battle started, but now they open and out pours the army on horseback, led by the Senapati of Kapilavastu. Yasodhara realizes only now that they have taken a long time to appear. Where have they been?

The Sakiya janata, seeing the approaching cavalry, let out a cry of triumph, thinking reinforcements have arrived. But once the troops reach the riverbank, instead of shooting arrows at the Koliya, or launching their horses into the river to throw spears at the Koliya rafts, or joining a party that has made it to the other bank further downriver and is now rushing up to do battle with their new enemies, the senapati and his soldiers go among the Sakiya and beat them back with whips, jabbing at them with spear tips, smacking bodies and heads with poles, horses trampling those who will not get out of their way. At the same time, on the opposite bank, a troop of soldiers has appeared, led by the local Koliya rashtrika, and they are beating back their own Koliya people; they too showed up, she thinks, conveniently at just the right moment. Probably they had gathered already in the forest beyond the bank and were waiting for the battle to get out of hand.

The soldiers on both sides finally force their way to the river's edges and form phalanxes, each facing their own janata. The armed Koliya villagers immediately melt away into the forest beyond the river, and some of the Sakiya janata also beat a hasty retreat to the top of the steep bank. Yet a contingent of them remain, along with the impoverished farmers. They are enraged at this betrayal by their own soldiers and begin to attack them with spears, stones, sticks, even hurling mud at them. Soon arrows are being shot at the soldiers. The sureness with which they find their mark tells Yasodhara that the archers are not villagers but trained warriors—of the Khattiya varna. And all at once, because the crowd has thinned out, she can see Khattiya nobles on horseback among the janata. She searches desperately among them for a glimpse of her brother, for Rahula mounted behind him, but it's no use. The soldiers are struggling to hold their own along the river's edge. Battle lust is high, fuelled by fear and frustration at the growing drought among the farmers and janata, fuelled by a lust for power among the Khattiya warriors, who support the Gotama Gotra and will benefit from their ascendancy. More and more of the soldiers are falling, pushed further back into the river.

Yasodhara has a vista of the battle and the river, and so she is one of the first to notice a raft coming upriver towards the battleground. As it draws closer, she sees that it is the ferry, poled along by the ferryman. And standing on it is Siddhartha, in his red robes.

The people at the top of the bank, who are not involved in the battle, begin to notice the ferry. They cry, "The Awakened One! The Awakened One!" As the cries grow louder, more and more Sakiya on the bank see the ferry. Those warring at the river's edge finally hear these cries. They stop fighting and begin to shout too. Soon even the soldiers are calling out, "The Awakened One! The Awakened One!" The senapati, whose sword has been raised all this time to spur his men on, lowers his blade.

The ferry stops a short distance from the combatants, and they fall silent.

The Awakened One gestures with a lifted hand in greeting. "Mitto, what is this quarrel about?"

Much to Yasodhara's surprise, and clearly to the surprise of the combatants and onlookers, his words can be heard distinctly. (Later, this will be attributed to the Awakened One's miraculous powers.)

There is a great swell of murmuring, then someone shouts, "Water." Soon everyone is crying out, "Water! Water!"

"And what is the price of water? Is it worth more than your lands and fields and houses?" Siddhartha's voice, even as it carries, has none of the hectoring of a noble or a raja shouting to reach the back of a crowd.

Again there is that muttering, and then some voices shout, "No," and soon the crowd is roaring, "No! No!"

"And what is the value of your lives?" he asks, in a tone that is simply curious. "The lives of your loved ones? The dependants you will leave behind defenceless, your mothers, wives, children, who will be unable to meet life's needs on their own and end up destitute? What is the value of these people?"

"Priceless!" the voices bellow.

"Then friends, why do you destroy your lives over something so trivial as water?"

The onlookers mutter again among themselves. But this time, no one has an answer.

"Help us, O Awakened One," someone cries, and soon the janata and farmers and warriors are crying together, "Bring us rain, O Awakened One!" "Don't desert your people in their need!" "Give to us what you gave to the Licchavis!" "Pardon us, O Awakened One!" "Grant us respite!"

Siddhartha listens to all this calmly and, when the clamour finally ceases, he raises his hand in acknowledgement of the pleas. Then he instructs the ferryman to take him back downriver to the Nigrodha Park.

Soon after, the janata and warriors disperse. The senapati gestures for his soldiers to set about repairing and restoring the sluice gate.

Desperately worried about Rahula, Yasodhara scrambles down the ladder into the dispersing crowd. She hurries through the city streets towards the palace and, turning down the lane to the women's quarters, sees the two young concubines, Visaka and Sanga, outside the street door, craning to peer through the crowd. She breaks into a run. They spot her and wave frantically.

"Rahula?" she gasps when she reaches them, clutching Sanga's arm.

"He's alive, sāmini," Sanga assures her.

"Not even wounded," Visaka adds.

Yasodhara lets go of Sanga's arm, huffing in relief. Yet she can tell from their expressions that Rahula is in trouble. "He's in the courtyard," Sanga whispers.

Together they hurry through the passageway that leads to the interior courtyard. Whatever has happened, she needs to be calm, even objective. She is sure, from the concubines' expressions, that a terrified little boy awaits her. In the courtyard, Rahula is seated on a bench with Devadatta. Prajapati is cleaning dirt off the boy's face and arms with a wet cloth, Tissa holding the bucket of water for her. "Ammé!" Rahula leaps up from the bench and runs to her. She takes him in her arms and he presses hard against her.

"Now, now," she says softly, "it's probably not as bad as you think." Holding him away from her, she looks from Rahula to Devadatta. "Tell me."

Devadatta glances at Rahula, then says glumly, "As you've probably guessed, the fight at the river was planned. Mahanama and Amitodhana plotted with the Koliya rashtrika on the other side, having got the approval of the Koliya raja, who wants our Gotama Gotra to continue to rule Kapilavastu."

She nods impatiently, knowing this already.

"In order to prevent the battle from ending too fast, something had to be done to keep the senapati from it." He looks away from her widening eyes. "This was Rahula's and my task. You see, we knew that the senapati, as the interim ruler, was working in the raja's receiving room. We also knew that in one of its corners, behind a curtain, was an antechamber with a small window. So, before the battle began, Rahula squeezed in through the window, taking his bow and arrows along with him."

Yasodhara turns to her son, gesturing for him to pick up the story.

"I . . . I held the senapati at bay with my bow and arrow while I let mātula in," Rahula says, in a small voice.

The women gasp at the audacity of this, but Yasodhara keeps her expression neutral, not wanting to frighten the boy any more than he already is. "What happened then, puthā?"

Rahula doesn't say anything, but glances at his uncle.

Devadatta's face darkens. "I was supposed to kill the senapati, but, well, I couldn't. It's one thing to kill a man in the heat of battle, another in our mātula's old receiving room. So, instead, we tied and gagged the senapati.

Then Rahula locked and barred the door from the inside, pushed furniture up against it and crawled back through the window. So it took the senapati's soldiers, when they came to alert him of the battle, some time to break down the door."

"But why?" Prajapati cries. "Why did you do this? Why did you get involved in such a foolish scheme?"

Neither Rahula nor Devadatta says a word. The answer is so obvious: desperation at the bleak futures that await them both.

Devadatta finally speaks: "Bhagini, the best thing for us is to ride into exile. Go to the Koliya Kingdom, where I know we will be welcome."

"But bhāta," Yasodhara says wretchedly, "you won't find refuge there. Our former home is also a part of Pasénadi's empire. The Koliya raja will have no choice but to turn you both over as fugitives. Also, the Koliya senapati and his guards, as the maharaja's representatives, will hunt you down."

Devadatta is silent for a long moment. Then he says, "Then my only option is the vana-dasas. I will go among them and live in the forest."

"I will, too," Rahula declares.

Yasodhara takes her son by the shoulders. "No, puthā. That is not the solution for you. I will beg the maharaja to excuse you on grounds of youthful folly. And bad influences," she adds, with a quick glare at Devadatta.

That evening, storm clouds gather and, by the first part of the night, just after the sun has set, it begins to rain. A miracle performed by the Awakened One to alleviate the suffering of his people. As Yasodhara stands at her window, watching the janata in the street below, running about joyfully in the rain, collecting water in buckets and barrels, crying out, "The Awakened One has saved us!" she knows that Pandu will want Siddhartha gone as soon as possible. Siddhartha too will be keen to leave, spurning this mantle of rain-maker.

Rahula is seated beside her in the window well, looking out pensively, a prisoner in these quarters now. Soldiers will not come in here to seize him. Such a violation of the palace women's privacy would enrage the janata, and she knows the senapati doesn't want further trouble. "Do you think he's really caused this rain, ammé?" Rahula asks.

"No." She takes his hand. "He said so himself."

"But that could be just . . . modesty." He cocks his head. "Don't you think he's a modest man, ammé? And look how he stopped the battle. Everyone is talking about it."

Yasodhara sighs and gets up. She begins to fold some shawls. "Yes, yes, I saw it all." Then she shrugs and says nothing more. If she talks about Siddhartha she will start to hate him again because he has left her alone, once more, to figure out their son's future. She has no energy left for hating.

As Yasodhara and Rahula are preparing for bed that night, a serving woman comes to inform her that Devadatta wishes to speak with her in the front courtyard. Rahula makes a move to come with her, but she signals him sternly to remain.

She finds Devadatta in the courtyard, standing in the shadows with his horse. She had come down unforgiving and angry, determined to wish him a curt goodbye, but now, as she goes towards him, she realizes that they may never meet again. Despite what he did to her son, she is filled with sorrow at the thought of losing him, this brother she has loved from the beginning of her life. They stand a moment, regarding each other. Then she reaches out and embraces him, and he clings to her. When they pull away, she places a hand on his cheek. "The vana-dasas have always been your people, bhāta. From the time you were young, you were drawn to their world. So, live well among them. Follow their laws and customs and try, really try, to be happy and fulfilled with your lot." Even as she says this, she knows she has said similar words before, when she left him in Mudgala; and recalling this, she again feels despair and worry for her intemperate brother.

Devadatta nods, his face stern, frowning to hold in his emotions. He finally manages a smile, a cheeky salute, then turns and walks his horse out of the gate. Yasodhara stands in the street as he mounts, watching how he's taught his horse to kneel so he can get on despite his bad leg, his gift with animals so evident in this moment. They give each other a last look, and he rides away. She watches him go until he is lost in the dark.

By morning, a message arrives from Savatthi. The messenger rode through the night to deliver it: the maharaja is on his way and will be in Kapilavastu this evening. Until such time, there is to be no punishing of the rebels or any actions taken by the senapati, except to maintain peace.

Yasodhara allows herself a moment of relief. The Senapati of Kapila-vastu is a cold and cruel man and she doubts he would have granted Rahula clemency because of his age. In fact, the general is likely to have been extra harsh with Rahula: to be taken captive by a mere boy has damaged his reputation. Pasénadi, she hopes, will be kinder.

The next day, she is working in her walled garden when she looks up to see Ananda and Anuruddha coming down the garden path towards her. She hastily stands up and washes her hands. They reach her now and, seeing their smiles, she catches her breath. To confirm her guess, Anuruddha says, "All is well for Rahula."

"How?" she whispers. "What has happened?" Before they can answer, she blurts out, "Siddhartha intervened."

The two men look at each other and shake their heads merrily.

"It is Ananda, ñātiké," Anuruddha says with a laugh. "He intervened on your behalf."

Yasodhara clutches Ananda's hand and squeezes it, even though such touch is forbidden to bhikkhus by the rules of the Order. "Well, well, now, you must tell me all, bhāta! I have missed your stories."

They sit in the shade of a tree as Ananda tells his tale:

Last evening, Siddhartha and his bhikkhus were preparing to perform their meditations in the Nigrodha Grove, seated cross-legged in a circle, when there was a clatter of hooves among the trees and a rider, followed by soldiers carrying flaring torches, cantered into the grove and came to a halt.

Siddhartha immediately recognized the maharaja. Gesturing his bhikkhus to stay seated and not be alarmed, he went forward. Seeing that the maharaja didn't recognize him, he cried, "Sāmi, it is I, Siddhartha. I am joyful to see you after all these years."

But Pasénadi simply frowned at Siddhartha and demanded, using his gotra name, "Do you, Gotama, claim that you have achieved total enlightenment?"

"Yes, sāmi, it seems so," Siddhartha replied, chuckling.

Pasénadi snorted. "Every samana who is head of this or that school, with this or that theory, has also declared themselves perfectly enlightened.

How can you, who are so much younger than these other claimants, who has practised for many fewer years, declare yourself enlightened too?"

"There are four things, sāmi, that you shouldn't dismiss because they are young: a warrior, a flame, a snake and a bhikkhu."

Pasénadi frowned again before letting out an astonished bark of a laugh, understanding it was a joke. "That is good, that is very good! A warrior, a flame, a snake and a bhikkhu!" Forgetting himself, he leaned down from his horse and slapped Siddhartha on the back. "I must remember that one!"

After that, Pasénadi got off his horse, handed his reins to a soldier and put an arm around Siddhartha's shoulder. "But come, come, let us talk. Enlightened though you might be, you're still a statesman. The advice of a friend, a wise friend, is very much what I need now." Siddhartha led him some distance away from the other bhikkhus to sit cross-legged under a tree. Facing each other, they began to discuss the situation in Kapilavastu, and though Ananda and the other bhikkhus couldn't hear what they said, they could see from the way the maharaja nodded that he was taking Siddhartha's advice.

When Pasénadi was finally ready to leave, Ananda asked to accompany him through the treed path of the Nigrodha Grove. As they went along, he pleaded Rahula's case, explaining that Siddhartha himself couldn't ask for such a favour for his son.

"But I thought bhikkhus were not allowed to intervene at all," Yasodhara says, when Ananda finishes his story.

Ananda and Anuruddha look at each other, amused. "What the raja decrees is not always what the amicis do," Anuruddha says, and Yasodhara laughs with them.

6

A Handful of Mustard Seed

THE NEXT DAY, after Pasénadi has met with the senapati, he issues a decree. As penance for engaging in battle, seventy-five Khattiya nobles must join the Awakened One's Order. The senapati will decide which men are to be chosen. This news is received with astonishment throughout the city. Everyone had expected imprisonment, even death, for the Khattiyas who had spearheaded the rebellion.

Yasodhara, hearing the news, immediately understands that Siddhartha has intervened on behalf of the men to save their lives. She goes to her room to tell Rahula. He is silent, taking this in, chewing on his lip.

Sometime later that afternoon, Rahula slips out of the quarters. When they discover him gone, the women are frantic. Although he has been forgiven, he is still vulnerable because of the continuing tensions between the Gotama and Pandu Gotras. Yasodhara is about to send a message to Anuruddha asking for his help when Rahula returns, flushed, an expression on his face that she can't read.

"Where have you been?" she cries, grabbing him by the shoulders.

He smiles. "I grew tired of being stuck here, ammé, so I went to play marbles with the stable boys." He produces the marbles from a knot in his dhoti to prove he is telling the truth. "Besides, aren't I forgiven by the maharaja?" Yasodhara regards him through narrowed eyes, certain he is lying.

A couple of days later, as Yasodhara anticipated, the Awakened One announces that, having spent nearly a month in Kapilavastu, he will depart the day after tomorrow. He has promised the Licchavi princes he will visit them in Vesali again, on his way back to Rajagaha. And Ambapali, the great courtesan of Vesali, has prepared her Mango Grove to be dedicated to the Order. He will give one last oration, he declares. It will take place in the palace's public courtyard on the invitation of the maharaja.

The women of the quarters decide they will go, excited to hear the Awakened One speak and yet sad this will be the last time. As she listens to them express their feelings about the upcoming oration at the morning meal, Yasodhara again wonders how they can be so forgiving of Siddhartha. Especially since, once he departs, they must truly face the bleak futures that await them; must, in the next day or so, pack and leave. And although she herself longed for Siddhartha to leave the city, now that he is actually going, she is surprised to find she has become used to his presence and will also, curiously, miss him.

After a quick midday meal, Yasodhara, Rahula and the women walk over to the public courtyard for the oration. As they go, Rahula takes her hand. She smiles. He has been unusually affectionate since yesterday, and last night even asked to share her bed and huddled close, like he used to when much younger.

The public courtyard is full, not just with noblemen and noblewomen but also with important Vessas. She spots Anuruddha seated further back and they raise hands in greeting. Notably absent are Mahanama and Amitodhana, whom she presumes are in disgrace. Nor is there the usual phalanx of Brahmin priests. Pasénadi, hearing of the argument during Siddhartha's last sermon here, decreed that the Awakened One, his friend, would speak without interruption or contradiction. As a result, only the disgruntled palace priests attend today, upset that the midday sacrifice has been cancelled yet again.

Yasodhara sits a few rows back in the gathering with the other women, Rahula beside her. As her companions chat away, she glances often at her son, aware that he has become pensive, frowning at the ground in front of him.

Now, a conch sounds in the courtyard and the gathering falls silent as Pasénadi, accompanied by Pandu and the Senapati of Kapilavastu, comes to sit on his throne. Other courtiers are already on the mats and cushions around him. After the maharaja is settled, Siddhartha and his followers file in, having been fed earlier in the formal dining hall. Yasodhara has eyes only for Siddhartha. This is, no doubt, the last time she will see him. He is too important for his wanderings to ever bring him to her rural exile. Much against her will, she feels a pang of sorrow go through her at this final farewell.

The bhikkhus sit as they did before, Siddhartha and his two senior monks on the dais, the other bhikkhus in rows before them. When they are all settled, the Awakened One takes a sip from the clay cup before him. Then he speaks:

"Mitto, today I will tell you a story. Four months ago, not long after I took up residence in the Bamboo Grove outside Rajagaha, I heard that a noblewoman named Kisagotami had lost her only son. Driven mad by her grief, this Kisagotami refused to let the dead child be taken from her but, instead, went through the city with the boy on her hip, going from doctor to doctor, seeking a medicine that would revive her boy. Finally, someone sent her to me. She came into my presence carrying the corpse on her hip and cried, 'O Awakened One, you claim to have achieved deathlessness. Then restore my son. Cure him of death.' So, I said, 'Yes indeed, I can heal your child of death.'"

A murmur of astonishment, of bewilderment, rumbles through the crowd, and people glance at each other. Yasodhara is astonished too, even as she understands this is a rhetorical trick. She leans forward, interested to see where Siddhartha will go with it.

"'But,' I told her, 'in order for me to effect such a cure, you need to bring me a handful of mustard seeds from a household where no one has ever died, where no one has ever experienced the tragedy of losing a loved one to Yama.'"

The audience chuckles, and people look at each other again, shaking their heads at this oratorical feat by the Awakened One. Yasodhara too is impressed, but then her eyes narrow as she regards him. Her breathing is suddenly shallow. She doesn't know exactly why, but she feels this story is directed at her.

"So Kisagotami went from house to house in the city, searching for a home that death had not touched. And slowly, as she continued her search, the truth about impermanence and the human condition came to her. Released from her delusion that anything is permanent, she gave her son for cremation, then came to me, and I accepted her as an upasika."

The Awakened One takes a long sip of water as the audience waits, expectant. Yasodhara leans forward, watching Siddhartha's every move, anxious for him to speak, in the way one is anxious to hear bad news quickly spoken. Her gaze slides to Rahula and he, feeling her eyes on him, gives her a quick frown and looks away, chin stubbornly tilted. Her apprehension climbs a level.

Siddhartha continues: "Some people, I understand, have been going around declaring that I say we shouldn't love anyone, because the more we love someone, the more we suffer through attachment. But I have not said this at all. Love has a very important and blessed place in the lives of all beings. Yet there is good love and bad love. Now the latter, bad love, is the kind that is based on the concept of 'me' and 'mine.' This love based on 'me-and-mine' breeds jealousy and anger and, yes, often hatred. It makes us cruel to those we claim to love, makes us possessive of them. Makes us punish them for 'their own good.' Even sometimes imprison them in our houses. This kind of love makes us discriminate and have prejudice, or just indifference, to anyone we consider not 'me-and-mine.' To anyone not of our family or gotra or race or nation. This kind of love makes it easy for us to kill or starve or enslave those who are not part of 'me-and-mine.' But then there is good love, the kind of love I do advocate, which is based on kindness and compassion for *all*. Loving someone in this way means putting their interests ahead of your own. With this kind of love, our goal is to selflessly bring happiness to others, to alleviate their suffering, often at the expense of ourselves. And this kind of love does not demand anything in return."

The Awakened One goes on to explain further this love, providing other examples of people he encountered, like Kisagotami, who at first loved in the wrong way but learned to love beyond "me-and-mine." Yasodhara listens, her fear building.

The oration finally comes to an end. The Awakened One gathers his robes around him and, in the silence, stands up. The audience watches him, remaining respectfully seated, as he steps off the dais and starts to walk away.

"Pita, give me my inheritance!"

Yasodhara turns, shocked. Rahula is up on his feet. Again, he shouts, "Pita, give me my inheritance!" He makes to go forward and she grabs him by the wrist, hissing, "Rahula, puthā!" He struggles out of her grip and stumbles onward, scrambling over the people in front of him to get to the Awakened One.

Laughter ripples through those gathered, although some faces are appalled.

Rahula reaches his father. "Pita." He falls to his knees. "Give me my inheritance."

Siddhartha smiles, unsurprised. He lifts the boy, touches his head, and takes his son by the hand. "Come, Rahula." They walk away together, and Rahula turns to look at Yasodhara. She is standing now, stunned. He gives her a nod, a grimace of a smile, and is soon swallowed by the crowd.

Yasodhara hears a woman shrieking, over and over, and it takes her a moment to realize the sound is coming from her. The voices of the other women, of the crowd, are deafening now. Arms grab her, but she slaps them away and shrieks again. Then she is being flung backwards down a shaft, the voices, the world, receding. The next thing she knows, she is opening her eyes to find her aunt and the women of the quarters peering at her anxiously. She is in her own bed.

Rahula now pushes through the other faces to stand closest to her. "Ammé," he whispers, stroking her forehead, "ammé." Her eyes widen as she stares at him. His head is shaven, he wears white robes. Her memory rushes back and she gasps, "Why, puthā, why?"

The women leave the room at a signal from Rahula, and for a time she sobs as he waits, silent.

After a while, she turns back to him. "But why, puthā, why?" she asks again, holding her hands out.

He doesn't answer because what he has to say is so obvious. He could not have gone to that isolated farm, where he would have had no future at all.

"But is it what you really want?" she whispers at last.

"No, ammé." He gives her a small smile, a shrug. "But I will never get what I really want. So this is the best choice. The only choice."

Prajapati and Mitta approach now, bearing food. "The boy should eat," Prajapati says gently. "There is no meal for him among the bhikkhus at this late time."

Yasodhara nods and struggles out of bed, sitting on the edge to retie her hair and gather the little strength she has.

She and Rahula sit for the meal on a mat, the table between them. They pick at the food, too miserable to eat. Finally, they both push the food away and stare out the window, where the sun is beginning his final descent.

"Ammé, I must return to the grove . . . the rules of the Order."

"Must you really go?" Yasodhara grabs his hand and Rahula lets her hold it for a moment before he gently stands, his fingers slipping from hers. He goes to the door and shuts it behind him as he leaves.

That night, Yasodhara's mother comes to her and stands at the foot of her bed, regarding her with sadness. She awakes, crying out with loss.

7

The Women Walk

THE NEXT MORNING, the city waits for the senapati and the maharaja to deliberate and for the list of nobles who must join the Awakened One to be proclaimed. The names are announced by midday. Yasodhara, like everyone else, is astonished at first to find that Mahanama and Amitodhana are not named, but then she understands: Pasénadi wants them around to nip at Pandu's heels, using their voting bloc in the sangha.

Soon after this, women from the noble families whose men have been chosen arrive to petition the maharaja at the palace, seeking exemption for their husband or father or son, pleading that they will be rendered destitute. The maharaja refuses to grant clemency. These women are distraught, and some of them faint before him. They are led, or carried, or come of their own accord to the palace women's quarters, where they gather in the courtyard. Yasodhara, Prajapati and the others offer refreshments and comfort, directing serving maids to lay out mats and carpets on the clay floor for the noble ladies who have fainted. Yasodhara has been numb with misery all morning but now she throws herself into this activity, taking comfort in the sorrow of these noblewomen, their keening echoing the sound in her own heart.

Once all of them are calm, they sit in glum silence, contemplating their lot. Finally, one of the women speaks: "It is a cruel sentence to pass on us women, who are innocent. What have we done to deserve this punishment? Because punished we are."

"Yes," another cries, "it is we who will bear the brunt of this sentence. The men will have lives of contemplation, free from domestic care, free from hunger. Free from the scrabble to feed and look after their children and dependants, which will now be our burden."

Yasodhara nods. Because truly her own life, too, will be a scrabble, whereas Siddhartha's will be one of glory.

"No doubt our men will be treated well," a third says, bitterly. "They will reside in shady parks in Vesali and Rajagaha and Savatthi, or wherever else they go."

"And be guests of the famous Ambapali! Enjoy the courtesan's beauty and grace!" a fourth adds sarcastically.

"While we continue to live in this city that is hostile to us now, struggling to survive without our male kin."

The other noblewomen murmur and groan in agreement, and Yasodhara groans along with them.

"Once again, the men have benefitted while we must suffer. Why should we suffer?" another woman declares.

"Yes, yes, well said"; "Why should we suffer?"; "Why should we bear the brunt of their sins?"—are the cries taken up by many.

"It's not just," Yasodhara declares too, wanting to share the burden of her sorrow, her anger. "They have everything, and we have nothing at all. I say so as the former wife of this so-called Awakened One." The other women lean forward, listening intently to her. "My husband abandoned me and now he gets my son too. My son who I raised and loved without any help from him. How is that just or right?"

One of the women turns to Prajapati. "And you, sāmini—even though the Awakened One wasn't of your womb, you fed him and raised him as your own. What does he do for you now, when you are on the brink of destitution?"

"Is this all his Middle Way has to offer his own mother? His own wife?" another woman cries, gesturing at Prajapati, at Yasodhara.

Collectively they vent their anger and frustration on the Order: "If any of those bhikkhus comes to my door, I will take off my slipper and slap their faces." "Hear, hear. I will, too." "I will set my dogs on them." "I will pour my chamber pots on their heads!"

Yasodhara feels a bitter strength in this combined anger towards Siddhartha and his Middle Way. Finally she is not alone in her anger, her grief.

The clamour rises fiercely, and Prajapati gestures for the women to calm down. When they have grown quiet, she asks, "But what would you have me do, women of our gotra, noble ladies? What can I possibly ask my son?"

The women are silent. Then Yasodhara speaks, an idea coming to her even as she says the words. "Ask that we be allowed to follow our sons, our menfolk, the way the women of soldiers or caravan merchants follow theirs." The other women murmur in surprise at this. "Yes, yes, why should we be left behind to suffer?" Yasodhara continues. "They owe us this, given how they've destroyed our lives." The women are listening to her intently now, nodding, faces set with grim determination, beginning to believe this is owed to them too. Their belief gives Yasodhara courage. "It will be a hard life, but at least we will see our husbands, our sons, and be under their protection. We *must* ask for this."

"Why should we merely follow them?" Mitta suddenly adds. "We should ask to be taken into the Order. The Niganthas allow samanis, and many women who join the Niganthas are, indeed, the wives and mothers and unmarried sisters of men who have taken the Nigantha path."

"Yes," Yasodhara cries, her voice cracking. "Yes, that is exactly what we should ask for!"

A hum of approval slowly grows, and the women nod at each other.

"Even in the Vedas," Mitta continues, "there are verses about female sages who took to the wandering life in the past. They are never recited now because men don't want us to wander, but I know those verses exist. I can name the female sages, because my mother was a Brahmin who learned this knowledge from her father. Ghosha, Lopamudra, Gargi, Maitreyi."

Now that Mitta has offered this historical precedent, from the Vedas no less, Yasodhara sees that the women are convinced, her own hope reflected in their faces. "Pitucché," she says to Prajapati, her voice hoarse, "let us go and ask the Awakened One now." Seeing the doubt in her aunt's eyes, she jumps up. "Noble ladies, let us go *now* to Nigrodha Grove."

The women turn to Prajapati, their devi. After a moment, she nods and rises, though her glance at Yasodhara says she doubts they will succeed.

That morning, the residents of Kapilavastu are stunned to see a phalanx of noble Khattiya women marching along the Uttarapatha, led by the devi and her daughter-in-law. They stop what they are doing and come to stare at the procession, and their astonishment makes Yasodhara quail at the boldness of this venture. These women seldom walk the city streets, travelling instead in palanquins and chariots; now, their dusty feet and clothes are a shocking sight for the janata. Yasodhara hopes desperately that the dusty dishevelment of the women will make Siddhartha and the other bhikkhus see they are serious and grant their wish. To the voice that contradicts this hope, she keeps saying, "The Niganthas allow this, the Vedas speak of it." Some shopkeepers and householders come running with sweetened water and other refreshments for the women, who sternly but politely decline. Soon a large crowd follows them. The city gates are shut because of the recent battle and, when the women reach it, the gatekeeper hurries out of his hut to see what this commotion is about. He is startled to find the devi in front of him, and immediately falls to the ground to touch her feet. When he rises, Prajapati says, "Sonanda, open that small door in the gate to let us through. Then shut and bar it. Also, put your guards before it to block the janata from following. It will not do to go forth in such a large procession." The man nods his obedience.

The women troop out the gate, across the bridge, and leave the city behind.

The Nigrodha Grove is an arduous quarter-yojana from the city. When the women reach its entrance, they stop to regain their strength, to drink water from a nearby stream. Then they turn off the main road and make their way through the trees, along the path that leads to the samanas' huts.

Quietly, Yasodhara has sent a messenger ahead on horseback to warn the monks, telling him to give the message to Ananda. Soon she sees her cousin hurrying towards them along the path, accompanied by the senior monks Moggallana and Sariputta. The procession comes to a stop. Prajapati steps forward and bends quickly to touch the bhikkhus' feet, even though she is the devi—making this gesture, Yasodhara knows, to show her seriousness. "I wish to speak with the Awakened One." It is more a command than a request.

Her aunt, somewhere along the walk here, has come to believe more fully in what they are doing. Ananda makes eye contact with Yasodhara: Be strong, persist.

The two senior monks nod and indicate for Prajapati to follow them. She signals the other women to remain behind, but gestures for Yasodhara to come with her. As they walk along, Yasodhara, apprehensive, glances at the huts scattered among the trees, taking in brief glimpses of red robes, the smell of fires and cooking rice and pulses, the rustle of wind through the trees. How peaceful it all seems, in such contrast to the roiling fear inside her. "Pitucché," she whispers, "you must speak for all of us. He will listen to you, as his stepmother, as our devi." Prajapati gives her a small smile to says she's already decided this.

They finally reach a clearing. Siddhartha is seated cross-legged outside his hut, awaiting them. Rahula is sweeping the area before the hut, and on seeing the women approach, he starts in surprise, then comes towards them, his face lit with joy. Yasodhara sternly lifts a hand to say he must remain where he is. He steps back behind Siddhartha, confused.

The two senior monks bow to Siddhartha and depart, but Ananda lingers, standing by the women.

Siddhartha doesn't rise to bow and touch his stepmother's feet. Nor does he smile; his face remains guarded. "Bhagini," he says with a nod, addressing both women as "sister," to put a distance between them.

Yasodhara gestures with her head to Prajapati that they should stand to one side of the Awakened One, as if before a raja—to convince him they have come in humility, in sincerity. When they have stood thus, Yasodhara glances quickly at Ananda and he nods his encouragement.

"Sāmi," Prajapati begins, speaking formally, her voice shaking slightly, "it would be a good thing if the women who have come here be allowed to go forth from the life of the house into the homeless life, following the Middle Way and its Eightfold Path."

For a long moment, Siddhartha remains silent, looking at the ground in front of him. Seeing his grim seriousness, Yasodhara understands, with a lurch within, that he is about to refuse them.

"It cannot be, Gotami," he finally says, addressing his stepmother by her gotra name. "I do not grant permission for the women to go forth into the homeless life in our Order."

Yasodhara signals, with an urgent movement of her head, for her aunt to try again, shooting a look at Ananda, who also nods subtly.

This time, Prajapati sets her lips in a thin line, and when she speaks, her voice trembles with anger. "I, the woman who was your mother when your own died. I, who fed you with my own hand, say again: It would be a good thing if the women gathered in this grove be allowed to go forth into the homeless life, following the Middle Way and its Eightfold Path."

The Awakened One gives both women a pained look. "It cannot be, Gotami."

"I, the mother who held your forehead when you vomited, who pressed cold cloths to your body when you were taken over with fever. I, the mother who clothed you with soft wool in the winter, with light cottons in the summer, who taught you your first words of the Vedas. I, your mother, say again: It would be a good thing if the women gathered in this grove be allowed to go into the homeless life!"

Yasodhara, breathless, watches the struggle on Siddhartha's face. Yet, after a moment, he says, "You have asked three times and I am refusing now for the third time. In our Order, women will not go forth into homelessness." He lowers his head and is silent.

Yasodhara and Prajapati stare at each other. They are truly refused. Dazed, they turn and stumble away. Rahula goes after them, slipping his hand into Yasodhara's and looking up at her with worry and sorrow.

They are walking along the path to the entrance when they hear Ananda call out, "Pitucché, bhagini," and turn to see him hurrying towards them.

He gives them an appealing look. "Pitucché, bhagini, I had hoped for this like you, but now the Awakened One has explained his thinking to me and I see he is right: tomorrow, seventy-five Sakiya noblemen will join us on a fifteen-day walk to Vesali. Seventy-five men unaccustomed to the samana life. So then, to have women on this journey too, ladies who have walked nowhere, would be impossible. Also, these Sakiya men must not be distracted by the presence of their womenfolk. A man needs to break from the old life and be reborn into the new."

"And what about us women? Are we not to be reborn too?" Yasodhara spits on the ground. "I despise your Middle Way," she cries to her appalled cousin. She turns to Rahula and holds her arms out. He goes to her and embraces his mother as, sobbing, she falls to her knees because he cannot even leave the grove to spend one last night with her.

Back at the palace that evening, Yasodhara is lying in bed, windows closed, her head heavy—expecting that soon her illness, with its light-sensitivity and nausea, will be on her—when Upasama, the concubine, knocks and tip-toes in. "Sāmini, a bhikkhu wishes to see you." From Upasama's wry smile, Yasodhara understands it is neither Ananda nor Siddhartha. "He waits in the front courtyard."

In the shadows of the rapidly descending dusk, Yasodhara sees the bhikkhu seated on an upturned barrel, in the white robes of a novice, head shaven. He rises, and she knows right away by his height that it is Anuruddha.

She goes to stand in front of him and, though it is forbidden, he takes her hands and smiles at her. She doesn't smile back. He too has now abandoned her; Siddhartha has won him also. "Why have you joined, Anuruddha? How can you, of all people, be happy in this wandering life? You who love the courtesan houses, the dice board."

"Ah, but my love has been shrivelling for a long while, ñātiké. It took Ananda's return to finally snap me off from the vine of desire that I was entangled in."

"But you won't be happy—you won't!"

Anuruddha is silent, arms crossed over his chest, eyes on the ground. "Yes, you may be right. The test of the samana life will tell." He looks up and regards her, eyes glittering in the dark. "I suspect it might be Rahula and his welfare that will keep me in the Order."

At last, Yasodhara understands. He is telling her that he has come with a promise: he will be Rahula's guardian in their new life. He will care for the boy as if for his own; and he will do so out of love for her. This might just carry him into true belief in the Middle Way.

After he is gone, Yasodhara sits on the barrel, bereft. Nothing—not even this promise—can compensate for her loss.

At dawn the next day, the women of the quarters return to the Nigrodha Grove, their hearts bitter with the memory of how hopefully they walked here yesterday. The other noblewomen who walked with them have also come to bid their men goodbye, and Yasodhara sees her own resentment and anger reflected in their faces. The women gather at the entrance to the grove, and soon the bhikkhus approach in an orderly line. Siddhartha is at the very back, accompanied by Ananda, Moggallana and Sariputta. The Sakiya noblemen in their white robes are also towards the end of the procession, and on seeing them, the women surge forward to embrace their men, weeping and pressing food on them.

Rahula pushes his way through the crowd to Yasodhara. Her eyes fill with tears. "Don't cry, ammé." Rahula kneels to touch her feet and once he is done, she draws him up and holds him close. "Puthā, don't forget me. I have told you where we will be living. If your wanderings ever take you even close to our new home, come and visit, please."

"I will come, ammé, even if I have to come on my own. I will find the way and I will come."

Yasodhara sees Anuruddha approaching now. He gives her a smile, reminding her of his promise.

Moggallana, the senior monk, claps his hands to say it's time to go. They must get on with their journey before it becomes too hot.

The sound of weeping increases now, and the women cling to their men even as they begin to move away. Some of the men are weeping too now. Yasodhara holds Rahula for a long moment, eyes shut, then pushes him to be gone.

"Come, daharā." Anuruddha takes the boy by the hand.

Yasodhara watches her son go among the bhikkhus. Soon he is lost in the throng of them. Among the final bhikkhus to pass the women is Siddhartha. When she sees him, she turns away, even as she feels his gaze on her. His handprints are all over her sorrow; he has brought her to this place.

8

Me-and-Mine

YASODHARA TAKES TO her bed, immobilized by exhaustion. This fatigue soon becomes her reality, and all her attention and energy are focused on not being submerged in it, on trying to tread water in a rushing river current. Any failure to pay attention, to battle the current, will drown her. Ah, but how she longs to drown, how she wishes she had it in her to stop treading water, to succumb. She thinks often of that noblewoman Kisagotami, and curses herself that some tough fibre of sanity, will not fray and give way this time. At night, she often has her old dream of being chased by an elephant and hiding in a well, clinging to a root as a python winds its way up that very root towards her, a forest fire raging outside, smoke filling the well, choking her.

Still, nothing lasts forever, and soon the disease begins to loosen its grip. Every day, there are little improvements: she manages to pull herself out of bed and get as far as the wash basin; manages to sit for a short while in the window well, warmed by the late evening sun, before fatigue takes her back to bed. Meals continue to be an ordeal requiring all her stamina: the conscious, tedious working of jaws, teeth, tongue, her body prickled with sweat from the effort. Soon, however, she is able to sit up for longer, to eat more, to do a few chores about her room. But now, without the distraction of illness, the bright void of Rahula's absence must be confronted. With her parents, she was able to fall back on the exigencies and compensations of her life—first, her work in Mudgala, the companionship and love of Siddhartha; then, later, when she lost her husband, raising Rahula, loving him so completely. But now there is nothing to grow or nurture and she is agitated by a restless boredom.

She starts to wander about the city again, like she did after Siddhartha left, hoping to tire herself out. Yet, even this walking to exhaustion can't disperse her frantic ennui. There are the children everywhere; and also the mothers with children. She stops often to stare, breathless: watches one woman bend down with casual annoyance to haul her whining child onto a hip; sees another rest a hand on her son's neck as they walk down a street; observes a third sit with a daughter between her legs, combing her hair. Don't these women know how precarious their hold is on their child? It seems incredible to her that they are so unaware, incredible that she was blind herself to the fragility of the bond. Rather than envy or longing, she feels helpless, like a person looking from a fire-destroyed home towards neighbours' intact houses.

During each segment of the day, she thinks of Rahula and imagines what he is doing at that time. The mornings are particularly hard to bear because she is haunted by the image of her son walking that yojana the monks complete barefoot every day. Though he is mature well beyond his age, in the way Siddhartha was as a child, at the same time his body is that of a ten-year-old. His young feet, not yet calloused and hardened from the samana life, will bleed from this walking. To make matters worse, the hot season has continued unabated, and the rains have not arrived. How can Rahula endure this heat when she can barely abide it, is depleted by her much shorter walks through the city? Her worry is a knot in her throat when she thinks of him begging outside households; she prays that some woman will take pity on her child and make sure he is fed that day. As the weeks pass and water becomes scarcer and the crops fail, her torment grows. There will be less and less food to give away to samanas.

Every day now she visits the Yakshi of Kapilavastu to prostrate herself on the ground, hair spread on the dirt floor as a sign of humility as she begs the Yakshi to guard Rahula. She also begins to visit trees that are famous for containing devatas, making offerings to these spirits of the air. As she performs these rituals, she takes bitter pleasure in knowing that the Middle Way forbids them, or at least frowns on such "superstitions." She becomes an ardent practitioner of the sacrifice. Each week, she offers two goats to Pusan, God of the Roads and Travellers, so that he will guard her son.

A month has passed now and, even though Pandu is installed as the new raja, Pandu's wife, curiously, hasn't come to arrange the transfer of the palace duties and to set a time for Yasodhara, Prajapati and the other women to leave. Periodically, her aunt mentions this in a murmur of worry and dread, saying, "When will she come, when will she come?" as if the waiting is worse than being cast out.

Meanwhile, the women who walked with Yasodhara to the Nigrodha Grove have been coming every day to the quarters to lament the departure of their men, to comfort each other. Yasodhara is happy to see them and, when she hears their voices in the courtyard, she always hurries down to sit with them, clinging to other mothers and weeping; and, like them, she expresses her anger towards the Awakened One. The women of the quarters join too. But, because they haven't lost their men, they are quiet, comforting the other women by bringing them sweetened water and other refreshments.

As the days pass, however, the women grow tired of venting their anger against Siddhartha and his Order. And finally one morning someone says, "But truly, that idea of us women going forth into homelessness was a foolish one. We would not have been able to meet the challenges of a samani's life."

After a silence, there is a grudging murmur of assent.

"But I would have met the challenges," Yasodhara says firmly. "I would have borne any hardship for my son."

"Indeed, indeed," the women murmur, but Yasodhara can see they are placating her. She adjusts her shawl, suddenly realizing she is alone now in her belief that Siddhartha has let them down.

A few days later, fifteen Sakiya men return, sent back by the Awakened One. They are too old or suffer from respiratory or back ailments and are unfit for the samana life. When Yasodhara hears this news, she runs with the other women of the quarters to the public courtyard, arriving as the noblewomen who have lost their men come rushing in through the heavy wooden street doors. They converge on the dusty, bedraggled men who stand or sit in the middle of the courtyard, drinking water brought to them by slaves. A few women cry out with joy as they embrace husbands and brothers and grandfathers, kiss their faces, their hands; but there are also cries of disappointment and sorrow from the other women, who weep, their pain fresh again.

Once everyone has calmed down and some food is brought, the men sit on the verandah and eat, the women watching them.

"Tell us, how are our men?" Yasodhara finally demands, not willing to wait until they are sated.

The men glance at each other and then the oldest among them speaks: "Our Sakiya men are truly struggling to adapt to this new life of wandering. The poverty, the last meal at midday, the sleeping outdoors—it's truly hard to bear, even for the stronger warriors."

"Then there's the daily walk of one yojana," another man adds, clutching his back to show the damage this caused him. "It takes a toll even on stronger warriors' bodies because we're only allowed those two meagre meals a day."

"And how is my Rahula, faring?" Yasodhara demands, her mouth dry.

The men glance at each other again. One of them, a much older cousin of Yasodhara's, says, "Ah, ñātiké, that is the joy, the strength of being a child. How their young limbs can keep going! It's a wonder to see. There, even our strongest warriors are struggling and your Rahula skips along on the daily walk."

"Rest assured, too, your boy does eat each evening," another man adds. "He is exempt from that stricture."

"And he is well cared for. Anuruddha and Ananda treat the boy like their own, always attentive to his welfare."

Yasodhara regards the speakers through narrowed eyes and they return her gaze with innocent smiles. Clearly, they are not telling her the truth. If the wandering life is hard on the Khattiya men, then it must be doubly hard on a ten-year-old boy. She makes a choked sound and hurries away. Prajapati and Sumana run to catch up with her. They touch her arms to implore her to stop. Turning to them, she cries, "I am his mother and I can do nothing for him!" She gestures for her aunt and the old concubine to leave her alone and rushes on—not towards the women's quarters now, but in the direction of the heavy street doors.

It's been a couple of days since she walked out into the city and, as she goes along, she gazes at the mothers with children, like always. Yet something strikes her for the first time, something she's never noticed before—just how many of the mothers look harassed or anxious or distracted, how many of them are harsh or impatient with their children, smacking or yelling at them, bellowing out orders in strident voices. The anxiety of failure, the fear of loss, the striving ambition—she recognizes all the things she once felt, too. *Me-and-mine.* She stops in surprise, insight blooming within her: it is true she loves Rahula with her whole heart, that she would lay down her life for him; yet, at the same time, she has also loved him as "me-and-mine." And her anger at Siddhartha has shaped Rahula; her anger is a vein that ran deep in him, is an essence he absorbed since he was an infant, so that, at just ten years, he was capable of being part of a scheme that involved the murder of the senapati.

Understanding this does not exonerate Siddhartha. Their son's actions, his anger, were also shaped by the discovery that his father was alive yet never contacted him, that he mattered so little to his father. "But yes, yes," she says impatiently to the angry voice that is starting up in her again, "let us for once put Siddhartha aside. It is *I* who hasn't loved Rahula beyond 'me-and-mine.'" Still, she wonders, as she passes yet another harassed mother, watches yet another mother berating a child for some small crime, is it actually possible to love beyond me-and-mine as a mother? "Ah, I would like to know if that is possible," she says aloud, thinking of her aunt and the women of the quarters, who love Rahula with an almost diaphanous pleasure because their own ambitions and anger are not attached to him.

Almost a month and a half after Rahula's departure, Pandu's wife does finally come to the palace women's quarters, accompanied by her daughters-in-law and unwed daughter. Yasodhara, Prajapati and the other women gather in the private courtyard to greet the entourage, anxious and sorrowful. After they've bowed to each other, Pandu's wife says in a brisk, friendly manner, "I wish I could allow you to stay longer, sāmini." She smiles apologetically, her eyes resting especially on Yasodhara. "But form and etiquette, unfortunately, require this change." Yasodhara nods at Pandu's wife, both to acknowledge her kindness in allowing Yasodhara this time of mourning, but also to confirm that yes, they cannot stay much longer.

Prajapati and Yasodhara take Pandu's wife around the quarters, show her the accounts tablets, call in the head servants to meet their new mistress. Through all of this, a greater and greater dread grows in Yasodhara. Now, truly, their exile from this home is real—made tangible in the way Pandu's wife expertly runs her eyes over the tablets before saying she will take them away to study better; in the way the head servants prostrate themselves before their new mistress. Pandu's wife is escorted to the granaries and introduced to the Master of the Granaries. As Yasodhara and Prajapati walk away, they glance back wistfully at their old servant, whom they've known for so many years, now leading his new mistress from grain trough to grain trough, from one large earthen pot to another. "Truly we are strangers now in our own home," Prajapati says.

Back at the quarters, the women are waiting, fearful, despondent. For a while, everyone stands in silence, looking around at this home that is already no longer theirs. Finally, Prajapati speaks: "It was kind of Pandu's wife not to hurry us out, but that was only a temporary reprieve." She glances at Yasodhara to confirm what they discussed on the walk back. "So, we have set a date for our departure. It will take place in a week."

The other women moan and murmur. "A week?"

"Yes, in exactly a week." Yasodhara nods sadly. "The constellation of the stars is good on that day for a journey, for change."

"I know that some of you told us your plans," Prajapati continues, "but we ask again, because we haven't discussed this in a while: Who comes with us, who doesn't?"

Sumana and Utara glance at each other and then at Tissa, who nods. "The three of us come with you, sāmini," Sumana says. "We're too old for the courtesan life and no one will pay to bond us as slaves at this age." For once the old concubine's face is sober, her tinkling laugh absent.

"I too have no choice but to come with you," Sundari Nanda says ruefully. "What else can the daughter of the former raja do? Certainly not the courtesan houses or bonded slavery."

Now Sanga and Visaka look at each other. "Our plan stays the same," Visaka says. "My mother Vimala will take us in."

"Mine too remains the same," Mitta adds. "A group of Niganthas arrived yesterday in the Nigrodha Grove. I've been to see them and asked permission to join. I will go with them when they move on."

All faces turn to Upasama now. The concubine shrugs and shakes her head. "I'm still looking around for a household that will purchase me as a bonded slave. Until that happens, the ganikā Vimala has kindly agreed to take me in as a temporary servant."

The women then fall silent, listening to the sounds around them: a koel calling from a tree in the walled garden, a slave singing in the next courtyard, the sounds of people passing in the street beyond the high mud walls, a man and woman flirtatiously bantering and laughing. Soon, this house will not know them anymore.

Although some of the women who walked to the Nigrodha Grove still gather every morning in the courtyard, their numbers have declined. Among those who keep coming, most are now in agreement that their decision to go to the grove was foolish. "It was right for the Awakened One to turn us away," they say. "We did not go in true seriousness; we would not have been able to make the journey." When they say this, Mitta always counters with, "Not true. I could have made the journey; I did go in true seriousness." A few of the other women murmur in agreement.

Yasodhara, as she goes about getting ready to depart, notices that the women who still come each day to meet with the women of the quarters have started to spend the morning in meditation. Then they recite and discuss the parts of the tenets they remember, and seek each other's advice on how the teachings might be lived out in their present lives. The women return again and again to the idea of the three fires. They confess to each other that they burn with anger, greed and the delusional expectation that things should stay permanent and unchanging; they confess their despair over the fact that everything does indeed change and change and change. Yasodhara doesn't join in these sessions, but the words of the other women echo within her.

One morning, on impulse, Yasodhara walks to the Rohini River and stands on its bank, watching the water rush past. An idea, a thought, has brought her here: all her life she's complained that she is nothing but a seedpod carried along by any river current. But that seedpod metaphor, she is realizing, is the wrong one. Rather, she is a woman who waded into a swift river and tried to dam it, tried to hold in place the rushing onwardness of life; a woman who tried to control and contain also the destinies of her husband and son, both of whom single-mindedly pursued their own paths. A radical understanding grips her: *Perhaps the time has come for me to truly be a seedpod, carried along by a river current.*

Mitta, in preparation for her departure, has shaved her head and donned the white robes of a novice Nigantha samani. Yasodhara invites Mitta to her room and, once her cousin is seated cross-legged on the floor, Yasodhara asks, "Mitta, how will you survive the life of a samani? Look at our men— they are barely managing, and most of them are Khattiya warriors. Look at the feet of the men who returned. How will you stand walking with such bloodied, wounded feet?"

Mitta smiles and tugs at the ends of her robe. "Faith, ñātiké. It is faith that will keep me walking, that keeps all samanas and samanis in the wandering life. Yes, the pain and discomfort will be great at the beginning, but then gradually it will get easier to bear." She laughs. "If Anuruddha can adapt to the samana life, anyone can."

"True," Yasodhara murmurs. "But tell me, Mitta, if we had succeeded when we went to the Nigrodha Grove, would you still be choosing the Nigantha way?"

Mitta makes a knot with the edge of her robe, but says nothing.

"So, then you go in half faith?"

Again, Mitta remains silent.

But, Yasodhara thinks as she studies her cousin, faith is not the only thing that keeps a person walking despite bloodied feet, despite hunger. There is love, there is desperation. And perhaps . . . there is also curiosity—to know something more about yourself, something that can only be found in the wandering life.

The next morning, Yasodhara sits in on the meditation and discussion in the courtyard. When the visitors are gone, she says to the women of the quarters, "It is true that we didn't go to the grove in seriousness before. But that doesn't mean we cannot go in seriousness now, that we cannot prove to the Awakened One we are capable of the samana life."

The others frown at her, not understanding.

"What do you propose, daharé?" her aunt Utara asks. Then adds, "The men, after all, are long gone now."

Yasodhara gestures to Mitta. "I propose we shave our heads, put on robes and walk to Vesali."

The women regard her in stunned silence.

She leans forward, anxious to get her point across. "And this time we *will* go in seriousness. We will walk to Vesali and prove our seriousness." She smiles, wryly. "Siddhartha, no matter that he's turned away from the world, is still very much tied to it. The world, whether Siddhartha likes it or not, whether he believes it so or not, does influence the Order, in the same way the janata influences our sangha. His wife, his stepmother, the palace women turning up in Vesali as samanis cannot be so easily dismissed." She looks gravely at Prajapati. "I . . . I know the enormity of what I'm suggesting, but not to try . . . ?"

"And what will we do if we're refused again?" Sundari Nanda demands. "We will be in Vesali where we have no kin, no friends. Who will take us in then?"

"I don't know." Yasodhara grips her hands together in her lap, face stubborn.

The women murmur in protest, in bewilderment. "You don't know, and yet you propose we all walk to Vesali?" Upasama cries. "Abandoning whatever future we might have here, or even at that rural estate?"

"Yes."

The women shake their heads at each other and examine Yasodhara askance, to check whether she's slipped into madness again.

"I know what I'm proposing is foolish, even reckless. I can't offer you a pledge of success. I can only offer you hope . . . and a chance to try for something. All our lives, others have determined what we will do, where we will live, who we will be. But now, we go of our own volition. That is all I can offer you, a chance to act, to choose, of your own volition."

"But it takes fifteen days to walk there," Prajapati says, thoughtfully. Yasodhara sees that her aunt is, for the first time, beginning to consider this plan.

"At a yojana a day, pitucché. Which one covers in a morning. Then one rests and only begins walking the next morning."

The women are silent again, thinking. It is Prajapati who speaks at last. "But who will feed us along the way? Where will we find rest?"

Yasodhara smiles. "Pitucché. The former devi and her daughter-in-law, the women of the raja's quarters, will not be ignored or allowed to starve. We are also the womenfolk of the Awakened One. Think of how already, on our walk to the grove, people came running with food and water."

"But to shave our heads," Visaka and Sanga protest, clutching at their hair as if Yasodhara will spring forward any moment and cut it off.

Yasodhara, desperate for at least one adherent, turns to her cousin. "Mitta, will you come with me?"

Without hesitation, Mitta nods.

Yasodhara nods at her. She looks around at the other women, challenging.

"I will come too," Prajapati says after a moment. "If I don't try for a better future, my failure of spirit will haunt me. It is better to try." She sighs. "But how will we accomplish all that walking when our men can barely manage?"

"Pitucché, haven't we women stayed up all night nursing a sick child or relative, then gone to do our daily duties, then returned again to pass the night nursing? Haven't we women borne our monthly cycle of pain and suffering without halting any of our duties? And hasn't that, along with the other humiliations we must endure as women, taught us fortitude? Then there is childbirth, a torment worse than anything a man could ever bear. And yet we endure." Yasodhara looks around the circle of faces. "And yet we endure."

A moment later, Tissa, Sumana and Utara nod hesitantly to say they will come. After some reluctance, Sundari Nanda nods too. Yasodhara understands that, with Prajapati committed to this course, these women really don't have much choice but to join. They come out of desperation, and she hopes this will be enough to keep them walking.

Only the three concubines, Visaka, Sanga and Upasama, hold out. They have other alternatives.

"Let us leave tomorrow before dawn," Yasodhara says. "If we linger another day, we will lose courage."

"I agree." Prajapati nods at the others.

Yet Yasodhara senses their hesitation. She jumps to her feet. "And to firm up our resolve, let us each go to our room and cut off our hair."

She unties her own locks with shaking fingers and lets them fall around her shoulders. If she doesn't win the women over now, they will not go. She picks up a knife, lying nearby after their meal, and hacks off a lock.

The women gasp.

Yasodhara looks pleadingly at her aunt.

After a moment, Prajapati stands and lets down her hair as well. The other women stare as the devi takes the knife from Yasodhara and hacks off a lock. "Come, dhītā," Prajapati says gently to her daughter. "Come, ñātiké, come Sumana." She beckons to Utara, Tissa and Sumana, and holds out the knife to them.

The four rise slowly and also let down their hair, then take up a few strands, caressing them. Sundari Nanda begins to weep softly and soon the other women weep too.

Yasodhara suddenly feels terrible. "I don't want to force this on anyone. If you don't wish to come, there is still our rural estate."

"Yes," Prajapati adds. "I will arrange for you to get there safely."

But at these words, Tissa nods to say she is resolved. Utara and Sumana also nod, though more reluctantly.

Prajapati reaches out and presses Sundari Nanda's shoulder. "Come with us, dhītā, you cannot go alone to the estate."

Sundari Nanda puts her head in her hands and weeps loudly. She, who was so attached to her beauty that she turned down numerous suitors, is now reduced to this.

Slowly, the women break apart and go to their rooms to cut their hair, Mitta trailing the older aunts so as to help them.

Yasodhara stands before her mirror. Then she sinks down on a stool. What has she started? What has she led the women into? She gazes at her reflection for a long while, at the glossy hair falling around her shoulders. *Enough.* She grabs a pair of spring scissors on the table and begins to saw off her hair.

When at last her hair is cut, she examines her image. The jagged ends, the outlines of her skull, make her look gaunt, frail. "What are you now?" she whispers. "Not a woman, certainly." She closes her eyes to steady herself; imagines Rahula's joy when he sees her again, the feel of his body in her embrace. And this time she will learn to love him beyond "me-and-mine." This is her goal, this will keep her walking.

The court barber has been sent for, and a serving woman announces he has arrived in the private courtyard. Yasodhara steps out of her room as the other women emerge too. They stand in their doorways staring at each other's changed appearances, haunted faces. Even the concubines in their doorways have that same haunted look, though they haven't cut their hair and aren't going with them. Yasodhara leads the way towards the stairs and the others troop behind her.

The court barber, seeing the palace women with their jagged hair coming down the stairs, steps back as if from some danger. Yasodhara approaches him ahead of the others. Pulling up a stool, she sits before him and orders, "Shave my head."

"All your . . . your hair, sāmini?" She gives him a stern look. After a moment he sets about his work, the hand that holds her head trembling.

He finishes Yasodhara, and Prajapati offers herself. While she is being shaved, a cloth merchant arrives, bearing bolts of white cloth Prajapati had sent a serving maid to order. The man ogles the women in disbelief, in horror.

Afterwards, he spreads the news in the city of what the palace women have done. Many of the noblewomen who went to the grove to petition the Awakened One come rushing in to see if the rumour is true. When they see the women in their new robes, their heads shaved, most are horrified and weep. But those who have continued to visit the quarters every morning look at the palace women with joy, with relief. They listen to the whole story, and one of them says to Yasodhara, "You have done for us what we couldn't do for ourselves." "Yes," another adds, "in this you're truly the Awakened One's wife. You have shown us the path that we too must take."

Then Yasodhara knows, beyond a doubt, that she has set the right thing in motion; her fellow women of the quarters will also not be travelling alone now.

Soon, Amitodhana and Mahanama visit the quarters to see if the rumour is true. "But why?" Mahanama demands, as if this development is a personal affront to him. Amitodhana frowns, irked.

"But it is you, both of you, who have helped bring us to this. So why do you ask why?" Prajapati replies.

The men flush at her accusation. "And what if you are refused by the Awakened One again?" Amitodhana demands sarcastically.

"Yes," Mahanama adds, "this is just typical women's foolishness."

"At that point, we will consider other options," Prajapati says calmly, though there is a slight tremble in her voice.

"The courtesan house or bonded slavery," Yasodhara adds, because she wants to make them squirm.

"You are of the Gotama Gotra," Amitodhana cries. "I forbid it."

"Then will you take us into your houses?" Yasodhara demands.

The men look uncomfortable. Taking women of such high status into their homes would cause friction among the other women in their households, who would be forced to give them precedence. After a few further half-hearted protestations, the two men slink away. "When our Gotama Gotra is back in power, I will send for you both," Mahanama says.

But Yasodhara knows they will never be in power. Their days are finished and already, as everyone in Kapilavastu knows, the Vessa bankers to whom Mahanama and Amitodhana owe a great deal have filed cases with Pandu to recover their money.

The next morning, before dawn, the six women gather in the courtyard wearing their white novice robes, eyes large with fear at what they're undertaking. As they stand in this nervous silence, they hear footsteps coming down the stairs. Turning, they gasp, then cry out in joy—because here are the three concubines walking down to join them, heads shaven and wearing similar robes.

"Oh, bhagini." Yasodhara goes forward to take their hands. "You lighten our hearts." This is the first time she has ever called any of these women "sister."

"A courtesan's life is tolerable," Visaka says, with a glance at Sanga, "but it's not a happy one—having to pleasure men one doesn't love or can barely tolerate. I will miss my mother, but really it is a gilded cage she offers me. And, if we do succeed, our lives will be our own."

"Like you, sāmini," Sanga says, addressing Prajapati, "we know we will be haunted for the rest of our lives if we didn't try for a better future."

"And I had no choice," Upasama says huffily, "once these two made up their minds. No courtesan house will take me at this age. And I doubt a respectable household will want a former concubine as a slave."

The first sign of light has appeared in the sky, and it is time to go. The women look around them at the place that was their home. Yasodhara thinks of all the years lived here, the happy and unhappy times. She and each of the others carries a cloth bundle tied to a stick. The bundles contain all that bhikkhus carry: a needle and thread, a sieve for straining pond and river water to drink, a razor for shaving their heads, and a begging bowl. The servants and slaves come forward to give the women food for their journey. After they present this food, they kneel to touch the feet of the women—even the feet of the concubines. Yasodhara looks on in wonder. All these women have turned holy because of what they have renounced already—their beauty, their status, their luxury.

At a signal from Prajapati, one of the servants runs to open the street door. They go through it one by one, each woman turning to look back one last time at the life she is leaving. Yasodhara sees on their faces the same numb terror she feels. But there is no turning back, nothing to clutch at. The current has caught them up and is sweeping them along.

The women expect to leave quietly as the city sleeps. Instead, outside their quarters, and all the way to the gates of the city, the janata have assembled to watch them go in silence, holding up lamps in the faint dawn light. As the palace women make their way through the streets, they are joined by the other women who have also committed to this journey, heads shaved, in white robes, bearing their bundles on sticks. And just as the servants and slaves of the quarters did, the janata see these women as holy too, for what they have already renounced. Mothers rush forward, holding up their children for Prajapati to bless; merchants thrust out their purses asking Prajapati to touch the leather pouches. She, as the devi, is used to dealing with the janata, and so she performs these blessings gracefully, though

Yasodhara knows that Prajapati feels she has not yet earned her holiness. "Yes," Yasodhara thinks again, as she watches, "I have indeed done the right thing."

By the time they get to the city gates, they have become a group of thirty samanis. The janata do not follow them any further but send them onwards with a roar of love and approval, crying, "Don't forget us, samanis! Don't forget your relatives and people!"

9

Seedpods

BY MIDDAY, THE women reach a potters' village. The residents are ready for them with water and food, alerted by merchants and horsemen who rode past the women on the Uttarapatha, staring back astonished. Yasodhara and Prajapati have been to this village a few times to buy pots on their way back from their estates, but at first the gambojaka doesn't recognize them with their shaved heads and robes. When they address him by name and tell him who they are, he peers at them, cries, "Sāmini!" and falls to the ground. The other villagers, who have also gathered to welcome the mendicants, gasp and crowd forward. They prostrate themselves as well, but Prajapati quickly steps back and raises a hand. "Please, no veneration, mitto. I am not who I was before, and you must treat me like any other samani." But the villagers are unsure, dumbstruck that she, the devi, has addressed them as "friends."

"Sāmini, you must stay with me," the gambojaka finally insists. "My family will give you our home and we will move in with various relatives."

"That too cannot be." Yasodhara smiles at them. "We are samanis and you must treat us thus."

Again, the villagers hesitate. Then one of the elders says, reluctantly: "There's the orchard where samanas usually stay when passing through our village. But it's unsuitable for ladies such as you who—"

Yasodhara waves her hand to stop him. "Then show us to the orchard."

When they reach the trees, Yasodhara sees that the fruit are few, and many are dried on their stems; the leaves on some of the branches are

brown. Yet, surprisingly, the grass is green and the stream that runs through
the orchard isn't as thin as it might be in this drought.

Once the villagers have left, the women sink down under the shade of
trees with sighs and groans, faces grimy, robes dusty, aware now that their
bodies ache, most of all their legs. Turning her feet over, Yasodhara sees
that her soles are beginning to bleed. The other women are also examining
their feet and now Upasama, the concubine, cries, "How will we ever walk
fourteen more days?" After a despondent silence, someone says, "I fear this
is a foolish venture. I set off with such courage, but now, I . . . I don't feel
I can go on."

"Yet another ridiculous attempt by us women," a second adds bitterly.

"We've only made a laughingstock of ourselves," a third contributes,
and the buzz of agreement is loud.

As Yasodhara studies the exhausted faces around her, she is sure some
of the women will not last. For herself, though, despite bloody feet, something in her will not allow a return. *Truly, the river has caught me up and is
carrying me along.* She is full of wonder that, after just one morning of walking, she has arrived at this place. And there are others who feel as she does:
her aunt Prajapati, Mitta and those women who walk out of true belief in
the Middle Way. For them, for herself, she must act now. "Come," she cries,
jumping up, "let us bathe at the stream and then I will teach you how to
soothe your feet. A trick I learned when I worked the fields in Mudgala."
Once they have washed in the stream, she shows the others how to smear
cool mud on leaves and wrap these around their feet, tying them with vines.
As they follow her instructions, some of the women continue to exchange
doubtful glances. "How will we keep walking on these bloodied feet?" one
demands. "What have we embarked on?" another says.

After they have attended to their feet, the women rest under trees.
Yasodhara shares the shade of a mango tree with her aunt, and no sooner
has she lain down than she feels the lumpiness of the earth beneath. She
lifts her body to move stones away but when she lies back down, the hard
earth presses painfully against her sore shoulders, shins and buttocks. Yet,
as if in compensation, the smell of grass and earth brings memories of
childhood, of lying under trees watching clouds pass by; also comforting
is the sound of the breeze through the branches above. "Pitucché," she

whispers, "I think we will lose some of the women. I . . . I don't know what I can do to hold on to them."

"Act confident," Prajapati murmurs back. "Pretend. Like I did as devi." She gives a little laugh. "Pretending my husband's actions didn't degrade me, pretending I didn't see the conflicts among the women, didn't see Siddhartha's humiliation; playing the happy wife to the janata. Pretending, oh Ushas, that I didn't see your unhappiness." Yasodhara presses her aunt's hand to acknowledge this confession.

Later that afternoon, the women of the village join them. As they sit in a circle, Mitta leads them in a meditation. Yasodhara gives herself over to it, following her breath in and out, letting the world with all its worries gradually subside around her, aware of her rushing thoughts and feelings but also a sense of peace from just being aware of them. The quiet that descends around them is broken by the sound of the stream, a few birds in the trees, the distant *thwok-thwok* of someone chopping wood. When she finally opens her eyes, she sees that the other women are calmer too, their worries soothed. Recalling her aunt's advice that she pretend confidence, she says, "Thank you, Mitta, I am calmed by this meditation, made surer of our mission." Then she adds, even as the thought comes to her, "I think it would be a good thing if you, Mitta, gave an oration, to firm up our resolve. Because you, more than any of us, have followed closely the tenets." She holds out a hand to her surprised cousin with a smile. "Teach us what you know."

Mitta frowns, staring at the earth, tapping it with a finger while she gathers her thoughts. Finally, she looks up and, beginning in the traditional way of orators and storytellers, says, "This I have heard, mitto: A woman, thinking a river to be calm and peaceful, enters it with a blissful mind, intending to cleanse and rejuvenate herself. Yet, the moment she has waded into deeper waters, she gets caught in a strong current beneath the surface and is swept away. Helpless, she watches as the surge carries her downstream; helpless she watches her clothes on the bank become specks in the distance. After some time, however, the river narrows, the banks are much closer, and she sees there is grass, sawgrass, reeds, creepers and bushes, all hanging into the river. As she goes past the grass, she tries to cling to it, but it breaks off in her hands. She clings to the sawgrass next, but it cuts her hands.

She clings to the creeper, even the bushes, but they give way and she is carried along by the river to her inevitable end.

"So it is with us, mitto. For, the river is the worldly life into which we enter, seeking comfort, only to be swept along towards our death. The grass, which is physical forms of all kinds—our loved ones, our wealth— breaks because it is the nature of physical things to break and wear out and age and be lost, including our own bodies. The sawgrass with its knife-sharp edges represents our feelings, and they cut us, causing such great suffering. The creepers are slippery and also break easily. They are human activity, which produces no permanent result or effect that we can grasp on to and prevent ourselves being swept along the river of life to our inevitable death. And the bush, which is surely the strongest of the plants along that shore, also cannot be clung to, because it comes out at the roots. The bush is our consciousness that is always with us and appears so permanent, but yet also dies with our bodies."

Mitta now falls silent, gazing modestly at the ground, giving her audience a chance to absorb what she's said.

Yasodhara examines her cousin, astonished, impressed; looks around also at the thoughtful faces of the samanis, and of the village women, each one of them considering the truth of this impermanency in their own lives. She never knew Mitta had this ability to capture an audience—yet realizes, even as she thinks this, that Mitta never had the chance before, as a woman, to display her talent. Her teaching has given some legitimacy, some solidity, to what was beginning to feel like a strange dream, an unfeasible venture. Mitta begins to speak again, explaining how the Middle Way might offer, through the Eightfold Path, a way out of the prison of their human condition.

"Yes," Yasodhara thinks, "even though I lack belief in the Middle Way, in the end it provides purpose and context. It will keep us all walking."

That evening, the women of the village come bearing more food and the samanis accept it. Managing on one meal a day is still something for the future. As they eat, Yasodhara says to her cousin, "It's interesting that you used that metaphor of the river current, Mitta. All my life that is how I've seen myself. A seedpod carried along by any river current." The women are listening to her intently and she continues, sharing her struggle to hold on to Siddhartha and then her son, each slipping between her fingers like grass. The women nod and murmur in commiseration, recognizing their own pain in her story.

That night, every rustle in the bushes and grass causes a frizzle of terror in Yasodhara that a snake is slithering towards her. Once, when an owl shrieks, the women shriek too, then fall into nervous laughter, a note of frenzy in their mirth. Yasodhara is sure she will never sleep, but the walking has exhausted her and she soon drifts off.

The next morning, they are woken very early by drops of water falling on them and the patter of rain on the canopy of leaves above. Yasodhara groans as she wipes her face with an edge of her robe. "Yet another challenge for us to face," she mutters to Prajapati.

"Yes," her aunt whispers back, "Pusan is certainly testing us." They grimace at each other, suddenly realizing they should have made a sacrifice to the God of the Roads and Travellers before they left.

As they sit huddled against tree trunks, Dawn creeps across the sky, unfolding her pink banners. Soon, the village women arrive again with food in clay pots, carrying banana leaves as umbrellas. The samanis gather under the largest tree and eat the gruel offered them as the villagers squat, watching them eat. The gambojaka's wife says, "Mitto, you will have to walk two mornings to get to the next village." The women stop eating and regard her, wide-eyed. The other villagers nod in commiseration, sighing gravely. "Today, the road will also take you through a forest and you *must* get through to the other side, where there is a pleasant meadow in which samanas rest."

"A forest? Are there many wild animals in it?" Then Yasodhara blushes, realizing how sheltered this makes her sound.

"No, no," a village woman assures her, "it's perfectly safe as long as you keep on the path. The elephant and boar are much deeper in the jungle, and we've hardly ever heard of anyone sighting a tiger or leopard."

Just as Yasodhara is feeling comforted to know this, another woman adds, "Still, if possible, wait for a merchant caravan and go through with them."

Yasodhara exchanges looks with Prajapati. She is sure now their hosts are lying about the safety of the jungle.

The villagers have brought enough food to last the women until tomorrow. Still, they apologize, explaining that they don't have much to spare because of the drought. The women thank them. But after the villagers have left, they regard each other apprehensively. No one gets up to begin the journey until at last Yasodhara stands up firmly. "Well, we must leave. It's important to get through the forest as soon as we can." She holds out one of the banana leaves the villagers brought, using it as an umbrella, and nods to her aunt. Prajapati comes to shelter under the banana leaf, taking the other end of it. They set off and, after a moment, the others hastily grab leaves and follow.

The road soon gets muddier as the rain increases and, before long, they are stumbling through sludge, trying not to slip. Yasodhara looks at the sky, listens to the thunder, and a worrying notion comes to her. "Pitucché," she whispers, "what if this is the rains, arriving late?"

Prajapati gives her a rueful smile to say she was thinking the same thing. "Let's hope not, daharé. Well, at least, not until we are in Vesali."

Finally, after what seems an interminable amount of walking, they reach the forest and stop before it, sheltering among the aerial prop roots of a large banyan tree. The women, despite the banana leaves, are dripping wet because the rain has blown sideways, soaking their garments and faces. They squat on the ground, squeezing out their robes, exhausted. After they have sat like that for a while, Yasodhara gives her aunt a long look. She and Prajapati stand up. The other women cry out in protest. "Mitta," Upasama says—for "friend" is how they address each other now, removing all distinctions of rank and relationships—"surely not. Why can't we just stay here until tomorrow morning or until a caravan comes?"

"We haven't walked far enough today, mitta." Yasodhara is sympathetic, yet she keeps her tone firm, confident. "We must do at least a yojana each day." She gestures to the rain. "This might be the rainy season arriving late. If so, we have to reach Vesali before the rains truly come. We cannot get caught in them."

The other women look terrified at this new danger, and Yasodhara silently curses herself for mentioning the rains.

"If the rains truly come," Sundari Nanda says in a small voice, "we'll be trapped. Unable to go forward or return home."

"But no," Yasodhara says, stroking her sister-in-law's shoulder, "that will not happen. It was foolish of me to even say it. Why, it's almost Sarada. The rains never come this late." Then she adds, because the women still look very skeptical, "I know of what I speak from ten years of cultivating fields, from absorbing village lore."

Finally, one of the women stands up. "I cannot go on. I will return to the village we left, and from there to Kapilavastu." Two other women murmur in agreement and also rise.

Their covert exchange of glances tells Yasodhara these women have already discussed the possibility of return. She looks quickly at her aunt: here come the desertions. "This is not an army. No one is conscripted." Her voice shakes and she looks around at the faces, waiting for others to also give up. Much to her surprise, though, no one else rises to join the three women. In the faces of those continuing onwards she sees resignation, apathy—and for Mitta and a few others, a firmer resolve, a re-commitment to their path.

The woman who first spoke up nods in farewell, and signals to the other two. They walk away with her, shamefaced. The rest watch them leave, envying their failure of courage, envying that they have the choice to return.

Silently the remaining women set off into the forest. The rain is immediately lighter here because of the covering of trees, and they lower their banana leaves. They have been walking for a short while when Yasodhara, to pick up spirits but also warn off any animals in the bush, begins a song she learned in Mudgala when tending the fields, one whose rhythm always kept her going beyond tiredness. After a few moments, the other women join uncertainly in the call-and-response.

Soon, one thin, cracked voice rises above the others. Hearing the other women taper off with little gasps, Yasodhara turns to see that it is Tissa singing. Her old aunt, who was struck dumb twenty-five years ago, has found her voice. She gapes in wonder as Tissa comes towards her, face radiant as she sings, clapping her hands in rhythm.

Tissa reaches Prajapati and Yasodhara and holds her hands out as if she is a performer, swaying her body from side to side as she sings. They clasp her wrinkled hands and kiss her fingers, filled with the heady joy of those who were previously despairing. "See, see," Tissa calls out in her cracked old woman's voice—so strange for Yasodhara to hear—"see what the Middle Way has given me. I am now truly a believer."

Tissa now starts a hymn to Pusan, God of the Roads and Travellers, and soon the other women join in, singing lustily as they continue through the woods, clapping their hands in rhythm with the chant. Tissa recovering her voice has given them new purpose and belief. Their undertaking, despite its difficulties, will cure their sorrows and failures, will alleviate the pain of their stunted hopes and loves. Yasodhara sings loudest, elated.

After Tissa's song is finished, Upasama starts a bawdy love song. The other women accompany her, stopping every so often to hoot with laughter over the words, their rowdiness amplified by this new burst of belief in their mission, and also by the awareness that, for the first time in their lives, they are not under the usual restrictions of their femininity. "No one watches us," Yasodhara thinks as she hoots with laughter too, shouts out the lewd lyrics. "No one judges us. There is no role of wife or mother or sister or noble lady to uphold here."

Soon the trees begin to thin, and then, abruptly, they are out of the forest and in a meadow, its grass cropped by deer and other animals that feed here. "Look," Yasodhara cries, pointing to some huts that previous samanas must have constructed, in the shade of trees. The women run across the grass to the huts, which turn out to be frail stick structures covered with leaves and palms. Still, the women huddle into them with pleasure. As they crouch down and open their food, the rain ceases and Yasodhara and her aunt smile at each other. They are going to be all right.

That evening it is Tissa who gives the oration. "This I have heard, mitto: If there is a large bonfire burning and a woman keeps flinging dry grass, wood and dried cow dung on it, the fire will grasp at this fuel and burn higher and higher. In the same way, if an oil lamp is constantly refilled and its wick replenished, the lamp burns on and on. So it is with us who, nourished by the fuel of craving, try to seek satisfaction in things and other people, thus creating for ourselves unhappiness, pain, mourning and desolation. Because all things and people, mitto, are impermanent—as I know so well."

The next morning, Yasodhara awakens and gets to her feet—and cries out in pain. Hastily sitting down, she examines her soles and sees that they are swollen and blistered. Prajapati too is examining her feet, as is Mitta, who shared the hut with them. The three women look at each other, worried. How are they to keep walking now?

Yasodhara hears cries of despair and pain from the other huts as well. She pushes herself up on her feet and hobbles out, lips set grimly, then goes about collecting brush and wood, and lights a fire to boil a little rice for their breakfast. The earth feels as if it is studded with sharp knives. She tries walking on the sides of her feet, on tiptoe, on her heels, but nothing helps. Yet she keeps going, knowing she must set an example, and soon the other women emerge from their huts and hobble around too, preparing their own fires to cook their rice. When Yasodhara finally does sit to get some relief, her feet throb and pulse with greater pain than ever.

After their meal, the women sit on the banks of a stream with their feet in the water, regarding each other forlornly. Finally Tissa, whose reedy old woman's voice is still strange for Yasodhara to hear, says, "Why don't we lance our boils? That, at least, will relieve the pain." And so they each set about doing so, using razors and needles. This does give them some relief, but then it dawns on Yasodhara that they are now in danger of infecting their wounds from walking barefoot. Some of the women, realizing the same, begin to sob at their miserable plight, at the fear of infection and even gangrene.

"Well," Yasodhara says quietly after a while, "we cannot just sit here. We walk back or forward, but either way we must walk."

As they hobble out of the meadow, Yasodhara watches to see if any of the women will turn back. A few do look towards the forest, but going through it alone, or even with a couple of other women, is too frightening a prospect. The rain yesterday kept the elephants and wild boar in the thickets, but today who knows what they might encounter on the road?

As they walk along, Yasodhara's feet throb and burn as if they are feverish, and soon she feels as if her entire body has been reduced to her feet, her entire body pulsing with pain. The sun rises higher, a blinding shimmer on the road, the air humid from puddles and water-filled gullies. The backs of her knees, her thighs and armpits are slick with sweat. She has to stop frequently, as do the other women, to wipe palms against robes so that the stick-bundle won't slip from her hands. Her robes are soon wet with perspiration. And now, as if this is a new pain, a new exhaustion to bear, it strikes her that Rahula must have suffered like this in those early days of his wandering. Delirious with heat and pain by this point, she is filled with a heavy horror, as if just discovering some terrible inadvertent crime she has committed, a crime that continues. She is unable to separate herself from her feelings, unable to convince herself that Rahula no longer suffers thus and is now safely in Vesali. She begins to cry, despite knowing her tears will lower the morale of the other women; and soon the women join her in weeping. After a while, Yasodhara finds something companionable in this choral keening; it is a comfort to know one doesn't suffer alone.

In this way, crying and hobbling and swaying in the heat, the women reach a hamlet. The local children come running to greet them at the thorana to the village and, as if they are used to the sight of weeping, limping samanis, take their stick-bundles and skip along merrily, chatting. Soon the women dry their eyes on their robes and answer the children's questions. When they reach the village square, the gambojaka and his committee are waiting to greet them. The gambojaka comes forward, crying, "We welcome you, sāmini. Who might you be?"

"We are on a journey to see the Awakened One," Yasodhara explains, and is relieved to see them nod in recognition of the name. "I am the wife of the Awakened One and this is his stepmother, the former devi of our kingdom." The men frown, chins tucked in, not sure whether to believe this or not. Yasodhara reaches hastily into her bundle and produces her royal seal. The men examine it, astonished.

"Now you are even more welcome!" the gambojaka declares.

"Though we've never met you, sāmini, we know your husband well," one of the elders explains to Prajapati. "He visited many times and saw to our needs. Come, come, let us show you one of his good works."

The men lead the women to a large well in the centre of the square. "See, sāmini," the gambojaka declares. "It was the former raja who supervised the digging of this well. Paid for the bricks from the state coffers. We have never forgotten his kindness and generosity."

Yasodhara feels unexpectedly blessed by sight of the well—it is as if Suddhodana watches over them from the Land of the Fathers.

The village women, who have hung back all this time, now surround the visitors. They direct the samanis to sit on a low mud wall by the well, then wash and wrap their feet in leaves that have healing properties. Other women bring food and the samanis eat as best they can, too tired and in pain to swallow much. They fall asleep that afternoon in the village orchard and are so exhausted they are only able to rouse themselves hours later, as the Sun begins his descent.

Yasodhara pushes herself against a tree and examines her feet. The swelling has come down and they don't throb as much, but her soles are still raw and bleeding, her nails cracked and filled with dirt. Beyond the orchard, she can see the villagers going about their routine in this charming village. She is reminded of her life in Mudgala, and longs suddenly to end her journey here, to live among these people and be one of them. But no, she cannot let the women down; and she will never be happy until she's reunited with Rahula. Truly, her old life, even Mudgala, has fallen away from her.

That evening, it is her aunt Prajapati who gives the oration to the village women. "This I have heard, mitto: There is a flayed cow, a cow without skin. And because its flesh is unprotected, wherever it seeks refuge it suffers. Whether it stands by a wall, or under a tree, or out in the open air, insects swarm it, biting and nipping, drinking its blood, feasting on its flesh. Finally, in anguish, it escapes into the water hoping for relief there, but fish and other water creatures also nip and gnaw at it, drinking its blood and feasting on its flesh.

"We, who are *nama-rupa*, name and form, inhabited by consciousness, are that cow, and the skinless flesh our six senses. Our hearing, touching, seeing, tasting, smelling and thinking are constantly in contact with the world around us, constantly gnawed by it. But, through the Eightfold Path, we learn to cover the exposed flesh of our senses."

After the village women have left, the samanis eat and do what they have fallen into the habit of doing after these orations: they discuss their lives in the context of the talk. It is Upasama, the former concubine, who speaks first tonight, saying with a sigh, "Yes, I was indeed that flayed cow." She tells them how, as she became older, she grew more and more frightened

at the loss of her beauty, wondering from day to day when the raja would
tire of her and want her gone, wondering what life of loneliness and struggle awaited her beyond the palace; and she confesses that these fears made
her bitter and angry, difficult to live with. Mitta joins in, adding her own
anguish about losing whatever little beauty she had after she got ill, her face
and body cratered with boils and pustules, knowing she would never find
love, never be married. Sundari Nanda, too, now confesses her vanity over
her beauty and then her panic when she realized too late that she had lost
it before she'd secured a husband. Soon the other women add their tales of
fear about their beauty. And Yasodhara listens, touched at their vulnerabil-
ity and friendship.

When they set off the next morning, Yasodhara finds that her feet feel less
painful—probably because her soles have hardened, she thinks. Or perhaps
it is because, having survived a morning of walking on swollen feet, she
knows she can survive another. Once again, the women have been warned
that there will be no village for a night's rest. They must stop in a meadow
by a river where some samanas built mud huts a few years ago.

When they reach the meadow, Yasodhara sees the huts at the far end,
a river beyond. Signalling the women, she leads the way forward but then
stops, peering ahead through the shimmering heat. Four samanas are
already gathered in front of the huts, around a fire. She starts to go forward
once more, but slowly, wondering what reception they will receive, and if
the men will share the huts with them. As she draws closer, she sees that the
ascetics are of the matted, filthy, naked variety.

The men notice the women approaching and jump to their feet, glaring.
They start to shout, shooing the women away as if they bring disease. One
picks up a stone and flings it. The stone hits the young concubine Sanga
in the shin. She cries out, and the other women cry out with her. For a
moment both groups regard each other in silence. Yasodhara clenches her
fists to steady herself, angry now. Her women have been walking a long
distance and need rest. *Deserve* rest. Those four men don't each require a
hut; they must be made to share. She pushes the end of her outer robe
over her shoulder and strides forward. The other women follow a short
distance behind.

The samanas have squatted down, thinking they have won the battle—but now, seeing Yasodhara continuing to approach, they jump up again and gesticulate, yelling. One picks up a stone and prepares to fling it at her. She holds her hands up to say she and the women come in friendship, but the man throws the stone nonetheless. She ducks and it sails past, falling in the grass. "We come in peace, samanas," she calls out. "Share the huts with us. We too are on a spiritual path. We too are tired."

The men look at each other wildly, then turn to growl at Yasodhara. They seem half-crazed with hunger or austerities and she can smell, even at this distance, their reek of dried urine and feces. It strikes her that they might not even be ascetics; perhaps they are just homeless lunatics. She calls again: "Mitto, share the huts with us." They growl and glare again. One picks up another stone, but before he can fling it, a rock flies past Yasodhara and hits him in the stomach. The man yelps in pain and surprise. "Lie down, mitta!" one of the women yells, and Yasodhara throws herself flat on the ground as sticks, clods of earth and stones fly past her, hitting the men. They cry out, arms raised, stumbling back.

With a shriek, the women rush forward with sticks and more stones and clods of earth. The men turn and flee, and the women give chase. On reaching the river, the women still in pursuit, the men wade in and swim across. From the other bank, they yell and gesticulate for a time, before finally giving up and limping off into the forest. The women are helpless with laughter, delighted by their courage, their success. They are learning to survive.

On the sixth day of their journey, they reach the Sakiya-Malla border. The crossing is at a shallow point on the Anoma River, across which travellers usually wade, waist-deep. Yet because of the drought, the river is merely a stream that rushes through rutted mud. Looking at the stream, Yasodhara wonders what food, if any, awaits them on the other side.

Malla guards stand sentry at the top of the other bank. As the women cross the river and clamber up the bank, the men watch their approach sternly. "Who are you and where do you go?" one of the guards demands.

"We seek the Awakened One, in Vesali," Yasodhara says, keeping her tone mild and respectful. The Malla are well-known for their hostility to outsiders.

At these words, the guards sneer. "Awake from what?" one asks with a guffaw. Another adds, "Awake from the long naps these lazy samanas take." They extend their spears to block the way, their faces stern again. "Where do you come from?"

"Mudgala," Yasodhara says promptly, because Kapilavastu is more splendid than the Malla capital and she doesn't want to give these men any further cause for hostility. "It's a simple little provincial town not far from here, sāmi," she adds, sure they won't know better.

The guards survey the visitors, then nod to say they accept this. By now, the women have lost all signs of physical refinement. Their manner of walking, which used to be small-stepped and elegant, is now crude and bowlegged because of their sore feet. None of them stands tall and graceful; their voices are cracked, uncertain; their robes are stained and grey.

"However, if you want to continue," one of the guards says, "you must pay the road tax."

The women cry out in protest and look at Yasodhara. She draws herself up. "We know the laws of the Middle Country. Samanas and samanis pay no road tax."

The guards glare at her but she meets their gaze. She and her companions have suffered enough, triumphed enough; they are truly samanis now. She will not allow these men to tell her otherwise.

Finally, the guards grunt and step aside to let them pass.

Beyond the banks is a road through fields. As the women set off along this road, they stare at what is around them, troubled. The drought is worse here than in the Sakiya Kingdom. The fields look burnt. As she passes some paddy stalks that lean into the road, Yasodhara, the only one among the women with expertise in cultivation, stops to examine the plants. The other women crowd around her. "Look," she says, and points out the little mites that cling to the dead stalks. "It's not just drought. A pestilence has shrivelled the crop." The women can see she is frightened, and they too become scared. "We cannot expect much food here, if any," Yasodhara continues grimly. "The best thing is to walk through as fast as possible."

"But the Licchavi Republic is six days away," one of the women protests.

"How will we survive that long?" another cries.

"We have no choice but to keep going forward." Yasodhara shakes her head as she looks again at the paddy stalk. "That's all we can do. Go forward."

In the fifth part of the day, when the sun is right above them, the women spot a village to their left in the distance. With reluctant, worried glances at each other, they turn onto the path that leads to the village, wondering what reception they will get, recalling the hostility of the Malla guards. As they draw closer, there is an eerie silence. Usually, by now, village dogs will have given the signal and children come running to greet them. "Perhaps we shouldn't . . ." Prajapati says.

"But we need at least water, pitucché," Yasodhara whispers, though she too is feeling more and more unnerved. She notices that hawks and crows circle above.

Reaching the thorana that leads into the village, they stop and peer at a deserted square with a well in it. They call out greetings but get no answer. Finally, their thirst is too great and they edge forward.

A few steps in, they smell the rotting flesh. And then, suddenly, there is a great flapping of wings, a hoarse crying and cawing and howling as dogs, crows, hawks rush out of the houses where they have been feasting on corpses—the dogs, tails between legs, each carrying a juicy bit of bone or meat in their jaws, the birds rising into the air with pieces of flesh in their beaks and talons. The women cry out in horror. They turn and run from the village, pressing robes to noses to keep away contagion and prevent themselves from vomiting.

Despite their painful feet they don't stop running until they are back on the main road. There they stand panting, gaping at each other, exhausted and hungry. After Yasodhara catches her breath, she says again, "There is nothing to do but go forward. That's all we can do. Go forward." And so, the women continue along the road, heads bent, each step and then the next their only reality—because if they don't keep their intent fiercely on one step, and then another, they will collapse.

As if trying to escape her fear and the pain in her legs, Yasodhara's mind flits from snatches of songs, to bits of past conversations, to fleeting images of things and people. At one point, she does the accounts of the fields in her head, laying out tokens on an imaginary counting board. Even the image of Rahula, the image that has kept her walking all this way, slips and slides from her mind; she confuses him with memories of her brother at that age, or Siddhartha, or even Anuruddha.

Finally, the women stumble across a copse that has a small pond and settle there for the evening. They dip their strainers in the muddy water and hold them over their begging bowls, but the water they drink is still silty, with a slight odour of rotten eggs. They fall asleep as soon as it is dark, no one tonight having the heart or strength to give an oration. Yasodhara's dreams are like her waking mind—images, moments, songs, actions, all rushing along like clouds flung forward by a storm.

The next morning, before dawn, Yasodhara sits up, clutching her cramping stomach. The moment the cramp releases its hold, she rises and stumbles away to the thicket, the others asleep around her. She is barely able to make it into the privacy of the bushes before she has to relieve herself, panting as she does so, nauseated by the foul odour. Once she is done, she rises to go and wash herself, but takes only a few steps before she has to squat down again and relieve herself. A cold sweat breaks out all over her body now and she feels light-headed, her limbs soft. It is all she can do to keep squatting. When she finishes and tries to stand up, she doesn't have the strength. Instead, she shuffles away from the foul mess and falls on her side, curled up. The world spins. She is terrified at how swiftly this illness has come over her, terrified it is the same sickness that killed the village.

When Yasodhara next opens her eyes, the women are bending over her. Prajapati shakes her gently. She tries to rise but finds she can't, and sinks back with a cry. The women reach down, lift her and bring her back to the copse. She has left her body now, is far above it, watching heavy-headed, heavy-lidded, as the women use their bowls to draw water from the pond, wash her face and body, then lay her out to rest in the shade of a tree.

When she next awakens she is in a hut, the room filled with menace, the very walls rustling with evil, alive with it. But no, no, the menace isn't in the hut—it lurks beyond the open doorway. She must drag herself over to the entrance; must shut the door before the evil comes in. She grunts with effort, pushes with her elbows, trying to get herself to move, but her limbs are inert, impossibly weighted. Finally, sweating, breathless, she gives up and lies on her back, eyes tightly shut, succumbing to her fate—hoping that whatever lurks out there will end her life swiftly.

The next time she wakes, she is lying on the floor of a cart with a covered roof. Seated cross-legged before her is a merchant who wears rings on each of his thick fingers, and chains around his massive neck that dangle and clink on his vast hairy chest. He watches her, smiling subtly, swaying with the moving vehicle. He licks his lips with a smacking sound, then introduces himself: his name is Naggaji and he is the leader of a caravan of merchants; his hometown is Rajagaha. "And now, sāmini," he says, waving his ringed hand towards the world outside, "you should know that we are passing through a forest which the people around here call the Waterless Wilderness. A dangerous forest ruled by a rakshasa." He gives her an amused look, a conspiratorial wink. "Now, a story: of how a wise old merchant once bested this rakshasa. Because it will give me great pleasure to tell this story, and it will relieve the tedium of our journey."

The merchant settles more comfortably, makes himself a wad of betel leaves, which he sticks in his cheek, all the while regarding her merrily with those hungry eyes. Yasodhara watches him, helpless, as if she is a trussed-up goat being taken to the sacrifice.

"Now, on this particular occasion I am speaking of, our wise old merchant and a younger merchant decided to take the same path through this Waterless Wilderness. The wise merchant, a man I shall not admit to knowing, but will simply say I greatly trust"—here he winks at her to say he is that very merchant—"this wise merchant felt that the combined needs of their two caravans would exhaust the grass for the oxen along the way, as well as the herbs needed for cooking. Also, so many wheels and animal hooves would damage the road. He thus offered the younger merchant the option of going first or going second, a month later. The younger merchant, being greedy and impatient, thought to himself, 'If I go first, my oxen will feed on the grass and we will have our pick of herbs for cooking. Also, the road will not be churned up from my fellow merchant's caravan going before me. Further, we will get to the water first on the other side of the wilderness.' So, he declared he would travel first. The wise merchant was secretly pleased at this. The other merchant's oxen and men would eat the old grass and herbs and, by the time he went through, there would be sweet new grass and herbs. As well, the road would be smoothed by the wheels of the younger merchant's many wagons; a water hole would await him on the other side, because the young merchant and his men would have had to dig one for themselves.

"Now the rakshasa of the forest"—Naggaji pauses to give her that same elaborate wink he used to identify himself as the wise merchant—"seeing the younger merchant coming through, discerned he was a fool. Using his illusionary powers, the rakshasa appeared on the road as a merchant with carts and men travelling from the opposite direction, all of them garlanded in blue lotuses dripping with water."

The merchant gestures widely and Yasodhara now finds herself in that caravan with the younger merchant. Then she *is* that younger merchant, watching through his eyes the approach of the disguised rakshasa and his carts. When the caravans meet, the rakshasa calls out, gesturing to his soaked clothes, "Fellow travellers, just ahead it is raining heavily and there is plenty of water." He holds out his garland of dripping blue lotuses. "There is also a large pond ahead, from which my men and I plucked these lotuses." Joyful at the news, she cries to her men, "Destroy the water pots. They are slowing down our progress. Water waits ahead!" They gleefully smash their water pots and she urges her men forward.

They travel on, looking ahead with anticipation for the glimmer of the pond around the next corner. But there is no pond. "The next corner!" she cries. "Have heart, my good men!" They go around the next corner, and there is still no pond; and around the next and the next, but there is still no water. Finally, dazed with thirst, she stares at the shimmering road ahead, forced to admit she has been duped. And now the rakshasa appears before her in his true aspect, horned and matted, teeth dripping with saliva. He lowers himself over her, mouth open wide like a cobra's, the entire world reduced to his gaping maw.

Then suddenly Yasodhara is back in the chariot and Naggaji the merchant is cackling with laughter, as if he has pulled off a wonderful joke on her. Who is he really, who, who? But before she can get an answer to this question, she has drifted off again.

When she next opens her eyes, she knows she is definitely dreaming, because her brother's face hovers inches above hers. She watches him for a little while, then closes her eyes, happy to give in to this illusion. She smiles; tells herself she is back in Ramagama and they are children. But then her brother calls her name softly and she quickly opens her eyes and stares at him. He nods and grins, and now she sees that this is real because her brother is dressed in the manner of the vana-dasas, bare-bodied except for a deerskin around his waist, many chains of animal teeth and hard nuts around his neck. "Daharé." Her aunt now comes into view, bending over her. "Daharé," Prajapati repeats softly, "do you know who I am?" After a moment, Yasodhara nods. She tries to pull herself up but Devadatta gently pushes her down. As she looks around, she sees that she is indeed in a hut, its walls made of leaved branches and creepers that rustle in the breeze, its roof of more leaved branches, an occasional animal skin hanging here and there for protection from the elements. Suddenly, she is unbearably thirsty and croaks for water. Her aunt goes to get it and returns with all the other women, who crowd in, smiling and nodding to tell her she is past the worst. She greedily gulps the water and then asks for something to eat.

Her aunt ushers the women out and she goes to get the food. Alone with her brother again, Yasodhara takes in his new clothes, his matted hair, his beard trimmed with a knife. She wants so much to talk to him, but is still too weak to do anything but smile and smile. Prajapati soon returns with a thin rice gruel, and her aunt and Devadatta help her struggle into a sitting position. As her aunt begins to feed Yasodhara, Devadatta tells her how she came to be here.

After she fell ill, some of the women went to stand on the road, hoping to get help. Soon a caravan of merchants came along and offered to take Yasodhara and the women in their carts and chariots. The leader, who knew the area well, told them that, further along, they would enter a forest and, once there, he would take them along a trail to a vana-dasa village whose inhabitants, because they foraged and hunted, did not depend on cultivation and were thus not very affected by the drought. When they reached the village, much to their surprise, the women found Devadatta among the tribe. He had been living with these vana-dasas since he left Kapilavastu.

"We have been here three days, and very well treated too." Her aunt nods to say she has reassessed her thoughts and opinions of the vana-dasas.

"And your bhāta has hardly left your side all this time." Devadatta laughs sheepishly and waves a hand, as Prajapati continues to praise him for his hospitality, the care he has taken of them all. Yasodhara can tell he is proud to have been able to do this, proud to show them he is doing well. She takes his hand and kisses it. "Ah, bhāta," she croaks, "you have found your true home, then."

Later, alone, she thinks over all her aunt and brother told her, recalling her dreams and hallucinations, wondering if the caravan leader would have actually related that story to her.

By the next day, she is able to stand and hobble outside, supported by the women. Seated on a mat, she takes in the village. It is set up in a jungle clearing, with a river running close by. Outside the various huts, women tend to their children, or grind seeds, or slice up root vegetables and fruit and leaves she has never seen before, foraged with expert eyes from the forest. In the centre of the village is a large firepit with an iron spit over it. A deer roasts on the spit. "Everything is temporary, the tribe moves all the time," Sanga whispers to Yasodhara. The young concubine's eyes are mischievous. "Nothing is permanent. *They* seem to have grasped the Middle Way even before the Awakened One." The women seated on mats around her laugh, and Yasodhara smiles.

"Imagine, mitta," Sundari Nanda says, gesturing to the women outside their huts, "the children trace their lineage from their *mothers*, not fathers. Because the vana-dasa women cohabit easily with their men, and paternity is hard to fix."

"So, the heads of households are senior women, not men," Visaka chimes in. "Imagine such a life, mitta!"

Yasodhara nods, as fascinated by this world before her as the others.

As the days pass, she observes her brother as he goes among the vana-dasas. She sees he is respected by them. He is sometimes in the company of a young woman and, though he says nothing to Yasodhara about this woman, she guesses he cohabits with her. Still, the fact that he never introduces the woman to her makes Yasodhara question if he is truly happy or comfortable. Finally, she says to him, "Bhāta, are you at peace among these people?"

"Of course, bhagini." Devadatta shrugs. "I have always loved the vana-dasas."

"But in the end, they are not your people. I see you struggle with their language."

"I learn it, bhagini, I learn it. This is truly where I wish to be."

"Ah, then I am happy to see you settled." She kisses his cheek, realizing it is cruel to question him further. For, no matter if he is happy or not to be here, he is still a kind of prisoner among them; he cannot leave the vana-dasas and go to any town or city, because then he would be vulnerable to arrest for what he did in Kapilavastu.

In a week's time, she is ready to walk again, but Devadatta insists that he will take all the women in carts through the forest to the Licchavi border. When Yasodhara protests, he says, half teasing, half mocking, "But you are not even a proper samani yet, bhagini. Once the great Awakened One decides you are, then you can live by his rules. But, until then, you are not bound by them." He winks at her. "I have advised the women, and I advise you as well, to say you walked all the way. It will make a stronger case for the great Awakened One having to keep you." After a moment she nods, smiles and agrees.

On the evening before their departure, as the women are eating, Prajapati says, "We must give an oration tonight as a token of our gratitude. One of the vana-dasa women says she can act as translator." The other women murmur in agreement.

"Which one of us will speak?" Mitta asks, and Yasodhara puts her hand up with a small smile. The other women laugh in surprise.

"You have led us through forests and meadows," Upasama says, "through drought and hunger. We were all wondering when you would finally lead us in the spiritual path."

That night they sit cross-legged in a circle, where they are joined by the vana-dasa women. Yasodhara looks at the earth for a long moment, gathering herself. "This I have heard, mitto." She nods to the translator and, once this woman has spoken, continues: "A woman who has wandered too far into a forest to gather firewood and herbs disturbs a male elephant, who gives chase. She darts through the trees, hoping the tusker will not be able to follow, but it crashes its way through the vegetation and gains on her. The woman recalls that there is a well on the edge of the forest into which a nearby tree has pushed its roots through the brick lining. Once she gets there, she clambers down one of the roots into the well and hangs in the gloom, waiting for the tusker to give up and go away. Soon, however, she hears a rustle and, looking down, she sees a python winding its way up that very root towards her. She searches around frantically for another root she might swing to but sees that, on the other four remaining roots, are four vipers, their red eyes glowing in the dimness. A gnawing sound makes her glance up: two rats, one white, one black, nibble at the very root on which she hangs. And now there is a crackling outside the well, and smoke begins to seep in. A forest fire has started and it will soon burn away the tree to which this root is attached. The woman, beleaguered by her desperate circumstance, hasn't noticed that a honeycomb hangs on the well's wall, just above her. But now the bees, roused by the smoke, begin to buzz about, and a few sting her. The honey, released by the heat, starts to drip down; and the woman, forgetting her hopeless condition, sticks out her tongue, greedily licking the sweetness."

Yasodhara waits for the story to be translated, then waits a further while, giving all the women time to absorb the story that she's told, based on that old dream of hers. The silence is filled with the murmur of wind through the trees. Finally, she speaks again: "The elephant is our fear of impermanence that chases us, the well the sensual life into which we slip to avoid this impermanence. The tree root is the things and people we cling to, hoping they will grant us escape and succour from the terror of impermanence. But the python, death, slithers its way towards us and the vipers are the four elements, earth, water, fire and air, also impermanent and often a danger to us. The two mice, night and day, gnaw away at our lifespan; the forest fire is sickness and old age that will burn our body away. The stings of the bees are the stings of our constantly changing circumstances. And yet, despite all this, mitto, we continue to indulge our sensual pleasures, forgetting our desperate condition."

She stops her sermon there. Unlike the speakers before her, she will not move on to show how the Eightfold Path will free them from pain. She doesn't have that belief yet, and she will not pretend, as it would dishonour the faith of the other women. When she looks up and scans their faces, she can tell from their knowing smiles that they have understood this.

Early the next day, as Dawn is throwing out her colourful banners, they reach the river that marks the Licchavi border. Yasodhara stands for a long moment holding her brother's hands, memorizing him. She is sure she will never see him again. "Our parents in the Land of the Fathers are happy that you looked after me, bhāta. They are proud. I will always love you and will never forget you. Nor your kindness to me."

"Kindness, bhagini?" He gently releases one of his hands and touches her face to say it was love, not kindness.

As she wades into the river to get onto the ferry, she glances back at Devadatta. He raises a hand in farewell from the top of the bank. She clambers onto the barge and looks back again—and he is gone.

10

Power and Possibility

AS THE FERRY takes the women across to the Licchavi Republic, they see ahead what looks like a wondrous land. And indeed, they alight into a dreamscape: the fields of paddy are waist-high, susurrating in the breeze, a soft sun over the green and gold; fruit trees in the orchards bear succulent mangoes; birds, who were silent in the Malla lands and rustled among the withered leaves listlessly, here sing lustily, whirring in the sky. "Do you think the Awakened One really did perform a rain miracle?" Sanga whispers.

"He says he didn't and we should believe him," Upasama replies. Yasodhara nods to agree with her.

As the women set off towards the Licchavi capital, the road beneath their feet feels cool from the rains and yet firm, the gullies on either side filled with water. A herd of cattle amble over to a fence to greet them. The women stop to admire and exclaim over the fatness of the beasts compared with the emaciated ones they left behind, stroking their glossy coats—and Yasodhara uses her expertise from Mudgala to check their ears and nostrils for good health.

Soon they pass Licchavi villagers at work in their fields. Seeing the troop of women, they leave their tasks and come running over, calling out, "Who are you, strangers? What brings you to our land?" They nod amiably, smelling of fresh soil and green growing things.

"We are from Kapilavastu." Yasodhara smiles, breathing in that nostalgic odour of cultivation. "And we come to ask the Awakened One to take us into his Order."

The villagers sigh in admiration and one of them says, "So it should be, so it should be."

"Indeed, indeed," the others agree.

Yasodhara, sure of Siddhartha's renown here, adds, "I am the former wife of the Awakened One, and this is his mother." She extends an arm towards Prajapati.

"Then I hope your request is granted, sāmini," one of the village women exclaims. "It would surely be a good thing for women to also go forth into homelessness under the patronage of the Divine One."

A quick look passes between Prajapati and Yasodhara: here, Siddhartha is regarded as divine.

The villagers insist the visitors must honour them by sharing their mid-morning meal. "Further good fortune will come to us from feeding the mother and former wife of the Divine One," they say.

Yasodhara bows her head, gratefully accepting for all of them.

As they lead the way along a bund through the paddy fields, the Licchavis praise all the goodness "the Lord" has brought to their lands. And in the village, seated in its square under a tree, Yasodhara marvels at the food their hosts bring them—of a variety and quantity she hasn't had in what feels like years. Other villagers come to gaze at the women, to ask for their children to be blessed by the former wife and mother of the Divine One.

When they have finished their meal, the women, knowing they are close to their goal, decide they will keep walking to Vesali, the capital. The cool landscape gives them a fresh burst of energy as they set off, waving to the villagers. Walking here is an easy trek, compared with the drought-ridden landscape they have passed through so recently. Their feet have also finally hardened, the rough, thick skin on their soles.

After some time, the women grow sober. When they stop for a rest, squatting under a tree at the edge of a field, they are all silent, inwardly turned. Finally, Upasama says, "Well, here we are, almost at the end of our journey." She sighs and her sigh is echoed by the other women. The possibility of being denied—which they have pushed away in order to keep walking—is now very real. Yasodhara looks out at the green fields in front of her. Where will they go if they are refused again? What will they do? Truly, it is impossible to return to the domestic world. They are changed in some fundamental way by this journey, have come through a dark passage and emerged reborn. She stands with a deep sigh and indicates to the others that they should move on.

They set off again and, when the Sun is just past the midpoint of his journey back home to his beloved Dawn, they see the ramparts of Vesali, capital of the Licchavi Republic. Though the ramparts are tall and strong, the city itself is small; Yasodhara has heard it does not possess the parks for leisure within it that Kapilavastu has. The Licchavis, though a wealthy people, are also a warrior race and live the ascetic, ordered lives of soldiers—even those citizens who are not in the military. As they draw nearer the capital, Yasodhara sees that the huts where the Dasas live outside the ramparts are clean and well-built in barrack-like rows, unlike the snarl of hovels bordering Kapilavastu. Yet none of this order and cleanliness lifts her spirits. The city is a further reminder that their future will soon be irrevocably decided.

From villagers along the way, they have learned that the Awakened One and his bhikkhus are residing in huts built for them by the grateful Licchavi princes, situated in a pleasant woodland called the Mahavana. They ask and are directed to this place. When they reach its entrance, Yasodhara pauses on the path that leads in, gazing at the woods. It is more royal park than proper forest, the undergrowth pruned so nobles on horseback might chase deer through trees. She turns to the other women, wide-eyed. Then she says firmly, "Be strong, mitto," and strides forward into the trees. Prajapati hurries to keep up with her. The other women scrambling behind begin to sniffle and soon they are all weeping, even Yasodhara, despite herself, as if knowing already they will be denied.

Thus weeping, worn out and dusty, the women arrive at the clearing where huts are scattered among the trees for the monks. An asoka tree is in bloom, its fragrance mingling with the odour of burning firewood from the midday meal that has just been eaten. Bhikkhus go about their tasks with calm, efficient movements, washing pots and pans, sweeping leaves from the grass, mending one of the huts, the *tap-tap* of hammers filling the air. Yasodhara watches all this, feeling frightened, excluded.

Soon the monks become aware of the women standing at the edge of the clearing. They stop their various tasks and stare.

Yasodhara glimpses now, through the trees, an open, gabled audience hall. A group of monks are seated there in a semicircle. Siddhartha sits on a small dais before them. At the sight of him, her throat constricts, as if he is a mighty king and she a subject brought for judgment. Yet she must go on, to the end of this journey. And so, dazed like someone going to her execution, she leads the women quietly forward along the path towards the hall.

The monks move towards the women, through the trees, drawing closer and closer. The women can now recognize husbands, brothers, uncles, sons. Many of them weep more openly now. They call out the men's names, holding out hands imploringly, breaking from the group. The men stop in their tracks. Then, with cries of amazement and joy, they run towards their women. Forgetting their vows, they seize their loved ones in their arms, hug and kiss their wives, mothers, sisters, daughters, cousins. Soon the women are showing their hardened, blackened feet as proof of devotion and love, and the men weep now too, some of them kneeling to kiss those blessed feet. Caught in this whirl of reunion, Yasodhara momentarily forgets her goal. "Rahula! Rahula!" she calls, and pushes through the melee of monks, searching frantically for her son. "Rahula! Rahula!" But no one responds.

By now, the commotion has attracted the attention of the monks in the hall. Yasodhara sees one of them rise and walk swiftly towards the entrance. She gestures to her aunt. "Pitucché!" Together, they rush towards the hall, reaching it just as the monk steps out onto the grass. Ananda! He peers at them, startled.

"Pitucché, bhagini, why are you dressed like this?" He wrings his hands in distress. "Why do you stand here weeping?"

The two hold out their arms, as if to say, "Isn't it self-evident?" And then, Yasodhara cries, her voice cracking, "The Awakened One wouldn't allow us women to go into homelessness because we didn't come to him in true seriousness. But now we have come in true seriousness. We have walked fifteen days, we have divested ourselves of all trappings of womanhood, to prove to the Awakened One that we are worthy."

Ananda stares at Yasodhara and Prajapati, speechless; he takes in the other women in their shabby, dusty robes. Then, with a quick frown, he signals them to wait and hurries inside. As if they are starving Dasas come to beg a pittance of food, Yasodhara and Prajapati watch him go quickly to Siddhartha and the other senior monks and bow before them. She strains to hear, hands grasping a pillar for support.

"Sāmi," Ananda declares to Siddhartha, "Sakiya women, including your mother and former wife, have arrived, walking all the way from Kapilavastu. They have walked for fifteen days. They have endured all the hardships of the wandering life, have divested themselves of their womanhood." He pauses to gather himself, then speaks formally. "Given the seriousness of their intent, O Awakened One, wouldn't it be a good thing if the women are allowed to go forth into homelessness?"

Holding her breath, Yasodhara watches Siddhartha—who has turned slightly to take in the women and men embracing, kissing, walking into the woods arms around each other, sitting under trees as if at a picnic. He turns back to Ananda and raises his eyebrows to convey his regret. "I have already given my answer. Women will not go forth into homelessness in our Order."

Yasodhara and Prajapati turn to each other, stunned. Yasodhara strains again to hear the discussion in the hall.

Ananda frowns. "But sāmi, the women have shown themselves worthy of this going forth. They have walked for *fifteen* days, have already lived as samanis."

"No, Ananda, I cannot grant this."

"Surely, sāmi, such devotion, such faith, proves a true commitment to the Middle Way? And what will the women do? They have already gone forth into homelessness. We know well the paths open to them: the courtesan's life or bonded slave."

Siddhartha is silent.

Yasodhara watches him, giddy with hope. Surely Siddhartha must change his mind now.

"Ananda, you have asked three times and three times I have refused. Do not ask again."

And so, it is over.

"Pitucché . . ." Yasodhara whispers.

"Oh, Ushas," Prajapati whispers back.

But Ananda, beloved Ananda, is not ready to give in that easily. After a respectful pause, he speaks again: "Sāmi, are women *capable* of attaining stream entry, of reaching the place of the Once-Returner, the Non-Returner, of finally realizing Nibbana?"

Yasodhara and Prajapati glance at each other, then lean forward to listen intently.

"Or, sāmi," Ananda persists, "is it only men, only half the human race, who can achieve this? Is your Middle Way for only half the human race?"

Siddhartha is silent for a long moment, caught off guard. "They are capable," he finally replies, grudgingly.

"If this is so, sāmi, then since Prajapati Gotami has served you well as mother in the absence of your own, since Prajapati Gotami dressed and fed you and helped you grow to manhood; since Prajapati Gotami has done all this, wouldn't it be a good thing for Prajapati Gotami, and hence for all women, to be given a chance to realize Nibbana, the highest bliss? Wouldn't it be a sad thing to deny your stepmother, and indeed all women, the highest bliss? And since Nibbana cannot be achieved in the household life but only by going forth into homelessness and practising the Eightfold Path, shouldn't then all women, starting with your stepmother, be allowed to do so, if they wish?"

"Ananda, just as a kingdom that has many women and few men is easily captured by another kingdom, so a samana path that allows women will not last long. I predict our Middle Way will die out in five hundred years if we allow women. Is that what you wish?"

Now it is Ananda's turn to be quiet, but his silence is obdurate, challenging.

"Ananda. Just as a field of rice, in which a blight of grey mildew takes hold, is soon destroyed, a samana path that includes women will soon wither and die."

Another loaded silence from Ananda.

Siddhartha sighs. He gestures to say he cannot deny Ananda's logic, at the centre of which is a vital question: Is the path to Nibbana only open to half the human race? "I will think on it and, in consultation with other senior monks, and indeed all our bhikkhus, offer a decision."

Ananda hastens to the door to inform the women, but their radiant, grateful faces tell him they have already heard. Yasodhara longs to press his hands, to embrace him, but she and Prajapati hold back and bow instead. He senses their impulse and nods merrily.

They hurry away to tell the other women, but have gone only a few steps when Yasodhara hears the cry, "Ammé!" Before she can turn, she feels damp arms flung about her waist. She spins around to take her freshly washed son in her arms, kissing his wet head over and over, crying and laughing. "Rahula, Rahula, look at your white robes already covered with dust from mine. You'll have to wash them all over again."

Rahula hugs her tight, then leans back and grins up at her cheekily. "And why will I have to wash them, ammé? Isn't that what you have come to do?"

Yasodhara gulps a laugh, cuffs his head gently, then grabs him again and rains kisses all over his face and head until he breaks away with a yell of laughter, of protest, and goes to embrace his grandmother, to touch her feet.

Anuruddha in his white robes now comes towards them, also wet from the river bath. When he reaches Yasodhara, he shakes his head, laughing. "Ñātiké, even as a girl you always pursued what you wanted."

"But will I get it this time, ñātaka?" They grimace at each other.

"My vote is with you, natike." Then Anuruddha bows and excuses himself to go about his tasks.

Yasodhara watches him, this dissolute cousin of hers, pick up a broom and diligently sweep outside a hut, then pick up mats and dust them. She turns back to Rahula. Her arm around him, they walk with Prajapati towards the other women—who are still seated under trees, chatting and laughing and embracing their menfolk as if they are nobility once again. One of the women has taken out a needle and thread from her bundle and is mending the edge of her husband's robe. Yasodhara stops a small distance away and regards this scene. When they arrived at the edge of this clearing, there was a sober, quiet, industrious air to the place, the men going about their work in tranquility. Now it resembles a harvest festival, a fair. She glances at her aunt and sees that Prajapati is thinking too of what Siddhartha said: how the Middle Way would die if women were allowed to go homeless alongside men. She detaches herself from her son and gives him a long, grave look. Then she and her aunt begin to call the women by name, one by one, beckoning them over. The other women, seeing Yasodhara and Prajapati's forbidding expressions, look frightened. They leave their men and gather quickly.

Yasodhara and Prajapati lead the group some distance away and, as the women cluster around, explain what has happened and the Awakened One's impending judgment. "I must tell my husband," one cries. "And I my son," another adds. But Yasodhara shakes her head. She repeats what the Awakened One has said about the Middle Way and how it will not last if it includes women. "We have to prove ourselves. Prove we will not be a blight on the Order. By walking here, we have already demonstrated much. But now, by our conduct, we must show the Awakened One, and the senior monks, that we are true samanis detached from worldly bonds. So, let us prove our seriousness by setting ourselves apart from the men." It is taking all her will to speak in this calm manner, because now that the immediate danger of rejection is past, she feels anger starting to roil in her against Siddhartha, against his cowardice in passing this decision on to all the bhikkhus.

The women sigh and reluctantly agree, casting longing looks at their menfolk, who are observing this discussion, apprehensive, from a distance.

Yasodhara and Prajapati retrace their steps back along the wooded path, and the women follow with glances of farewell at their men.

Once they have left the clearing and walked a short distance, Yasodhara spots a trail that leads to the river, glimpses water in the distance. She signals the women and they turn off along this path. The woods thin out the closer they get to the water and soon they reach a clearing dotted with trees. "Let us build huts here," she says to the women. "Let us show the men what we have learned on this journey. Show them we are true samanis."

The women nod and start to forage for sticks and branches and broad leaves. Within a short time, they have constructed huts for themselves. They stand back, looking at their handiwork, and one of them says what is on all their minds: "Surely our judges will be impressed." Then they go down to the river to bathe.

Later that day, Ananda, Moggallana, Sariputta and a monk Yasodhara hasn't met before come to visit the women, who are clearing the area with quiet tranquility. Prajapati and Yasodhara go to welcome them. The other women watch from a distance. Moggallana and Sariputta greet Prajapati and Yasodhara warmly, clasping their hands together, bowing and smiling. They introduce the other bhikkhu as Maha Kassapa, and he gives them a short, stern bow. The women, to show they are devoted samanis, kneel and touch the earth before the monks' feet. Then they rise and gesture towards the copse. "Come, bhikkhus," Prajapati says. They lead the men around the clearing, showing them their handiwork. The other women follow Prajapati and Yasodhara's example, touching the earth before the monks' feet as they pass—men who are much younger than many of the women and might not be from noble backgrounds. Ananda, Moggallana and Sariputta express how impressed they are by the huts; Maha Kassapa, however, remains unrelenting, examining the structures sternly as if looking for flaws.

Some of the women have foraged deeper into the woods and returned with fruits, root vegetables and leaves for a meal, which they are now cooking, as the group did not eat at midday. Moggallana, Sariputta and Ananda are very interested in these foods, which they were ignorant of. Maha Kassapa pretends indifference, but Yasodhara can tell he is also curious. "Oh, these," she says casually, waving a hand towards the harvest, "we learned how to find them from our friends the vana-dasas, who we encountered in a Malla forest." She turns to Maha Kassapa. "But I'm sure that you too, sāmi, have encountered and been the guest of these vana-dasas on your wanderings. You haven't?" She continues in mock astonishment. "Why, they are very good people, generous with all they have. And drought or no drought, they always have food because they know how to forage. We even preached the Middle Way to them." The nearby women bend their heads to hide their smiles, and the other monks smile too at Maha Kassapa's discomfiture as Yasodhara ribs him.

Before they leave, Maha Kassapa says to Prajapati and Yasodhara, "Whatever the Awakened One decides must be voted on by the whole sangha." For a moment Yasodhara is bewildered by the term "sangha"; she and Prajapati exchange a quick look. How ironic that Siddhartha is now using the term "parliament" for his Order.

Ananda stays behind after the other monks return along the path. Yasodhara and Prajapati lead him to the privacy of a tree some distance from the women. Seated cross-legged under it, Ananda gives them a sober look. "Pitucché, ñātiké, you should know that the possibility of women being admitted to the sangha is causing much division among the bhikkhus. Particularly between our Sakiya men and the Brahmins. They have not been getting on at all. These Brahmins are much keener on asceticism and purity than our Sakiya men. Your arrival has only added to their conflict. Our Sakiya monks will, of course, vote to allow women into the sangha, but the other monks are against it. Maha Kassapa, also a Brahmin, leads the resisting group. I'm sorry to say, he has great influence over the majority of our bhikkhus."

"But we are trying, we are trying in every way," Yasodhara cries, frightened again.

"Yes, I know you are, but . . ." He shrugs helplessly.

She looks at her hands, twisting them in her lap, trying to gain control of her anger. "It is unfair that these men, who know nothing about us, get to decide our fate. Do they not realize, bhāta, that there is a tie between evil and those who have power over the fates of others? That evil, like a shadow, trails after those with power?" Ananda is clearly startled by her words, but he nods to say he sees her point.

Once they have escorted Ananda to the main path, Yasodhara and Prajapati walk back slowly to their clearing, hands behind backs, lost in their thoughts and fears. After some time, Prajapati murmurs, "How much like a kingdom it is here. Power and possibility, the fate of the ruled so dependent on the whims of the sangha."

Yasodhara regards her aunt, head cocked. "So, if it is indeed like a kingdom, pitucché, and everything depends on the vote of the sangha, then the thing to consider is how the sangha might be swayed by popular opinion."

The next morning, the women wake before dawn, light their fires and have their breakfast, making a quick porridge with some rice the monks have given them. They then practise meditation for the rest of the morning, until it is time to go beg for their midday meal. They form a line and head down the path, on their way to Vesali.

The gatekeeper admits them without question, bowing respectfully. News of their arrival has by now travelled through the city. The women cluster around him to ask directions to the homes of the Licchavi princes who rule the republic collectively, there being no single raja; and also for directions to the house of Ambapali, the great courtesan of Vesali. The women then gather some distance from the gate to decide who will go where.

"I have always longed from my girlhood to see the great ganikā." Yasodhara smiles at the other women. "If no one minds, I would like to go there." The others murmur their agreement. "Sanga, Visaka, will you come with me?" The young concubines say they will, quickly grasping why Yasodhara has invited them.

The three women set off through the city and, because it is small, by asking directions a couple of times they quickly find the ganikā's house. It is tucked away discreetly at the end of a cul-de-sac, though Yasodhara is sure everyone in town must know where it is, and where anyone going down the cul-de-sac is heading. They reach the big wooden street door, ring the bell and wait. Soon a serving maid opens the door. She starts in surprise, but then nods to say she too is aware of their arrival yesterday. "Please step in, samanis." She ushers them into the courtyard and rushes to get her mistress. As they wait, Yasodhara and the former concubines look around, agog at the beautifully painted designs on the wood façade, the elaborate fountain with its many spouts, the jets arranged to rise through bamboo pipes in ascending order, the flower bushes pruned to look like dancing women.

And then there she is coming towards them: Ambapali, the Great Courtesan of Vesali, dressed simply in a white dhoti, a golden shawl around her perfectly formed shoulders, a string of jasmine in her hair. Yet, despite this simplicity of dress, despite the fact that she is well into her fifties, her beauty is unearthly; it cannot be reduced to finely arranged features, a skin the colour of golden sand, a perfectly proportioned body. No, there is something beyond that, some spirit, some fire, that lights her in a way Yasodhara has never seen in another woman. Easy to see why she has been ascribed divine origins, deemed the child of an apsara.

"Ah," Ambapali says with pleasure when she reaches Yasodhara and her companions, "the entire city has heard of your arrival and your quest. I am honoured you grace my house on your first day."

"The honour is ours, sāmini." Yasodhara bows low.

"But will you stay and eat with us? Surely, being women, you are allowed to dine with us, unlike the bhikkhus who won't even cross our threshold?"

Yasodhara nods quickly. This is, after all, the great advantage they have over the men—they can enter these quarters and develop intimate friendships with other women.

As Yasodhara, Sanga and Vivaka eat with Ambapali and her courtesans, they reveal who they are. The ganikās are awed that Yasodhara, sitting here among them, is the former wife of the Divine One. "And what do *you* seek from joining the Order?" Ambapali asks her.

Yasodhara is quiet a moment, thinking on this. "I came because I wished to be reunited with my son, to check if I might be able to love him beyond me-and-mine." She cocks her head to see if the ganikās understand this concept, and they smile to say that they do. "But there is something this journey has taught me: our lives *are* in constant flux. In this, the Middle Way is true. So the sensible thing is to try and live with calmness, with patience, even with happiness, in the midst of this flux. I wait to discover how, or if, this might be possible."

The courtesans are quiet for a while, absorbing this. Then they bend forward to quiz Visaka and Sanga as to how they, as concubines, one even trained as a ganikā, found in themselves the ability to destroy their beauty. The two women explain their journey: how they began the fifteen-day walk out of wanting something more than the ganika life offered to them, and how, as the days passed, they grew to believe more and more in the Middle Way. Yasodhara listens to them, heartened to hear their story because it surely means there is hope for their cause.

After the meal, Yasodhara, Sanga and Visaka, knowing well how the Middle Way has failed women, knowing well the unquenched thirst of women drawn to its path, lead the courtesans through a meditation. Following that, Sanga gives a short discourse on the Four Great Realities, and Visaka talks about the Eightfold Path.

As Yasodhara listens to the concubines, she marvels at how the younger women have changed: there is a new peace to them; they have truly become, like Mitta, one of the faithful.

Later, the ganikās cluster outside to bid them goodbye, and Ambapali insists that they must come visit tomorrow too. "Perhaps someone else will come, sāmini," Yasodhara says, bowing. "I think the stepmother of the Awakened One might like to meet you."

Ambapali sighs with pleasure. "I will look forward to that very much."

As Yasodhara and Sanga and Visaka begin their walk back to the Mahavana, they are glowing with success. In the days to come, thinks Yasodhara, we will make it harder and harder—impossible—for the sangha to vote against us.

And so, in the days that follow, the twenty-seven women visit all the noble houses in the city and the houses of the important Vessas as well, winning over the women in these homes to their cause. The rules of the sangha have changed since the monks were last in Kapilavastu. Now the lay public are allowed to visit the bhikkhus in the evenings, and a discourse is offered by the Awakened One or another senior monk. The ruling princes, generals and rich Vessas come often to listen. But frequently now, on their way to the discourse, they stop their chariots and palanquins beside the path to the samanis' huts, so that their women might go visit with the female ascetics. Before long, the samanis' leaf huts are replaced by more permanent mud huts with thatched roofs and raised floors. Ambapali leads the way with this generosity, and soon the other Licchavi women are vying with each other to build huts.

The Licchavi women's gratitude goes beyond their thanks for this new access to the Middle Way: Yasodhara and her fellow samanis have become the Licchavi women's advisers and confessors, and are sought out for private hearings during which the women of the city pour out their sorrows, their troubles, and ask for advice. Sometimes all they want is a sympathetic listener. Yasodhara finds that she, in particular, is visited by widows and by women whose husbands are unfaithful, who have abandoned them in every way but name. And she finds she has much to offer these women from her own life.

Ananda's intercession on behalf of the samanis is well-known by now among the Licchavi women, who also know of the impending vote. And they are not fools. They understand why the samanis visited all the important houses in Vesali first. Ananda begins to receive gifts of new robes from the women and, since a bhikkhu is only allowed to own three sets of robes, he soon distributes his gifts among the other monks. Hearing of this through an amused Anuruddha, Yasodhara thinks, "Ah, good. The world is impinging on the sangha with its demands and desires."

Ananda has not come to see Yasodhara or any of the women since his initial visit. But one evening, two weeks after their arrival, Yasodhara sees him approaching through the trees and knows he comes with the verdict. The women stand from where they have been sitting or straighten up from their tasks and watch him approach. Yasodhara holds her breath watching him draw ever closer, as the other women huddle around her and Prajapati.

When he reaches the group, Ananda takes a moment to survey their faces, then simply smiles and nods. The women stare at him, stunned. "We won?" Yasodhara whispers. "We . . . we have won!" In unison, the women shriek, then hug each other, weeping with relief. A few rush to touch the ground before Ananda's feet in gratitude. Yasodhara longs to embrace her cousin, and the impulse is so strong she has to wrap her arms around herself instead, laughing.

When the women calm down, Ananda gestures for them to sit in a circle with him. His face is sober now, and they watch warily, knowing something bad is coming. "Mitto," he says at last, "there are eight extra rules you will be expected to follow, in addition to all the other rules bhikkhus abide by."

He is looking at Yasodhara, and she nods impatiently for him to go on.

"A bhikkhuni—for that is what you are to be called from now on—no matter what her age or how long she has been in the sangha, must rise, reverentially greet and pay homage to any bhikkhu. No matter his age, or even if he was admitted to the sangha the day before."

Some of the women gasp, and Ananda clears his throat nervously.

"A . . . a bhikkhuni must not spend the rain retreat in a place where there are no bhikkhus. A bhikkhuni sangha cannot decide when the important dates should be, such as the Upasotha day, but must wait to be told that by the bhikkhus. When, at the end of the rain retreat, all members of the sangha meet to invite and accept criticism of their conduct by their fellow members, the bhikkhuni must do so before both the male and female samanas, whereas the bhikkhus will do so only before their own sex."

The clamour of disappointment among the women is louder now. Yasodhara anxiously hushes them, wanting to hear all the bad news. "Let Ananda finish, let him finish!" The women's voices subside, though some of them still mutter angrily. She gestures for Ananda to go on.

"A bhikkhuni, where she has committed a grave offence, must make penance before both male and female monks, whereas a bhikkhu does so only before his male counterparts."

The women groan at the humiliation of this.

"A . . . a woman who seeks admission must get permission and approval from both the assembly of bhikkhus and bhikkhunis, whereas a man does so only before the bhikkhus. A bhikkhuni must never find fault with or abuse a bhikkhu."

Further groans from the women, though by now some are giggling at the absurd unfairness of these rules.

"And finally, a bhikkhu is allowed to address orations to a bhikkhuni, but the reverse is forbidden."

The women fall quiet now, fully absorbing their subservient role in the sangha. "Must we really rise to any bhikkhu and pay homage, even someone who is in their youth or adolescence?" Yasodhara asks. Rahula will be ordained in a few years; impossible to imagine falling to worship at his feet.

"I am afraid so," Ananda says, apology in his voice. "It was a struggle for the Sakiya men to get this acceptance from the Brahmins and, like two enemy kingdoms meeting to settle on a peace treaty, there are unpalatable compromises."

The women grumble. "Yes, yes, as always we women are offered up as the compromise." "Worship my own son?" "Worship my younger brother?" "Worship my nephew, my grandson?" After a while, though, they become quiet again. They meet each other's eyes and slowly agree. "Bhikkhuni sangha," someone says with a sigh of accomplishment. "We are our own sangha."

"Subservient but still independent," Yasodhara says. "And that is something we must remember. *Independent.*" Then, as the thought comes to her, she adds, "Like the vassal kingdom we were born into." She smiles. "What the maharaja orders and what the raja and his sangha do are not always the same thing."

The others laugh gently. "Yes, indeed," one of the women cries and Yasodhara sees they understand that although these rules are a humiliation, they have won something truly important for themselves. Also, since they don't live with the men, their contact will be fleeting and occasional, like the maharaja's with his vassal kingdoms. To make sure they understand this, she adds, "And there won't even be a senapati to see that the maharaja's wishes are done."

"Indeed, indeed." The other women chuckle.

"Then we agree to the terms?" Yasodhara asks. The women nod, one by one around the circle.

The final woman to give her assent is Prajapati, seated to Yasodhara's right. "Mitto, we have accomplished something that will benefit women for all time," the former devi says with a small smile, her chin lifted.

Yasodhara turns to Ananda. "Tell the Awakened One that, just as in my former life I accepted with delight a garland of jasmine or lotuses, in the same way I accept these eight rules and all the others, not to be transgressed during the course of my life."

The other women smile at the irony in this ornate declaration. Then one by one they declare, "I accept with the same delight." Ananda grins and bows to accept their vows.

Once he is gone, the women continue with what they have been doing, but now a gentle happiness spreads among them. Yasodhara and Prajapati had been on their way to wash their clothes and so now they pick up their dirty robes and continue. As they squat in the water, scrubbing and beating their robes against a rock, a mild breeze ripples across the river. After some time, Yasodhara sees Rahula in the distance, hurrying along the shore towards them. When he reaches them, he says, his face shining, "You are to stay with us, ammé!" Then he holds out his dirty white robes with a smile that is filled with happiness, love, mischief.

She takes them with a laugh. "Come here, Rahula, let me show you how a robe is washed. Soon you will be ordained and then you cannot come as you like to see me."

"But I will, ammé, I will. I don't care what the rules say."

"Rahula," she chides gently. "When you enter a kingdom, you must try to live by its rules."

She gestures for Rahula to squat beside her and then sets him to wash his own robe, supervising him. Once they have laid the clothing out on the grassy bank to dry, they sit under a tree watching life on the river, the passing boats, the fishermen.

"Ammé," Rahula says after a moment, "in all the time you've been here, my pita has never come to visit you."

"Ah," Yasodhara says, realizing for the first time the truth of this. "You are right, puthā. And here I wasn't even aware that he hadn't come." After a moment, she corrects herself. "Not unaware, but rather not expecting." She squeezes water from the edge of her lower robe. "Not really caring."

She travelled for fifteen days, endured heat, bleeding feet, starvation, thirst, illness—even the Waterless Wilderness. She is no longer the girl of sixteen who married her cousin. She is not the wife who struggled to keep her husband in their marriage but failed. She is not even the same kind of mother she was a few months ago. One self left Kapilavastu; a different self sits here on the banks of this river. And this new self is also changing—yes, she can feel it—becoming less seedpod and more river.

"Pitucché," Yasodhara says, turning to her aunt, "I've been thinking. When this rainy season is done, we are free to wander as we wish. I would like to visit Ramagama, to see again that beloved city of my youth."

Prajapati nods happily. "The beloved city of my youth too, Ushas. I also long to see it."

"I have never seen Ramagama," Rahula says and links his arm through Yasodhara's. "I will come with you, ammé."

Yasodhara laughs and gently disengages his arm from hers. "If you want to go to Ramagama, Rahula, then you must persuade your mātula Ananda or Anuruddha to take you there. But, puthā, you will not come with us."

Author's Note

THE PALI CANON, the earliest Buddhist text, was composed and recited orally until it was committed to writing in 29 BC (approximately 454 years after the Buddha's death). It says very little about the life of Siddhartha Gotama before he left on his spiritual journey. The well-known story of the cossetted Prince Siddhartha who didn't know, until the age of twenty-nine, that all human beings grow old, get sick and die first makes its appearance somewhere between the second and fifth centuries AD, according to various scholars. While this story might not make human sense in an era where death happened so easily (including that of Siddhartha's own mother), and while it might not fit the conventions of a realist novel, I do love the story as a narrative metaphor of the tenets of Buddhism and I have incorporated its tropes into this novel.

The Pali Canon does, however, offer a clearer picture of Siddhartha (now the Buddha) post-enlightenment. We see a man who is a sophisticated diplomat and skilled administrator, who understands very well the importance of public opinion and how it might be swayed; who cultivates the friendships and patronage of the great kings of his world; who knows well also the power of silence and inaction, of giving his enemies enough rope to hang themselves. He is also humble: quick to admit when he doesn't know something and seek advice, quick to change his opinions and rulings if they are proved wrong. He is a great and often humorous orator. All these qualities allowed him, on his death, to leave an efficiently run sangha, which survived long after all the other ascetic schools that flourished at that time (with the exception of Jainism) had died out. This is the Siddhartha I have turned to when creating my fictional version.

Of Yasodhara, the early version of the Pali Canon says very little, and she is often referred to simply as Rahulamatta, "mother of Rahula," which further erodes her identity. We get no sense of her feelings or opinions on being abandoned, nor her feelings about any of the other events in her life. She first starts to enter Buddhist literature around the first century AD and has fascinated bards, poets, playwrights and novelists since—as she fascinates me. I have drawn on some of this work in creating her. Paradoxically, the Canon is full of vividly portrayed women who speak their feelings and opinions, particularly in the *Therigatha*, the Songs of the Sisters, in which the women sound remarkably modern in their understanding of their subjugated position. Various scholars have also gathered together good historical evidence about the lives of women in this era, which I have used. Though women had a lower position to men, they were freer in this time than Indian women have been for many centuries since. In Yasodhara's world there were no child brides or widow burning. There were bride prices, rather than dowries. Widows remarried. Women moved around freely and there was no seclusion and veiling. They owned property, ran businesses and chose whom they married. It is sadly impossible to imagine Indian women walking unmolested through India today, as female ascetics did in Yasodhara's time.

My characterization of Ananda, Anuruddha, Mahanama and the other personages of the Buddha's story is completely fictional, as there is very little known about their early lives. I have built some characters from a small trace: with Anuruddha the story of his boyhood gambling and the cakes, with Mahanama the story of Vasabha and Nagamunda. For Ananda, I was struck by the fact that he was very good with a needle and ran sewing circles for the monks—the skill of a travelling man? There is also a sense of the outsider about Ananda, the one who doesn't quite fit, too busy looking after everyone to have time to pursue enlightenment. Then there is his championing of the women. Giving Prajapati just one child, rather than two, is for artistic economy, not ignorance or an error.

A note about Buddhist terminology. Generally I have used the Pali words for Buddhist concepts rather than the Sanskrit. The one exception is karma, which is *kamma* in Pali. "Karma" is one of the few words that is commonly understood by everyone, so I've kept its Sanskrit version.

I changed the "Four Noble Truths" to the "Four Great Realities" after listening to a talk by Bhikkhu Bodhi, who explained that the term *sacca* means "that what is." "Truth" suggests a relative thing, but "Realities" suggests something that simply is.

What gets me interested in starting a novel, what keeps me going, and where I end up are all different. One thing, however, stayed constant in writing this book: my ongoing interest in seeing how the tenets of Buddhism (such as the three poisons of greed, hatred and delusion, non-attachment, etc.), as they are captured in narrative tropes in the early stories, might be melded with the tropes of Western realism to create a hybrid form. My fictional characterization of the personages from the Buddha story illustrates these tenets, as their fictionality did in the early Buddhist stories—like that of the spoiled Prince Siddhartha.

IN THE SIXTH CENTURY BC, the fertile basin of the Ganges in North Central India (called the Middle Country) was under the control of two empires, the Kosala and the Magadha. They ruled over the tribal republics of the Middle Country, among which was the Sakiya Republic. The kings (rajas) of these vassal states governed with the aid of a council of ministers (amicis), and an oligarchy of nobles (the sangha) who met to discuss and vote on important issues in a parliament (the santagara). The raja was not a hereditary title. He was voted in by the sangha. His powers were limited as he had no army, just his palace guards. It was the emperor (maharaja) who kept an army in each state, headed by a general (senapati). At the time of the Buddha, there were two maharajas: the Maharaja Maha Kosala of the Kosala Empire, who was succeeded by his son Pasénadi (the title was passed hereditarily for the emperors); and the Maharaja Bimbisara of the Magadha Empire.

This was an oral culture, as a written language had not yet developed in India. Some primitive symbols and numerals, however, were used for account keeping. Time in a day was measured in roughly ninety-minute segments. There were eight daytime segments and eight nighttime segments. The day segments began at what we would regard as 6 a.m.; the night segments began at what we would deem to be 6 p.m. I have followed this in describing time, with the exception of "afternoon," which is a word from our way of keeping time.

The final "a" in Yasodhara is pronounced like the vowel in f*a*r.

Other than her name, the final "a" in all the other character names, like Siddhartha, Ananda, Suddhodana, etc., is pronounced like the vowel in th*e*.

The final "i" in character names such as Prajapati, Pasénadi, etc., is pronounced like the vowel in p*i*t.

The language the Buddha spoke has long disappeared. I have used Pali for my foreign words in the pages that follow, because scholars guess that this is closest to the language he spoke.

ahavaniya: one of the hearths in the daily sacrifices

Ajivaka: a member of an ascetic sect

amici: minister

ammé: mother

anustarani: an old cow or goat used in the funeral ceremony

apsara: nymph

Atman: soul; pl. Atmans

ayyaka: grandfather

ayyakā: grandmother

ayyé: husband or wife; a formal term of address

bhagini: sister

bhāta: brother

bhikkhu: Buddhist monk

bhikkhuni: female Buddhist monk

bisaj: doctor

caara: spy

Chandala: low caste who carry corpses

chaturanga: a board game similar to chess

daharā: boy, or child

daharé: girl, or child

Dasa: the lowest caste, not of Aryan descent; pl. Dasas

devata: spirit who lives in trees and the air

devi: queen

dhītā: daughter

dhoti: a garment consisting of fifteen feet of cloth that is wrapped and pleated around the lower body

dukkha: a term that covers everything from irritation to tragedy, depending on its context

gambojaka: village headman

ganikā: courtesan

Gimha: the hot season

Gotama Gotra: the Gotama clan

gotra: clan consisting of extended family

Hemanta: winter

janata: the populace, the people

Khattiya: the warrior caste; pl. Khattiyas

maharaja: emperor

Mahasetthi: head of the board of merchants

mātula: uncle

mitta: friend; pl. mitto

naga: mythical creatures who are half-human, half-snake and live underwater; pl. nagas

ñātaka: term of address for male relative

ñātiké: term of address for female relative

Nibbana: enlightenment

Nigantha: member of the Jain sect; pl. Niganthas

pita: father

pitucché: aunt

puthā: son

raja: king

rashtrika: governor of a district or province

samana: wandering male ascetic; pl. samanas

samani: wandering female ascetic; pl. samanis

sāmi: my lord

sāmini: my lady

samitr: slaughterer at ritual sacrifices

sangha: assembly of nobles

santagara: parliament building

Sarada: autumn

senapati: commander of the army in a vassal state

setthi: rich merchant

Sudda: lower caste; pl. Suddas

thorana: elaborately carved wooden doorway or entranceway

uparaja: regent

upasaka: lay male follower of the Buddha

upasika: lay female follower of the Buddha

Uttarapatha: one of the main commercial routes through India

vana-dasa: forest aboriginal tribe

varna: caste

vesiyā: prostitute

Vessa: merchant caste

Yama: god of death

yojana: a measure of distance about fifteen kilometres

ACKNOWLEDGEMENTS

Behind this writer at his solitary work stood a community of helpers and guides:

Lynn Henry (at Knopf Canada), first and foremost. With much love and thanks, Lynn, for making me appear a better writer than I am, not just on the sentence level but also in terms of structure—particularly the way you've helped me incorporate Buddhist narrative tropes into my novels, sometimes knowing what I'd like to do even before I've expressed it, or understood it myself. Christoph Emmrich at the University of Toronto who immediately and intuitively understood the kind of research a novelist needs to do, and also introduced me to guides and scholars in Nepal, who helped me see the distant past in the present. Ranjini Obeyesekere, thank you for introducing me to Yasodhara through your *Yasodharā, the Wife of the Bŏdhisattva*, and also for all your other inspiring translations. Rishika Williams, Judy Fong Bates, Kathy Page and Merilyn Simonds—thank you for your insightful early readings that helped this novel grow draft upon draft. Anne Blackburn at Cornell University and Nadeeka Rathnabahu at the Postgraduate Institute of Archaeology, University of Kelaniya, thank you for your help with the Pali words and glossary. At Westwood Creative Artists: a warm thank you to Bruce Westwood, Meg Wheeler and Michael Levine. My undying gratitude to all the Buddhist scholars throughout the past two centuries, whose painstaking work was so valuable to me. They are too numerous to name but I have provided a bibliography on my website. A few, though, must be singled out: Nayanjot Lahiri for her patience with my stupid questions and for making me aware of the trade routes during the Buddha's time; the late Senake Bandaranayake, dear lost friend, who taught me how to see the traces of the distant past in the near past, and who sent me off to see the wooden Padmanabhapuram Palace in

Tamil Nadu. In Nepal, many thanks to Nutan Sharma and Basanta Bidari. Grants from the Canada Council for the Arts and the Ontario Arts Council gave me the best gift of all: writing time. Mary Renault, where would the imaginer of ancient history be without your work? The epigraph is taken from *First Buddhist Women: Poems and Stories of Awakening* by Susan Murcott (Parallax Press).

⚘

I wanted to stick to only professional thank yous, but this acknowledgements page felt incomplete without this personal one: Amrita (Pieris), thank you for your love and friendship; for ignoring my pleas of work with a "Don't be so boring" and taking me off for lunches and foot massages and boozy nights and fun trips to your lovely country house near Puttalam. Post-war, through our work on WTR and GLF, we got to discover those parts of our country that had been closed off to us because of the war. I am very happy I got to do that with you.